THE OTHER MAN

BOOK I OF THE ROSE GOLD SERIES

NICOLE FRENCH

Copyright © 2020 by Raglan Publishing

ISBN: 978-1-950663-07-1

Cover Design: Raglan Publishing

Cover Image: Rafa Catala

OVERTURE

JANUARY

It wasn't necessarily odd for Nina Evelyn Astor de Vries Gardner to be standing on a New York City sidewalk. After all, this was where she lived. Lexington and East Ninety-Second Street. The heart of the Upper East Side.

It *was* odd, however, for her to stand outside her apartment building for nearly an hour. Clutching a bouquet of red roses. Unmoving while the petals swayed in the whistling winter wind and the doormen peering curiously from beyond the old brass-fitted doors.

It was one in the afternoon, but Nina's clothes were more appropriate for evening. In fact, they were the same pieces she'd worn the night before: an ice-colored silk shirt and A-line skirt from Chloe, plus her favorite Zanotti heels, three-inches of waterfall-colored leather. Winter whites. Flimsy for the frigid January weather, mitigated only by a heather gray cashmere coat left open despite the wind.

Nina barely noticed. It might have been thirty-three degrees, but she was burning up. Just looking at the red bricks stacked to the sky, at the thick glass-paned windows that never seemed to open, made her heart beat faster. Made her skin prickle. Made her eyes water.

She couldn't understand why.

After all, this was her home.

Wasn't it?

For a decade, the Upper East Side had been the kingdom below her apartment on the twentieth floor, though one that had never and would never belong to her. That was what happened in the de Vries family when you were the second-born grandchild, and a girl to boot. You were stowed safely in your ivory tower, afloat in luxury. Wrapped in chains of diamonds and gold. Told exactly what to be and where to be it and when.

And Nina had hardly ever bucked those edicts. Until last night. When her entire perfect world seemed to splinter into pieces, then reconstruct itself unrecognizably for a few hours of passion-colored pleasure, just to shatter all over again.

And now she was here. Back in this same world. The same life. To put it back together.

The problem was, she wasn't sure she could.

Nina Evelyn Astor de Vries Gardner sighed. It was a mouthful, those names. She'd always hated them. Even the first. "Nina" was short and almost lazy, considering in some languages it just meant *daughter*. As if that was all she was. And yet, wasn't that fitting? Someone's granddaughter, someone's daughter, someone's cousin—that was all she had ever been.

Someone's wife.

She wrapped a hand around her left wrist, which only a month ago had been circled with bruises she had carefully hidden with a gaudy Bvlgari watch she only kept for just that reason. Calvin had a strong grip, and that night, it was locked with bourbon. They had a rule, of course. Never her face. She couldn't act on behalf of De Vries Shipping if she looked like a bruised peach. And her grandmother, Celeste de Vries, the venerated head of one of New York's oldest families, would have roasted Calvin on a spit before allowing something as untoward as "abuse" to touch her family's pristine legacy.

But now Grandmother was dead. Mother, per usual, was awash in gin. Eric, Nina's cousin and new head of the family, was in jail for a crime he didn't commit. And his wife was missing somewhere in South Korea.

The de Vrieses were no longer pristine. And deep down, Nina knew the truth: it was all her fault. Complicity was just as bad as the crime. She was the coward who still hadn't fessed up to her parts in her family's mess. Instead, she had escaped her own guilt in the arms of a stranger and broken every vow she had ever made.

Her real name should be Deceit.

That's not fair, doll.

Nina started at the voice chiming in the back of her mind. A man's voice. Lilting, self-assured, mischievous and earnest all at once. Mostly polished, but roughened with slightly rounded Ls and Rs, occasional overemphasis of the letter O. The kind of voice she previously heard only from taxi drivers, doormen, workmen. A voice that, despite belonging to a complete stranger less than twenty-four hours ago, was now so ingrained that it was acting the part of her conscience. Reminding her not to let anyone say anything bad about her.

Not even her.

Do you believe in love at first sight?

He'd asked her in the early morning hours, when they were so exhausted that the line between asleep and awake was thoroughly blurred. The question had roused her anyway, sultry as a siren's call. And like a ship, she'd crashed right into the rocks.

Not until I saw you.

Even now, Nina was hardly surprised she had said it. Love was such a foreign concept. Her family said the word maybe once every five, ten years, when expected, and usually in front of cameras or other relevant audiences. Nina honestly doubted they understood what it meant. She wasn't sure she ever did.

Until last night, baby.

Yes. It *had* been the truth in that beautiful hotel room, on that plush, soft bed, with his green eyes reaching the depths of her with just one look. Love had poured out of her like everything else. Curiosity. Desire. Humor. Lust.

Love, though, was the reason, when he had wondered come morning just why they couldn't make a real go of it, she'd gone against every instinct she had.

She told him the truth.

Broken his heart and hers.

And run away as fast as she could.

Because Nina knew if he looked at her like that again, she wouldn't have been able to leave him. Not then. Not ever.

Matthew.

She thought the name silently to herself. Then thought it again. Drew her mouth around its consonants like she was sucking on a piece of candy, letting its sweet nectar glide over her tongue. And for a moment, Nina allowed herself to conjure his face.

A long, straight nose with just a hint of a break at the bridge. Two green eyes framed by a sooty fringe of lashes. The lush, full mouth always hooked by a slight smirk. An impossibly square jaw dusted by a five o'clock shadow.

Nina pressed a hand to her aching heart, to a bruise he had left. One of many she actually wanted. She'd managed to cover most of the spots on her neck and arms with concealer. But that one, bright as the roses she held, safely hidden under her shirt, she'd kept.

Slap me, he'd ordered again under the lush fall of the shower, not for the first time that night. *Slap me. Like the dog I am.*

He wasn't a dog, but he certainly turned her into an animal. And so she *had* slapped him that time, surprised by the surge of power when her hand found his cheek. The sight of her fingerprints on his olive skin was intoxicating, almost as much as the way his body vibrated, like a guitar string that had just been strummed. He loved it so much that she asked him to do the same for her. Just to see what it was like.

Matthew had pressed her against the shower wall, spread her wide as he found her depths again and again, and then, like a vampire, bent to her breast. He sucked the delicate skin between his teeth. And bit.

Do you ever wear red? he had asked her, again and again as he drew a single rose bud up and down the length of Nina's bare arm, leg, hip, thigh. *Would you do it for me?*

Pleasure. Pain. It all danced through her, echoes of the first primal ecstasy she had ever experienced in her twenty-nine, almost thirty years. Her fingers pinched at the spot through her shirt, hard enough to expand the bruise. It wasn't *his* lips, *his* teeth, but considering she would never see Matthew Zola again, it would have to do.

I can't take them with me, Nina had told him when he ordered the bouquet up to the room. And yet, as she fled, she captured them too. The final remnants of their scarlet night.

Nina pressed her face into the roses, the scent taking her back to the room at the Grace Hotel. As scarlet as the letter she should be wearing. Then, with regret she didn't bother to fight, she set the flowers down on the sidewalk and fished her wedding rings out of her purse. For a moment, she cradled them in her palm, observing the way the afternoon light blinked off the facets of the diamonds. Ten carats on a simple white gold setting, paid out of her own trust). She would have been fine with a much smaller ring, one that Calvin, on his respectable, but mid-level salary at the time, could have afforded.

He had insisted that a ring like this was needed. If only to look legitimate. Legitimate…for a bride of only twenty.

So pure and clean. So full of lies.

In more than one fit of rage, Calvin had grabbed her ring finger and twisted cruelly. Once she had required a splint.

"Don't test me, princess," he'd snap before taking a rough handful of her hair and yanking. "Otherwise I'll spill *all* your secrets. You know I will."

Had it really been ten years of that?

Could she survive ten more?

Nina slid on the rings.

It was time to go in. To face her life. Her husband. Her…home.

Nina left the flowers on the pavement for someone else to enjoy. She had known from the start she couldn't keep them. Color like that simply didn't belong in her life.

PART I

RECITITAVO

CHAPTER ONE

Matthew

"SO THIS IS WHAT REAL MONEY BUYS."

Derek Kingston, my investigative partner with the NYPD, and I stared up at the gleaming glass tower just a few blocks from the raging bull of Wall Street. A year ago, if you'd said I'd be on my way to the top of the De Vries Shipping building—a company that had been running the shipping industry in the tristate area since the seventeenth century—I'd have told you to have a few more, why don't you?

And yet, here I was. Matthew Zola. Middle-class Joe. One-time jarhead. Assistant prosecutor with the Brooklyn District Attorney's office. Somehow doing favors for one of the most powerful men in New York.

"Come on," I said. "I told Eric we'd be there at noon. It's five after."

As we started down toward the sunken lobby of the DVS headquarters, my phone rang in my pocket.

"Hold on." I reached for it, but it immediately slipped out of my gloved fingers to the marble steps.

"Here you go, buddy." Derek handed me the phone. He arched one brow. "Who's 'Lady Godiva'?"

I snatched the device away, frowned at the caller ID, and swiped it off. "No one special."

"Special enough to earn a spot in your contacts, though. I don't know the classics well enough. Why Lady Godiva?"

Lady Godiva was the wife of a medieval nobleman who supposedly agreed to ride through the town naked if her husband agreed not to overtax the people. The Western world's first exhibitionist, I guess.

I rolled my eyes. "This one likes to be watched."

"Is that what they teach you in law school? Dirty stories about old ladies?"

I ignored Derek's amused stare while we walked the rest of the steps down into the lobby.

Finally, he shook his head. "Man, you have all the fun. Maybe I should start trolling bars for married chicks too."

"It's not all it's cracked up to be," I said. "Matter of fact, I'm trying to break the habit. There are enough fish in the damn sea without that mess."

Derek just laughed. "I'll believe it when I see it. The day you stop cruising for married chicks is the day I become Mayor of New York. Unless..."

I looked up sharply. "Unless what?"

Derek pushed his sunglasses down his nose to eye me up and down. "I'll put it this way, my friend. Did the fisherman get caught?"

Before I could answer, a flash of light over his shoulder caught my eye. Bright silky hair, like a waterfall of gold. I shoved Derek to the side and took off after the girl.

It was her. I knew it was her.

Two weeks ago, I'd wandered into my friend Jamie's bar on the Lower East Side, drenched by rain and pretty sure I would end up going home with some random and probably taken woman. As Jamie and Derek both love to taunt me, I did have a, uh, pattern. It wasn't that I went looking for chicks with diamond rings or boyfriends living in the next state. They just happened to find me. Was it my fault they weren't getting what they needed at home? They knew the score, and so did I. No one got serious, and no one got hurt.

So, yeah. I thought I knew exactly what I was getting into that night when I stumbled into Jamie's bar, soaked and lonely.

Instead, I met her.

Tall, blonde, with looks as classic as the red rose I'd played over her naked body and a mind as sharp as its thorns, Nina Astor was a dream incarnate. She wasn't just the perfect woman. She was perfect for me.

It had been nearly two weeks since I'd met Nina Astor at the bar Envy. Since we spent half the night talking over wine and tapas—something I honestly *never* thought I'd do with a woman. I wasn't the up-all-night type. I was more the love 'em and leave 'em type. After hours of trading quips and small plates, neither of us could take it any longer.

———

"AND IF I TOLD YOU...IF I said it could only be one night?"

What? Inside, I reeled. One night? How could something like this only last for one night? This was already the stuff of legends. Nina and I hadn't done anything more than kiss, but I knew it would take years, decades even, to penetrate the depths of what we could be together.

One night? She might as well have asked for one second.

But her gaze didn't waver. She was completely serious.

The tip of her nose had reddened in the cold, and her lips were swollen from our kisses.

"One scarlet night," I murmured as I swept my thumb over her plump lower lip. "Well, if that's all I get...I'll take it."

My heart plummeted the second I said the words, but I knew they were true.

———

HOME.

The word had echoed through my mind the moment I'd slipped inside her, the second warm, slick welcome had squeezed my cock, the instant her flower petal lips touched mine.

It never occurred to me before then why we call it "coming." But it's true, you know. When you do it right, and with the right person too, it really is an arrival. Her body was like coming home.

But God has a funny sense of humor. After too many years of helping others break the ninth commandment, of course I fell for a married woman. Given my track record, that was just a matter of probability.

Two weeks ago, Nina Astor and I met by chance. But come the next morning, Cinderella disappeared into thin air. What did that make me, the prince?

Not fuckin' likely. People had called me a lot of things in my sad, sorry life. Bastard. Asshole. Homewrecker. Sinner. Prince Charming definitely wasn't one of them.

Maybe that's why I kept trying to find the girl even after she told me not to. By some crazy magic, love makes you a better version of yourself. I still wasn't ready to go back to what I was before.

Unfortunately, neither I nor the extensive tools at my disposal could locate her anywhere. And I'd been looking for her ever since. Of course, when I didn't have my other job to do.

She was gone. Poof.

Until...now?

"Nina!" I called as I dodged around people exiting the elevators. The blonde girl slipped inside along with the waiting crowd. "Nina, wait!"

She didn't respond. But it was her. I knew it was her.

Until it wasn't. The elevator doors closed, but not before the girl turned, revealing a face that was pretty enough, but which definitely did not belong to the woman who had cast her spell. One corner of her lips tugged upward in a half-smile, and she offered a little wave at me just before the doors shut. Like so many of them, it was her little way of saying she was mine for the taking.

Except like all the others, she wasn't the one I wanted to take.

"So that's her name, huh? Nina?"

I swallowed as Derek approached behind me. I hadn't actually uttered the name to anyone. Not since I'd spoken to her. Not since that night.

"I don't know what you're talking about," I said flatly. "*She* doesn't exist." I jabbed one of the call buttons with more force than necessary. "Now, come on. We have to get our heads in the game."

————

"Jesus. Fuckin'. Christ."

Obediently, I passed my fingers from forehead to chest, then shoulder to shoulder. Spectacles, testicles, wallet, watch, or so they said. Hey, it wasn't like I never took His name in vain, but it couldn't hurt when Derek continued cursing at the newest evidence from the craziest case either of us had ever worked on. I could practically feel my grandmother, *Nonna*, shaking her fist next to me. Better safe than sorry.

Eric de Vries, Chairman of De Vries Shipping, spread a selection of photos across his entire desk. "My bodyguard took these when we found them," he said quietly.

In spite of his designer suit and the glinting edges of his top-floor office, Eric had the pale, numbed look of a man still recovering from a war zone. It was something I was familiar with, having served in a few myself before becoming a prosecutor with the Brooklyn DA's office.

It wasn't Iraq, but the man had been through it over the past six months. Heir to one of the wealthiest dynasties in New York, he had returned from years away to marry Jane Lee Lefferts and claim his birthright. The only problem was that Jane turned out to be the illegitimate daughter of the de Vries family's sworn enemy—a fact she hadn't even known until she was about to walk down the aisle.

Jonathan Carson was a verifiable madman. Demonic as the devil. Slippery as an eel. And as the leading munitions manufacturer in the country, he had half the armed forces in his back pocket, which meant most of the federal agencies too.

Maybe they should have walked away. But that was never an option. And if you saw them together, you'd know it too.

Unfortunately, they were still suffering the consequences of that decision. Despite the fact that the de Vrieses have more money than God and enough evidence for the FBI to lock Carson up and throw away the key ten times over, all they had was…me. Apparently I was the last government employee *not* on the take from John Carson. And Eric and Jane's last hope in vanquishing this psychopath.

If it had been anyone else, I would have walked the fuck away. But Jane and I had been casual friends for years. And truth be told, I had a soft spot for true romance. So despite the fact that Eric could be an imperious dick, even he deserved a shot at real happiness. So few of us get it in the end.

Oh, Matthew. You will.

That voice. That breathy, smooth, silky voice, husky with pleasure, full of promise. For a moment, she was here with me again. Urging me not to settle for less than she believed I deserved.

Why, I thought to a woman who wasn't there. *You coming back to me, doll?*

She wasn't real, of course. So there was no answer.

"Walk me through it one more time," Derek said to Eric, gesturing at the pictures. "You're locked up, so Jane goes to Korea to get her mom?" He shook his head. "What the hell was going on again?"

"Carson had me framed for securities fraud," Eric said dryly. "Without bail, thanks to a bribable justice. Once my lawyers were able to change the judge, the suit was dropped. But it took almost two weeks."

"And so he used that time to, what, kidnap your wife?"

"Her mother, actually."

Eric pointed to one of the pictures, where a frail, glassy-eyed Asian woman I took to be Jane's mother was curled on a stained cot. Sedated, obviously. I didn't know Yu-na Lee Lefferts, but if she was anything like her daughter, she wouldn't have gone without a fight.

"She was bait. For Jane. And then for me, I guess."

"So she goes to Suwon, gets taken hostage, and then he waits for you so he can, what? Hit you up for some shipping deals?" Derek asked. "Seems like a bit much."

"It's a little more complicated than that." Eric gestured to the pile of notes he and Jane had brought back from Korea a few days earlier, which he'd mentioned on the phone.

"Carson was building a plant on the border between North and South Korea," I told Derek. "In conjunction with the Russians, potentially. We're pretty sure he was getting ready to produce and sell nuclear weapons to the North Koreans."

Derek looked up from the pad of notes he was leafing through. "*What?*"

Eric nodded. "You heard right."

"But that's...that's..." my friend sputtered.

"Treason?" I filled in for him. Yeah, I'd been there. When Eric told me about these new revelations a few days ago, I'd just about lost it myself. I still wasn't convinced there wasn't *someone* with the feds who couldn't help here. International arms deals were a bit above my pay grade.

But those calls had been met with silence. Copies of Eric's notes had been received and filed away.

Meanwhile, John Carson was still at large.

"Carson's only problem was that he couldn't transport them across the border," Eric continued. "The South Koreans couldn't be bought, and DVS has nearly exclusive contracts on all private ports there. His plan was simple. Steal my wife and mother-in-law to make me ship his weapons north."

I peered at him. "Would you have done it? If…" I gestured at the photos.

"I would have given him whatever the fuck he wanted to get my wife back," Eric said softly. "Unfortunately for him, I found her first. Like that."

All of us turned back to the photographs near the edge. These were the worst. Jane lying in a pool of her own blood. Face whitened, eyes starry and glazed. Black hair matted to her face from dried sweat and who knew what else. Alone. Scared. On the precipice of death.

The idea that his own flesh and blood mixing with de Vries DNA had proved to be too much for the sycophant. When he had discovered that his daughter was pregnant with Eric's child, Carson had abandoned his plan of catch and release in favor of something much more gruesome.

"What kind of man takes a woman's baby right out of her body?" Derek wondered.

"The kind who isn't really a man at all," Eric replied. "The kind who's a fucking monster."

His voice was stone.

Eric had this look about him, like he would do just about anything to end this madness. I'd seen it before. Men clutching a maimed arm or leg. Screaming "make it stop!" until a medic was able to run a sedative. Ready to cut themselves open or anyone else just to make something happen.

"Eric," I said slowly. "This is…look, I hate to say it. But I think you need to keep trying with the CIA. Maybe not the director right now, but there are still good people over there. I still have a friend from the Marines I can check in with. And you know we don't have jurisdiction with any of this."

Eric's gray—and right now, irritatingly familiar—eyes sharpened like steel. God, Nina's eyes...they did the same thing. Shone like silver in some lights. Glowed like ice in others.

I blinked. I needed to focus. Forget the girl. Get the fuck back to work.

"So you've said," Eric snapped. "About ten times. I'm traumatized, Zola, not an idiot."

I held up my hands in mock surrender. Okay, I should give the guy a break. Eric de Vries was a kingpin in a city with plenty of illegitimate ones. But I couldn't help it. I generally liked the guy, but there was something about him that made me want to knock him off his high horse. We'd known each other for going on five years now, friends of friends of friends. And even though I was helping his family out with this case, I couldn't help goading him here and there. Even at a time like this.

I told you. Not a good guy.

Matthew...

I shook my head. God, she was driving me crazy, and she wasn't even real.

"We tried your friend with the CIA," Eric was saying. "And the FBI. And the NSA. Carson bought them all. No one gives a shit, Zola. Except you, apparently."

Derek rubbed the back of his head and sighed as he scanned the pictures once more. "Not much for neat crimes, is he?"

"We already knew John Carson liked a spectacle," I said. "The man literally stopped Jane and Eric's wedding in front of a thousand rich New Yorkers. His grudge against the de Vrieses was all over the *Post* for weeks."

"Well, that gives you a motive, doesn't it?" Derek tapped his finger on a picture of Jane wrapped in Eric's arms. The moment of rescue.

I stared at it for a long time. Eric, like all these types of suits, generally wore the inscrutable mask of the ultra-wealthy. He was terse and unreadable, just like the rest of his caste. But in the photo, with equal parts pain and love were all over his face like they had been etched with a knife. He clutched the girl like he'd never let her go again. Like he'd been certain she was gone forever.

Do you believe in love at first sight?

It had just fallen out of my mouth in the early morning hours, as instinctual as the way my fingers stroked her skin.

And then, to my utter fuckin' shock, she'd answered.

Not until I saw you.

Fuck it. You only met the love of your life once. Some of us only got one night. But others might get a lifetime.

If they were lucky.

Who was I to watch someone else tear down that chance when I might be able to help?

"We can't do anything about this," I said, ignoring the way Eric's shoulders slumped in defeat. "We just need to find a crime *here* to prosecute."

"What're you thinking, Zo?" Derek asked.

"One thing is bothering me. Eric, do you know who actually turned you in for securities fraud? If you were indicted, it should have gone to discovery. Were any witnesses named in the documents?"

"No. That's why it was dropped. There was no documentation, and the single witness's testimony was both anonymous and without corroboration." Eric shook his head with disgust. "It shouldn't have made it to trial to begin with."

"You don't have any idea who might have offered testimony, though? Someone close enough to you to actually *be* a witness?"

Eric opened his mouth to protest, then shut it again. "Well—no."

"What were you going to say?" I asked.

He looked uneasy, but decided to go with it. "Look, it's just a feeling. No one ever came out and said anything—not after the will was read. But I'm fairly sure at least some family members weren't exactly happy I inherited the company after so long away. The accusations about securities fraud were linked more to requests made by Carson...but the evidence for them could have come from a few different people."

I looked at Derek, who nodded and made some notes. It was vague, sure. But it was still a motive. Eric's gut might lead us in the complete wrong direction, or it might give us exactly what we needed to close this bitch of a case. There was only one way to find out.

"I gotta get going, but I'll look into it," Derek said. He nodded at Eric on his way out. "Mr. de Vries."

We waited until Derek was gone and the door had closed to speak again. Eric had already picked up his coat from the back of the chair, no doubt eager to get back to Jane.

"How is she?" I asked.

The Jane de Vries I knew was a vibrant woman with more attitude than a teenage rebel. The ghost in these pictures was her polar opposite.

Eric expelled a labored breath. "She's..." He stared out the window toward the New York City skyline for a long time. "She's as good as can be expected, I suppose." He glanced toward the door again, then back at me. "But it might be better if you come to the house from now on. Aside from the fact that you really shouldn't be seen here in case Carson has people watching, I think it would be good for her to hear about your progress for herself."

I nodded. I really couldn't promise to do much. After all, Derek was right. For me to be any help at all, I needed to find a crime that John Carson committed within Kings County. And then he needed to be in New York for Derek and his guys to make the arrest. It was a long shot, if there was anything at all.

But the look in Eric's eyes—the pure, unadulterated sorrow—kept me from saying as much.

Instead, I extended a hand. Tentatively, Eric reached out, and we shook.

"I'll do whatever I can," I promised. "I'll be in touch."

CHAPTER TWO

NEARLY SIX WEEKS AFTER MY MEETING WITH ERIC DE VRIES, I FOUND MYSELF in Manhattan, having just finished a meeting in midtown interviewing a witness for another trial. As I sometimes did on days where I worked out of the office, I had my assistant forward my calls to my cell phone for the rest of the afternoon so I could wander. And just like all those other times, I was walking circles around the Upper East Side.

Up Fifth Avenue to the northeast corner of Central Park. Take a right into the farthest, fading reach of Spanish Harlem, then walk back down Lexington Avenue until I reached the upper Sixties. Hang another right past the Church of St. Vincent Ferrer, and repeat.

It was early March, so the trees hadn't quite started blooming. The last of winter hung over the city like a chilly dream, including a few heaps of snow from one final blizzard just a week before. But small buds hanging off the branches held the promise of color and light again. Tiny signals that change was afoot. Something was about to happen.

Just like the rest of New York, I was thoroughly tired of winter. Even so, the storms and the snow hadn't kept me from my patrols of these tired city blocks.

It was a dream that did it. A dream that woke me in the morning feeling like a part of me was missing. My chest would ache, my jaw would be tense, my throat tight with her name on my tongue.

It usually started with one part of that night or another. The things that were burned into my memory. A heated gaze. A prolonged conversation. Sometimes even the feel of her body, clenched around mine so tight I'd cry out in my sleep.

———

"Do you ever wear red?" I found myself asking, despite the fact that I'd never see her in it, even if she did. "Like this?"

Nina just watched the progress of the bud as it traveled down her side, over one leg, to flirt with the delicate curve of her ankle. She cleared her throat. "Well, no. Not really."

"Not even lipstick? Maybe your nails?"

"Grandmother always thought it garish. Unfitting for someone like me."

"Someone like you?" I drew the flower over the hook of her heel.

Nina shrugged. "Someone of my 'station,' she would have said."

"She probably knew you'd attract a trail of lovers. Like the pied piper, except with color instead of song."

As I trailed the rose back up her other leg, I found myself wondering what Nina would look like with a bright red mouth, puckered with want. Scarlet fingernails digging into my skin. A crimson silk negligee, begging to be torn off.

Christ, I was hard at just the thought.

And yet, despite our frenzy on the street, despite the way Nina was watching the progress of the rose like it was a piece of kindling that might literally burst into flames...I stayed where I was, drifting the soft petals up and down her equally soft skin while I studied her reactions. The way her breath hitched slightly when I found a particularly sensitive spot. The way her lean curves tightened in anticipation of something I wasn't quite ready to give.

"What do you want, beautiful?" I murmured. "What can I do for you?"

Nina's eyes brightened as I drew the rose back up her chest. I played it over the line of her bra, feathering it over her breasts. She wasn't a Coke-bottle pinup, far too slender for that. But I knew without checking that each breast would fit perfectly in the palm of my hand.

"I don't know if anyone has ever asked me that before."

I dragged the flower over one nipple, causing it to perk through the silk. Nina squirmed and bit her lip. All right, then. Clearly that was something I needed to do more of.

I leaned over her, enjoying the way she arched slightly in anticipation. The rosebud traveling over her other nipple. She moaned. Just barely.

"I'm asking now," I said, hovering my lips over hers. I wanted to kiss her. God, I wanted to kiss her. I wanted to feel that give of her body against mine again, see what happened when the fire there was allowed to burn unfettered.

But.

Not yet. Not. Quite. Yet.

"Tell me, sweetheart," I said, as I placed a soft kiss on her jaw. Then another on the other side. "What do you like?"

————

LAST NIGHT it had continued until I'd shouted loud enough that my sister Frankie had come running from her bedroom across the hall. Embarrassed, I'd snapped at her to get the hell out, then tossed and turned until I finally resigned myself to watching the sunrise glimmer over the roofs of Red Hook rowhouses like mine.

I did whatever I could to escape what haunted me. Trudged over to one of the bars in Gowanus, or even to Jamie's joint in Manhattan. Had a few too many drinks. Gone home with one chick or another. Women who were usually blonde. Thin. Eager. And, because I was predictable as fuck, usually taken.

Even so, I often ended up here.

Because just like all the others, the dream ended the same way. Nina holding the bouquet of roses I'd given her. Looking up to where I stood in our hotel window. Raising a delicate hand before disappearing into a big black car. Into the city for good.

And I was left with a gut-twisting feeling I was truly coming to hate for its stubborn fuckin' tenacity. That I needed to find Nina Astor. That she needed me to find her too.

But she was nowhere to be found.

The problem was that I had so little to go on. I knew she was rich. I knew she was more or less local. But other than that? Not a whole lot.

The name, for instance, had to be a fake. I'd combed through New York city and state records until I was blue in the face. Marriage. Divorce. Even, with a heavy heart, death. According to public databases, the only Nina Astors in the general tristate area died during the Depression. So I'd gone to ground. Interrogated the front desk of the hotel for over an hour before I finally left. Interviewed people on the damn street trying to get the plates off the car she left in.

But like a buster, I always ended up on streets like this, hoping to run into her. I couldn't have told you why I thought Nina was from the Upper East Side, but the prim, polished neighborhood seemed to fit. She was as classic as the nineteenth-century buildings and stately brownstones, as clean as their sleek facades, so different from the stained gray stonework of the Bronx neighborhood where I grew up or the pile of red bricks I now called home.

The funny thing, when this neighborhood was first built, it was as middle class then as Belmont or Red Hook were to me now. Buildings full of French flats—single-family housing where the upper-level working class of New York's gilded age lived before they were usurped by the city's bourgeoisie.

Nina had told me her family was wealthy, but she didn't say who they were. Astor, though. Everyone in New York knew that name. Streets, buildings, subway stops. It was everywhere.

Unless, of course, that's where she got it. Grasping for a fake name to offer, she'd taken one in plain sight.

It was a hard pill to swallow, thinking the woman who had stripped me bare might have lied to my face.

I stared up at a particularly fancy building on a tree-lined street off Madison. It was complete with gargoyles scowling at the corners and a green-tinted roof curling at the top.

I scowled back. Was this where she was hiding?

Or was I kidding myself? Nina probably wasn't even in New York anymore. She probably never would be again.

Before I could keep walking, my phone rang with my assistant's ring tone. I flipped on my Bluetooth and answered.

"Zola."

"I know who it is. I called *you*."

I rolled my eyes. Tiana was the best assistant I'd ever had. She didn't put up with my shit, which was a very good thing. But she also came with a truckload of attitude.

"Ti, what's up?"

"I just sent a file via the secure server. I would have waited, but it was straight from Ramirez. He said given all the work you've been doing on"—she paused before speaking the next word in hushed tones —"*Carson*...this was a natural extension."

I frowned and pulled out my phone to look at the file. Since Derek and I had met with Eric downtown, I'd made hardly any progress on the Carson case. I had a few friends in high places, but it was clearer that any help I could offer those two would come from me and me alone. But that would require a break I hadn't found yet.

"This is a file on a prostitution ring. Why wasn't it sent to Human Trafficking?" I flipped through a few more pages. "Jesus, they don't even have charges filed? What the hell does this have to do with John Carson?"

"Do you really think I know the answer to that?"

I groaned. I didn't have time for this. I had a case heading to trial next week and another ready to go before a grand jury. Like just about every other government employee, I was overworked and overtired. I didn't need this goose chase on top of everything else.

"Before you dig into it, though, I have a Caitlyn Calvert for you."

I made a face. "Ah, no. Tell her I'm out."

Unfortunately, no such luck. "That didn't work this morning either, Zola."

My scowl turned into a full-on death glare. I'd met Caitlyn Calvert during one of my late-night runs into the city. With her honey-brown hair and diamond earrings, she dripped polish and wealth. So close to the other perfectly bred creature I had been seeking. And after a bottle of wine, it was close enough.

We had gone to a hotel in Chelsea to get what I thought we both needed. For her, it was an escape from her humdrum life of committee meetings and planning a wedding she apparently didn't even want. For me, she was just close enough to the woman I *actually* wanted to pretend for a few hours that I'd found her. One night was enough for me, though —I was never into fakes.

Ms. Calvert, however, had other ideas. I'd given in the last two. But today, I was in no mood.

I scowled. "Come on, Tiana…"

"Don't give me that look—she's been calling all damn day. You're taking this call, Zola."

"How do you know what my face looks like?" I shook my head. This wasn't even a video call.

"Because I know," Tiana said shortly. "I'm putting her through."

And before I could say another word, the line clicked over.

"Z? Are you there?"

The single-initial thing bugged me, but she'd been doing it since we met. I pegged it as her weird little way of establishing intimacy, the way rich women did when they couldn't do it with hugs or kisses like normal people.

"Caitlyn, I'm at work," I huffed. "I need to get back. What is it?"

"I was surprised, that's all, when you declined my invitation," Caitlyn said. "I honestly thought it was too good to be true. Imagine it. You and me? Alone? A whole weekend away from your sad little shack?"

On the other end of the line, I could hear Caitlyn's nails clinking against her glass. If I remembered correctly, they were French tipped, painfully white at the ends, paired with diamond rings so bright they could probably be seen from space.

I frowned. Insulting the house in Brooklyn that I scrimped and saved for wasn't the best way to get on my good side. Sure, the house I shared with my sister and her kid was no palace. But in a city of renters, owning my own place was so far the crowning achievement of my financial life. I didn't even remember telling Caitlyn about it, but that didn't mean a few glasses of wine hadn't loosened my tongue at some point.

"Like I told you," I said, kicking my foot in the direction of a bunch of pigeons that instantly scattered. "I can't get away this weekend. I'm buried in work, and I just don't think—"

"Lover, please. It's been eons since our last night. Don't make me beg. It turns me into a dreadful bore."

I rolled my eyes. We'd seen each other three days ago. I hated the ones who talked like this—like they were characters out of *The Philadelphia Story*. Katherine Hepburn without the smarts. Cary Grant without the swagger. I wasn't any more special to Caitlyn than she was to me—but like so many trust funders and trophy wives, she thought she was entitled to plenty. Including my company.

"Look, we had some fun, honey, but now we can just leave it at that," I said bluntly. "I don't have time for anything more than the one night, and you're, well, engaged, right? This was never going anywhere."

There was a long pause. Long enough that I might have wondered if Caitlyn had hung up if it hadn't been for the sound of her breathing. Good fuckin' God. These kinds of people really couldn't take the word no.

"I see," Caitlyn said finally, although I wondered if she really did. "I —well, I'm not one to beg."

Aren't you? After all, hadn't she been doing just that in a suite downtown just last week?

I had the good sense to keep that to myself. It was hard, let me tell you.

"You're a class act, Cait." I decided to be generous instead and lie. "I hope you and your fiancé can work it out. And if not—you'll find what you need in the end. You deserve it."

"Thank you."

Her voice was suddenly soft, and I felt bad. I forgot sometimes how vulnerable women like her really were. So many of them were neglected, stuck in their posh apartments like museum pieces, pretty things for their husbands to look at when they tore themselves away from the stock markets and men's clubs. Caitlyn was desperate for someone, anyone, to make her feel seen. Loved, even.

But the truth was painfully clear. I was useless to any woman but the one I couldn't find. In the meantime, I was just another asshole, another sinner using them as much as they were using me.

"You take care, Cait."

Maybe one day she'd find a real Prince Charming to rescue her. But that prince wasn't me.

No sooner had the conversation ended than my phone rang again.

I groaned. "Tiana, what now?"

"Oh, no. You did *not* just 'what now' me, Mr. Attitude. I am just doing my job, and you think it's okay to serve me that kind of mouth?"

I sighed. This fuckin' day was never ending. "Tiana, I'm sorry. I'll bring you a whole cheesecake from Junior's on Monday. Thank you for dealing with my mouth."

She sniffed. "That's more like it. I have Leona Parker for you."

I stood up straighter. That was actually someone I wanted to talk to. "Put her through, please."

Leona Parker was a classmate from Officer Training School who had turned her time in Special Forces into a thriving career at the CIA. She and I had known each other for fifteen years, and she was one of the few people I would trust with my life. Mostly because I already had. After meeting with Eric, I'd sent her the full file on the de Vrieses with hopes the feds would *finally* pay attention to the fuckin' disaster that was the Carson case.

"Lee," I answered. "Tell me it's good news."

The long sigh told me my request was not going to be granted. "I'm sorry, Zola. I wish I could."

"Fuck. The director too?"

We had to speak in veiled terms. I worked in a government office whose lines were probably monitored 24-7, even via cell phone. Leona was a legitimate G-man. Or, G-woman, I supposed. She lived her life under surveillance. And a conversation about John Carson wasn't something we wanted tracked back to us. Not immediately, anyway.

"We said that's how it might go. He's powerful, Zo. You know that. Lots of ties to *lots* of people. People in government. People with very deep pockets."

I understood immediately what she meant. John Carson's company held about forty percent of the U.S. government's munitions contracts. The armed forces needed him as much as he needed them.

"Still, though," I said. "Even after Korea—"

"Stalled," she interrupted.

When they had come home from South Korea in January, Jane and Eric had enough evidence against John Carson for ten indictments. Kidnapping. Conspiracy. But the worst by far was nuclear arms production. And here was Leona telling me that the CIA still couldn't be moved.

"I'm so sorry I don't have better news," Leona said. "But that's just the way the cookie crumbles, my friend. You know the director isn't going to act against the DOJ. This isn't the first time this has happened. Think about Guantanamo."

Again, her meaning was clear. The president, in all his glory, was basically wielding the attorney general like a shield for anything he wanted. Carson had been one of the president's largest campaign contributors. And now he was reaping the benefits.

I sighed. This was bad. Maybe not wholly unexpected, but bad, nonetheless.

Another dead end.

"Better take it back to Ramirez. He's got the *cojones*, so to speak, and he's supporting your investigation. These days a lot of justice seemed to be happening...where you are."

I rubbed my forehead viciously. I honestly didn't know what else to do. This was all state-level attorney generals and district prosecutors had been hearing since the last election. Suddenly our job wasn't just fighting the bad guys in our own communities. We were doing what the feds couldn't—not with corruption infecting Washington like a virus. I'd been an ADA for seven years, but these days, it felt more like twenty. Talk about added stakes.

I considered the file Tiana had just sent. What had seemed like yet another task in my overworked life now felt like a final ray of hope.

"Thanks, Lee," I said. "I'll, uh, let him know."

"Sorry, Zola. Say hi to your family for me."

"Sure," I said. "Tell Greg what's up."

With that, we hung up, and I pulled up the file to read on my way to the subway.

A few minutes later, it was obvious why Ramirez had sent it. The NYPD had been running surveillance on a trafficking suspect with ties in Downtown Manhattan, Hunt's Point, Jamaica Queens, and, yes, Brooklyn, at an address located right smack in the middle of "The Hole"—one of the last crime-ridden no-man's lands on the boundary between Queens and Brooklyn where even law enforcement barely dared to go.

Some called it the second Wild West, both for its apparent lawlessness and because it was home to the New York Federation of Black Cowboys. Rumor had it, there were actually fuckin' horses out there. In New York City.

I scanned the names that had been attached to the trafficking. No one new. Small-time crooks, people we'd tried to pressure time and time again on a variety of investigations over the years. New York was a big city, but the organized crime scene was relatively small. This felt like old news.

Until I came to a name at the bottom of the list.

Someone new.

Someone important.

Jude Letour was the heir to a DC-based import-export empire. His family had deep pockets in Washington, but they hadn't yet handed the reins over to their son, who was a bit of a black sheep.

Looked like he was doing his own import-export work of the human persuasion. Letour had been spotted coming in and out of the trafficking address in Brooklyn at approximately two in the morning, and the detective on the case had gotten at least three of the lower-level henchmen to name him specifically as the head of the trafficking project.

But I was more interested in another element. Eric had mentioned him more than once because he was part of Janus, a secret Ivy League society that originally connected the de Vrieses to the mess they were in. As it happened, Jude Letour happened to be the right-hand man to John fucking Carson. If he was doing underground business here in the city, there was a good chance his boss was too.

"I see you, motherfucker," I muttered as I paged through the notes. It was too late now to call the detective assigned to the case, but first thing Monday morning, I'd get Derek on it.

I turned back toward Central Park. Instead of going home, I'd be making another stop on the other side of the island. This was the kind of thing I needed to tell Jane and Eric in person.

CHAPTER THREE

It was nearly dark and starting to rain when I emerged onto Central Park West. I pulled my favorite fedora low as I wove through the heady mix of buskers, shoppers, tourists, and businesspeople, crowded by the ring of pedicabs and horse-drawn carriages looking for the last few fares.

The Upper West Side was one of those places that was just plain nice. It still had hints of the grit that coated New York—you could never completely escape that anywhere—but it lacked the marks of poverty and neglect that tore at other parts of the city, like mine.

Here, the bases of the buildings were washed and white instead of tagged with graffiti and filth. The sidewalks were clean and mostly uncracked. Across the street, the greening trees of early spring waved in the breeze like friends instead of people who wanted to mug you. Above, rain clouds threatened, but right now, it was just a nice place to walk around.

You fuckin' liar.

I shook away my subconscious, cloaked in the voice of my best friend, Jamie Quinn. Over the last few months, I'd developed an alarming recurrence of internal monologue, usually taking the form of someone close if it wasn't her. A friend. A sister. Someone who knew me well enough to call out my bullshit.

Go the fuck away, Jay, I told him mentally.

Not until you admit what you're really *lookin' for.*

Or who, I thought with him. Fine, fine. Fuck the pretty brick buildings. I was walking an extra twenty blocks under the threat of a downpour for the same reason I often got off halfway between Brooklyn and Belmont every Sunday just to meander Central Park. The reason why I'd suddenly started visiting every museum on Fifth Avenue more than I went to Mass.

———

"Can you walk a bit, doll?" I asked Nina as she hurried on a gray cashmere coat. "Might warm us up. I need a bite to eat after all that wine."

"I—yes, I could eat. Somewhere close, though?" She looked at her feet. "I'm so sorry, but I'm afraid these shoes weren't made for long treks."

"Don't ever apologize for those shoes."

I was rewarded with another mild blush and a murmur of something like, "I'm glad you like them." I took Nina's hand, and for a split second, the cold disappeared as a shock of heat passed through my fingertips. Jesus, Mary, this was some kind of electricity.

Nina started as if she'd felt it too. Her bright eyes found mine, then drifted to my lips. For a moment, I considered kissing her. I'd wanted to for hours at that point, and I was pretty sure she wanted it as well. But she had a skittish quality that reminded me of the stray cats by my house, like if I took a step too soon, she'd bolt.

Instead, I raised her hand to examine it. Her skin was so fair, almost translucent. I could practically see her pulse moving. Slowly, I pressed a kiss over the lace of veins that crisscrossed just below her knuckles.

When I dropped our hands, she had her other one pressed to her shirt, as if to hold her heart in place. I couldn't blame her. One brief touch, and mine was practically jumping out of my chest.

"You all right there, beautiful?" I asked.

She nodded. "Yes, I—I just thought…"

I cocked my head. "You thought what?"

She blinked, looking a bit embarrassed. "I thought you were going to kiss me."

I knew it.

I shrugged. "I thought about it. But I figured I'd be a gentleman and wait until you asked."

At that, amusement danced over her glossy features. "A gentleman from the Bronx," she murmured.

Her. It was always her.

But Nina Astor was a damn mirage, to the point where I wondered if she had been real at all.

Two months after the night that changed my life, I was searching for a ghost.

It was time to accept it.

Nina Astor didn't exist.

The rain was really starting to rap on the brim of my hat by the time I reached Jane and Eric's brownstone on West Seventy-Sixth Street. I pressed the buzzer and faced the security camera. It took a few minutes —Eric and Jane had a team set up downstairs to vet any visitors. A few minutes later, the door buzzed open.

"Hey, Tony."

The security head nodded at me as I jogged up to the fourth floor. The whole place was a giant construction mess. Eric had recently bought out the building and was having it restored to a regular house for the two of them. I sniffed. Some house. It made my little brick place in Red Hook look like a fuckin' storage shed.

Two minutes later, Eric opened the door, clearly just off work himself in the remains of another impeccably tailored suit. Takes one to know one, I suppose. Just because I was a civil servant didn't mean I had to look like one. But there was a big difference. I bought my Armani threads from my sister's secondhand shop uptown. Eric probably had his made custom, brand fuckin' new.

Still, he wasn't flashy the way you'd expect someone worth several billion dollars to be. As far as I knew, he had worked hard to hide the fact for a long time. I'd heard the stories, of course, of how Eric de Vries had walked away from his birthright. Gone to law school, like me. Started his own firm in Boston, only to be lured back to New York to save his family's fortune. But I could have saved the guy a decade and told him he wasn't ever going to be anything other than the head of a powerful family. Money has a funny way of weaving into people's DNA. You can't hide that kind of breeding.

"Hey," I said as I followed Eric inside. "I was on my way uptown and thought I would drop in. I, uh, have some news."

"That so?" Eric shook my hand. "Need a glass of wine to tell it?"

"It is after five o'clock." I nodded toward the couch where Jane was sitting. "Hey, Jane."

Eric went to get us all drinks in the kitchen without another word. I'd been here enough to where my unannounced visits weren't much of a surprise anymore. For the same reason that Leona and I usually spoke in veiled terms, I made these updates in person.

Jane got up from the couch to greet me after I took off my trench coat and hung it with my hat.

"Hey, you," she said. "Been a minute."

"You're looking good," I told her honestly.

And it was true. When Eric had brought Jane home from Korea, she'd been completely traumatized, much too thin and ghostly. Now the color in her cheeks had returned, along with her trademark cat-eye glasses and penchant for needling her husband. We had the latter in common. I didn't linger as she gave me a kiss on the cheek—as much fun as it was to rile Eric, I knew all too well how protective he could be over his wife's affections. It was only last Thanksgiving that he had tried to clock me over the turkey for offering her a hug.

That, thankfully, seemed to be firmly in the past as Eric joined Jane and me by the flickering fire, delivering us both red wine while he stayed with vodka.

"Damn." I wasn't well-versed in French wines, generally preferring Italian, but I knew Eric only bought the best. "This is why I really come here. What is this, a Margaux?"

Eric nodded, though Jane shrugged.

I chuckled. "You don't know?" I asked her.

"This one has the fancy tastes. I'd probably just bring home Three-Buck Chuck every night, but Eric thinks he's allergic to it."

I grimaced at the idea. I didn't have the cash to drink one of the best wines in the world like house grog, but I was with Eric on this one. I appreciated the life people like the de Vrieses led. The perfectly tailored clothes. The spacious, yet comfortable home. The best food. The best wine. The best of everything.

"Nice work if you can get it," as they say. And if you can, why the fuck not?

"I just don't see the point of drinking garbage," Eric was saying while he played with his wife's dark hair.

"Why, my dear Rockefeller," Jane teased. "What a charmingly privileged thing to say. Leave the swill to the slums, is that right?"

In a split second, Eric's expression went from casually opaque to completely transparent. I'd seen it before. It was their ongoing act—Jane would say things that would purposefully get under Eric's skin until his implacable facade broke. And when it did, she obviously relished the consequences.

The hand in Jane's hair tightened, and the atmosphere in the room crackled. Eric growled something in his wife's ear that made her turn just a few shades lighter red than the wine in her glass. He looked just as fierce as ever, but it was clear by her expression that whatever threat he'd just made was something Jane was more than happy to receive.

I shifted in my seat. Fuck, maybe I'd blown Caitlyn off too early. I could call her now. Meet up at a hotel on the East Side. Anything to scratch that goddamn itch.

And yet, I also knew that whatever charge had just passed between them wasn't just about sex. I knew it because for one night, I had felt it too. Something happens when two souls join the same way bodies do. Nina Astor and I had given each other everything we had that night. For the first and only time in my life, I'd been completely naked with a woman and allowed her to do the same to me.

I'd been cut open. And so fucking deep.

Do you believe in love at first sight?

Not until I saw you.

There was no going back after that. Unfortunately, it also meant nothing else could replace it once it was lost.

I shook my head. I'd already been down that rabbit hole too many times today alone. Right now, I needed to focus on the two very *real* people in this room who needed my help.

"So, what's up?" Eric pulled me out of my daydream. "What's the news?"

And into something worse.

"Well, I'm afraid it's not very good. I got a call from my friend at the CIA. They, um, are declining to prosecute. They won't be sending anything to the DOJ."

"*What?*"

Eric exploded off the couch, nearly tossing Jane to the floor. She barely saved her wineglass, but looked too crestfallen to reply.

"What the fuck happened?" Eric demanded. "We practically gift-wrapped that indictment for them!"

I waited while he continued to spout. Jane's normal air of mischief had completely shuttered while she toyed with her wedding rings, still loose around her fingers.

"Look," I said once Eric had calmed down. "We've talked about this. You know as well as I do that the current administration is basically in Carson's pockets. A pardon was always a possibility. Now it's just…a reality, I guess. Unless he's prosecuted here. At the state level."

"We should take it to the press," Eric said. "I'll give an interview to the *Times*. Try his ass in the court of public opinion. Isn't that how they got that campaign manager indicted in 2017? Where's the fucking accountability?"

"I'd wait on that for a minute," I said. "There's another way to go. One that won't give away your hand."

"Like murder?" Eric muttered.

Jane elbowed him in the ribs.

To be honest, I couldn't really blame Eric for the joke. If it had been the love of *my* life targeted in this way (Nina's face again appeared in the back of my mind), I'd have probably taken my Marine-issued Beretta to the streets a long time ago.

"Kidding," Eric said with a long drink of his vodka. "Sort of."

"Look, maybe the feds aren't prosecuting, but the Brooklyn DA sure as hell is," I continued.

I proceeded to outline—vaguely—how my boss intended to pick off the people surrounding John Carson, mafia-style. The Brooklyn DA's office had been going after New York's worst gangsters for over a hundred years. We had a process. You go after the small fish first. You cut off the whale's food supply. And then, when he comes down to find out where his chow went, you swoop in with the net.

Maybe Carson could buy off the feds, but he didn't have any leverage with my boss or me. We just needed the right crime. The right confession. The right jurisdiction.

I didn't mention the file that Tiana had sent this afternoon. I wasn't really supposed to be discussing the details with them anyway; I only wanted to give them a little peace of mind when I could. They deserved at least that much.

Eric, though, had his own ideas. Stage a secret meeting of their so-called "society." Lure the whale into the net instead of waiting for him to swim buy.

Jane wasn't having it.

"*No*," she snapped. "He'll know what you're doing. He's thought one step ahead of you this whole time. Eric, he will know."

Eric just stared at her, clearly getting his argument together. I wasn't sure where I stood.

On the one hand, I was plenty interested in investigating the Janus society. From the outside, it sounded like a rich-boys' club that also sounded an awful lot like the mafia. Its members met in defunct grave-yards, smuggled booze and other goods, and in general took pleasure in fucking with regular people. If Eric wanted to give me the goods, I wouldn't argue. Especially since getting a list of members wouldn't just help the case—it would probably make my career.

On the other hand, I understood Jane's trepidation. It wasn't the safest plan when both she *and* Eric had already been abducted by these assholes.

Before he could answer, however, the buzzer announced another visitor.

"We're not done," Eric said on his way to the call button. "Yeah?"

"Mrs. Gardner is here." Tony's voice vibrated through the fuzzy speaker.

"Oh? Sure, send her up." Eric unlocked the door. "This should only take a minute, Zola. It's just my cousin. She's been a huge help with all of this shit."

I shrugged and took another sip of wine. "Fine by me."

Heels soon clicked up the marble stairs. A second later the door swung open, and a bluster of white, blonde, and sparkle wrapped in a familiar gray coat whirled into the apartment with the force of the rainstorm outside.

"Hello, hello, I'm so sorry to interrupt your evening." The visitor's back was to us as she shook out her umbrella and set it by the door. "I'm a bit desperate, and I needed to see Jane immediately. I—oh!"

When she turned around, I could barely hold my glass. I couldn't speak at all.

It was her.

The woman I'd been seeking for months.

The elegant work of art I'd been dreaming of every night since January.

She stood by the door, her large gray eyes locked with mine. She was a statue. I was a statue. Only the bit of pink at the tip of her nose and the crest of her cheekbones betrayed the fact that she was human. And that she was as surprised—or more—to see me too.

"Matthew."

The word was so faint, it was barely audible. But hearing my name from those lips at last, I managed to find my own voice as well.

"Nina."

CHAPTER FOUR

Nina.

Nina Astor.

Was here.

In this apartment.

Staring at me with the *exact* same expression she'd worn just before I kissed her for the first time. Lips partially open. Jaw dropped an inch or so. A dewy sheen over her plump bottom lip.

Kiss me, she seemed to say.

And I couldn't. Fuckin'. Move.

"You two know each other?"

Eric's voice knifed through the tension, and with regret, I watched Nina assume a mask I'd noticed her cousin take several times. Family trait, apparently. She smoothed her dress—a fitted white thing, conservative but for a tasteful slit above her knee—and turned to pick up a binder she had set on the entry table.

"We've met." Her voice was calm as she crossed the room to stand by the couch. "Calvin made a donation to Juan Ramirez's campaign last year. It was at the fundraiser, wasn't it, Matthew?"

I couldn't stop staring at her legs long enough to answer.

"Nina, wine?" Eric asked from the kitchen.

She nodded, though she didn't look up. Not at him. And certainly not at me.

Finally, I managed to move enough muscles to swallow and clear my throat. It wasn't easy. "Oh. Yeah, um, yes. Yes, that was probably it. Good to see you again, doll."

I couldn't help it. It slipped out. The seemingly harmless moniker had come as naturally with her as breathing. It was special, "doll." The name my grandfather used for *Nonna* when he was still alive. The one that made her blush well into her seventies. The one that made her his.

Not everyone grows up with that kind of model for a relationship. But I did. My parents were good for fuckin' nothing, but the two people who raised me, staunchly Catholic Italians who took on five kids in the Bronx, had been in love with each other since they were teenagers and stayed in love until my grandfather's last breath.

"Doll," he called her even on his deathbed, like he was about to whisk *Nonna* off to see Frankie Valle at the Copa. And she squeezed his frail hand and blushed and chattered at him in Italian, like they were still kids.

Fools in love until the bitter end.

Maybe I should have been more careful. But the second I met her in that goddamn bar, Nina was "doll" to me. For better or for worse.

Nina focused on her binder, but the tinge of pink on her cheeks spread. *Good*, I thought. At least I wasn't the only one feeling something here.

Eric returned with Nina's wine, and we all watched awkwardly as she took a very long drink. When about half the glass was empty, she cleared her throat.

"Ah, yes. Yes, it's nice to see you too, Matthew."

She looked me over for a few seconds longer than necessary. I resisted the urge to drag her out of the apartment like a fuckin' caveman.

Nina blinked, like she had just remembered where we were, and turned. "Actually, Jane, this isn't purely a social visit. I have a dreadful favor to ask you."

Much to Eric's obvious irritation, Nina took his seat on the couch beside Jane. He sat in the other chair while I remained transfixed by the way Nina's skirt rode up her thigh. You would think it had been three years since I'd gotten laid, not three damn days. You would have thought I'd never seen a woman's legs before tonight. All I could think about was the way her skin felt under my hands—velvety and smooth, taut and responsive. I remembered sliding my palms up those limbs, memorizing the lean curves of muscle and bone as I went. Up, up, up to the promised land waiting between them.

As I sipped on my wine, I could barely even make out the conversation. Something about a gala. An event Nina desperately needed Jane's help with. Fancy, rich-people shit.

It only reminded me that I was the odd man out here. Eric and Nina were old money, the sort that didn't know anything different. Jane was from more middle-class stock like me, but if this apartment was any indication, she'd taken to extreme wealth like a fish to water, shitty taste in wine aside. Being a de Vries obviously had its benefits.

That was when it hit me. De Vries. Nina was a de Vries. Eric had mentioned his only "cousin" often enough, the daughter of his aunt, his deceased father's sister. Nina was the other grandchild of one of the oldest families in New York, a genuine heiress to a shipping dynasty.

In other words, from a completely different world.

———

"De Vries. Is that your last name?"

Was it my imagination, or did she recoil?

"No," she said emphatically. "It is not."

I frowned. "You sure?"

Something as sharp as a knife flashed in her eyes. They might be the color of cooing doves, but they turned hawkish in a second.

"Do you think I don't know my own name, Mr. Zola?"

———

Oh, she was a sly little fox, wasn't she? Bits and pieces of our actual conversation, wine-soaked as it was, were coming back to me. I'd known even then there was a connection between Nina and the de Vrieses. And she had lied, point-blank, even while cultivating my sympathy for her plight.

———

"GRANDMOTHER WASN'T PARTICULARLY...SOFT. She cared for me, of course. Not as much as my cousin, who lived with her. But she did. And then they fell out, and I was the one who stayed behind when he ran off. I took care of her and visited when she was ill."

———

So. Nina was an heiress.

———

"AND WHEN E—WHEN my cousin returned after years away and got married, Grandmother left him everything. Our family's entire business. Our properties. All of it."

———

WAS, then. That's right, I remembered that too. Celeste de Vries had died last November and willed the company to Eric—his reward for getting married. Huh.

Her hands moved gracefully as she paged through the files she had brought. Every so often, though, she darted a look at me I couldn't quite read. Suspicious, maybe. Fearful? Confused? Yeah, that made two of us.

I downed the remainder of my wine, then sat back in the armchair, brooding until Jane and Eric's bickering pulled me out of my daze.

"Nina," Eric was saying. "Look, I get that this is a big deal, but we were kind of in the middle—"

"Shh, Petri, take a Xanax, all right?" Jane interrupted. "No one delays the Met Gala."

Eric and I both frowned at her. I vaguely knew what she was talking about—some big party at the museum that shut down the Upper East Side every spring. Was she really talking about a fuckin' social event like it was more important than my updates about John Carson?

"The Met Gala," Jane repeated, like we should completely grasp the gravity. When we clearly didn't, she went off. "Eric! Come on, I would have expected better from you, at least. *The Met Gala.* First Monday in May. Fashion prom. It's the giant fundraiser of the Costume Institute of the Metropolitan Museum, overseen by the editor-in-chief of *Vogue* magazine. One of the most exclusive tickets on the planet, and something you do *not* say no to. *Ever!*"

By the time she finished ranting, Eric seemed to know what she was talking about. I, however, was still more interested in Nina, who had gone quiet. From what I recalled, this was a woman who knew fashion. Organizing a fancy event with a bunch of designers seemed like something she'd be capable of doing—more, probably, than a novice like Jane.

Nina seemed more interested in studying her nails than meeting anyone's gaze. I followed hers. Right to the rock on her left hand.

––––––––

"Is there someone else?" My heart pounded as I asked. But I had to. I probably knew the answer all along.

Guilt flooded her beautiful face. "I—yes. I'm so sorry, Matthew, but yes, there is."

Every cell in my body deflated. Fuck. Fuck.

I sighed, but forced myself not to look away. "Married, or just…"

Her shoulders hunched. "I'm married, yes."

––––––––

The memory faded, but I still felt like I'd been punched in the gut.

"Okay, so what's up?" Jane asked Nina, who jerked out of her own daze.

"It's awful, just awful," she said in a strange, rushed voice. "I took over Grandmother's seat on the committee, of course. There wasn't time for them to find someone else. I had intended to give it to you—I think that's what she wanted, since the two of you spent so much time at the Institute in her last days, and to be honest, I don't really know much about fashion beyond the houses I like myself. But you and Eric had so many...challenges...lately, I thought it best to do it myself this year. Except I'm absolutely all wrong for it!"

I sat back in my seat again and continued to study her. Call me crazy, but me thought the lady protested a little too much.

"Wrong for what, Nina?" Eric wondered.

Nina flipped to a large picture: a black-and-white photo of a man about to break his guitar over the words *London Calling*. "Wrong for this. I can't help organize an event around this theme. I know absolutely nothing about it."

Everyone bent to look.

"Oh my merry Mick Jones," Jane murmured. "You have got to be kidding. Have I died and gone to heaven?"

"What?" Eric wondered.

"Is that The Clash?" I asked with a grin. "Hey, I like that song." Hell, I was just glad to contribute *something* to this conversation.

"It's the theme," Jane practically sang. "They choose one every year for the exhibit and the gala itself, and this year it's 'London Calling.' Cora Spring and the Metropolitan Museum are using *The freaking Clash* as their inspiration!"

"Which is why I don't know what I'm doing!" Nina burst out.

Okay, so she lied about who she was. And no, I didn't exactly believe that she was *that* stressed about planning any kind of fashion event, punk-themed or not. But in that moment, I didn't really care about what lies Nina Astor-de Vries-Gardner-whatever-her-name-was had to tell. I heard the note of true panic in that beautiful voice of hers, and all I could think was *make it better*.

My hand shot out before I could help it, and barely stopped before it landed on top of hers. Nina stared. Jane and Eric stared. And by some Herculean effort, I managed to pull it back into my lap and pretend that nothing happened. Except something already had. Less than five minutes, and I was like a magnet. Good fuckin' God, I needed to get out of here.

"So you see," Nina turned the conversation awkwardly around with a single nervous glance my way. "You have to take my spot, Jane."

"Come again now?"

I stared at my hands while the three of them went back and forth. I should go. I needed to go. But the truth was, as long as Nina was sitting in front of me, I wasn't going fuckin' anywhere.

"Just to be clear," Jane said. "You are asking me to help the editor of the world's most prestigious fashion magazine and a bunch of the other most stylish people in the world plan the world's most exclusive fashion event?"

Without a flinch, Nina nodded. "Please, please, please. I look like a fool."

I frowned. Not fuckin' likely. I had a feeling that the calm, competent woman sitting in front of me had never looked like a fool in her entire life.

"Well, I only have one question," Jane said. "Do I get to go too?"

"Oh, of course! You and Eric are already on the guest list. Heather and Mother too. Didn't I tell you? The family always has a table."

"Ah, no! You most certainly did not!"

And then Jane started screaming the same way my sisters did whenever one of them won five dollars on Keno tickets. Eric and I sat back like we were being blasted by a fog horn. Jane launched herself at Nina. And Nina...grinned.

Every iota of irritation melted off me at the sight of that golden smile. It fuckin' transformed her, and the ice that covered most of her appearance suddenly glimmered, like she'd been dipped in gold. Caught in Jane's embrace, pure happiness made Nina glow.

————

"Do you know how long it's been," she wondered as she watched our fingers slowly, slowly entwine, "since someone held my hand?"

————

HER LONELINESS that night had been palpable. The way she'd responded to my touch made me wonder how often she touched others at all.

———

"Now I feel like I've seen something different. And loneliness doesn't feel like an exchange for other privileges. It simply feels unbearable."

———

SHE'D BEEN TALKING about them. Funny, how knowing these two had affected us both the same way. We'd both been so lonely that night, and part of it had been because knowing two people as passionately in love as Jane and Eric reiterated the lack of it in our lives.

As Jane wrapped Nina in a bear hug, it was clear that Nina's plea tonight might have been motivated by a desire to get closer to her cousin and his wife. She had felt partially responsible for their plight, I remembered now. Why, I still wasn't sure. But I wanted to find out. Hell, with everything I was working on, I needed to find out.

"You look way too happy about this for a man who just committed his wife pretty much full time for the next three months," Jane told Eric as she returned to her seat. "First Monday in May is right around the corner."

"So it is," Eric said, "which also gives me an idea." He tapped a pen on the coffee table. "Maybe…we don't need a secret lair to trap the big fish. Maybe we just need a really exclusive event. And the right date to toss out a lure."

"Uh-oh. Someone is going Scooby-Doo on us," Jane said to Nina. "Who do you think is under the mask, Fred?"

I snorted. Eric didn't even respond, too obviously happy with his wife's glee. Nina, unfortunately, just looked confused. Dammit. Not even Scooby-fuckin'-Doo? What else had she missed out on as a child, growing up in this family?

"Who are you thinking?" I asked. I was already following Eric's logic. "We've tried the Jane card before. Yu-na too. He's not biting."

We were talking about Carson. Over the last few months, we'd done everything we could think of to bring the man into New York, if only to see what he would do. No dice.

Something about the gala had Eric's mind whirring.

"No," he said. "But we haven't tried my mother."

CHAPTER FIVE

THE PLAN WAS SIMPLE ENOUGH. MAYBE TOO SIMPLE.

As it turned out, John Carson once carried a pretty big torch for Eric's mother, who now went by Heather Keeler. Enough that Eric wondered privately if the man had been responsible for his father's death long ago.

"She says he acted like she belonged to him," he said.

Jane curled into herself at the thought, no doubt reminded of her own recent traumas.

"Hey," I found myself telling her. "We're going to get him, one way or another."

I wished it were true. I wished it could have been a promise.

"He's a narcissist who loves big public displays," Eric said. "He won't be able to resist a big public invitation from the woman who rejected him again and again. For him, it's the ultimate victory."

Soapy enough for you? Yeah, me too.

My job was to get the warrant in order, and to be there waiting with the police. Not too hard, really. But I had my doubts.

While I genuinely thought Carson would respond—we knew the man was nothing if not obsessive about this family—I definitely did not think he would show up. I'd been investigating John Carson for more than six months at this point. He was as slippery as an eel, but ten times smarter.

Still, I was willing to play along. Mostly because I wasn't going anywhere while Nina Astor—or Gardner, apparently—was sitting across from me. Nina kept trying to leave, but every time Jane would rope her back in with another question. Since the gala was the entire reason she was there, Nina would cast me a furtive glance, swallow about half a glass of wine, pour more, and keep talking.

"Great." Eric stood after we re-hashed the plan for the last time. "I'll call my mother tomorrow. Jane, you and Nina need to get her invite ASAP." He picked up the empty wine bottle. "Damn. Do I need to open another?"

"I need food, not wine," Jane announced. "Unless you're trying to get me drunk, Mr. de Vries…"

The playful lilt in her voice was unmistakable.

I hid a smile. I had known Jane a long time, and she still had a ways to go in her recovery. It was good to hear her joking again.

Nina rose and smoothed the fabric of her skirt over her long legs. Again, I found I couldn't look away, particularly once I caught the silvery gray shoes that seemed extremely familiar. Probably because I'd seen them before. And felt them digging into my back.

Fuck. Me.

She adjusted a delicate platinum watch around one wrist. Iced, just like her.

"I should be going, actually," she said. "I just wanted to make sure everything was taken care of. Jane, I'll call tomorrow. The committee meets at one. I'll introduce you to everyone, and then…it will be in your hands, I suppose."

Was that a note of melancholy I heard?

Jane nodded, though her attention rested with Eric, who was rubbing his thumb meaningfully around the top of the wine bottle. Suddenly, it felt like they were the only two people in the room. Nina and I were obvious intruders.

"Shall we order out? Eat by the fire tonight?" Eric asked. "What do you think, pretty girl?"

Jane just bit her lip.

I had heard Eric use the nickname on a couple of other occasions, and it never failed to make Jane squirm exactly like she was right now. In fact, the whole fuckin' place crackled right along with the embers in the fireplace.

Nina swallowed, darting yet another glance my way. I didn't even bother hiding my stare.

"I'll call tomorrow," she said again with a bit more force than strictly necessary. "Eric. Jane. M-Matthew."

And before anyone could respond, she practically sprinted out of the apartment, her heels echoing down the staircase before the front door shut.

"Zola?" Eric asked as he eyed his wife like prey. "You, ah, need anything else—"

"Nope." I was already up, tracking the door like a dog on the hunt while I retrieved my hat and coat. "I'll drop by next week, maybe with Derek. Just let me know what Heather says. I..." I stopped when I caught sight of the umbrella leaning by the door. "I'm going to see if I can catch Nina. She left this."

I didn't wait for a reply, just snatched the umbrella and skipped down the stairwell two at a time. *Not again, not again.* The words were a pounding refrain in time with my feet. I couldn't fuckin' miss her again. Not when I knew she wasn't just a figment of my imagination.

But when I emerged onto the street, Nina was nowhere to be seen— probably having already disappeared into one of those big black cars people like these seemed to have waiting for them all the time. I was cursing myself out when I turned toward and spotted a flash of white. Tall and leggy. Striding toward the black of the park.

"Nina!" I shouted, taking off down the street, jumping around left-over puddles while I clapped a hand atop my hat. The rain had stopped, but every so often I felt a threatening, fat drop. "Nina, wait!"

Finally, she looked over her shoulder. Her eyes grew about three times their size, and she doubled her pace.

"What the..."

She was avoiding me. Like a scared bunny, she was taking to the woods. In the middle of New York fuckin' City.

"The hell with that." I broke into a run, straight into the traffic hurtling up Central Park West.

"Get the fuck outta the road, asshole!"

A parade of horns followed me into the park, but I didn't care. I couldn't lose her again. I just fuckin' couldn't, and that was that.

"Nina! *Nina*! Goddammit, will you just wait!"

It was amazing, really, just how damn fast she could walk in four-inches heels, especially on a surface that switched erratically between pavement and cobblestones. Even if I hadn't figured out exactly who she was, I'd have known she was a veteran of New York sidewalks. Very fast. But not fast enough.

"Nina!"

I lunged forward and managed to catch her hand just as she started to cross the Seventy-Seventh Street Bridge. I snapped her back hard enough that she toppled into me, forcing me to wrap my arms around her just to stop us both from smacking the pavement.

The effect was immediate.

Lightning.

Shock.

Electricity.

Fire.

Look, I was still mad. Livid, in fact. I didn't chase after women, much less an Upper East Side princess who had done her best to pretend I didn't exist for the last two hours. If she were anyone else, I would have let her go, and good riddance. And maybe I was that much angrier *because* I couldn't let her go. Because she'd been stuck in my mind for months.

But the second I touched her again, none of that mattered. Because it wasn't a mirage in my arms. It wasn't a dream where I'd woken up shouting in the dark. She was the real thing. And she felt better than I had ever imagined.

"If you don't mind!" She wriggled out of my grasp with a huff and immediately started brushing down her coat, which was now rumpled from the chase. "Matthew, just what do you think you're doing, grabbing me like that?"

And just like that, the anger was back.

"What do I think *I'm* doing?" I repeated. "What do you think *you're* doing, huh? It's eight o'clock at night. In Central Park."

The sky above us was pitch black aside from the lights of the buildings ringing us. The park was a dungeon compared to the glowing city.

Nina stopped de-rumpling her coat and looked at me. That mask was back. So like her cousin's, but somehow sharper. More...imperious. For some reason, I was taken back to one particular moment in the bar, when we'd first met.

———

"What did you call me?"

"Princess," I said with a sly grin as I leaned on the bar just a few inches from her. I was invading her space, and it made her uncomfortable. I didn't give a shit.

I reached out and twirled a bit of her golden hair around one finger. "You're all dainty and shit, sitting on your throne, sipping on your wine. Like a princess. It fits."

She swallowed, looking fairly angry, although the way her tight nipples were pointing at me through her

blouse said she felt a lot more than that. Inwardly, I shrugged. Angry sex was just fine by me.

"I don't like being called princess."

———

She was right, of course. I had thought it funny at the time, but right now it was painfully obvious: Nina Astor wasn't anyone's princess. She was a queen.

A queen without her crown, I realized, thinking of Eric's unintentional coup. A monarch without a kingdom.

"I brought you this." I held out the umbrella like a knight offering fealty. As if I should kneel or something, and allow her to touch the umbrella to my shoulders like the edge of a sword.

"Oh." She took it. "Well, thank you. That was kind, but unnecessary.

Eric would have sent it over, or Jane could have brought it to our meeting tomorrow."

"Why were you running away?" I demanded bluntly.

Nina touched her mouth as she took a step backward. "I wasn't running. These shoes wouldn't let me."

"Po-ta-to, po-tah-to. Skipping. Trotting. Cantering like a fuckin' horse if that's what you want to say. But you were getting away from me as fast as those chopsticks would take you."

She looked down. "I thought you liked high heels, Matthew."

"I *love* high heels, doll. Especially on you. But not when they're taking you away from me."

She started again at the use of the nickname, just like she had in the apartment. But she didn't answer. The ferocity that had been on her face a moment before tightened into something more patrician. Something much more guarded.

I fuckin' hated it.

"Nina." I took a step toward her. "Come on. You couldn't have thought I'd just let you leave without talking."

The mask fell a bit, though now she was inordinately interested in the empty-branched oak trees surrounding us. "Oh, but I wish you would. It's—Matthew, it's better this way."

"Better? You wanna walk me through that one, sweetheart?"

She didn't answer as our gazes finally locked. This wasn't stolen glances across the coffee table. We were in the middle of Central Park on a cold, dreary night. The trees swallowed the sounds of the city. Right now, it was just us here on this bridge.

"I—" I took off my hat, put it back on. Then did it again. "I just wanted to make sure you were safe, all right?"

Nina tipped her head. "Matthew. Really."

"Okay. *Okay.* But what the fuck did you think I was going to do? Months, Nina. I've been looking for you for *months.*"

"I told you not to do that."

Her tone was bitter. But not as much as mine.

"I don't remember that part. I remember telling you I'd walk you down after a shower, but when I got out, you had fuckin' disappear—"

"You couldn't have possibly believed I would stay," she cut in. "I said one—"

"And just when I'm thinking about giving up, the fuckin' door opens in some random person's apartment—"

"Jane and Eric are *not* random, and—"

"And like the Mother Mary herself just answered every one of my damn prayers, you walk in out of nowhere, so—"

"I was there for my own reas—"

"The hell if I was just going to let you walk out again without a word. I have some questions, Nina, and I'm not leaving until you fuckin' answer them!"

By the time we had finished cutting off each other's sentences, both of us were seething—me in a more obvious, chest-thumping way with my favorite hat now crumpled in my hands, Nina with that ice queen glare of hers.

She crossed her arms. "You have questions. Like what, pray tell, Mr. Zola?"

I *hated* the crisp formality. It reminded me of a judge on her last case of the day. Or the headmistress at the parish school where I had lasted exactly two years before being kicked out. The only time I ever wanted to hear Nina address me *that* way was on her knees before I taught her some fuckin' respect. Right before she begged for more...discipline.

"Like...like..." I was gesturing wildly by this point. Fuckin' Christ, the woman flustered me with just a name.

As she folded her arms again, the light from a streetlamp caught one of the facets of her diamond.

"Like *that*," I said, pointing at it.

She looked down at the stone, then back up at me. "That's an engagement ring. And a wedding ring."

"I know that."

"I told you I was married."

"I know that too."

"I fail to hear a question, Matthew."

I stomped my foot. Like a fuckin' child, I stomped my foot right there on the bridge. I already knew Nina could make me crazy, but I didn't realize she could be like this. Full of stubbornness. Intransigence. Using her ability to reduce a man to rubble out of spite.

Okay, so she was part of one of the oldest, richest families in New York. Okay, so she was suddenly back in my life after months. I was a lawyer in the greatest city in the world. I went in front of judges, reporters, jury members every damn day. I wasn't going to let one spoiled little girl get the best of me.

And this time, I wasn't going to take it easy on her.

"Your name," I said. "What's your name?"

She rolled her eyes, looking for a moment like I imagined she must have at about sixteen. All pretention and privilege. No fuckin' respect.

"You know my name."

"I know your first name, *Nina*. But that night in the bar, you told me point blank you weren't a de Vries. Ms. *Astor*, is it?"

She opened her mouth, then closed it again. "I—okay, yes. Fine. My surname is not de Vries. But I told you that because it's the truth."

"Is it?"

"It *is*."

"You gave me a fake name."

"I did not."

"You *did*," I snapped. "I'm an investigative prosecutor for the Brooklyn DA, Nina. I didn't lie to you about that. Or anything else, for that matter. First thing I did Monday morning was run your name through the system. Again. And again. Nothing. Astor isn't real, is it?"

"It's my father's name!" she finally broke. "And if you recall, we don't exactly have the best relationship. I didn't lie about that either."

"My father is gone too," Nina said at last.

"I'm sorry to hear that. When did he pass?"

"Oh, he's not dead. He simply left the country when I was a little girl. He lives in London now, I believe. My mother was never particularly parental, so I was largely raised by my grandmother too, as it happens."

Her voice was low, almost as if it was the first time she had ever admitted any of this. In just a few words, Nina established that she and I had more in common than I thought. Fucked-up childhoods.

Absent parents. What had she gone through since? Had she wondered through the years if there was anything else she could have done? Had she chased her father's memory as I'd chased mine, with as much hate as desire for his approval?

And yet, as questions flurried, only one lingered: who in their right mind could leave a woman like this?

How the fuck could he?

I'd probably never meet Nina's father. But if I did, I knew I'd hate him.

———

"So, what?" I said. "People don't just abandon their parents' names because they skip town."

"If you must know, when he left, I requested to have my name legally changed to de Vries because I was so angry. My mother never changed hers, and I wanted to be a part of the family who actually raised me. It was a girl's naive quest for belonging. And, as it happens, an absolute waste, considering I wasn't allowed to keep it when I married."

I remembered the story about her dad now. I could easily imagine Nina, a beautiful girl of sixteen or so demanding her birthright, even if it was just in the form of a name.

The grandmother too. The great Celeste de Vries. The matriarch of New York who had ruled this city with a diamond-encrusted fist until her death last fall.

By the time she was done, Nina had turned away in a huff, facing east toward the side of the city where she belonged. She clutched at her coat, pulling it tight.

"So?" I asked, forcing myself back to the here and now. "What is it?"

Nina turned back with a frown. "What's what?"

"Your name. Your *real* name."

"Oh. It's...Gardner."

Was it my imagination, or did she sound almost reluctant to admit it? Like she wished she didn't have to say it? Like she wished it didn't exist?

But it did. It was the same name Eric had used before she'd walked in. The one I'd been turning in my head over and over again for the last hour. I knew what it was. I just needed to hear her say it.

Nina stared at the ground like the black pavement might reveal something else important. When she looked up again, her eyes shone with frustration. "My husband's name is Gardner. So, yes. I was a bit misleading. But considering you and I barely knew each other, I hardly thought the complications surrounding my surname were any of your business."

"Misleading? I asked you point blank that night if you were part of the de Vries family. You said *no*."

I didn't know why I was so angry. Actually, that wasn't true. When I really thought about it, I knew exactly why.

Like so many people who grew up in this city, I understood the con of New York. Everyone had an angle. Everyone had a story. I knew you couldn't always trust people to tell you the truth because I didn't always do it either.

How many times had I given women wrong numbers when I didn't want them to call? Made up excuses so I wouldn't have to see them again? I sugarcoated the worst parts of my character, brushed off my excesses like they were nothing. And I told these stories, lived these falsehoods because everyone in this city did. Putting on an act was as natural to New Yorkers as catching a cab.

But for one night, with one woman, I'd dropped it all. At that bar, in that restaurant, in that hotel room—Zola disappeared. Mattie was gone. All the things I'd ever said and done ceased to exist.

With her, I was only Matthew. The Americanized name given for my grandfather, per old Italian custom. I'd split open my chest, my heart, everything I was for this beautiful woman I had only just met, for one critical reason:

I believed she had done it too.

"I said I wasn't a de Vries," Nina cut back in a voice that shook. "And I'm not. Or have you forgotten the rest of that conversation too?"

———

"*So you're an heiress,*" I said, *again trying not to be too impressed. It seemed like a word out of one of my sister's crappy romance novels, not a real thing.*

"*That's just it,*" Nina said acerbically. "*I'm not an heiress anymore.*"

"*That doesn't seem fair,*" I said. "*Especially if you were the one there, taking care of her. I'd be pissed off too.*"

"*Yes, well. I wasn't happy about it at first, it's true. But it was Grandmother's choice.*"

————

NINA'S VOICE SHOOK THEN, just like it was shaking now. Her emotion made her tremble, like a string that had just been plucked. I took a step forward so there was less than a foot between us.

"Baby, I didn't forget a *second* of the night I spent with you."

Nina shivered even more in the brisk night air, but her face was flushed. Her lips parted, and for a moment, I considered stealing a kiss. Her chest rose and fell with each breath, and by the way her eyes kept drifting down to my mouth, I was pretty sure she wanted it too. It would have been so easy…

But.

I was no gentleman. Not then. Not now. Maybe not ever. But even standing here in the middle of Central Park, piss mad at her and in no mood for generosity, something about Nina still made me want to be better.

So I stepped back again and checked my watch. "Seven o'clock. What do you say, dinner?"

Did she look slightly disappointed by the new distance?

"Dinner? Oh, no. I have to get home."

"And home is…"

Her eyes narrowed with suspicion.

"Relax, doll. You know I can find it out on my own if I want to, right?"

Now she was practically squinting.

"Nina," I said. "You're not walking through the park at night by yourself, no matter how much you want to get away from me. But you better face it, we'll be seeing a bit more of each other if we have a shot in hell of helping Jane and Eric. So you might as well answer my questions now instead of later."

Her heart-shaped mouth opened and closed a few times before pressing into a tight line. She didn't like being pushed into a corner, that much was obvious. But like her reaction to the name princess, this only made me want to do it more.

"Fine," she gritted out. "You may walk me to the traverse for a taxi. But *only* if you promise to keep things purely professional, Matthew. That night..."

She was looking for something I'd never be able to give as the price of her company. So I did the only thing I could think of. I lied through my teeth.

"Never happened." I held out my hands in surrender.

Nina didn't look convinced, but after a moment her shoulders relaxed. With a bit of amusement, she gestured toward my hat. "You look like...I don't know. A film noir character in that hat. Like you're expecting a femme fatale to enter your life."

I tipped the brim at her. "Who says she hasn't already?"

Nina was silent.

"It's a classic," I said, trying to make her more comfortable. "Every man looks better in a good hat."

She tilted her head, but there wasn't a trace of derision in those sparkling silvers. "Some certainly do," she said softly.

I held out an elbow for her to take so we could continue across the park. "Come on, doll. You called me a gentleman once. Let me see you home."

CHAPTER SIX

MY GRANDFATHER USED TO SAY THAT WHEN HE MET MY GRANDMOTHER, IT was love at first sight across the train platform. *Nonna* was in the opposite car, on her way downtown for a catering gig. He was going home after a Yankees game. They were both seventeen. It was 1957.

Before the doors closed, *Nonno* jumped out of his car and caught the door of hers. He jammed himself into the car, grabbed the strap above her, and rode with her all the way to Brooklyn, a full two hours in the opposite direction from Belmont. Then he waited all night until she finished serving canapes at a wedding so he could see her home, back to the apartment off Arthur Avenue that happened to be less than four blocks from his own.

Less than a year later, they were married. And for more than fifty years, he never stopped seeing her home.

"*Why?*" I asked him, time and time again. As a kid, a teenager, even a young man, I couldn't fathom running across the platform for something as ridiculous as a girl, much less riding hours out of your way and then sitting around for more than four hours while she worked. New York was fifty-two percent female. Pretty girls were a dime a dozen. But the trains running on time? That was priceless.

Because, he'd say, each and every time, a lilt of Italian left over from his childhood in Naples coloring his speech just so. *That's what you do when you meet the love of your life, Matthew. You treat her like a lady, not a broad. You protect her. You keep her safe. You see her home.*

———

NINA and I made our way toward the Seventy-Ninth Street Traverse, staying on the main lit path while I kept her hand securely in the crook of my elbow. I scanned the trees while we walked—I wasn't kidding before about the potential for crime. How many times had my office prosecuted shootings in Prospect Park or similar spots? Places that seemed G-rated during the day could be death traps in this city at night. I could handle myself, but her? In those shoes? No fuckin' way.

In spite of the possibility of threats around us, neither Nina nor I were walking very fast. In fact, we both seemed to be dragging our feet. A lot.

"So, who's the bum?" I asked after a bit.

I was going for light-hearted, but I couldn't quite keep the bitterness out of my voice. Nina's left hand was clutching my arm, the diamond on her ring finger so big it was practically a flashlight.

Maybe a part of me had hoped she was lying that morning. Maybe a part of me had hoped they were on the rocks even now. Separated, maybe. That our night together was so life-changing and earth-shattering that she had gone straight to the courthouse and filed for divorce.

God knows if she had stayed, I probably would have begged her.

Nina cast a sideways look at me. "I'm—you know, I'm not sure I want to tell you."

I sighed. Getting any of this story out of her was going to be like pulling teeth.

"It was just a joke," I said. "Really, though. I want to know. Who's the lucky guy who snags *you* for life?"

She snorted lightly. It was an adorable quirk of hers I remembered from before—a distinctly unladylike snort when she thought something was funny, but forced herself to stifle a bigger laugh.

"What?"

She shook her head. "Nothing. It's just…well, you talk as if we just got engaged. But actually, Calvin and I have been married for quite a while."

"Calvin? That's his name?"

The investigator in me was already taking notes.

Calvin Gardner.

Spouse to Nina Astor/de Vries.

Grade A motherfucker.

Okay, the last part was just an assumption. But I was already itching to get back to my office and run the bastard's name through the system. Find out every dirty secret he had. Everyone had a few.

Now it was my turn to shake my head. I needed to let this go. For her sake. And mine.

"And how did you lovebirds meet?" I prodded, again trying and failing to sound playful. So much for letting it go.

Nina cast another skeptical look. "Do you honestly want to know this?"

"Sure, doll. Of course I do. I just want to know if you're happy."

It wasn't until I said it that I realized it was true. Because the woman I met two months ago had been so desperately *un*happy, she was practically tearing apart at the seams. Women who were happy with their husbands didn't seek out trouble on a Friday night. They didn't take off their rings in a bar. They didn't come looking for me.

I remembered her face that night. The way her eyes, large and soulful, had been slightly red-rimmed from crying. The way she had quivered at my touch as something foreign, almost frightening, before it became something she relished.

———

"Do you know how long it's been," she wondered as she watched our fingers slowly, slowly entwine with each other, "since someone held my hand?"

That ache in my chest throbbed again. Her voice was so sad, so fuckin' tragic. I would have done just about anything to see her smile. I wanted to hear that shy laugh. Just one more time.

But the truth? I realized then that I'd take her tears too. I'd take anything this beautiful woman had to offer me tonight. Anything at all.

"Why don't you tell me what happened?" I asked.

I brought her hand to my knee so I could cradle it between both of my palms. Nina emitted a soft sigh, but she didn't pull it away.

"Go on, doll. I got all the time in the world."

———

I STILL DIDN'T KNOW why she had been upset that night. Had it been this Calvin? What had he done to her? Because he *had* fucked up somehow. That much I knew for sure. But as much as I wanted Nina's marriage to be so terrible she'd come running back to me all over again, I found something else to be true.

I'd probably do just about anything to make Nina happy.

Even if it wasn't with me.

"Of course I'm happy."

She was lying.

Even if years of interrogating criminals hadn't taught me to sniff out lies like a bloodhound, I'd still have known it in a second. Even if the words hadn't tumbled out of her mouth just a little too quickly or her back hadn't straightened too much. It was something innate, something deep inside me on a cellular level that could sense the fact that Nina wasn't telling the truth.

I knew this woman instinctually.

Just like, I suspected, she probably knew me.

"I suppose you want to know why I was at Envy that night," Nina said as we started walking again. *Something. Finally.*

I shrugged. "Only if you want to share." *Tell me every fuckin' detail.*

Nina opened her mouth a few times. She did that when she was thinking, like the wheels churning in her head controlled her jaw too. It was cute. Another sign I was cracking that carefully wrought facade of hers.

Up through the trees, lights flashed from the cars making their way across the park. I slowed my steps a bit more. She didn't seem to notice.

"Well, you know about what happened to Jane and Eric..." Nina gave a wistful smile. "I was trying to stay vague that night, but now I see I could have just told you everything."

I nodded. Now that I thought about it, January's events started to line up and make sense.

"We met, what, a couple of days after New Year's?" I asked. "Eric was in jail..."

Nina nodded. "Yes. I was at the party where he was arrested."

"You were damn upset, I remember that. Even then, I could tell it was about more than just your friend messing up their wedding, but I didn't know...I didn't want to press..."

Now I was the one holding back. Because to be honest, if I had known then what I knew now, I would have been forced to walk away or risk compromising my entire career. I don't think it's a choice I could have made. God help me, I'd have sold more than my soul for that night with Nina. Even if it was the only night I was ever going to get.

Something else was bothering me, though. Something else was missing. Not from that night, but from the morning. Before she left...

———

"Oh, Matthew," she said softly. "What am I going to do?"

"Why don't you tell me what happened? You never know. Maybe I can help."

She watched me for a moment. "It's my cousin's wife. The one I told you about. She's—well, she's done something very unwise. And he's not available to deal with it, so I have to."

———

"The next morning." I looked up to the skyline with sudden awareness. "That was when Jane left for Korea, wasn't it? *That's* why you left in such a hurry."

"That's right." Nina nodded again. "I was staying with her at the time, while Eric was at Rikers. Sometimes I think if I had been there...I could have convinced her to stay. And she...well, she wouldn't have lost the baby."

Everything about her sudden escape that morning made much more sense. As did her apparent guilt. The atrocities that Jane had suffered as

Carson's captive in Korea weren't easy to swallow. It was by the grace of God that Eric had been able to get to her. That she had lived at all.

"Is that why you offered Jane the gala thing?"

Nina's glance grew knife-sharp. "What do you mean?"

Now it was my turn to stop. I turned her toward me. I wanted to read her face clearly.

"Nina, we didn't have a lot of time together, but I remember one thing. You like fashion. You like clothes. Enough that you could pick out the vintage Armani suit I was wearing in a crowded bar with just a glance."

She didn't reply, but the shadow of guilt across her face told me I was on the right track. So I rattled on.

"And if this event is as big as you say it is...well, let me ask you this: Of the two of you, one a lifelong socialite who probably organizes these kinds of things with her eyes closed, the other brand-new to this world and recovering from a traumatic kidnapping to boot, who is going to be more qualified—or welcome on the committee, for that matter—to put this shindig together?"

The shadow darkened. Nina bit back a smile. *Bingo*.

"She's been sad," Nina said as she started walking again. "Eric's been worried about her. She's been sitting in that apartment alone all day, every day, for almost two months. Most of the event is already planned anyway, and it seemed...it just seemed like the least I could do."

I knew it. She was doing this out of guilt. I knew something about that. It's hard to forgive yourself for things when you think you might have been able to fix them. It's even harder when you know you were responsible.

"You sure you're not Catholic, baby?" I joked.

As we arrived at the traverse, Nina turned with a woeful smile and raised her hand for a cab. "Maybe in another life."

Before I could answer, a taxi pulled over. I surprised Nina by piling inside the car with her. Suddenly, I was engulfed by her scent as it filled the backseat. Roses. She still smelled like roses.

"What are you doing?" she asked as I shut the door behind me.

"I need to get the train on the east side," I lied. "You wouldn't make me walk in the rain, would you? Don't forget, doll, I wear vintage."

"From your sister's shop, right?"

I grinned. "Good memory, I see."

Nina peered out her window. The ground was still wet, but there were no more drops threatening. When she turned back to me, her mouth twitched with a hidden smile.

"Incorrigible," she mouthed at me before turning to the driver. "Ninety-Second and Lexington, please. The west side of the street."

The cab took off into the night, and for a few minutes, we sat quietly as the park raced by, the lit buildings of the Upper East Side beckoning us forward. I stared at Nina's lap, where her hands were folded together, the diamond on the left flashing with every passing streetlamp.

"I still don't understand," I said. "The night I met you, you said it was your fault. But I know this case, Nina. I know it like the back of my hand. John Carson is a fuckin' monster. And Jane and Eric are two of the most stubborn people I've ever met. I don't really see how you could have caused anything that happened to them. But you were upset. You kept saying something about how it was your fault. Even before she was taken."

Nina tensed visibly, but didn't look up. Nor did she answer. I was quickly realizing she had that strange ability people with power possessed to control a conversation simply by pretending it hadn't occurred. It happened on the witness stand a lot. I'd ask a question, and the rich assholes or kingpins would give an answer to a completely different one. Or sometimes they would act like I hadn't said anything.

But it was for that reason that I'd also learned to drill down until I got the answer to the actual question.

"Nina," I said again, watching her face very carefully. "Did you feel personally responsible for what happened to Jane and Eric in January?"

She blinked. "I didn't have anything to do with Eric going to jail. Or with Jane going to Korea, if that's what you're asking."

"That's not my question. I asked if you felt personally responsible."

"I—" She shook her head back and forth. "I don't know how to answer that."

"It's a yes or no question, baby."

"It's not that simple!"

The car turned up Madison, barreling past the patrician apartments and posh storefronts that were mostly closed for the evening. I had no problem imagining Nina wiling away her days here. Pointing her elegant finger at shop girls. Sipping on a cappuccino before starting her day.

It was a wonder, really, that I hadn't run into her all the times I'd walked around. Something in me knew from the start she belonged here.

But honestly, I had no idea what Nina de Vries did with her days. Whether she was a vapid socialite who shopped and spent money, or if she had a real job, even if it was one that didn't pay anything. I didn't know who she was at all.

The guilt etched across her face told me I needed to find out.

"Listen," I said as the cab took a right onto Ninety-Second. I only had a few seconds. Then who knew when I was going to see her again? "If you have any additional information about what happened with Jane and Eric, anything at all, I need to know about it. They don't have to know we talked, but, Nina, if I'm going to have any chance at putting this asshole behind bars, we do need to go over this. You want to do right by your cousin? Make up for whatever part you think you played? Tell me what you know. I can help. Right now, I'm the only one."

The car stopped at the corner of Ninety-Second and Lex, in front of an old, impeccably maintained brick building that was partially sheltered by restoration scaffolding.

"This all right?" the cabbie asked in a thick accent.

Nina looked between me and the driver. "I...oh, this is fine, thank you." Her eyes widened, but she didn't move. She seemed stuck in place. "I...do you need the car?"

"Here." I slipped the cabbie a twenty through the plastic barrier, then nodded for Nina to get out.

I followed her across the empty street until we were standing under the awning of what I assumed was her building. Through shining, brass-trimmed doors, a doorman looked at us curiously. Nina waved at him and maintained a careful distance from me. Much too far for my preference.

"Well?" I asked. "You know I'm not going anywhere until I get my answer."

"You must be very good at your job."

I just tipped my head. "Nina. Come on."

She opened her mouth to speak, but before she could, a voice interrupted us as the door to her building opened.

"Mommy?"

Nina's eyes widened, and she turned. "Oh! Hello, darling. What are you doing up?"

I stared at a small blonde girl who was yanking on the arm of a very tired-looking middle-aged woman.

"Patricia said we could come down and wait for you after you texted, Mommy. We thought you'd be home forever ago!"

I watched, dumbfounded as Nina carefully embraced the girl, whose head rose approximately to her rib cage. She was slim and delicate, with ribbons of wavy blonde hair that reached her shoulders. I wouldn't have noticed much else about her until she set her eyes on me. Those eyes. They were wide and curious. Completely familiar. Completely mesmerizing.

"Who's that?" she asked.

I started to reach out, but Nina gently turned her away.

"I'm glad you came out to greet me," she said, "and I'm sorry I'm late. But it's really time for bed, my love."

"I'm sorry, Mrs. Gardner. She really wanted to see you tonight," said the older woman with a curious glance my way.

"That's perfectly fine. We don't get to see enough of each other as it is." Nina stroked the girl's hair away from her face with a tenderness that made my chest ache. "Go with Patricia, darling. I'll be up to kiss you good night."

"Okay, Mommy."

Mother and daughter hugged again, blonde touched blonde before Nina set a kiss to the little girl's forehead. The girl scampered back to her nanny, and it wasn't until the doorman ushered them both inside that I finally found my voice again.

"Who—who was that?"

Nina turned back to me, those bright gray eyes shining again, wide and without guile. "I should think that clear from the way she addressed me. That was my daughter."

"Your..."

Suddenly, it all made sense.

Her caginess. Her guilt. Her insistence that she was happy when she clearly wasn't.

Nina wasn't just married.

She had a daughter. A family.

And the little girl was absolutely perfect. Just like her mother.

Guilt shot through my chest, and at first, I didn't understand it. After all, I wasn't the most upstanding guy. Considering my track record, it's not like I'd never been with any moms. Caitlyn Calvert, for instance, had two children herself.

But in those situations, the kids were an idea. A theory, at best. This one was very, very real.

I watched the girl disappear into an elevator, then looked back at Nina, whose gaze hadn't wavered. Something had changed. She wasn't scared of me anymore.

Progress, I thought. But toward what? This woman was as off-limits as it got. Not only was she a daughter of one of the most powerful families in the city, she was married. She was a mother. And she was now part of an investigation.

Chasing this one was a suicide mission, plain and simple.

"Nina." I still didn't completely know what to say.

Mild surprise played across her porcelain features. "Yes?" Was she...*entertained* by this?

"I—"

I was struggling. Floundering. I should have just said good night and walked away. Let her remain on the periphery of my life where she belonged.

But I couldn't.

"Dinner." The word fell out of my mouth like a bouncing ball.

Her brows knit together with confusion. "I'm sorry?"

I pulled at the knot of my tie. *Get yourself together, Zola.* "I'd like to have dinner. Tomorrow, if you're available."

She stepped toward her building with regret. "Oh, Matthew, I don't think—"

But I shook away her excuses. "No, no, not like that. Look, there's a lot more to discuss, like I said. About the gala, the plan, everything. You said you wanted to help Jane and Eric. This is the way to do it, all right?"

I was chattering—who was I kidding? I had questions, so many more now that this angel-faced bombshell had been dropped in my lap. But I wasn't lying. If Nina could help at all with this case, I needed that too. There was some kind of involvement she was leaving out, and I needed to know what it was.

"Look," I said. "I'm doing my best, but I could use all the help I can get. Would you be willing? Dinner. Tomorrow night."

She inhaled deeply, then exhaled, long and low, glancing from side to side. She was nervous. Of course. Any idiot could sense the tension between us.

"All right," she said. "But not tomorrow. Next Friday. I'll meet you at—"

"Farina," I interrupted, and then with a smirk: "In Chelsea. I promised you Italian the next time, didn't I?"

"Matthew…"

I held my hands up. "Jokes, baby, just jokes. It's pasta, not sex."

"Matthew!"

"Sorry, sorry. I'll be the perfect gentleman, I promise."

I took off my hat and put it back on, tipped slightly to the side, just the way *Nonno* used to wear it. Nina watched the movement with her bottom lip clenched between her teeth. Shit. I really needed to get out of here. Remind myself why I really *did* need to keep things purely professional with this one.

"All right," she said slowly, still staring at my hat. "Seven?"

I smiled. "Seven…would be heaven." Then I winked. Like the corny bastard I suddenly was, I winked.

Nina laughed. And every worry I had evaporated into the night. How in the fuck had I forgotten the sound of that laugh? Like the fuckin' bells of heaven.

"Seven at Farina," she agreed. "I'll see you then. Good night, Matthew."

"Night, doll."

I watched her disappear into the lobby, waiting until she'd entered the same elevator as her daughter. Then, as I started toward the nearest subway, I pulled out my phone and, against my better judgement, googled Nina and her husband, under the correct names this time. And immediately felt like a fool.

Nina Astor had turned up nothing for months, but Nina de Vries had been making *Page Six* since she was a teenager. Nina Gardner even more. There she was at Eric and Jane's big engagement party last year. Again at their splashy society wedding. She always wore a lot of white, silver, and very light blues. Colors that almost weren't colors. And yet she stood out on every page, often on the arm of a short, melon-shaped man who looked at least twenty years older than her.

I expanded a picture of the two of them at the New Year's party where Eric had been arrested. Nina stood by while Eric was carted away, delicate hand covering her shock-opened mouth. God, she was beautiful. Even in distress, even in the harsh glare of a paparazzi picture, fuckin' stunning. Her hair was pulled up in some kind of twist, while the ice-blue gown she was wearing made her eyes glow.

Calvin Gardner, however, looked like a mushy cantaloupe in a bad tux. I squinted. He was watching with a pinched face, but he didn't look particularly surprised to see his cousin-in-law being taken away by the FBI. Or even that upset. Actually, he even looked a little...satisfied.

Immediately, I dialed Derek.

"What up, Zola? Tell me you're not still at the office."

"Nah, D. I happen to be out. How's your Friday night, man?"

"Well, I *was* planning to go out in a bit until you called."

"Liar. You're at home watching the Knicks, aren't you?"

"It's a good game tonight. Did you read that file Ramirez sent over?"

"I glanced through it, yeah."

"Heavy shit, but looks like some solid leads. You want me to look into Letour's businesses?"

I worried my mouth a minute, pausing outside the entrance to the subway. "Yeah, I do. But first...I have another name for you."

"Shoot."

I turned around to look up at Nina's building. I wondered which of the lit windows were hers. If her husband was there now, lying through his teeth. It was just a hunch. I had no real official lead on the guy. But everything in my gut said he was involved in this. And I had been doing this too long not to trust my gut.

She wouldn't like it. She wouldn't want me to get involved.

Fuck it. I said I'd be a gentleman. But I never promised to be a saint.

"Remember Calvin Gardner?" I asked. "Eric's cousin's husband?"

"Yeah. But you said that was a no-go, so I never looked into him."

"I was wrong. And I have an address. 9211 Lexington. He's connected to all this shit. I know it."

CHAPTER SEVEN

"So, what's it for?"

The next day, I stood in my living room while two of my sisters and my four-year-old niece watched me try on a suit. It was a familiar scene. My house in Brooklyn, which I currently shared with my sister Frankie and her daughter, Sofia, was a second home base for our family, especially when they wanted to get out of the Bronx. Kate, who owned the vintage menswear store that had provided me with the Armani Nina mentioned, often passed through on her way back from scouting estate sales in Connecticut or Long Island on the weekends. And like a good sister, she always put the best aside for me first.

I turned from side to side, examining the charcoal gray secondhand Prada. Maybe it was used, but a good suit makes a man look like a million bucks. And in a city like New York? Money talks. Loud.

I turned to where Kate was sorting through a pile of handkerchiefs with Sofia. "What do you mean? Hey, keep that one for me. I like it."

Sofia handed me a red paisley pocket square, but Kate kept right on talking while I tucked it into the breast pocket.

"Mattie, come on. All of a sudden, you need a new three-piece? What's it for? Or, I should say, who?"

"Maybe I just wanted to spruce things up a little." I turned back to the mirror on the wall and pulled at the lapels. Were they too thin or just right? I didn't usually go for a peak like this, but I was kind of feeling it.

"You've turned down everything I've put aside for you since January because you said you had to save money."

"Hey, the holidays are expensive when I have five sisters and six nieces and nephews, all of whom like nice things."

"Is that why you gave me a crappy gift card?" Frankie chimed in. "Because I like nice things?"

"Amazon has all sorts of things, Fran," I said. "I didn't see you giving it back to me."

"Yeah, well, beggars can't be choosers."

I didn't press her on that fact, because I knew on some level, it hurt Frankie's pride that she and Sofia lived with me because she couldn't afford a nice place for the two of them on her teacher's salary. But I happened to be very proud of what my sister did for a living, and it wasn't her fault that Sofia's dad was a worthless piece of shit who ran out on them. Most of the time, I was happy to have them here. They made my house a home.

I redid the tie with a bit more concentration than necessary. What my sisters didn't know was that I'd pretty much blown my spending budget for months that night with Nina. Even though she'd taken the hotel bill, entertaining a woman like her still hadn't been cheap. I'd sprung for the best wines, the best food. For hours. After needing to repair my furnace the following month, I'd only *just* managed to get my bank account back to normal.

Kate peered at me over her librarian glasses. "Frankie says you've been out a lot. Anyone special?"

I scowled into the mirror at Frankie, who avoided my gaze. "Francesca! Why do you have to share my business all over town?"

Honestly, my sisters were worse than reality show contestants, the way they gossiped. Living with one of them meant my every damn move was on display.

Frankie just chuckled and got up to go to the kitchen. "I didn't know your extracurriculars were a secret, big brother."

I pulled the tail of the tie through the knot. "You don't know shi—I mean nothing." I winked at Sofia, whose little mouth had dropped when she sensed a curse word coming. "No swear jar, Sofs. I caught myself that time."

"*Zio!*"

"All Frankie said was that you don't come home most weekends, and that sometimes you get up and leave in the middle of the night," Kate said.

"What?" Frankie called when I shot her another murderous look. "You don't!"

"So I'll ask again," Kate continued. "Who's the girl? What do you think, Sofs? Should we finally get to meet one?"

"Yes!" Sofia cried as she tossed several folded handkerchiefs into the air like confetti.

I finished with the tie, then fastened the first button of the jacket. The suit was only fifteen years old, not true vintage like most of the stuff in Kate's shop. It would be perfect for Friday night. I fingered the red silk pocket square. Crimson. Just like a rose.

"There's no one," I lied as I turned around. "You know me, girls. I just like to look good."

Right on cue, Kate's skepticism melted away as she checked me over. It wasn't much different than when we were kids—me, a grouchy four-teen-year-old stuck babysitting his little sisters, her at eight, forcing me to wear *Nonno's* suits so we could play wedding or ball or whatever would keep my pack of little sisters from screaming bloody murder at me.

I had to hand it to Kate now, though. She saw the craze for flash menswear coming a mile away. After *Mad Men* got big, she used her part of our grandfather's bequest to lease her shop in Riverdale. Eleven years later, my little sister's business had been mentioned in just about every local paper as *the* place to go for men's secondhand fashion in the city. She had regulars from pretty much every major costume design house, television studio, and stylist group in town.

"Well?" I asked, turning from side to side. "Is it adequate?"

Kate tipped her head. "The lines are good. Your cute little Italian butt was made for Prada."

"Cute butt!" Sofia shouted.

I threw another pocket square at her, which made her giggle. "My ass is not cute or little, Kit-kat."

"*Zio*, that's a swear!"

I tossed a crumpled dollar into my niece's chubby little hands. She immediately rolled over and waved it at her mom.

"Is that why *Nonna* still tries to grab it every time you come for dinner?" Frankie asked as she helped Sofia put the dollar in the mason jar on the counter.

"*Nonna* just wishes I was still five years old." I turned back to the mirror so Kate could look me over better.

"I think you should have Jerome taper the hems a bit more," Kate added, referring to the tailor I used by my office. "And take in the back of the jacket maybe an inch. Prada was ahead of the game in 2004, but it's still a little too early aughts."

"You mean I shouldn't look like a Backstreet Boy?"

"Too late!" Frankie called from the kitchen.

"Yeah, you already went through that phase once," agreed Kate.

"I did not. The Marines wouldn't allow it." I let her pull the jacket from my shoulders. "What about the suspenders? You don't think they're a little too grandpa?"

Kate gave me a look through the mirror. "Mattie, you wear a fedora every day of the week, so I don't really think grandpa fashion has ever been an issue for you."

"Hey, my hats look great."

"Your hats make you look like those old movie characters you love so much," Frankie said as she sat back down with Sofia, a glass of wine in hand.

"Nothing wrong with that," Kate said. "Suspenders are all the rage right now. And those pants weren't made for a belt."

I slipped my thumbs under the waistband. She was right. These didn't have belt loops, and while they would stay up just fine without the straps over my shoulders, the buttons sewn into the waist certainly meant they were supposed to have them. They were old-fashioned. Traditional.

Some people liked that.

———

"An undershirt," Nina remarked as she pulled my shirttails open. "Most men don't even bother."

"Most men are content to look like fuckin' heathens. I like to think I'm not most men, doll."

"No," she said, desire thick on her tongue, "you are definitely not."

———

I WASN'T INTENTIONALLY TRYING to remember all the ways Nina seemed to enjoy the more old-fashioned aspects of it, like my favorite fedora, modeled after *Nonno's*, or the double-breasted vest I wore under my jacket that night.

It was a little too easy to imagine the look on her face if she caught sight of a pair of suspenders. The way she might reach out and pull one side of the elasticized leather. Out, out, out...then *snap!* It would land hard enough on my chest to leave a mark.

I turned away from my sisters. They didn't need to see the almost immediate effect that particular fantasy had.

"See?" Frankie said to Kate. "Look at that. He's *definitely* got a girl."

Too bad I couldn't hide shit from them if I tried.

"There's no fuckin' girl, Fran."

"*Zio!*"

I sighed and tossed another dollar at Sofia.

"I'll take them," I told Kate as I pulled the straps over my shoulders, one at a time. "The square too. I'll take the whole kit." I checked my watch. "But can you make it snappy? I'd like to catch Jerome before he closes. See if he can do the alterations before Friday."

Kate was already done with the pocket squares, and it was clear by her expression that I wasn't fooling her. Not in the slightest.

"Friday, huh?" she asked as she started putting things away. "Sure, there's no girl. Just you wait until we tell everyone tomorrow. We'll get it out of you, Mattie. We always do."

———

I DIDN'T STAY home after dropping off my suit. Something had been bothering me since running into Nina the day before. I had some things I needed to get off my chest, and since I had to be uptown tomorrow for Mass anyway, I figured I'd give Frankie the house tonight and kill two birds.

So I took the train all the way up to the Bronx. I walked into Christ Our Redeemer, where I'd spent a solid part of my childhood daydreaming on the hard wooden pews and making trouble in catechism classes. Where I'd spend the next morning kneeling beside my family, trying to figure out how to be a better man than the one I always seemed to end up being.

Now that I was grown, I wasn't sure I believed all the stuff I learned within these brick walls. But I still went to confession, if only to appease my grandmother, who was a *very* devout Catholic. And, if I was being truthful, I still went for myself. A little absolution never hurt anyone, and there were days, like today, when I needed it a little more.

Like when you run into a woman who would tempt Christ himself, I thought to myself. Who was I kidding? In less than a week, I'd be sitting across the table from the definition of temptation. This was an emergency.

Quickly, I crossed myself as I knelt in front of the latticed screen and tried not to sniff. This thing had always smelled damp, somehow. Like a colony of moths lived under the kneeler.

"Forgive me, Father, for I have sinned. It's been..." I looked up at the rickety wood beams, trying to count just how many days it really had been since I'd sat in a confessional. Fuck. I mean, damn. I mean, crud. Whatever. I'd add mental profanity to the list and give Sofia a twenty when I got home. "Three weeks? Maybe four?"

The familiar, patient breathing of Father Deflorio wheezed slightly from the other side. Great, so the priest had a cold too. The silhouette of his head tipped in recognition of my voice.

"Hello, Matthew. Nice to have you back." *Finally.* He didn't have to say it.

"We've got a bit to catch up on, don't we, Father?"

The priest said nothing, just waited for me to speak. He wouldn't rush me or goad me, like some might on a Saturday afternoon with several other people waiting to confess before Mass the next day. I'd known the unflappable Father Deflorio my whole life. He was a vacuum of personality, to the point where my sisters used to compare him and his soutain to *Nonna's* drapes. But you know, that's not such a bad thing when you're divulging all your mortal secrets in hopes of having a shot in hell at heaven. Ah, you know what I mean.

"Let's see…" I flipped my fingers in front of me, trying to recount all my sins. "Between all five of them, I told my sisters to fuck off at least ten times since February. I yelled at Frankie twice last week alone for throwing her towel on the new couch. Took the Lord's name too many times to count. Um…a fair amount of sex with contraceptives—a few of them were involved, one engaged. And I lied to Kate when she asked me who I was buying a suit for."

"A suit?"

I rolled my eyes. *That's* what he picked up on?

"A suit, yeah. It's for—well, I said it was for no one. But it's not. It's for this woman. This—well, I told you about her, Father. The one-night stand. The one who's married."

"Forgive me, Matthew, but there have been a few like that before."

"The blonde, Father. The princess. The…doll. Nina."

I practically choked on the word now. That word I had never used before I met her.

There was a long pause. Then: "I remember."

I'm sure he did. I came up here after our night together and spent a fuckin' hour in the confessional. It wasn't so much about telling him everything Nina and I did. Father Deflorio wasn't some dirty voyeur— he just needed the facts so he could dole out a punishment to fit the crime. Me, I just needed to process. Figure out what the hell had happened.

Some people talk to therapists, but I was Catholic, so I talked to my priest. And that day after Nina's and my scarlet night together? Well, it took a while. And several other times since. Because you can't really repent if you don't regret. And I still couldn't find it within myself to regret anything I had done with Nina Astor…de Vries. I winced. Gardner.

"I saw her again," I said. "Yesterday. For the first time since January. I was at a friend's apartment, and she walked in. Turns out she's his cousin, right under my nose. Can you believe that, Father? That's some divine intervention right there."

Father Deflorio's sigh, again, was audible. Yeah, he knew where this was going.

"She's helping on a case. Afterward, I walked her home across the park. We just talked, Father, honest. But we couldn't finish, so I asked her to dinner."

"Matthew..."

"It's not like that, I swear it."

His silence told me he didn't believe a word. I couldn't blame him. I didn't believe myself either.

"Okay, okay, maybe it is a little," I admitted.

"Have you continued to have impure thoughts about this woman?"

Impure thoughts. Ha. Yeah, that was putting it mildly. "You could say that. One or two times since yesterday?" Right, well, that was only true if you counted all last night and all day today as one "time" each, but since it was constant, I figured it was technically true. "And, yeah, I mastur-bated in the shower thinking about her. Twice."

"Matthew, God is quite clear about this matter. It's there in Exodus. Deuteronomy. 'Thou shalt not covet your neighbor's wife.'"

Thou shalt not covet. Yeah. Sometimes it felt like all I ever did was covet. "Well, she's not really my neighbor's wife."

"'Thou shalt not commit adultery,'" added the priest.

"I mean, does it really count if *I'm* not the adulterer? She's the one who's married, Father. I had to stare at the rock on her finger for three hours, so I know it's true."

It was like I was thirteen all over again, sitting in catechism classes and picking apart every piece of logic. That was the first time anyone every suggested I should be a lawyer. If it hadn't been for the good priests channeling my healthy questioning of the Church, I might have never gone the route I did.

That didn't mean I was going to win this case, though. Then, as now, Father Deflorio couldn't be moved.

"'Every one who looks at a woman lustfully has already committed adultery with her in his heart.'"

I studied my hands. Fuck. If that was the truth, I'd been committing adultery with Nina nonstop since she walked into Eric's apartment. I was going to burn for those petal-shaped lips alone.

I shook my head viciously. "Right. Yeah."

"Is there anything else?"

I thought for a moment. "No, I think that about covers it."

"If I might…"

I prepared myself for a lecture. Maybe a whole rosary this time around. We'd been talking about Nina for months, and Father Deflorio knew—maybe better than anyone—that my thoughts weren't any closer to salvation-worthy than they were when we started.

"Spend some time revisiting your catechism. Go home. Review Part Three, Section Two on the Ninth Commandment."

"You got a page number there for me, Father?" I teased. "Maybe a line?"

"Matthew."

"Sorry, sorry. No, you're right. I'll give it some thought."

"Really consider it. Sit with God's Word. Try to remember: the problem isn't with her, Matthew. It's in your distance from His decree. There is an emptiness in a Godless life that you're looking to fill with her instead. But it won't work."

Was that the problem? Sin begets sin, so it just made me want to sin more? Like sugar or cocaine?

I frowned. If that were the case, it shouldn't matter who was under the sheets with me. Caitlyn or any of the other practically nameless women I'd been seeking out lately, trying to fill this void. Anyone should have sufficed. Nina should have become nameless too.

Yeah, I wasn't convinced that void was caused by a lack of God in my life. But then again, I wasn't exactly an authority on the matter.

"You got it, Father. Thank you."

"Also, *five* Hail Marys this time, Matthew."

I smirked, though he couldn't see me. I knew he wouldn't let me off with just the standard three. "Thanks, Father."

"Anything else, Matthew?"

"No, that's it." I murmured the Act of Contrition I'd had memorized since I was a kid.

"Give thanks to the Lord, for He is good."

"For His mercy endures forever." I crossed myself again. "I'll see you at Mass."

"Very well. But, Matthew?"

I stopped just before opening the confessional door. "Yeah, Father?"

"For Heaven's sake, son, don't go to that dinner."

I swallowed. I couldn't lie to a priest. Not right after cleansing my immortal soul. But at the same time, I wouldn't make a promise I couldn't keep either.

"I'll think about it," I said and left the chamber to another hopeful sinner.

CHAPTER EIGHT

"*Why do you always wear a hat, Nonno?*"

I sat on the end of my bed, kicking my feet back and forth while my grandfather got ready for his date. That's right, my stodgy old grandparents still had "dates." It was a custom in our family to watch them go through the motions every week. Get ready. Get "picked up." Escort each other to dinner at Tino's or, if Nonno got good tips that week, maybe to a show.

Nonna was upstairs with my sisters—females needed more space, Nonno would say. And he was right. I had snuck up there once before to see for myself all the crap the girls used to get themselves together. Razors and nylons and something called a girdle that looked like a restraining device. Kate said it was to make Nonna look skinny, but I didn't understand why that was needed. She was only five feet tall, could fit into one of Nonno's pant legs.

Nonno kept his stuff in my room for this reason. I watched from the bed while he slapped on his aftershave and combed oil through his salt-and-pepper hair until it shone almost black again. Then he put on his clothes and transformed himself from the humble chauffeur into the swanky man I'd seen in his wedding pictures.

Undershirt, over-shirt, socks, pants.

"Two shirts!" I exclaimed the first time I watched him. "What the heck do you need two shirts for, Nonno? Aren't you hot?"

"I'm not a heathen," he'd said. "She don't need to see my nipples through, capito?"

Tie, tie clip, vest, handkerchief. Shoes I could see my reflection in, then jacket. It took a lot of clothes to look as good as my grandfather.

"A gentleman always wears a hat, Matthew," he said, his faint Neapolitan accent thicker after an extra negroni. "You go out without a hat, you look like a farmer. Like you're just getting off work. You want to show the girl you love you don't care about how she sees you? Love is respect, Matthew. You remember that."

———

"I'M SORRY, SIR," the hostess said again. "I really can't seat you until your entire party has arrived."

I checked my watch—it was my good one, my grandfather's Rolex that I only brought out on special occasions. I already felt like an idiot. This was supposed to be a casual dinner, but somehow I'd still managed to wear the new suit I'd picked up from my tailor yesterday and get a fresh shave after work before heading into the city. All dolled up and no one to meet.

Nina was late. Thirty minutes, to be exact—long enough that I was starting to wonder if she was going to show at all. It had taken every ounce of charm I had to stop the hostess from giving up our table fifteen minutes ago. Farina wasn't the most stylish restaurant in New York, but this was Friday night. Everywhere was either booked or busy, and there was a throng of people waiting on the sidewalk.

"She's going to be here any minute," I lied before turning on my best charm offensive. "If she doesn't, maybe you can join me, sweetheart."

Cheesy, sure. But it still worked. I couldn't lose this table.

"Sir…" The hostess, a pretty young thing with curly hair and freckles, giggled.

"Come on," muttered one of the customers waiting behind me.

I ignored them and winked at the hostess. "Do me a favor, honey? Five more minutes. If she doesn't show, you can give these jokers our table and I'll buy you a drink when your shift is up."

"My. I didn't know I was so replaceable."

The hostess's grin disappeared at the sound of Nina's voice. I swung around to find the crowd had parted around her like the Red Sea. And why not? The woman was a vision of light in a parade of black.

"Did you expect me to eat alone, doll?"

She examined me a moment more, then relaxed her shoulders. "I wouldn't dream of it. I'm sorry I'm late. The traffic across town was absolutely terrible. Thirty-Fourth was a parking lot."

"Should've taken the train. I'll stand with the rats if it saves me twenty minutes."

Nina wrinkled her long nose. I wondered if she had ever actually been inside the subway system.

"I'm sorry," she said again.

"Think nothing of it." I leaned in to kiss her cheek. "And *no one* could replace you, doll."

There was a slight hum in recognition. The faint scent of roses washed over me.

"I'll show you to your table, sir."

I stepped aside to let Nina pass and give myself a minute to recover —well, as much as I could watching her sway through the restaurant. She turned more than a few heads just by her grace. It wasn't the color— again, she wasn't wearing any, just a simple coat a few shades lighter than sand, which she handed to the hostess to reveal a cream-colored dress with bell-shaped sleeves. Nothing fancy, nothing flashy, other than a few diamonds glinting at her ears and another hanging from her neck. And, of course, the rock on her finger. But everything was subtly perfect. There wasn't a golden hair out of place.

Real money, I was starting to realize, wasn't loud. It was in the details. It was in the sheen.

"Can I take your hat, sir?"

I gave the hostess my trench coat and fedora, noting the way Nina's eyes followed them from my head to her hands.

"Do you always wear a hat like that?" she asked as I sat down. "I don't remember it the night we met, but you had it on last week, too."

"Usually, yeah," I said. "It was pouring that night. I think I left it home to dry."

"You don't see a lot of men wearing them anymore."

I shook my head, overcome with a sense of déjà vu. Another conversation about my penchant for traditional menswear. One that led to more...suggestive moments.

"It fits you," she said as she fingered my tie. Her thumb drifted over the clip, toying with the chain. "It's very...dignified."

"Dignified?"

She tugged on my tie, and the pull sent a current straight down to my dick. Goddamn.

She cocked her head. "It fits you. Even if you do have lovely...hair."

Nina's hands slipped around my head and sank into my hair.

Then she brushed her lips against mine, and this time she took control, her mouth setting the pace of a kiss that practically stopped my heart. Jesus Christ. This wasn't some innocent angel. She was a temptress after all.

"Matthew." Her breath danced around us in clouds of white. "Please. Somewhere close."

Close, close. Where the fuck was nice enough down here that I could actually take a woman like this?

"The Grace," I blurted out. "It's maybe two blocks away."

Nina finally relaxed, and her smile bloomed, transforming her as much as her laugh. "Take me there."

"It's a hat," I said matter-of-factly. "It keeps my head warm." Good fuckin' God, I needed a glass of wine, if only to ward off the flashbacks. Every other word out of her mouth was bringing them up like grenades.

We perused our menus for a few minutes, though I already knew what I wanted. I just needed time to recover myself.

"It's very pasta-heavy, isn't it?" Nina remarked.

"It's Italian," I said. "What did you expect, sushi?"

She looked up. "Of course not."

"You can just peck at an appetizer if you want, doll, but you'll look like an asshole."

"I'll look like a *what*?"

I grinned. "Excuse my French. A very pretty asshole, but an asshole nonetheless. I just mean you'll look like a jerk." I waved around the room. "This place is old school. You don't just waltz in, order an entree that could fit in your palm, and make a meal on Chardonnay so your pearls still fit."

"That's rude. I'm not even wearing pearls."

"I'm just saying, you need to be willing to eat like a real person. What do you think, can you do that, princess?"

I couldn't help it. I was goading her on purpose just like I did with her cousin. Maybe there was a gene in this family that made me predisposed to fuck with them. Maybe it was the two cocktails I'd pounded around the corner. Maybe it was the mind-fuck of waiting half an hour for a woman I had no chance in hell of fucking again. But it was all getting to me. She was sitting there like the Queen of fuckin' Sheba, without even a strand of hair out of place. All I could think about was what a mess I'd been since I met her.

And how I wanted to mess her up too.

Her face flushed. Not with desire. With anger. "Perhaps this was a bad idea."

She rose and placed her napkin calmly on the table before turning to leave. My heart turned to stone.

"Nina, wait."

She stilled and looked over her shoulder. Her eyes were cold, but hurt. The fact that I'd done that killed me.

"I'm sorry," I said, and extended a hand, though I knew she wouldn't take it. "Please sit down. I'll control myself."

She turned fully, ignoring the curious glances at us. "If you came here for some kind of ill-advised revenge for that night," she said quietly, "please be assured, I have regretted it ever since."

I wasn't sure what killed me more—the fact that she genuinely thought I wanted to hurt her, or the fact that she regretted what we had done.

"Have you really?" I asked. "Regretted it, I mean?"

Those big gray eyes shone with remorse. "Oh, yes. Matthew, it was very wrong, what we did. I'm married. I have a daughter. A family."

I swallowed and sat back in my seat. Well, that brought me back to reality in the space of a millisecond. The face of the tiny blonde girl I had seen last weekend flashed in my mind's eye. I still hadn't forgotten that bewildered little face. Fuck. Nina was right. What we had done was very wrong. And for the first time since that night, I truly felt it.

"I—I'm sorry," I said again. "You're right. And I'm the asshole, not you, sweetheart. I didn't ask you here to interrogate you, I promise. I'm trying to help your cousin."

"Are you sure that's all?"

No. "Yes."

I wanted to take her hand, assure her that I meant what I said. But I didn't totally mean it. And I was also pretty sure that if I started touching her, I wouldn't want to stop. Which I very much needed to do.

"Are you staying?"

The perky voice of the server interrupted our strange little detente. But I didn't move my gaze from Nina.

"What about it, doll?" I asked. "Give a guy a second chance?"

Nina examined me for a moment, then to my relief, slid gracefully back into her seat. "Just don't call me princess."

"On my honor." I turned to the server. "We need wine. Let's have a bottle of the—" I cut myself off and turned to Nina. "Do you mind if I order, doll? I just know the menu, that's all. The chef is a friend."

One side of Nina's heart-shaped mouth tugged with pleasure she was trying to hide. "Please."

I nodded. "Great, yeah. We'll have a bottle of the *Valpolicella*, and I can give you the rest too."

The server whipped out a pen while I rattled off my favorite dishes. If I couldn't cook for Nina myself, this was the next best thing.

"We'll start with the *asparagi con salsa di uova sode* and *pomodori e acciughe*," I said, pointing to the asparagus and tomato salad items in case the girl didn't actually understand the Italian menu. Thankfully, she seemed to be as authentic as the rest of the place. "Then we'll have the *tagliatelle* and *agnolotti*, followed by the veal and the market fish. It's bass tonight, right?"

The girl nodded as she finished writing. "Yes, *marsala*."

I nodded back. "Very good. Tell Noel that Zola stopped by."

The server bobbed. "Of course. I'll put your orders in and be back with your wine."

When she left, I turned back to Nina, who had been watching me curiously. Okay, so I was showing off. I couldn't seem to help it. I had been so fuckin' stunned when I saw her at Eric's the other night that now I wanted to make up for lost time.

"That was quite the mouthful."

"I can tell you what it is if you want."

"I read along with you," she replied. "But you ordered enough for a small army. I would have been fine with a salad."

I scowled. Hard. Nina's mouth twitched again.

"The chef and I went to Sunday school together," I said. "The guy who trained him in Belmont was rumored to be Sofia Loren's personal chef. We're not insulting Noel's menu by ordering fuckin' salad."

I didn't know why I was taking it so personally. I had been out with a thousand other women who ate like rabbits, and I'd never had the compulsion to micromanage their dietary preferences. And truly, if Nina said she honestly didn't want to eat anything other than greens, I wouldn't have stopped her.

But food was one of the few universal pleasures everyone could experience, from any background. People lost control of themselves when they ate really, really great meals. I already knew what Nina looked like when that happened. And since it wasn't going to happen again, this was probably the next best thing. I didn't just want her to enjoy the meal. I wanted her to give herself up to the pleasure. Just like she'd done the night we met.

———

"Want a piece?" I asked, offering the baguette.

She shook her head. "Oh..."

"Come on, doll. You already broke your diet for me. The broth is amazing. You have to try it."

She sighed with a doleful grin. "You're a terrible influence."

I smirked. "I'm the best, baby. Now, open up."

She did, and I delivered another soaked morsel into her mouth.

"Ohhhhh, that's so good," she said after she swallowed. Her eyes closed with pleasure, and again, I had to adjust my pants. Good fuckin' God, if that's what she did when she ate, what would she sound like when she came?

I fully intended to find out. Tonight, if possible. Again and again, if she'd let me.

———

Jesus, I really had a problem. Two minutes back in Nina's company, and I was turning into Bacchus himself with these thoughts. The god of wine. And hedonism.

Maybe salad was a safer bet.

The wine arrived, and we sat awkwardly while the server poured out, then eyed each other over our glasses.

"I—this is nice," Nina said. "I've never been here before."

I looked around the restaurant, which wasn't really anything special. A basement-level place, dimly lit with white tablecloths. A simple backdrop to traditional Italian food.

"Do you take a lot of dates here?" Nina asked.

I narrowed my eyes. "Do you really want to know?"

"I'm just trying to make conversation, Matthew."

"About my sex life?"

"Matthew!"

"How long have you been married?" I asked abruptly. Apparently the promise not to be an asshole was going right out the window.

Nina sighed and set her wineglass on the table. "Matthew, do we really—"

"Yes, we really, Mrs. *Gardner*." I couldn't—quite—keep the acid off my tongue.

"I thought you asked me here to help with Eric and Jane."

"I asked you here because I need information about your family. That includes you. And your—husband. And considering I didn't get the whole story when we first met, I plan on getting it now."

Her eyes grew steely. Yeah, I recognized that look. I had thought it was a response to being challenged, but now I knew it meant she didn't want to give something up.

Everyone has their tells, baby. You just keep giving me yours.

"Nina." I leaned over the table. "I could look up everything there is to know about you. Your vital records. Your speeding tickets. That time in high school you and your friends sniffed lines at the Vineyard. I could find out every fucking secret you have, baby, and there isn't a thing you could do to stop me."

She could have shied away. I was giving her my best "bad cop" right now, and a lot of people would have cowered at the idea of a criminal prosecutor digging up all their dirt.

But instead, Nina just stuck out her chin. "Is that so, Mr. Zola?"

My pants tightened. I nodded. "That's so."

"Well, then," she said. "Why don't you? It would probably save us both a lot of time and stress. Not to mention embarrassment in the middle of a crowded restaurant."

I took a leisurely sip of wine, trying and failing to get my heart rate under control. I had never felt like this before. Irritated, sure. Angry, even. Really fuckin' turned on. Crazy in lo—no, fuck that. *That* was not what was going on here.

Fuck it. I might as well tell her the truth.

"Because I want to hear it from you." I tipped my head. "You said you didn't lie to me that night. Other than your real last name, anyway."

"I didn't." Her voice was hurried and quick, but more out of panic, I thought, than because she was lying now.

"Good," I said. "Then I want the rest of the story. From your lips, not an investigator's. Let's start with…how about the little one who calls you Mommy?"

Again, her shoulders tensed. "Olivia."

"Olivia. Pretty name."

It was, too. I liked the way it sounded. Off my tongue, in my head.

Though I couldn't have told you why. I'd be lying if I said I hadn't thought about the little girl more than once this week. Especially around dinnertime, when Frankie and I were going through Sofia's meal routine. I wondered about that girl's life in that fancy building. Wondered if she was happy.

"How old is she?" I asked as the server brought our appetizers. "Six? Seven?"

"Olivia is nine."

I balked. "Your daughter is nine years old? She seemed tiny."

Nina raised a brow as she forked a few pieces of asparagus onto her plate. "She's average height for her age. Don't you have a niece at home? And five sisters?"

"Sofia's three. My other sister's kids are all boys. I guess I don't remember what a nine-year-old girl looks like."

She giggled at my apparent ignorance. Maybe she was right. I had grown up in a house full of girls. You'd think I would know all about it.

"Olivia is nine," she repeated. "Her father and I were married the year before she was born. We'll celebrate our tenth anniversary this June."

I gaped. Ten years. *Ten years.* Nina didn't look old enough to have a nine-year-old kid, much less to be celebrating a fuckin' tin anniversary.

What did they say about the tin man? That he didn't have a heart?

Maybe it fit after all.

"So you, what, stay at home? Take care of her when you're not doing…whatever a socialite does?"

More wisps of conversation were coming back to me.

"She attends a boarding school outside of Boston," Nina said. "When you saw her, she had just arrived home for the week. Her spring break." She offered a grim smile. "She goes back Sunday."

I had heard of people doing that sort of thing, of course. Rich people shipping their kids off so they didn't have to raise the kid themselves. But frankly, it surprised me. Nina didn't seem the type.

Just showed how little I really knew the woman at all.

My bewilderment must have shown, because Nina set down her fork and sighed.

"Matthew, if you're determined to hear my entire life story, I'll tell it to you. But it's not very interesting. I truly have nothing to hide."

I took a big bite of asparagus, then a long drink of wine. "All right," I said once I finally composed myself. "I'm ready to listen."

CHAPTER NINE

SOME OF THE STORY I ALREADY KNEW FROM OUR FIRST MEETING. SOME I'D
pieced together this week after discovering her real name.

She was christened Nina Evelyn Astor, the only daughter of two
distinguished New York families. Her father, yes, was a distant relation
of *the* Astors the ones for whom half of New York was named. Apparently I wasn't wrong in thinking the name was lifted from the street
signs. As she told me the night we met, he had left her mother when she
was a child and gone to live in London. Her parents never divorced, but
Nina had only a passing relationship with her dad.

Her mother, of course, was Violet de Vries, New York socialite and
only surviving child of the late Jonathan de Vries (gone before Nina was
even born) and Celeste de Vries, one of the last great dames the city's
wealthy were still mourning since her death last fall. Violet was a lush—
my word, not hers, but given the number of times Nina referenced white
wine while describing her mother, I pieced it together. It was her grandmother, Celeste, who had raised Nina, along with a bevy of nannies.

Like me, she had been abandoned by the people who were supposed
to love her. Like me, she had lost the ones who had. Only her loss was
much more recent.

"Celeste, I've heard about from Eric. Well, him and the papers. Her funeral in November was massive." I put a scoop of *agnolotti* on my plate, then served some to Nina. "No, you don't get to wimp out on the pasta, sweetheart. It's house made, and the sauce is a double *brodo*—this reduced stock that's to fuckin' die for."

"I forgot how much you like food."

Nina watched as I took a bite of pasta, looking, if I wasn't mistaken, pretty damn jealous.

"Food is a universal pleasure," I replied. "We only have five senses. Seems like a waste of this short life to deny one of them." I looked pointedly at her plate. "Go on, then."

Nina obediently put one of the lamb-filled pockets in her mouth and immediately closed her eyes in pleasure. "Oh *my*," she breathed. "That is excellent. My compliments to your friend."

I smiled with satisfaction. I sort of wanted to order another plate just to watch her make that face for the next hour.

"Celeste willed the company to Eric, right?" I asked as we continued to eat.

Nina nodded. "Yes. He was always the favorite."

"Despite being the black sheep?"

She nodded again with more than a tinge of resentment. "Yes."

I'd heard the basics of Eric's re-entry into his family multiple times at this point. Crazy, rich-people drama, the kind you'd expect to see on one of *Nonna's* daytime soaps. Rich matriarch gets a bee in her bonnet about the family legacy. Promises the whole kit and kaboodle to the prodigal heir, but only if he gets married.

She didn't, apparently, anticipate Eric and Jane being targeted by a homicidal maniac as a result.

"And your mother? She wasn't available to take things over instead? I mean, why Eric?"

Nina shook her head. "Mother has never been the most...reliable person. I would be shocked to learn if she had ever been under consideration. Her skills now generally revolve around Sancerre consumption and auction attendance. Uncle Jacob—that's Eric's father—was the one who was supposed to take things over, but of course he passed when we were children…" She shook her head. "I honestly don't think the family ever recovered from that, you know?"

I frowned. I had heard that story too. The fact that Eric was the only son of the only son, and that his father had died in a tragic sailing "accident" when Eric was just a kid.

"So Eric loses his dad, the family never recovers, and he takes off as soon as he can only to be rewarded for it ten years later. Have I got that right?"

Nina gave a curt nod.

"But you were the one that stayed around?"

"For the most part. I was actually at Wellesley for school and spent part of that time abroad before I got married. But I was still home quite a bit."

"And you already had a kid, an heir to the family. Plus, you changed your legal name to de Vries after your dad left." I tapped my fork on my plate, thinking. "I guess I still don't understand why Celeste didn't leave everything to you. Why drag Eric back into the family kicking and screaming when she had another grandchild ready and willing? Didn't she care at all about loyalty?"

"I thought she did."

I paused mid-bite of pasta. Like any good prosecutor, I knew when to press a witness, and when to wait for them to speak on their own. Nina was staring at her plate, but the wheels in her head were turning so hard, they were practically shaking the room.

"I asked her once," she said quietly. "Before she died. I didn't want to. After all, it was her fortune. She didn't technically owe me any of it, and the terms of her will didn't exactly leave me destitute. But Calvin—my-my husband, I mean—he pointed out that I deserved an explanation. After everything I had given her, all the time I had spent with her. He said it should have been me. And I thought perhaps he was right."

Calvin, huh? Well, that cast a different light on things. Derek was still working on his report on Nina's husband, but I already knew from my own poking around that the guy was relatively clean. Calvin Gardner's origins were still a mystery to me, but he had existed on the periphery of New York high society for years. First as a student at NYU's business school, then later as an investment banker, hopping from firm to firm, fund to fund, until he made his fortune during the late nineties dot-com boom. After he married into the de Vries family, it seemed he checked out of the finance world for good. To do what, I still wasn't sure.

Now I was starting to wonder...

"So," Nina continued, "after Eric came back, I asked her why."

"And?" I couldn't help it. She was talking so quietly, I was afraid the story would get buried in the din of the restaurant.

"According to Grandmother, I wasn't a de Vries anymore," she said. "Not once I became a Gardner."

"She didn't like Calvin?"

Nina's gaze sharpened. "What?"

I shrugged. "I was just asking. This seems like a punishment."

"She thought...she thought Calvin was perfectly acceptable, under the circumstances."

"And what circumstances were those?"

Her gray eyes flashed like a blade. "Matthew, I know you'd like me to say that my husband is a terrible person, but he's not. The circumstances were that he asked me to marry him, and I said yes. I was young, but it was a good match. And frankly, it still is."

Is that why you ended up in bed with me? I wanted to snarl. I couldn't fuckin' help it. Every instinct I had was telling me that Calvin Gardner was a piece of shit, and I didn't even know the guy. Something was very wrong about him ending up with Nina, but I couldn't see what it was.

Maybe it's you, you jealous fuck.

I cleared my throat. I needed to remember the real reason I was here. It wasn't to go into a jealous fit about the pretty woman across the table. I had one purpose, and one purpose only: to figure out this family's connections to John Carson. Whatever they might be.

Nina felt guilty about Eric's persecution. And I still didn't have a solid reason why.

"If you don't mind me saying, you're taking being passed over pretty damn well." I took another tack. Return of the good cop, so to speak.

Nina sighed, but relaxed visibly. "At first...well, I won't pretend I was pleased. But Eric and I grew up together. He's more like my brother than a cousin. Even after he left...well...I think it's fair to say that I could never hate him. And he didn't ask for any of this."

I tipped my head. "Seems a little odd that the two of you would have been so close. You're what, three, four years younger?"

"Not quite three." She shrugged. "We were all each other had."

"Wait a second," I said. "Back up. When I met you, you said you were twenty-nine."

She raised a brow. "And I was. For three more weeks after that too."

"I missed your birthday."

For some reason, the idea really fuckin' stung. Not because Nina wasn't some twenty-something ingenue anymore—honestly, that never really fit the bill for her anyway. It was because the idea of missing any of her milestones gutted me. Like I should have been there. That I should continue to be there. For the big moments, like turning thirty. For the small ones, like a haircut.

When it came to Nina de Vries, I didn't want to miss a fuckin' thing.

Except she's not yours to miss.

I offered my glass in toast, hoping the bravado would mask the sting. "Well, happy birthday, Mrs. Gardner. And to thirty more, and thirty more, and maybe even thirty *more* after that. *Cincin.*"

Nina waited a moment, then clinked her glass to mine with a sadness she didn't bother to hide. There was something about her response that made me wonder if anyone had bothered to celebrate with her.

"Your husband," I said. "What does he do? Is he involved in the family business too?"

It hadn't escaped me that in telling her story, Nina had avoided the biggest elephant in the room. She'd touched on all the major highlights of her life—her illustrious family, her daughter. But beyond our brief exchange, the man hadn't really come up.

"Calvin?" she asked.

"Yeah, good old Cal." I hated his name already.

She frowned. "Calvin."

"How did you and *Calvin* meet?" I pressed on, though the idea made me sick. "Lots of mutual friends?"

"Not exactly."

I waited, but it soon became clear she wasn't going to offer any more than that after she stuffed two agnolotti into her mouth, then two more in quick succession. So I decided to fuck civility and pull out my phone for a quick Google search. Not just of him this time. Of them both.

Photos of the two of them immediately came up, thought nothing yet about their courtship. It was probably buried by features on the Gardners at symphony premiers. Hospital benefits. Gallery openings. Everywhere you'd expect two wealthy benefactors of the city to show up.

Nina, of course, looked stunning in every shot. The woman couldn't take a bad picture.

"You look like Grace Kelly here," I said, pointing at one. "That dress is like the gold one she wore in *To Catch a Thief*. More white, of course, but with that same gleam."

Her husband, however, was a far cry from Cary Grant.

He wasn't as terrible looking as I'd originally thought. Just incredibly...ordinary, but like a man trying his absolute hardest *not* to look ordinary. He had a snub nose and a mustache that came and went depending on the year. His skin had that orange, weathered tinge of someone who spent too much time at tanning salons, with a reddish nose that betrayed a penchant for too much booze. His suits always fit just a little too tight around his midsection, and his hairline conspicuously grew about an inch forward about five years back. Plugs probably. And dyed too. When Nina wore heels—and she should *always* wear heels with those legs of hers—she had about two or three inches on him, which only enhanced the feeling that he was compensating for something.

As always, it was impossible to hide my shock. *This* was the guy who snagged the goddess of the Upper East Side? *This guy* bagged the work of art in front of me?

Ten years they'd been married, she said. Ten fuckin' years chained to a guy who looked like a round of stale focaccia.

"Put it away."

I looked up to find Nina watching me. Her expression wasn't surprised—maybe just disappointed. My reactions had clearly been playing all over my face, and she didn't like what she saw.

I ignored her command.

"He just looks...different than what I imagined."

Nina's eyes narrowed. "He looks exactly how a man of forty-eight should look."

I was right. That *was* quite a little age gap there. Which would have made him thirty-eight and her...twenty when they got married. Which meant she was probably a teenager when they actually met.

Nina. A doe-eyed eighteen or nineteen-year-old.

Then walking down the aisle with a moth-eaten motherfucker old enough to be her father.

Jesus. Fucking. Christ.

We examined each other for a moment, both of us obviously aware that we were about to have two separate conversations simultaneously— one on the surface, the other in subtext.

"Well," I said as I tucked my phone away. "Now I know what kind of guy ends up with Nina de Vries." *Your husband looks like he lives under a bridge.*

"He's changed a lot over the years. As most of us do." *He wasn't always an ogre.*

I took a bite of pasta. "So, how did you meet?" *How did Shrek land a twenty-year-old goddess?*

"Mutual acquaintances introduced us." *It was practically arranged, but I'm not going to admit it.*

"Was it a big wedding?" *Did your family hate him as much as I already do?*

"Not like Eric and Jane's, but it was nice. We were married at St. Mark's and had a small reception at the Waldorf. Just family and a few friends." *No one was excited to watch me kiss an orc.*

"And Olivia?" *Was it a shotgun wedding?*

"She was born the year after." *Maybe, but I'm not going to admit that either.*

"Why haven't you had any more kids since then?"

Nina set her fork down on her plate. "Are you finished with the third degree, Matthew?"

I dropped mine too. "Actually, no, I'm not. I have a lot more questions, *Nina*. And I'm going to keep asking them until I get the whole story."

"*What* whole story?"

"The one you're not telling. By my count, I've pursued at least four separate lines of inquiry tonight that you've completely ignored."

"What in the world does my marriage have to do with helping my family free themselves from John Carson?"

"I don't know yet. But those connections have a way of making themselves clear under the right circumstances."

"Oh, for goodness' sake." She pushed several pieces of pasta around on her plate until finally sitting back with a huff. "Just what do you think I'm hiding?"

"I don't know. You look like you. He looks like him. Something doesn't add up."

"You clearly haven't spent much time in my part of town," she said dryly.

"It's the norm for a jailbait socialite to run off with a guy who looks like a shoe?"

"My husband is middle-aged," Nina snapped. "It happens. Does that mean I should love him any less?"

"Maybe not if I thought you loved him at all."

"Stop it."

"Come on, Nina. Women like you don't just marry men like *him*," I rattled on. "You were the heiress, not the other way around, so it's not like you needed the money. If anything, old Calvin's the gold digger in this situation."

Nina pushed her chair back with a screech that startled a few other people eating around us. The restaurant dimmed slightly as she stood.

"I think I've had enough," she said. "Matthew, it was definitely *not* a pleasure. And if you want to do any more digging into my personal history, you won't have my help. Good night."

Before I could answer, she turned on her three-inch heel and walked away.

"Nina," I called as she strode out of the restaurant. "Goddammit, Nina, wait!"

"Is everything all right, sir?" The hostess appeared.

I watched Nina yank her coat from the rack at the front of the restaurant. "Shit. I mean, no, thank you. We're going to have to cut this short."

I flipped a couple of bills onto the table. "That should cover the meal and the tip. Tell Noel I said hello."

"But, sir, your second course."

"Box everything up. I'll come back for it." I dodged around the tables and servers, grabbed my own coat and hat off the front rack, and chased Nina onto Tenth Avenue.

CHAPTER TEN

"HEY!" I CALLED AS I CAUGHT UP WITH HER. "I'M GETTING A LITTLE TIRED of chasing you onto the street, Mrs. Gardner!"

Nina whirled around with a face full of fire. "Well, *I'm* getting a little tired of *you* throwing insults at me like Molotov cocktails, Mr. Zola!"

I held my hands up in surrender. "Whoa, whoa, whoa. I'm sorry, all right? I'm just trying to help your family."

"No, you're not!" Now that Nina had gotten started, she wasn't stopping. "You didn't ask me a single question about the two people you're *claiming* to help. Any discussion of Eric came as an afterthought, and John Carson didn't come up once. You took advantage of the fact that I care about my cousin a great deal to lure me to this dinner and force me to—"

"Force you to what?" I prodded. "Eat fresh pasta and drink some decent wine?"

"Divulge my life story to a perfect stranger!"

I took a step back like I'd been slapped in the face.

"Stranger?" I asked. "I'm a perfect *stranger*? Is that what you usually say to a man who's been eight inches deep?"

Her hand flew out and met my cheek with a crack hard enough to throw my jaw to one side.

"You," Nina seethed, "are *no gentleman.*"

I worried my jaw, my hand touching the mark she'd no doubt left there. "Baby," I growled, "you got that right."

And then, before I could stop myself, I snaked a hand around her waist and kissed her.

It wasn't a nice kiss. Not even close. More like something to take the fuckin' edge off. Like we were junkies feening for our next hit, and once it was offered all we would do was jab the needle in deep.

Soon both of us were clawing at each other right there on the street. Mouths feasting, tongues warring, hands grabbing, pawing, smacking at each other. I hadn't realized how much I needed it until that moment.

I was tired of talking. It was all just bullshit. I didn't want to act like a nice guy when I wasn't. I didn't want her to pretend she was innocent when she wasn't.

We were both angry. Maybe more at ourselves than at each other, if we were being honest. But for the first time all week, maybe in months, that anger had somewhere to go, and the hell if it didn't feel fuckin' great.

"Mmmph!"

Nina's fingers gripped at my shirt collar hard enough to choke. That, of course, only turned me on more.

"Stop." Her breath was a hiss, shaking her entire body.

"You stop," I growled again. "And let me kiss you, goddamn it."

But before my mouth could find hers again, she shoved me away. Her own chest heaved with the action, though the hand on my collar couldn't *quite* let go. I stared at her lips—swollen, puckered, still dewy from the kiss.

I stretched out my jaw. "Nina…"

"I…I…" She was staring at my mouth too, like she was starving and I was the buffet.

Yeah, baby. I know the feeling.

I leaned in. The hand at my collar tugged me closer. But right when I was about to hit money all over again, she started to sputter.

"What—what—we—no!"

Suddenly, with both hands on my chest now, she pushed hard enough to make me fall back on my heels, then ducked out from under my outstretched arms. Her chest still rose with the effort of each inhale, but she had wrapped her arms across her body like she was barring me from entry to her person.

"D-don't chase me. Please, Matthew. Don't."

I considered ignoring her. Christ, lust was ringing in my ears like an entire fuckin' bell tower. A chorus, not a solo, and deafening at that. But it was the look on her face that stopped me in the end. There was desire, sure—she couldn't get rid of it that easily. But the heat was written over with fear. Chilling. Cold.

Nina's eyes were ice-glazed moons in the night air, blinking steadily, like she hoped she might only be stuck in a dream. Like she was willing herself awake, over and over again.

Like I was a nightmare.

I held out my hands. "Hey, hey. It's okay. Nina, it's okay." I spoke slowly, like I was approaching a spooked animal. "Baby, I won't do anything, all right?"

"D-don't call me that." She stuck out her chin. "I'm not your baby. I'm not anyone's baby."

The bitterness at the end of that sentence punched me in the gut.

"Oh, really?" I asked. "What about that husband of yours?"

"Do not bring Calvin into this. Not after *that*. We are happily married, and you just kissed me!"

"You really think I believe that? No one kisses another man this way when they're happy with the one they've got!"

"*Fine!*" she spluttered. "What do you want me to say? That we can't stand each other? That we fight like cats and dogs? Would you like me to tell you that he beats me too and ties me to bed posts for fun? That he locks me in a dungeon like a princess just waiting for rescue?"

My skin prickled. "Is it true?" Just the possibility turned me feral.

She scoffed like it was an insane notion. "Are you crazy?"

"Maybe," I snapped. "I've been walking around this city like a fucking ghost for the last two months because the woman of my dreams vanished into thin air."

"I'm married, Matthew, not a ghost."

"I don't give a shit!"

"I'm *married*," she said again. "Why can't you get that through your thick head? I have a husband!"

I leaned close so she could hear my lowered voice. "Were you thinking of that husband when I was giving it to you up the ass, baby? Or when you were screaming my name to kingdom come?"

I stepped away with a smirk, too full of myself to be prepared for what was coming.

Nina's hand swept across my cheek once more with the heat of a bullet and fury of a house fire.

I snapped back like a rubber band, hand clutched to the searing spot. "What the hell, Nina! Stop fuckin' doing that!"

I won't lie. This wasn't the first time a woman had given me exactly what I deserved. Sometimes I even asked for it. Hell, I'd asked *her* to do it, and like a champ, she had delivered, all night long.

But this was different. This was the first time I regretted it.

"I love my family very much!" Nina shouted. "What right do you have to question that? Or are you going to throw my *one* indiscretion in my face every time I bring them up? You can't erase them, Matthew, no matter how hard you try!"

"I—"

All manner of blithe comebacks rose to my lips, but they faded immediately as I watched Nina's desperation rise and fall through her body. She was mad, yes. But she was also as confused as I was.

"Why?" she demanded. "I'm not available for you, Matthew. Why can't you just leave it alone?"

"Because I can't...I can't stop thinking about you!"

The words erupted from my chest and propelled me backward onto the steps of a brownstone. I collapsed against the bottom stairs and buried my face in my hands.

"This is going to sound crazy. But that night, in that hotel room, with you in my arms...Nina, it felt like I had been wandering my entire life and I'd *finally* found my purpose. Like I had found a, a, a calling, I guess is the best word for it. That action I can do better than any person on the planet. Be with you. Worship you. Love—"

"Don't say it."

Her voice was kind. Gentle. As gentle as the touch that feathered over my knuckles and pushed my hands away from my face. Wordlessly, she asked me to look at her, to see the earnest admonition there.

"Don't say that," she said. "Not when I'm not worth it. And not when it isn't true."

"*You* said it," I replied. "I asked if you believed in love at first sight. And what did you say, Nina?"

———

It wasn't just the sex. I mean, it was. Even lying here, exhausted and depleted, I still wanted her as badly as I had in the bar. Her hair was tangled, skin blotchy from my attentions. She looked as worn out as I was, but somehow, even more beautiful.

But yeah, it wasn't just the sex. It was every conversation in between. It was the way she felt when I held her. The twinkle in her eye when she laughed at one of my stupid jokes. Her quiet wit when she thought I wasn't listening.

There was so much more to this woman than I could ever discover in one night. I needed to memorize these final moments. Do everything I could to capture this feeling. I didn't know if I would ever see her again, but one thing was for sure: I went out looking for something missing in my life, and I had found it. Maybe it wouldn't last with her, but I wasn't going to settle for anything less. Not ever again.

We lay there for a while longer, and eventually, Nina's eyes drooped shut. Her lashes cast shadows just below her eyes, and her mouth fell open slightly.

God, she was so beautiful. Relaxed. Perfect.

"Do you believe in love at first sight?" I wondered as I gazed at her. "Or is that just a story old men tell at the ends of their lives when they wish they'd lived them better?"

I stroked her sleeping face. She shifted, then nuzzled my palm.

"Not until tonight," she hummed. "Until I saw you."

———

"Matthew, stop."

I wasn't exactly a taciturn guy. A lawyer, I made my living with words, twisting them around in a million different ways to make whatever argument I wanted. But with her, I couldn't twist the logic. And I didn't want to manipulate her. Ever.

I couldn't force her to say the things I wanted to hear.

Nina took a seat next to me on the steps. "That night..." She shook her head, like she was shaking away cobwebs. "I really do try not to think about it."

The admission was a shot to the heart.

"Wow," I said. "Okay."

"Not for the reasons you might think," she continued. And when she looked at me, those expressive gray eyes were shining all over again. "Because if I go there, I'm genuinely afraid of what I might do. The way you feel, Matthew...I understand it. I do. There, in that room, it was the first time anyone ever looked at me like you did. You struck down every wall I had. I felt accepted. I felt whole."

She reached over tentatively and picked up my hand. That somewhat familiar shock of electricity passed through us again, but neither of us flinched. It was like we were ready for it.

"You were right," she said quietly. "That night, I *was* very unhappy with my marriage. I wasn't sure I would be able to go back to it. I thought Calvin had done something..."

"What?" I asked sharply. "What did you think he had done? I'll find out if he did, Nina—"

"He didn't do it. And it's not important now."

I had never been less convinced.

"Nina," I said. "The night we met, Eric was in jail. You were wracked with guilt. You felt responsible."

She nodded. "Yes, I did."

———

"My cousin," she said. "His wife. They're—they're in danger now. He's gone, and she's—" She shook her head, clearly warring with herself. "I can't really talk about it, but it's my fault."

I frowned. "What do you mean, it's your fault? Sounds like it was your friend's fault for almost ruining the wedding, not yours."

"It's not just that," Nina said. "They've mostly recovered from that. But

other people close to me...they've continued to wreak havoc in their lives. And I've done nothing to stop it. Because I'm a coward. Just like my father. My mother. Just like everyone else in my godforsaken family."

————

I BLINKED as our conversation came back to me. "Who was it?"

"Who was what?"

"The person who continued to mess with Eric." A light went on. "Was it Calvin? Is that why you were angry with him?"

It made sense. If she thought her own husband had something to do with Eric's persecution, I could understand why she would have been so upset. I could tell her right now there was nothing she could have done, but she wouldn't have thought that at the time.

Which still begged the question: what the hell did her husband *do*? Maybe he was the key to bringing down John Carson once and for all.

Nina watched me for a long time. I didn't move an inch. She was going to tell me what I needed to hear. I knew it.

"Matthew," she said, "you can demonize my husband all you want. But that won't change what he is. My *husband*."

And just like that, my hopes deflated, right along with my self-righteousness. Fuck, I'd be in confession for half a day after this conversation. Because really, who wishes that another man was a criminal just to make his wife available?

It wasn't just coveting. It was mental sabotage.

"That night, I was referring to my friend. You remember, I told you about her."

"The one who tried to ruin Eric's wedding?"

Nina nodded. "Yes, that's the one. She was there the night he was arrested. I think she was rather enjoying herself."

Fuck. I was a terrible person. A really no-good, fucked-up scumbag. I didn't deserve a woman like this. Not when I was doing everything I could to make her life sound uglier than it was.

"You gave me a gift," she said quietly. "And I am so grateful. Without it, I don't know if I could have returned to my life."

"Yeah," I muttered as I rubbed my hands over my face. "Okay."

"But I did need to go back," she continued. "To be the mother my daughter needs. To be the person my family needs."

She squeezed my hand, then stood up. She brushed off her coat, and it was like we had never been crumpled there on the sidewalk together. The princess of the Upper East Side was back, and she was more immovable than ever.

I stood too. The evening was over, now that I had royally fucked it up. She was right. About everything.

It was time to go.

"I'm sorry about those shitty things I said," I told her. "It's not an excuse. I'm just jealous that he got to you first. I'm jealous because I convinced myself I deserved you more. I was wrong."

It was the truth. Even if it did hurt like a barbed spear.

"Oh, Matthew," Nina said sadly. "You don't deserve to have me. Not because you're a bad man, but because I'm just not available to be had."

"I don't want to have you," I said and suddenly realized it was the truth. "You're not a fucking object, Nina. You're not some pretty toy I want to have on my shelf to take down whenever the mood strikes me. You're a person. I just…wanted to know you. Because you are worth knowing, doll. I don't know much, but I do know that."

I must have hit a nerve, because suddenly she turned, and her eyes shone brighter than the rock on her finger, silvery and wet under the night sky.

She cleared her throat a little too loudly. "Well. It seems I'm letting everything go tonight. I've answered all your questions, Matthew. Is there anything else you want to know? My bank account numbers? Maybe my social?"

Everything, I wanted to say. *Anything. I want to know what you look like when you wake up in the morning. I want to know if you prefer coffee or tea. I want to know what kind of eggs are your favorite and whether you say prayers before you fall asleep and if you'd ever think about walking away from this life to be with a poor fuckin' nobody like me.*

"Just—just one thing," I lied. And maybe I shouldn't have asked at all. But I had to know. I suddenly needed the answer like I needed my next breath. "Is he good to you?"

Nina stared like she hadn't understood the question.

And then, to my utter fucking horror, she burst into tears.

"Fuck, fuck, *fuck*." I scrambled across the sidewalk, shooting glares at people clearly wondering just what the hell I had done to make the girl cry.

Without thinking, I gathered Nina close, cradling her between my arms, stroking her hair, urging her face into my shoulder so I could soak up every morsel of pain she was currently feeling. Fuck. *Fuck*. Normally it wasn't like this. I was an asshole, sure, which was why I made do with other assholes. Other men's girlfriends, wives, who had even fewer scruples than I did.

I didn't even care about kissing her anymore. I was just glad I could hold her again, even if it was to offer her comfort against what I had already done.

How fucked up was I?

"Shhh," I crooned. "I'm sorry, baby. It's going to be okay."

Nina hiccupped and swiped under both eyes with quick, vicious movements. Then slowly, she disentangled herself from me with a long sigh.

"Sometimes," she said. "I do forget. What it's like to have someone who…cares. I don't have many friends these days, you see. The cost of coloring outside the lines of my set, as it were."

"You mean what happened with your other friend?" I asked. "The one who liked Eric?"

"Turned the rest of them against me." She pulled a compact out of her purse, took a look at herself, and sighed again with resignation. "Look at me. Like a bloated punching bag."

She looked fucking beautiful.

Bitches, I thought. Catty shrews, all of them.

"You need a friend, doll?" I asked gently.

More tears appeared, and though she sniffed them back, a few still managed to escape, then a few more when I wiped the first off her cheek with my thumb. For a moment, she closed her eyes, almost like she wanted to lean into my touch.

But she didn't. And against every instinct I had, I pulled my hand away.

"Friend," she murmured. "Really? Would you be friends with someone who slapped you twice in one night?"

"I've been friends with a lot worse," I offered, trying to sound as light-hearted as I could. "I'll be your friend, Nina. You need one, let me do the job. Please. It's the least I can do after what I've put you through."

She offered a shaky smile as she pushed one final tear from her cheek. "Just friends?"

I bit back a cheeky grin. "Just friends. I promise."

She examined me for a moment. "All right. Friends."

We looked at each other across the pavement for a long time. I waited with her while she called a car to pick her up, but decided not to pressure her anymore. I didn't want to break Nina de Vries. If anything, I yearned to make her stronger. I wanted to see that fight in her again. And I was patient enough to wait for it.

So when she pulled away from the curb in a big black SUV, I waved a guilty wave, knowing I would have to pay a visit to the priest again, but also that it wouldn't be the last time. It didn't even bother me that I was well on my way back to Brooklyn when I realized I hadn't come up with a reason to see her again.

Or that she hadn't answered the final question I asked about her husband. And her used-to-be friend.

INTERMISSION I

MARCH

NINA'S PHONE BUZZED IN HER LAP, TEMPERED BY THE LAYERS OF HER SILK charmeuse skirt, where no one would notice it. She had been sitting in Sylvia Blake's parlor for over two hours, staring at a catered lunch with the planning committee of the Manhattan Children's Autism Foundation. They were supposed to be finishing up the final stages of the invitation design, among a few other things. But of course, these ladies, friends she had known most of her life, were using the luncheon to tipple a few too many glasses of pinot grigio and gossip.

"Did you hear about Dennis?" Camille St. Croix was saying as she pushed a piece of lox around her plate. "Ran off with his secretary. She's only twenty-two! Younger than his daughter."

"I told Samantha she should have gotten that procedure after she had the baby," Angela Crane replied. "I did it after we had our second. Alex *swears* everything is tighter than before I had children."

The women all laughed in that way they did about anything more risqué than their cardigans. The irony, of course, was that they all led double lives. Nina happened to know that both Camille's and Angela's husbands were regulars at the Benedict House, a hundred-year-old members-only establishment on Eighty-Ninth Street that catered to the more...elusive...sexual proclivities of Upper East Side males. Just like she knew that Angela had been having a six-year affair with the maintenance man in her building, and that the female "cousin" Camille entertained every few months was actually her husband's favorite call girl whose presence was written into the terms of their prenuptial agreement.

Nina knew these things because her grandmother had known them. Celeste de Vries was dead now, but she had taught Nina the importance of secrets. The importance of keeping them, yes, but knowing them as well.

"Ridiculous," Nina agreed after swallowing a spoonful of consommé. She could barely get it down. "Poor Samantha."

Usually she liked the thin broth at the Venetian—an appropriate luncheon choice for a woman expected to maintain a sample size. Lately, however, this choice or any like it had distinctly lacked…flavor.

With a covert glance to make sure her friends were more interested in Samantha's divorce plans than her own attention, Nina swiped for the new message:

Maya: Saw this and thought of you.

Soon after, a photo appeared. A plate of spaghetti, perfectly coiled on a dinner plate, blood-red sauce dribbled over the noodles.

Nina smiled to herself as her stomach grumbled. Matthew sent pictures of food almost daily—mostly pasta—his way of making up for the fact that even in the last few weeks, he *still* hadn't gotten her to eat any again.

Friendship she had begged for, and friendship he offered. His idea of friendship was… entertaining, at least. He teased her mercilessly, forced her to talk about politics and religion and basically everything you *weren't* supposed to discuss in polite company, and did his best to make her blush the few times they met for coffee or lunch. And no matter how many times she chided him for it, he wouldn't stop calling her "doll."

Nonetheless, Nina enjoyed his company. Maybe all the more for it.

Because Matthew, it turned out, was an extraordinary friend. It wasn't that the sexual attraction was gone. If Nina were *really* honest with herself, she was probably more attracted to him now than she had been when they met. But that wasn't the only reason she liked spending time with him.

He just…listened. He asked her questions. Meaningful ones. About her family. Her life. Even her husband. And when she answered, he listened and responded thoughtfully, either with an anecdote of his own, a reflective request for her to explain something, or another question that seemed designed to probe corners of her mind that most people never bothered to explore.

He offered her a safe space to think out loud. And, to her surprise, never seemed to judge her for it.

In just a few short weeks, he had become a true friend. Maybe the best one she'd ever had.

Nina checked her tablemates again. The conversation had switched to a debate about centerpieces. Quickly, she typed back a reply. The exchange was almost instantaneous.

Nina: You're funny. I still haven't eaten any, you know.

Maya: Tempted?

Nina: More than you know.

She almost didn't send the last one. Especially when the sleeve of her blouse slipped up, baring the bruise encircling her wrist. A remnant of an argument, two nights ago. Calvin had come home late from some sort of "meeting." She didn't know what for. She didn't *want* to know.

He had stumbled into her bedroom, the one she had used separately from him since their wedding. The moment his footsteps reached her door, she had woken, knowing what was coming.

But this time…she had said no.

And that, of course, was her greatest mistake.

Not the face, not the face.

He had stayed true to his word. *After all,* he told her later, when she was lying on the bed, bruised in all number of places while her husband mopped the sweat off his spray-tanned face. *I am a gentleman.*

His thin lips, which had always reminded her of worms on a hook, curled in jest. And then he had left her to tend to her wounds. Ice her neck and wrist. Contemplate clothing that would hide the bruising for the next week until it healed.

Her phone buzzed again.

Maya: Friday? Say the word, and my kitchen is open.

Nina stared at the last message for a long time. Matthew was a busy man. The fact that he even made it to the city during the week for the occasional coffee or lunch was impressive. Days would pass when, beyond the random culinary photograph, she wouldn't hear from him at all. And then, just when she considered giving in and calling just to hear his voice, something like this would pop up. Something more than twenty minutes in a safe, public space full of other people. And, just like now, she'd be paralyzed by the implications.

"Nina? Nina!"

Nina started and looked up. "Hmm?"

Sylvia, the chair of the committee, tapped her perfectly manicured nails on the white linen tabletop. "I *asked* if you would be willing to hire your florist for the event. Whoever are you chatting with over there so intently?"

Nina fingered her phone, drifting her thumb over the name on the screen. "No one important."

"I doubt that, N."

Nina fought the urge to lean away as Caitlyn Calvert, her once-best friend, leaned close to examine the message chain. Nina didn't move. If she closed the screen, it would look like she was hiding something.

"It's from someone named Maya," Caitlyn announced. "Who is Maya?"

Nina paused. She should have been prepared for this. The fact was, she didn't know a Maya. Neither did any of the other women at this table, women who knew just about every name in their extremely limited social circles.

But that was the reason for the pseudonym, wasn't it? Maya was a safe name. A name no one would suspect. Although the texts and phone calls she traded with Matthew had been relatively harmless—well, as harmless as they could ever be when he was calling her names like "doll" and "sweetheart," or using that absurdly deep voice of his to make her stomach twist into knots—there was always going to be the possibility of...more.

Or maybe, Nina thought to herself, that was just wishful thinking. She had been to enough therapists to know when she was supplementing. Projecting her desires onto others' actions. Wishing they meant more than they actually did to make up for the absence of real intimacy.

After all, she'd been doing it her entire life.

"She's a new acquaintance," Nina said. "A friend of Eric's wife. You remember Jane."

"Ohhh."

The hum of disapproval was universal, as it always was when Jane Lee Lefferts de Vries came up. The fact that Eric, the most eligible (and for ten years, missing) bachelor in their milieu had up and married an outspoken, pink-haired, half-Korean nobody within six months of returning to New York would be gossip fodder for years to come. It didn't help that in doing so, he'd tossed away Caitlyn's affections. In the eyes of these women, Jane's existence was a complete affront to their way of life.

"Is it true she elbowed her way onto the Met Gala committee of all things?" Caitlyn sneered.

"Celeste sat on it for years before she died," Sylvia pointed out.

"I think it's positively ghoulish," Caitlyn rattled on. "Celeste de Vries hasn't even been gone for six months, and that little hussy is taking over her life? Who does she think she is?"

Nina brushed her thumb over the now dark screen of her phone, trying and failing to ignore the ache in her chest whenever anyone mentioned Grandmother. Celeste de Vries had been neither warm nor kind. Ruthless. Calculating. These were more apt descriptors. Ones that Nina came to know intimately. Her upbringing had been full of sharp-tongued critique instead of hugs and kisses.

But she couldn't say her grandmother hadn't cared. Perhaps she was the only one who ever had.

In the end, too, Celeste herself had welcomed Eric's unorthodox wife fully into the family. No one else had said a word, but Nina had seen the grand society wedding for what it was: Grandmother's stamp of approval. Compared to the spectacle of Jane and Eric's wedding, Nina's own small ceremony was practically a servant's affair.

She could have been bitter. But in the end, Nina had become quite fond of her cousin-in-law. It wasn't difficult. Jane was candid, funny, and warm—everything Nina secretly wished she could be. More than that, Jane was unabashedly herself, no matter what. Something no one at this particular table could ever claim.

Nina opened her mouth to say so, but found that every beady eye was focused on her. Waiting for her to parrot their snide righteousness back to them or suffer the consequences.

Nina sighed. In moments like these, it was just easier to play the part. "Eric is chairman now. It seemed polite to step aside."

"And now she's pestering you for more?" Caitlyn cast a knowing look at the rest of the committee. "Forcing you to play nice with her sad friends too? Pathetic. There's nothing worse than poor relations, is there, girls?"

Another hum, this one of assent, circulated the table. Nina frowned, biting back a retort about how Caitlyn had risen from humble origins in New Jersey herself, a scholarship student at Nina's private school. Had she forgotten about the year she had lived with Nina and her mother? When her parents had been deemed unfit by the state?

It was how the two of them had originally become close. How many times had Nina given the girl her clothes? Her jewelry? Helped her mimic her own hair and makeup, even when they were older and Caitlyn no longer needed the gestures, only wanted them out of cama-raderie and friendship?

Or so Nina had thought.

"Well, go on, then," Caitlyn snickered. "Put poor 'Maya' out of her misery."

Nina blinked. "I'm sorry?"

Caitlyn rolled her big blue eyes and tossed a honeyed lock of hair from her shoulder. She'd started lightening it again, Nina noticed. Looking more blonde than brunette these days.

"N, honestly. It's one thing for Eric to expect you to be nice to his *wife*, but it's unrealistic to expect you to do the same for all her random little friends. The Upper East Side is members-only, darling. Better cut her loose sooner than later."

All seven pairs of eyes around the table watched and waited for Nina to do the dirty deed. And so, though she didn't want to, Nina found herself tapping out a terse reply to Matthew's request.

"'Sorry, I have plans,'" Caitlyn read as Nina typed. "Poor thing. Of course you do. Just not with her. Ever. Am I right?" She tittered with the other women. "*So* oblivious. Ooh, she's already writing back! What is she, staring at her phone? How desperate."

Miserably, Nina watched the three moving dots in the corner of the screen while Matthew wrote his response. *Please,* she begged silently, though she didn't know for what. *Please don't believe me? Please ask me again? Please send me another picture tomorrow when I'm not around all these hateful women?*

And then, like she knew it would, his message appeared while Caitlyn continued spying:

Nina: Sorry, I have plans. Thanks for the offer, though.

Maya: Any time, doll.

"Doll?" Caitlyn's chirping voice was suddenly covered in a layer of doubt. "She calls you *doll*?"

Nina swallowed thickly. "She's, um, from the Bronx." It was the best excuse she could think of.

Another round of knowing murmurs rounded the table. The Bronx only solidified this group's larger assumptions about a friend of Eric's uncouth new wife. For this set, any borough but Manhattan was completely unacceptable. It was why the few who couldn't claim to be true island natives did whatever they could to mask the fact. Below Fourteenth Street was a descent into madness, and above 110th didn't exist. Nina might as well have told them "Maya" grew up in a landfill.

Good lord, had she been like this before? So horrifically classist? So willing to look down her hyper-straight nose at anyone outside her social set? Had she always been this miserable?

She was beginning to think the answers were all yes.

"I'll take care of the florist," Nina said as she dropped her phone back into her purse, away from prying eyes. "Is that everything today?"

Her consommé had grown cold and looked like a vital fluid. Nina's stomach turned. She craved a large bowl of the pasta Matthew had shown her. It would be the perfect antidote to this group's poison.

The others quieted immediately, clearly taken aback by Nina's sudden change of tone. This was breaking protocol. Nina was supposed to chime in. Add a few salacious tidbits about "Maya," this woman they had never known but would take such pleasure in berating behind her back. She was supposed to laugh and giggle and taunt until they all bored with it and finally turned back to planning the next boring event full of the appropriately boring members of their set.

Maya was a made-up person, but Nina was suddenly quite protective of her.

"N?"

She turned to find Caitlyn watching her intently.

"Are you all right?" she asked in a low voice, only between them. "You seem a bit…distracted."

It was a nice way to say, "What the hell is wrong with you?"

Nina masked a smirk. Matthew's sardonic candor—and profanity—was seeping into her thoughts.

"I'm fine," she replied, grasping for an excuse. "It's just…" She leaned closer, praying Caitlyn would remember at least *something* of their former friendship. "Calvin arrived on Monday. I should get home before he does. It's—he wants me home."

That unfortunately, wasn't a lie. It was the truth she had been ignoring all day while dread built in the pit of her stomach. Calvin would likely be leaving again on another trip soon, but until then, Nina sensed she would have to deal with his…tastes…more than she would ordinarily.

Recognition flooded Caitlyn's features. "*Oh.* And Olivia…"

"Still in Boston."

"How long until he leaves again?"

"Next week. Maybe this weekend."

Caitlyn gave a curt nod. "Good. You can handle it, then."

Nina's shoulders sank with relief when Caitlyn didn't say anything more or expand upon the conversation to the group. Very few people understood the true nature of the Gardners' marriage, but Caitlyn was one of them. Or had been. Nina had no reason to believe Caitlyn had betrayed *that* particular confidence. And she needed to make sure their relationship stayed that way.

"Yes, you *should* be going. You have a lot to do." Caitlyn turned to the other committee members, whose noses were all back in their wineglasses. "Ladies, our beloved N needs to get home to greet her husband. You know how it is, when they manage to tear themselves away. Priorities, priorities."

Another round of amenable remarks like "Of course, Nina, dearest" and "Oh, certainly" circulated the table as Nina stood. They understood this obligation, at least. Nina would have wagered each of their marriages had their own shameful dimensions too.

"Thank you, darlings. I'll see you next week."

She pasted on the brightest smile she could as the others responded in kind. Glass painted facades, all of them. As expensive and fragile as crystal. A mere pebble would shatter them all.

The saddest thing? She was no different. Nothing but a beautiful glass veneer threaded with cracks.

ACT II

ENSEMBLE

CHAPTER ELEVEN

"ZOLA. ZOLA."

My assistant probably said my name ten times before I finally snapped away from my computer screen. The sudden movement made the pigeons on the windowsill disperse in a burst of wings. "Are you all right?" Tiana stood in the doorway of my closet-sized office, holding a manila file and eyeing me with something close to pity. "Do you need a cup of coffee or something?"

"What? No, I'm fine. Just focused, that's all. I have to get this motion done by four, or else we'll miss the judge." I checked my watch. "Derek should be here soon."

"The Kominsky case isn't going to trial until next week." Tiana tipped her head. "You've been 'focused' a lot lately."

I scowled. It was three o'clock on a Friday. Derek and his partner were finishing a stakeout in The Hole, which *really* needed to come up with some evidence if we had any chance of getting an indictment in time for Carson's arrest in four weeks.

On top of that, Nina's last text, a neat little brush-off if I ever saw one, had been echoing in my mind nonstop. And I couldn't figure out why.

It wasn't like I'd never had a female friend. Maybe not one I imagined naked half the time, but I kept that under control. Maybe a flirty

text here and there, but the few times we'd hung out since meeting in
Eric and Jane's apartment had been purely platonic. A walk in the park
after I visited her and Jane at the Met. Nothing preplanned. We meandered around Sheep Meadow, and Nina slipped off her heels on the
grass to walk barefoot before calling her car home. The second time, we
grabbed coffee too. That time, she wore flat shoes, so we made it all the
way around the reservoir.

As for the thoughts that went through my head every time I saw her
(and, sure, usually a few more times a night, often in the shower)? They
were between me and my priest. So what was so bad about a plate of
pasta and some table wine, I ask you? It was as innocent as it got, especially since I had Frankie and Sofia around to suck all the romance out of
the room anyway.

Usually she brushed me off with a bit more pizazz. I'd heard the "I
have plans" thing before, but it usually came with a phone call later.
She'd giggle at my dumb jokes, and I'd make more of them until neither
of us could think of a reason to stay on the line.

It had been two days since my last invitation, and I hadn't heard from
her at all. Truth be told, I was getting used to talking to Nina de Vries (I
still couldn't think of her as Gardner) almost every day.

"I'm *fine*," I said again. "Can I get back to work now?"

"I guess. If you don't care that there's a Nina Astor down by
security."

I frowned. "A who?" I glanced at my phone, sitting on the desk. No
messages. "Did you say Nina Astor?"

Tiana's eyebrow tugged up. "That's right."

"She didn't want to be put through?"

Tiana shrugged. "She just asked me to tell you she's waiting. Stop
giving your booty calls this number, Zola. It's getting embarrassing."

"She's *not* a booty—"

But before I could finish my retort, Tiana had ducked out with a flash
of her palm at me. I didn't have to hear her say "Bye, Felicia" to know
she was thinking it.

"Christ," I muttered even as I grabbed my jacket, hat, and the motion
to walk over to the clerk's office. "I'll be back in an hour," I said to Tiana
on my way out. "If Derek comes, have him wait."

———

I HALF EXPECTED the call to be a prank. But instead, true to Tiana's word, I found Nina pacing outside the building under the canopy that protected the courtyard next to my building's security office. On the busy, if fairly unremarkable street, Nina looked out of place.

Downtown Brooklyn was brass tacks. Nondescript concrete buildings, utilitarian benches. You had to get out of this part of the borough to find its tree-lined charm. In the middle of the neighborhood's unflinching practicality, Nina looked as ever like she had walked out of a fashion magazine in a conservative white dress and off-white cashmere coat.

One thing, however, was different.

Instead of a glossy, nondescript pink that matched the rest of her relatively colorless aesthetic, her lips. They were red.

———

"DO YOU EVER WEAR RED?" I found myself asking, despite the fact that I'd never see her in it, even if she did. "Like this?"

Nina just watched the progress of the rosebud as it traveled down her side, over one leg, to flirt with the delicate curve of her ankle. She cleared her throat. "Well, no. Not really."

"Not even lipstick? Maybe your nails?"

"Grandmother always thought it garish. Unfitting for someone like me."

"Someone like you?" I drew the flower over the hook of her heel.

Nina shrugged. "Someone of my 'station,' she would have said."

"She probably knew you'd attract a trail of lovers. Like the pied piper, except with color instead of song."

As I trailed the rose back up her other leg, I found myself wondering what Nina would look like with a bright red mouth, puckered with want. Scarlet fingernails digging into my skin. A crimson silk negligee, begging to be torn off.

———

I SWALLOWED and yanked at my collar. Was she trying to kill me here?

Did she remember that bit of conversation, just before I'd made her entire body flush from want under mine?

Nina turned then and caught me looking at her. My thoughts must have shown plainly, because that flush reappeared.

Yeah. She *definitely* knew what she was doing.

"Fancy seeing you in this neck of the woods," I said as I leaned in to kiss her cheek. Roses. Always roses. "This is a hell of a surprise, doll."

Nina accepted my kisses shyly. I stepped back before I embarrassed myself.

"I—I was just in the neighborhood," she stammered as she looked me over. She thought she was being covert, but her gaze practically seared over my navy Tom Ford. When she returned to my face, "Another Kate find?" she wondered.

I smiled. We'd talked about my sister before, but I hadn't realized Nina knew her by name now. *Thank you, Katie.* I owed her a nice dinner out just for Nina's reaction alone.

"That's right. You remembered?"

She nodded. "She has very good taste."

"She's just the dealer, sweetheart. I'm the one who picks them out."

When Nina didn't reply, I cocked my head. "So, to what do I owe the pleasure?"

"I told you, I was just in the neighborhood, and—"

"*You* just happened to be in Brooklyn? I thought this was a flyover state on your way to the Hamptons."

Nina shoved my chest playfully. "It is not! I've been to Peter Luger's at least five times, I'll have you know."

"Bah. Williamsburg is practically the Village these days. It doesn't count."

The jokes died down, and for a moment, we loitered awkwardly on the sidewalk.

I checked my watch. "I have a little time. You want to walk around?"

Nina looked at her feet. "Um…"

"Shoes. Right. Did you bring your car?"

She shook her head. I frowned. I wasn't sure if I'd ever seen Nina without the big black Escalade following her like a shadow.

I turned to the street and raised my hand. There weren't always a lot of cabs in Brooklyn, but I could usually find a few downtown. Luckily, there was a line at the hotel next door, so we were able to get off pretty quickly.

"Fort Greene Park," I told the driver. I winked at Nina. "Just a stroll, I promise."

———

LESS THAN TEN BLOCKS LATER, we entered one of my favorite parks in the area, a small, but tree-filled thatch of green where I sometimes spent my lunch breaks on sunny days like today. Spring was popping in New York. There was still a chill in the air, but the sky was blue, and the trees were almost all abloom.

Nina had been quiet on the short cab ride. Something was up. I couldn't have told you why. After all, I still didn't know her *that* well. I couldn't read her body language intuitively—yet—but some part of me knew there was somehow more to this visit than just "happened-to-be-here."

"If you want to know the truth," she said as we passed under some chestnuts. "I felt terrible about your invitation. To dinner."

My brows knit together. "What?"

The sunlight glinted off her gold hair. "Friday? Well, today, I suppose? Remember, you sent me the picture of spaghetti and invited me over…" She shook her head. "Perhaps I'm overreacting."

She came as an apology. For my invitation. I wasn't going to lie. I was kind of pissed about it at the time. But now…

"No, doll, you misunderstand," I said. "I'm just surprised that you came here because of a text."

"I didn't come here for a text." She stopped under a big maple to look at me. "I don't like texting. I think if you really mean to say something to someone, you should say it to their face."

"And what, exactly, did you want to say to my face?"

Nina took a deep breath. "I—well, that I'm sorry. I brushed you off for reasons that—well, it doesn't matter why. But I'm sorry. I just wanted you to know."

It was the last thing I expected. In all my life, growing up around stubborn New Yorkers who were as likely to spit on you as ignore you, I wasn't sure I had ever met anyone this willing to say they were sorry. Because she meant it. Because apparently I was important enough to warrant it.

It was so small, but suddenly the gesture almost felt like too much.

"It's nothing," I said as kindly as I could. But it was everything. She couldn't know that, but it was.

Nina turned toward a playground that was full of children, ringed by caretakers and strollers. In this neighborhood, that meant a few nannies, but mostly stay-at-home moms and preschool attendants. Some kids wore neon pinnies over their clothes, marking them as a part of one program or another. Their raucous shouts filled the air. Some were happy, some were sad. But it was a hive of all types of energy.

"Livy would like that." She pointed toward the children.

"A playground? Yeah, most kids do. Sofia would yank my arm off if she were here."

A smile played over Nina's lips, followed by another shadow. "I meant the monkey bars. But now she's grown mostly out of them. I think."

We started to walk again, but the uncertainty of Nina's final words kept echoing with every step. *I think.* How could you say that about your own kid?

"You miss her," I said.

Nina continued watching the kids until we were past them. "Well, yes. She's my daughter."

"I mean, right now especially. You're missing her right now."

She took careful steps. I wondered if she was trying to avoid scuffing her shoes. They were pretty—delicate suede things so light green they were almost colorless.

Almost.

When she looked back at me, her eyes weren't wet or anything, but pain still sparked there. "I—well, yes. I suppose I am. But what mother wouldn't miss her daughter, Matthew?"

"Mine," I said frankly.

Nina winced regretfully. "I—yes, I remember something about her. When we—met—you said she wasn't around much."

I could have teased her about the way she stumbled over the word "met," but chose not to. As much as I liked hinting about that night, it usually only made Nina uncomfortable. And I sensed now wasn't the time for that.

"Ah, yeah. You could say that. She up and left when my youngest sister was two."

Nina's eyes widened. *"Two?"*

I nodded. "That's right."

"And you were..."

"Fourteen." I shrugged. "That's when we moved in with my grand-parents. Me and five bratty little sisters."

"I see," Nina murmured. "We have that in common too."

"You're talking about your dad?"

She had told me once before about her father. The man, Something Astor, who had left when she was small. The one who still lived in London and whose lights I'd love to punch out for making his daughter grow up like I had. Without a father.

"My mother too." Her mouth quirked sadly. "There is more than one way to be absent."

I nodded, thinking of my own father, who was a lousy drunk even when he was alive. "Don't I know it."

"And so you were there to help...with five sisters?"

"I couldn't let my grandparents have all the fun, you know."

Nina raised a hand to her mouth in shock. I was about to tell her it was all right, that it was long past and I was over it. But before I could, something else caught my eye.

"What's this?" I picked up her wrist. There was a ring of bruising around the delicate skin, mostly turned yellow, but a few darker spots remained underneath a diamond-encrusted watch that, to be honest, was a little tacky compared to the rest of her minimalist style.

"Oh, lord." Nina jerked her hand away. "It's—it's nothing."

I tipped my hat back. "Nothing?"

"Yes, nothing."

Every internal alarm bell I had was going off like fuckin' sirens.

"That's what my mother used to say after my father left cuts on her cheek," I said. "Shit, I'd use it myself sometimes when he gave it to me instead."

"Matthew!"

"No one believed us then either." I pulled her hand back to look more closely. "Nina, these look like fingerprints. Who the fuck did this to you?" A thought occurred to me, one that made me feel suddenly murderous. "Was this Calvin?"

For a half-second, I almost wished it was. Not because I would *ever* want anyone to do something like this to her, but because it would mean I wasn't crazy. That the suspicions I had about the guy weren't just because I was stupid jealous, but because vilifying Nina de Vries's husband somehow made me the good guy here. That there was something about this marriage that was off, and I *was* supposed to be pulling it apart.

Nina, however, cast me a long, dry look as she took her hand back and shoved it resolutely into her pocket. "Matthew, honestly. You can't be serious."

"My office has its own separate bureau for domestic violence, sweetheart. We see shit like this *all* the time."

"Do you really think that people like me end up in court cases undertaken by *your* office?"

I narrowed my eyes. I didn't like what she was implying. I didn't like it at all. "We see all types, Mrs. Gardner. All fuckin' types."

She opened her mouth like she wanted to argue back with me. And I half wanted her to. I liked Nina pretty much any way I could get her, but she was especially fun to rile up. I got the feeling she didn't let herself do it too much. And you know what? Sometimes it's good for a person to get a little mad. You can't bottle everything up forever. Otherwise the glass breaks. And everyone gets hit by the shards.

"My horse did it," she said finally.

"Your *horse*." I shook my head. "I've heard some tall ones in my times, doll, but that about tops them. What are you going to tell me next? The sky is actually falling? Is the emperor wearing clothes?"

"It's true!"

She chuckled as she shoved a hand against my chest again. I fought the urge to trap it there, both so I could keep her close and also to examine those marks a bit more. She was laughing, but I couldn't shake the feeling that this was some elaborate ruse to throw me off the scent.

"If you can tell me where you keep a horse in New York City other than Central Park, I'll call you the Queen of England for the rest of your life, baby."

But she pulled her hand back and examined her wrist in the open. "Not here, silly. Long Island. I went to our estate in the Hamptons last weekend. Too cold for the beach, of course, but the horses were happy to see me. Unfortunately, I made the mistake of wrapping the reins around my wrist. Petrosinella was stung by a bee and threw me—the leather bruised my wrist."

I examined her, waiting for more. Most lies were easy to spot—they were either too detailed or not enough.

But Nina didn't continue. She let the story sit while we walked a bit more.

Fine, I thought as we stopped for a pretzel. Maybe she was telling the truth.

It wasn't until I had eaten a solid half of the warm bread that one particular detail occurred to me. "Wait a second. You named your horse 'Parsley'?"

She hid a smile. "And here I thought your family was from Naples. Don't you know the most famous story from there?"

I blinked, frowning. Something about that was familiar...finally, it hit me. "Oh! That's the original Rapunzel, isn't it?"

Nina grinned. I swear to God, it was brighter than the springtime sun.

"Very good." She tipped her face up toward the rays and basked in the glow. "It's my favorite fairy tale. When I was in college, I wrote a paper on it. There are so many other variations than just the Grimms' version. But I really liked the original from Naples. At the end, after the prince helps her down from the tower, she uses these three enchanted nuts to attack the ogress as they escape." She smiled dreamily. "She doesn't just need the man to rescue her, you see. They work as a team. He helps her, and she helps him right back."

"You are kind of like Rapunzel. Gorgeous. Blonde. Stuck up in your tower."

Her face darkened, though I meant it as a joke. "I—I'm not—"

"Jokes, doll." I frowned at her wrist. "You're here, aren't you? So you're not totally stuck."

She rubbed a thumb over the diamond on her ring finger. "Sometimes I do wonder…"

A few children shouted from the playground behind us. Nina glanced back at them.

"I never wanted my daughter to feel that way," she admitted quietly —maybe to the point where she didn't intend for me to hear her.

"Is that why you sent her away?"

She looked up. "What?"

I tore off some of the pretzel and held it out to her. "Is that why you sent Olivia to Boston? To get her out of the tower?"

Nina examined the bit of bread for a long moment. I was tempted to feed it to her directly, but I sensed that this was one of those moments where she would prefer to do things herself.

"Maybe," she said finally as she took the bread. "Maybe not."

We continued to walk.

"Why, then?" I asked. "If you miss her so much, why send her away? There are loads of good private schools in New York. And it's not like you can't afford them."

Nina winced, like the mention of her family's money caused her pain. We didn't talk about it much, but it was a fact. She came from everything. Me, not so much.

"Perhaps it's because I'm not a good mother," she said. "Did you ever think of that?"

"I would if it were the slightest bit true."

She stopped. "How can you say that? You have no idea what I'm like with my daughter or what kind of person I even am at heart. The women in my family—they aren't warm, Matthew. They are calculating and cold at best, vapid and neglectful at worst."

I turned, and immediately tossed my pretzel on the ground for the squirrels. The expression on Nina's face told me she needed my full attention.

"I don't need to witness you with your daughter to know basic things about your personality, doll," I told her. "I know you're kind. I know you're thoughtful. I know you're the kind of person who cares enough to come all the way across the city just to say you're sorry."

We stared at each other for a long time. But the pain I'd seen before had disappeared, or at least lessened. Something I said had landed, and that terrible sadness in her had lifted a bit.

"Did it work?" Nina asked. "My apology?"

I smirked. "Are you asking if I forgive you?"

"It's customary after you receive an apology to tell the person everything is all right."

I shook my head. "I don't know. My feelings were pretty hurt, Ms. de Vries. I think I'm going to need some amends made."

"Amends? Like what?"

"Well, I did invite you to dinner..."

She examined me a moment more, then cracked another shy smile. "You are incorrigible."

"So I've been told. Is it working?"

She shook her head, but her smile deepened. "I'll think about it," she relented. "I promise."

CHAPTER TWELVE

"YOU REALLY DON'T THINK YOUR COVER WAS BLOWN?" I ASKED. "IT JUST seems weird. Two weeks you've been hearing about these assholes coming and going on Thursday nights. First time you're there, zip?"

Derek tossed his Mets hat into the air, twirled it around his thumb, and tossed it back into the air. After nearly forty-eight hours in The Hole, my detective was beat and looked like he needed a six-pack of beer and a long shower. Instead, he had come to my house to debrief like a good soldier.

Nearly a month of investigation of Jude Letour's operation had helped us identify the house as a likely center for his trafficking operation. We had a few accounts of Letour and his associates, but we had designed the stakeout based on the comings and goings of the neighborhood in order to get some eye-witness corroboration. Planted the car. ID'd the suspects. Snuck Derek into the backseat of a rusted Chevy Nova with two days' worth of food.

All for nothing.

Twenty-four hours sitting in a neighborhood that reeks of raw sewage, and my man saw jack fuckin' shit. So he stayed another twenty-four. Still nothing.

"I do not," Derek argued for the tenth time. "No one even looked at the car. You know if someone recognized me, they would have at least glanced my way. Do you have any idea how many people squat in their cars up by The Hole, Zola? I was a chameleon, I'm telling you."

I groaned. As we had done countless times together, Derek and I were back at square one, sitting on my deck in the afternoon sun, reviewing the evidence and trying to determine our next step. People always think cops just run out and do whatever the fuck they want. Maybe the shitty ones, sure. But the good ones work with their prosecutors. Do things right from the start.

"So, let me get this straight," I said. "First witness, two weeks ago. The pawn broker across the street. He saw this Roscoe Jackson cat get into a cab and return with four girls in a car registered to an LLC owned by Letour. So we think he's the point man in the neighborhood."

"That's right," Derek replied. "They go into the house. And the guy doesn't see them come out."

"Doesn't mean they didn't," I said.

"Or maybe it does," Derek countered. "The pawn broker never leaves, Zola. He lives in his shop. Sleeps there. And he's a nosy motherfucker too. He would have seen them unless they're still there or gone... some other way. It's not like people don't 'disappear' all the time in that part of town."

I frowned. Insinuating murder was a bit of a stretch, even for two people as suspicious as we were. The girls could still be down there. They were hostages, after all.

The pictures of Jane flashed in my head, and I bit back the desire to run up to The Hole and knock on the door myself. It was hard sometimes not to get a white knight complex with this job. But suspecting and knowing were two different things. To do things right, you had to be careful.

"Okay," I said. "Witness two."

"So, the next night, a lady says Roscoe came to her restaurant on Sutter strung out as fuck. He orders coffee and curried goat and starts bragging about all the girls coming through the neighborhood. And when someone told him to shut up, he went off, talking about how these big shots were backing him with as many guns as he wants for his trouble. Says that if anyone messes with him, they're going to disappear too, just like the girls."

I wrinkled my nose. The guns thing—that had shades of arms deals about it, which *could* be connected to someone like John Carson. But it could be any number of low-level crime-ops in the area. At this particular intersection of Queens and Brooklyn, nearly every major criminal organization festered. The mafia. MCs. Gangs. You name it, The Hole had it.

"Back to the broker," I said. "What did he have to say then?"

"He says three nights ago, Junkie Roscoe is waiting outside the house to meet another car. This one comes in threes. Two big black Escalades. And a tall white guy with a black chin-strap beard."

"Which matches the pictures we have of Letour," I said with approval.

"Exactly."

"But no plates," I added.

"No plates," Derek confirmed.

"Because the broker needs glasses."

"The broker needs glasses."

"Which is why he couldn't ID anyone if we wanted," I said.

Derek snorted. "Everyone says that."

"Everyone wants to stay alive." I leaned back in my chair and set my feet atop the table as I enjoyed the late afternoon sun. "We both know what's going on here. Carson is feeding guns to the area, not just girls. There's too much organized crime in New York for him not to get a piece. Every major manufacturer has things fall off their trucks, so to speak."

"Exactly," Derek said. "Which is basically why Junkie Roscoe gave up the goods with his little rant when he said Jude's first name."

I frowned. "Wait, he named him to the Jamaican food lady?"

Derek nodded. "That's right."

"Still. We don't know he was talking about Carson with the gun thing. And we still have no one who can directly corroborate the fact that Jude Letour has been using a house in The Hole to stash girls and liquor, much less ammunitions from Chariot. Or any of John Carson's other jockeys."

I tapped my finger on my notes, which bore a list of Janus society members provided by its once-golden son, Eric de Vries. Derek and I had started digging here, but these guys basically lived in vaults. And there was no point in giving the game away. Not when they would go straight to the kingpin and blow the whole thing.

"You said it yourself, Zola: they're like the mob," Derek said. "They don't do the dirty work themselves. They hire it out to the underlings. Street-level gangs. Hustlers. Sharks. Junkies."

"Roscoes."

"Bingo."

I tapped my finger on my mouth, considering. "What does the trafficking unit say?"

"Zola, you know what they say. They don't think Letour is involved in the operation beyond being a dirty landlord. But we both know he is. That's three times now people have heard Letour mentioned in connection with these deals. With de Vries's testimony, we can send this straight to the jury."

"So they can send it right back?" I shook my head. "It's solid, but not beyond a reasonable doubt, my friend. We need more than one source."

"Zola, the pawn broker isn't a bad witness, and de Vries is foolproof!"

It was a common refrain between Derek and me over the years, not to mention many DAs and the precincts they worked with. Sometimes I wanted to have "beyond reasonable doubt" printed on my undershirt.

"The pawn broker is half blind, and Eric de Vries has a grudge, King. Jude Letour was part of a group that framed him for securities fraud, kidnapped his wife, and killed his unborn child. That's hardly foolproof. Other than them, the diner lady will get cast as no better than hearsay. Especially since you and Cliff didn't see *any* of it." I clicked my tongue, thinking. "*And* we still don't have any direct connection to John Carson. Sure, he owns a stake in that property along with Letour, but that doesn't mean he's culpable for what's going on there."

"Zola, come on…"

I shook my head. "Letour's not the target; he's just a liaison. We need the big fish. Ramirez only gave us leave to do this because he wants Carson, and so do I. If we can get a little more—something that will legitimately bring him down—then we might be able to take it to the grand jury before the gala."

Derek groaned. I didn't blame him. It was obvious to us both what was going on—one of the gangs in The Hole was running the door on a house trading drugs, prostitutes, and a number of other illicit items through the neighborhood. Rings like this usually had several different safe houses, but Derek had obviously identified one of the main hubs. Still, we needed more.

"I say we raid the joint. We're not going to get the evidence we need following junkies like Roscoe around Brooklyn," Derek said. "And if Carson's potential pickup is in only four weeks, we need evidence. Fast."

"Too fast, and he doesn't show at all."

I was hesitant to request a warrant for a full raid before we had the goods on the rest of the people running it. We had one shot at the element of surprise. We needed to make the most of it.

"Junkie Roscoe," I said. "When he was with the girls, how did he look?"

Derek raised a brow. "How do you think he looked? He's running girls for drug money and smoking that shit around the next corner. Roscoe Jackson is a grade A crackhead. What are you thinking? Raid his apartment instead?"

I twisted my mouth around. "We could make it look like something less...suspicious. He would be a bad witness though. If he's so wasted he can't even keep his mouth shut, the defense will tear him apart."

"So we get him sober," Derek chimed in. "Dry him out for a few days. Get the names we really need."

I frowned, weighing the pros and cons. It didn't take long. We were backed into a corner, and with barely a month until the gala, I was under pressure from both Ramirez and the de Vrieses to make some meaningful progress.

"Write it up," I said. "And keep watching him. I'll get a warrant for a raid on his place next week. We'll make the fucker talk. I want to be present during the interrogation, all right?"

Derek rolled his eyes. I knew as well as he did that a lot of cops didn't appreciate prosecutors in the interrogation room. But this was my case as much as his. I wasn't going to be sidelined.

"All right," Derek said. "I need to go home and clean up before I go back there. It's a motherfuckin' wasteland, that part of the borough. Sewage and horse shit all over the street. Actual horse shit, man. Fuckin' nas—"

"Ziiiiiiiiooooooo!" Behind us, the front door banged open, and before Derek could continue his rant, my niece's cartoonish voice filtered through the house and out the back door screen.

Derek smiled. "Sounds like responsibility."

"Sounds like trouble," I said as Sofia bulleted out onto the deck and into my arms. "Hey, peanut, you're back!"

"Mommy said you'd be home today," she squealed.

"Sure, I am, bean. It's Saturday." I squeezed her tight.

"Princess Sofia," Derek greeted her, having met her and Frankie a few other times.

"I missed you!" Sofia smacked a loud kiss on my cheek. Might have embarrassed some guys, but

Derek just watched with familiarity.

"It was just two days with your cousins, Sofs," I said.

"Two rotten days." My niece screwed up her face like a pug's. "Those boys is no good."

I raised a brow. That sounded like her mother talking.

"Sofia." Frankie's voice was sharp as she appeared at the door, arms crossed.

"But that's what you said! When they pulled on my braids and called me a *girl*!"

"You are a girl, Sofs," I told her. "Next time they do that, just say, 'Lucky me. Otherwise I'd look like you bozos.'"

That produced a giggle, and immediately the little girl started rehearsing the retort under her breath.

"Mattie, don't teach her that," Frankie said. "She's going to start calling all her friends clowns now."

I shrugged. "Lea's kids are clowns, and those animals deserve a taste of their own medicine. Just wait until I get up there on Sunday. Then they'll really get it."

"I can't wait until you have kids. You're going to have three little girls, and they're going to call you names all day long the second you try to discipline them."

Beside me, Derek straightened in his chair. "Ah, hey, Frankie. How're you doin'?"

Frankie's sharp gaze softened on the detective. "Oh, hey, Derek. Anything new?"

"Nah, Frankie," I said after Derek stared at her for a moment too long. "Just sorting out the usual things. Same day, different case."

"All right. I'll try to keep this one out of your way, then. Come on, Sof, you can play with your Legos while I get dinner started."

Sofia slid off my lap like a wet noodle, but stopped at the door before going inside. "*Zio*, can we play Barbies tomorrow?"

I cocked my head. "Barbies? How about I be the G.I. Joe instead?"

"No!" Sofia shrieked. "She don't need a man to rescue her, you bozo!" And then she rocketed inside.

Derek just chuckled.

I eyed Frankie. "She got all of that from me, did she?"

Frankie's cheeks reddened. "She's a smart girl."

I hid a smile. "That she is."

Frankie ducked in after Sofia. Derek watched her go while I went back to studying my notes.

"Yo, man. Your sister. You, um, you think she'd take my number?"

I looked up. "What, like for a date?"

Derek shrugged. "Yeah, why not?"

I frowned. "I mean, she's my sister. If you're looking for some easy fun, I'm not the person to be asking."

"No, no," Derek said. "I...she just seems cool. If you're not okay with it, I'll step back. No harm, no foul."

I eyed him for a moment, taking note of the way he followed Frankie's movements through the house. But before I could answer, the buzz of my phone on the glass tabletop interrupted us. I took another drink of my beer and swiped it open.

Doll: I thought about it. And I'm hungry.

I stared at the message for a long time. Part of me wanted to ask where and when. Another part wanted to ignore it completely.

Because being Nina's friend was hard. Her texts, her voice, her whole presence just reminded me of what I was missing. I'd never felt it more keenly than yesterday. The bruising around her wrist, horse or no horse...I couldn't stop thinking about that either.

I looked up to where Derek was still watching Frankie through the screen door. Well, no sense in two people I cared about missing out too.

"Frankie!" I yelled. "Can you set another place? Derek's staying for lunch."

Frankie popped back onto the deck. "Big brother, I am *right* inside. You don't need to shriek at me like a heathen."

"I never shriek." I grinned. "Will there be enough for Derek?"

My sister shrugged. "I'm just heating up a lasagna. We have enough to feed the whole block." Without waiting for an answer, she ducked back inside.

Derek immediately turned to me. "Yo, man, I didn't mean right now! I look like a hobo."

He pointed at his undercover wear, which included baggy pants, a t-shirt, and a hoodie, along with the hat he'd been tossing around—things that kept him from sticking out in The Hole. He looked a far cry from the neatly dressed detective I generally knew.

"Relax," I said. "She's met you before. Plus, Frankie works with little kids who eat glue all day. Her standards for menswear are not particularly high."

"She grew up with you," Derek retorted. "Somehow, I doubt she thinks ENYCE knockoffs are acceptable for dinner company."

I shrugged. "Honestly, the fact that I like a good tailor probably works in your favor. She's not in a hurry to date her brother."

"But—"

"Don't worry, man. It'll be casual. I'll be around—"

Just as the words escaped my mouth, however, my phone buzzed with the last message I was expecting tonight.

Doll: Are you busy? You may have convinced me to come over for pasta after all...

"Oh, shit," I murmured.

I eyed the message like I thought it was going to jump off the screen and run away. Texting and coffee was one thing. A walk in the park. But despite the fact that I'd already invited her, suddenly dinner...at my house...for an unnamed period of time? It seemed like something different entirely.

I peered inside, where Sofia was jabbering away while Frankie moved around the small kitchen. Yeah, there was no way I could bring Nina here, much as I might want to. Not if Frankie was around. Not if my coworker, a career investigator, was too. They would both see right through me, and I was *not* ready for that particular third degree. I had a solid masochistic streak, but even I had limits.

With that in mind, I sent a response.

Me: Bad timing, doll. My sister has company. House is off-limits today.

And immediately regretted it.

Me: I could meet you somewhere, though.

Three dots appeared almost immediately, and I stared at them before they disappeared. Nothing. I scared her off. Maybe she was rethinking things too. Like the fact that we probably weren't nearly as discreet about our attraction as we thought we were. Like the fact that she, a regular on New York's society pages, probably shouldn't be seen with a sleaze ball like me.

Smart girl.

"Who's that?" Derek pulled me out of my stupor. "Your latest victim?"

"What?" I looked up from my phone.

"You still getting calls from those chicks uptown?"

I grimaced. I never should have told Derek about Caitlyn. She *still* called from time to time, much to my embarrassment and irritation while Tiana gave me long looks and told her I was in court. But after running into Nina, I had to admit I'd lost my taste for that particular set. Or maybe just everyone. I hadn't been to Envy in almost a month. I hadn't been laid in even longer.

"Nah," I said. "This one's just a friend."

Derek rolled his eyes. "Yeah, I heard that one before. Ha. 'Just a friend.' Whatever's clever."

I sighed. I hadn't actually talked to anyone about the fact that my new "friend" was someone I still couldn't stop imagining naked. It didn't help that I knew exactly what to imagine, right down to the diamond-shaped birthmark on her inner thigh and the exact hue of her nipples. I stared at the sky while I polished off the rest of my beer. This was the same debate I'd been having with myself for weeks.

Nina was a married heiress and mother to boot. I was an off-color cop with a penchant for self-sabotage via seduction. Together, we were the definition of wrong.

And yet, like I told the priest damn near every Sunday, I couldn't shake the feeling that everything about us was *right*. Whether or not we were supposed to be lovers, I was certain that Nina and I were supposed to be in each other's lives.

Which was why, when I received her response, I already knew my fate that night was sealed.

Doll: I'd love to. Just tell me where.

"New plans, tonight, Derek. You and Frankie are officially having your first date." I stood and gave him my best older-brother stare. "Don't fuck with my sister, and we'll be good. I need to get to the gym and get out of here."

"What?" Derek recoiled. "Zo, come on. You can't do this to me. I didn't mean right fuckin' now!"

"Sorry, brother." I shoved my chair back. "Look, we won't be able to get the search warrant until you actually observe Roscoe with an illicit substance. Go back tomorrow and tail the asshole. Get it on record, and we'll write the affidavit. As for Frankie…you're on your own. *Carpe diem.*"

"But—but—"

I stopped at the door. "Word to the wise: help with the dishes. Household chores are the way to Frankie's heart."

And with that, I left Derek sitting on the porch to contemplate exactly just which chores might help him snag my sister. But before I went upstairs, I sent one final message to the lady uptown:

Me: Your wish is my command. Envy at 7.

CHAPTER THIRTEEN

THIS TIME, I WAS THE LATE ONE. AFTER WORKING OFF AS MUCH SEXUAL frustration as I could and then spending way too much time choosing shoes to go with my Varvatos pants, I found myself striding down Orchard Street with a distinct sense of déjà vu. I

'd have been lying if I said I wasn't a little nervous. Nina and I were on every street corner of this neighborhood, stamped on concrete curbs and blurry streetlights. Over there, I could see the first time I'd touched her skin. That was where I kissed her and managed to cop a feel the first time. And then, of course, just a few blocks down, was the Grace.

Ironic, really. We met in a bar named after one of the seven deadly sins, and then committed the worst of all of them in a hotel named for salvation.

Sin. It was a funny thing. I still couldn't come to terms with the fact that what we had done together was wrong, no matter how many times Nina, the priest, or even I said it was.

I felt like God Himself when I was inside her. So maybe it was that pride, no matter what *Nonno* said, that would get me in the end.

"Hey, Jamie," I greeted my best friend as I approached the bar.

Jamie Quinn and I had grown up just a few blocks from each other in

Belmont, and now he owned Envy, my favorite bar and the place where Nina and I met.

"Zo. Been a minute, man." He slapped me on the back. "Good to see you."

"You too, Jay. Listen, I'm meeting someone, but I'll have a—"

"She's over there," Jamie interrupted, pointing toward a booth in the lounge's far corner.

I followed his finger to where Nina was sipping on a champagne cocktail and staring at her left hand. She turned it back and forth, letting the facets of the diamond catch in the light. She looked like she wanted to rip it off her finger. Or maybe that was just my wishful thinking.

"It's that same broad you went home with in January, right?"

I turned back. "How in the fuck do you remember that?"

Jamie shrugged. "You'd remember too if you'd watched me trip all over my tongue for two hours straight. I know bad when I see it, Zo. And you got it bad."

I frowned. That night, sure. But Jamie was talking in present tense.

"It was a one-night thing," I said. "She's just a friend."

He glanced back at Nina, whose ring gleamed under the lamp above her table. "A married friend now?"

"Happens to be," I grumbled. "Not that it matters."

Jamie sighed. And for once, I saw no trace of the humor that usually accompanied his friendly jibes.

"Look," he said. "I've never said anything because you always had things under control. You had your fun, and it was funny, really, to hear stories about you shimmying down fire escapes in Armani vests or whatever. But you never looked at any of those bored housewives the way you're looking at her right now."

I snapped my gaze back at him. "Like what?"

Jamie looked at me like I was stupid. And I don't know. Maybe I was.

"Zo, come on," he said quietly. "Don't make me say it."

But it was too late. Already, I was two steps away from the booth, drawn to her ice-white flame like a moth in the dark. The trick, I told myself then, was to stay just far enough away that I wouldn't get burned.

"Hey, doll."

Nina looked up from her drink in brief surprise, but her face warmed immediately with a smile, and her hands dropped as she stood to greet me.

"Sorry I'm late, beautiful," I said as she leaned in to kiss my cheek. I slipped a hand around her waist—just for a second. The faint scent of roses floated around us.

When I let her go, Nina's cheeks were the color of petals.

"You're not late," she said. "I was early enough for a cocktail." She pursed her lips and exhaled while holding back a grin. "It seems to have gone to my head a bit."

The effect only brought out two small dimples on either side of her mouth, painted red again once more. I found myself wanting to tickle her just to see them deepen.

"We should get some dinner, then," I said. "I was thinking Tribeca—"

"What about another walk?" Nina interrupted. She looked down at her feet. "I came prepared."

She had eschewed her typical heels for another pair of flat black shoes with pointed toes.

"Oh."

I couldn't hide my disappointment. At all. They were nice, sure. But they weren't really her.

"Ballet flats," Nina informed me. "Terribly practical, I'm afraid. I didn't have time to change after spending my day at the museum with Jane."

As I drew my gaze up the rest of her, my disappointment faded. In a white shirt wrapped around her waist, a fitted Burberry jacket, and sleek black pants that stopped just above her ankles, Nina made comfort look damn good. Like she'd walked right off the set of *Roman Holiday*. And what did that make me in my vest and tie? Gregory Peck?

"Well, well, well," I murmured. "Hello, Audrey."

"Hepburn?" Nina looked down at her clothes again, like she was sizing herself up. "If you say so."

"I do. Come on, doll. Let's put those walking shoes to good use."

———

ONCE AGAIN, I was taken back to the night we met as we meandered around the Lower East Side—not hand in hand, though every few steps or so, our fingers would brush against each other, and neither of us made a move to step apart. We passed the Grace, however, and Nina overtly turned her head, like the hotel didn't exist. I considered making a joke about expensive penthouses and unforgettable nights, but decided against it. Much as I liked teasing Nina, I didn't want to embarrass her completely. She still hadn't forgiven herself for that night. Maybe she never would.

"So what were you and Calvin up to last night?" I asked as we hooked a left to walk north on Clinton. I stopped in front of a pretzel cart closing up for the night and purchased two—one for me, and one for me to eat in about thirty minutes, after Nina took three bites and ignored the rest.

Nina's mouth quirked to one side. She knew our pattern just as well as I did. Food had become this pleasant give-and-take with us—as in, I'd do my best to stuff her full of things she never ate otherwise, she'd fight me, then give in. But only for a moment.

"You do realize I have to fit into a custom Valentino this month, not to mention my gala dress," she said as she gingerly accepted the pretzel between two buffed fingers.

"Oh yeah?" I asked. I didn't even have to feign interest. "Big date?"

She rolled her eyes at me. "My husband will be accompanying me this time, if that's what you're asking. He won't like it, but he'll do it."

"Gala? Benefit?" Honestly, I was just throwing out words that seemed close. "Were you doing something like that last night too?"

Nina cocked her head. "What do you mean?"

"When I asked you to dinner. You said you had plans."

For some reason, when she said she had "plans," I always assumed it was her husband. Otherwise, she usually said who it was with. Lunch with Jane. Meeting with one of her many charity groups. Dinner with her mother.

Calvin was the only one Nina never talked about, which was fine, since I didn't like hearing about him. But some things inevitably came up. Things that weren't on the whistle-clean background check I ran on him a month ago.

Based on our conversations, I had a whole list of random personal traits about Calvin fucking Gardner I would have much rather forgotten, all of which made me hate his guts even more.

I knew, for instance, that his favorite vegetable was broccoli, but it had to be cooked to death for him to eat it. You know, like a toddler.

I knew that he had a nose for poker, but only five card draw. Like an eighth grader.

I knew he worked and traveled constantly, which meant he left his wife, the most beautiful woman in the fuckin' world, alone. Except for when either he or her *horse* were leaving bruises around her wrist from time to time. Like an asshole.

"Oh," she said. "Well, he was home this week until this morning." She offered a lopsided smile. "He's in Paris right now, though. And then Rome, I believe."

"And he didn't think to take you with him?"

I didn't mean to snap, but really, the idea of being in cities as gorgeous as Paris and Rome without your wife when she was *this woman* was fuckin' absurd. I'd give just about anything for a chance at that. My chest tightened as I realized I'd never get it.

"Matthew."

I hung my head. "Sorry. Well, I'm sorry you didn't get to go."

She shrugged. "Oh, I've been. Several times. Didn't I tell you that I studied abroad in Florence?"

I jerked. "You did?"

She nodded with a quiet smile. "Just before I had Liv, yeah. During my second year at Wellesley."

I examined her for a moment. "So you speak Italian?"

Her smile broadened a bit. "A little. What I picked up while I was there. It's a very beautiful city." She shoved her hands into her coat. Was I mistaken, or was she a little reticent to talk about Florence? Most people loved to gab about the places they had been, especially rich kids who studied abroad. But Nina didn't offer hardly anything.

"Have you been?" she wondered.

"To Italy? Oh, sure. Once when I was a teenager—my grandfather took me to visit his family in Naples. And then later I was stationed in Sicily for a bit before Iraq."

"You were in the Marines, right?"

"Yep. Semper fi and all that."

Nina looked like she wanted to ask me more, but the roar of Houston took over the conversation while we crossed into the East Village. We walked another few blocks, and I was just starting to think again about where we might go for dinner when she spoke.

"How did you end up in the military? Was it just because of your grandfather?"

I swallowed. I didn't talk a lot about my time in the Marines. Not because I wasn't proud of it. I was. I was proud that right after the city of my birth was attacked that morning in September, I was one of the first to line up to fight the bastards. I finished school and went straight into officer training school.

But what came after...things that happened when I was actually there...well, there wasn't a soldier, sailor, airman, or Marine who served active combat and didn't have some regrets.

I shook my head. She wasn't asking about that.

"It was something to do with him," I admitted. "He told me to be better. To make him proud. But at the time, I had no fuckin' clue how to do that. I was at SUNY getting some shitty degree in Communications that qualified me for pretty much nothing. I had no plans." I shrugged. "Then 9-11 happened. I saw a direction. I took it."

"How long did you serve?"

"Just four years after I graduated," I said. "Not as long as some, that's for sure. But I still managed to get a few promotions."

Nina blinked, looking appropriately impressed. "So you're..."

"Captain Zola, at your service."

I gave a mock salute. Was that another blush that stole its way across her cheeks? Nina's lashes fluttered.

To be honest, it sort of took me off guard. I had plenty of lines at my disposal when it came to women, but my military service wasn't one I often used. I understood its effect. Plenty of women had the hots for servicemen. I grew up in New York. The girls in my neighborhood would go crazy every time Fleet Week rolled around.

But for whatever reason, it never felt...well...honorable to use it like that. And so it wasn't something I really talked about with the long series of one-night stands I tended to follow. Most of the women I had been with didn't even know I had served. Because I wasn't interested in being some girl's officer and a gentleman. Especially since I wasn't a fuckin' gentleman. Not even close.

So I had forgotten the look some women could get when they discovered that part of my past. And I really hadn't anticipated seeing it on Nina's face.

I liked it.

I liked it a lot.

"Are you still a captain?" she asked. "Do people still call you 'Captain Zola'?"

"The rank is permanent."

"That's not what I asked."

I eyed her. "Technically, I'm a reservist." Another thing I didn't talk about much.

At that, her silver eyes grew into full moons of panic. "What? But there—there's still a war on. You could be called up. Matthew, you could be killed!"

Was it fucked up that I almost wanted to languish in her worry for a bit? Maybe even pretend a little that there was a legitimate chance I could be called up again for active duty? Just to see a woman like Nina fall all over herself at the thought of me in harm's way?

Yes. Yes, it was.

"Relax, baby," I said gently, hating and loving her obvious terror at the same time. "It's not exactly 1941. No one's been drafted since Vietnam. Drones do half the work of the infantry now anyway, and I'm thirty-six, which in military terms politely means 'old as fuck.'"

Immediately, she relaxed. "Oh, good." She tipped her head almost dreamily. "I bet you look handsome in your uniform, though."

I shrugged, still a little uncomfortable. "Some thought so."

"Did you have a girl back then?"

I could feel the shadow cover my face—the same one that always cropped up anytime anyone mentioned Sherry. How in the fuck did this conversation get here? "I—yeah. I did."

"Who was she?"

I gave her a look. "You jealous, doll?"

She narrowed her eyes. Fuck, who was I kidding? I wanted her to be jealous. Maybe that's why I let her ask me about the only person who had ever managed to rip out my heart.

"Yeah," I said. "I had a girlfriend, Sherry. We knew each other in high school. Grew up together, even though we didn't get together until college. Actually, it didn't really happen until I'd made the decision to leave."

"You enlisted and found a girlfriend?"

I snorted. "Don't be so surprised. It happens more than you might think."

"Everyone loves a man in uniform," Nina murmured.

"Do you?"

"I think the man makes the clothes, Matthew, not the other way around."

We stared at each other for a long time, and then, in a molasses-slow movement that seemed to last for hours, Nina drew her white-gold gaze slowly down my body, taking in each little quirk and peccadillo of the clothes I happened to be wearing. I had eschewed a tie and jacket tonight, but still wore a pair of gray fitted pants and a vest over a white shirt. I straightened, fighting the urge to stand at attention, as if I were under inspection once again.

Her sharp eyes didn't miss a thing, lingering over the hem of my pants, my carefully polished shoes, the hat tilted over my brow. She drew it down my legs, then back up to my chest before finally reaching my mouth again.

Jesus fuckin' Christ. Is this what girls experienced when I gave them the up-and-down? I felt like Nina de Vries had just peeled every piece of clothing from my body with a simple expression, and now I was standing on this Avenue A sidewalk stark naked.

"Yes," she said, more to herself than to me. "It's definitely the man."

And then she walked on, leaving me on the street corner for more than a second before I jogged up to meet her, wondering what the hell had just happened.

"Okay," she said once I'd caught up. "So, what happened? You went off to war, and the two of you just drifted apart?"

"Not exactly, but sort of. After I completed OCS, I stayed at Quantico for another six months of training, then D.C. for another year before I was deployed. We made it work while I was still stateside. She'd come down when I had liberty, I'd go up for a day or two on leave. It was kind of romantic. Hot, even."

Nina didn't look impressed.

I shrugged. "She probably liked the cammies, like you said."

"You're downplaying something."

I peered at her. "What makes you say that, doll?"

"Don't patronize me, Matthew. Especially not with...that...name."

She was irritated with me. But it was the way her voice cracked at the end that really gutted me. The acknowledgement—without actually saying as much—that the nickname was special. She knew it. I knew it. And though neither of us had the right to say it, the meaning was clear: don't joke around with that shit. Don't use it to play her for a fool.

I sighed. "All right, all right. But what do you want me to say? That I thought I was in love, but I was too stupid and naive to understand what love really is?"

"I don't believe that. Your grandparents—from what you've said, you had a wonderful example."

I shook my head. "Tell that to the guy who came home after his first tour to find his girl doing the bodega owner down the street. In the bed he was hoping to share with her."

She stopped. *"What?"*

I shrugged. "Look, it wasn't her fault. When I got back from deployment, I was different. She could feel it. I could feel it. Problem was, neither of us wanted to talk about it. Especially not me."

Nina shook her head. "Different how?"

"It's...hard to explain. But you change...out there." That was about all I was willing to say.

Hmm. Well. Regardless, I don't understand how she could do that. You were at war. You were a soldier—"

"A Marine," I corrected her gently.

"You were fighting for our *country*," she sputtered. "Of course you were different when you came home. But how could she not have been there for you?"

"Not everyone can deal with what happens to service members in combat, Nina."

She stopped again to look at me. This time, I didn't look away.

"Tell me what you mean."

It wasn't a request. And for some reason, her entitlement to that story irritated me even more.

"When I got back from Iraq, I went to confession every day for a month. Trust me, Nina. You don't want to know about all the things that happen at war."

"Don't I?"

I narrowed my eyes. "No. You don't. And you know what? Neither did Sherry."

We stood there for another minute or two, engaged in some strange staring contest over my service record, of all things. Nina and I both had our pasts. Our secrets. Things we would rather not revisit. She hadn't opened up about hers, but she was asking me to share some of the worst atrocities I'd ever been through right here on the open street?

For a moment, I wanted to walk away. I wasn't sure anyone was worth reliving those moments. Not even her.

But in the end, she broke away first, and we took the next few blocks in silence. Somehow, this had turned into something different than our average casual lunch date. I didn't know how or why. And the idea scared me.

"Did you—they talk a lot about the soldiers—service people—" Nina stumbled over the correct phrasing, the way a lot of civilians tended to do. "The ones who come back. Did you ever have it? PTSD?"

I snorted. "You make it sound like a virus. Like it's catching."

"Well, it is an illness, isn't it?"

"It's complicated."

Post. Traumatic. Stress. Disorder. The first three words of the acronym, I always understood. The last word—I didn't like that one so much. I wasn't okay with walking around thinking something was wrong with me or the men who served with me. Like we were clocks that couldn't keep time anymore.

Nina didn't press, but her presence pushed me anyway. It was funny. Some of this I hadn't even been able to discuss with the shrink my CO recommended when I left. And by "recommended," I mean he said he would kick my ass if I didn't see him.

"I don't have PTSD because my family won't let me," I said finally. "But a lot of guys aren't so lucky."

This time, she was patient, just waited for me to talk.

"I don't think anyone there could really explain—the right way—all the things that happen." I blinked. "But the worst was the way everything could change on a dime. One day we might have been patrolling. We'd say hi to the local kids. The next, we were shooting at their houses. Cleaning up their bodies from the road, praying to God they were able to forgive us once they were gone. It would go from, well, definitely not heaven, I'd say, but something livable, and then straight to hell in the space of a second. And I could never quite shake the feeling that I was causing the latter."

"Don't say that." She reached out and straightened my collar, tugging on it slightly. "You're a hero, Matthew."

My eyes pricked like they hadn't since I was a kid. I found it hard to swallow. For years, people had used that word when they talked about me. But it had always felt like a lie. I was never sure, not completely, that the other things I did, the mistakes I had made, didn't outweigh the good.

"I'm not a hero, Nina," I said. "Just a man."

"Well," Nina said quietly. "I can't imagine what kind of woman wouldn't want a man like you."

"Most women don't want a real man. They just want the act. The fantasy. And you know what, sweetheart? I'm happy to give it to them. I haven't needed anything else since." My words were harsher than I intended. But I was tired of this conversation.

Nina just kept watching the parade of emotions running across my face. For a moment, I wanted to run off into the night. Play a coward, because I hated the way one look from her seemed to spear through all my layers of bullshit and stir up things I made a point *never* to think about.

"Honestly?" she said. "You were right. I am jealous."

"Jealous?" I asked incredulously. "You're jealous of *that*? A fucked-up life of overcompensation?"

"I'm jealous that you've truly accomplished something." She stopped again. This part of the Village was darker, a bit more deserted than the rest. "Look at you. You're a self-made man in the truest sense. You served this country with honor. You continue to do so with your profession. Even my family owes you a great debt."

I opened my mouth to argue, but to my surprise, she wasn't done.

"What am I?" Nina demanded as she strode on. "My money, my education, my entire life has been handed to me from the highest point of privilege. I can claim no accomplishments that are truly my own. I am mediocre. If that."

I couldn't take it anymore. I didn't know why hearing her talk about herself like that drove me so crazy, but I really couldn't fuckin' handle it.

I grabbed Nina's hand and pulled her back to face me. To my surprise, I found her eyes shining under the bright afternoon sun. The ice princess was gone. Melting away beneath my touch.

I cupped her face. "Listen to me, all right?"

"Matthew—"

"Just listen. Nina Astor Astor de Vries *whatever*. You are anything but mediocre. You are fucking..." I took a moment, searching for a single word that could explain what I thought when I saw her. "Extraordinary."

I brushed my thumbs over her cheeks, wishing to God I could kiss her. Even now, we were walking a very thin line. If someone we knew saw us like this, they would see in a second what was written across both our faces.

But I couldn't let go any more than I could say the word thumping through my chest. I was too scared it would send me into some strange chasm I'd never be able to climb out of.

"I have never met anyone like you," I said honestly. "Mysterious as you are. Cultured. Sharp. Impossibly beautiful, inside and out. I wouldn't change a single fuckin' thing. Not one."

And then, because I couldn't stop myself, I pressed my lips to her brow. Nina sucked in a breath.

"Oh, Matthew," she whispered as her hands curled around my collar. "This isn't...I don't know what to do with you."

I laid my cheek against her forehead and closed my eyes, inhaling her sweet scent.

"There's nothing to do, baby," I said. "Just know that you have someone in your corner. That someone out there thinks you're incredible like no one else. Know that, and remember it when you're feeling down." I stood up straight again. "And don't waste your tears on me, doll. I'm not worth them."

The idea only seemed to make her eyes shimmer more. "I'm not the only one with a diminished sense of self-worth. If I have to remember all of that, then so do you."

I shrugged. I should have stopped stroking her hair, but I couldn't. This was how it was with her. I was an addict. I would convince myself that all I needed was a tiny hit to take the edge off, but once I started, I couldn't stop.

I took a deep breath and pulled my hands away, shoving them deep into my pockets where they couldn't find her waist, her elbow, her shoulder. Anything to touch.

And then, as if the universe knew we needed an interruption, Nina's stomach growled. Loudly.

She broke away and covered her face, looking mortified.

I had to laugh. "Damn. I need to feed you, don't I?"

Suddenly, the idea of tucking her away in some dark restaurant where no one we knew would ever find us seemed like a travesty. Nina wasn't a woman who should be shoved in a corner. She was a light, a beacon in this dark city. She deserved to shine.

"Come on," I said, pulling her hand, this time toward the curb. "We're going uptown."

"Uptown?" She backed away, alarmed. "Why ever would *we*—"

I turned. "You said you wanted to get out of Manhattan, right?"

"I—well, yes."

I chuckled, shaking my head. "We're going *uptown* uptown. I'm talking about the Bronx. Come on, doll, I promised you pasta. If we hustle, we'll make it in time for dinner."

CHAPTER FOURTEEN

"I DON'T KNOW ABOUT THIS," NINA SAID FOR THE HUNDREDTH TIME IN thirty minutes. "I'm *really* not dressed to meet family."

We stood on the sidewalk of Hughes Avenue, looking up at the house where I had been raised.

"Nina, this is my grandparents' house, not the governor's mansion. The last time anyone updated it was about 1975, and half the current occupants will have tomato sauce on their cheeks. Trust me, you're good."

Nina gazed at the house that faced Ciccarone Park, one block from the heart of Belmont. Just north of us, Fordham University loomed. Five blocks east, we'd end up at the Bronx Zoo. To her credit, Nina hadn't looked terrified when she discovered that by uptown, I meant the Bronx, the way most people from outside the city might have. She was, in spite of her tower, local. But that didn't mean she had actually spent much time up here.

Nina looked toward 187th, which, even in the dark, was still dancing with strung lights and the sounds of people enjoying the many Italian restaurants in the area. Raucous shouts and laughter of the neighborhood enjoying itself echoed from the other side of the street. It was a typical Saturday night in Belmont, which meant that while the bakeries and markets were long shut up, the rows of Italian restaurants would stay open until the chefs decided to go home. And given how often most of them drank with their last customers, it wouldn't be for a long time.

"You're sure it's not too late?" She checked her watch. "It's nearly nine o'clock. Won't the children be going to sleep?"

I snorted. "Not likely. The baby might be in the bedroom, but the kids are probably still going nuts."

As a kid, I didn't think I'd ever seen the lights in anyone's apartment go out until after eleven or midnight. At Tino's, a restaurant owned by a distant cousin, reservations peaked around nine at night—especially on the weekends—and meals could last for hours, particularly if Tino brought out the *Strega*.

More often, however, it was us who would serve meals until two in the morning. My grandmother would cook for an army if she could, and as her and *Nonno's* families slowly followed them to this neighborhood over the years, they were often called on to host the hoards. Kids in our family learned to sleep where they could, crumpling at their mothers' feet or on the couch. When my sisters or I complained about being tired, *Nonno* would gesture at the beaten wood floor before lighting his cigar and say, "You're tired? There's your bed. *Buonanotte*."

The Zolas lived in a true house, with crowded wood slats over a brick base and a big front porch where my friends and I used to lounge as teenagers until my grandmother chased us to the park with her broom. *We don't share no walls*, Nonno always told anyone who cared to hear. In New York, that was a real accomplishment.

Lights shining behind the crooked blinds informed me people were home, if the hum behind the door didn't already. *Nonna*, plus at least a couple of sisters. Joni and Marie, probably. Lea often brought the kids over on Saturdays too.

"You grew up here?" Nina said.

"From fourteen on, yeah," I said. "My youngest sisters, they don't remember anything else. But my parents' apartment was about five blocks away. This area...I guess you could call it home."

Compared to her palatial building on Lexington, this house was the definition of shabby. It had been years since I noticed the peeling paint, the rusting iron railing, the slightly crooked porch stairs. Fuck. I should have fixed them by now. These were the types of things I'd been doing since *Nonno* died. I couldn't let them go.

"Are there a lot of people here tonight?" Nina asked nervously.

"Tonight? Probably not. It's a Saturday, so there might be ten in there at most."

Nina's eyes widened. "Ten is *small*?"

I nodded. "Oh, sure. You come on a Sunday, that's when my aunts, uncles, cousins—everyone stops by after Mass. It's a madhouse."

"Do you—do you go every week?"

I shook my head. "No, although I'll never stop hearing that I should. But I come when I can. Every few weeks or so."

Nina touched her hair, which was tied casually at the base of her neck, allowing a few blonde tendrils to frame her features. Tear-shaped pearls dangled from her ears. She might have felt like a mess, but I honestly wasn't sure she had ever looked more alluring. Of course, I seemed to think that every time I saw her.

She took a deep breath and exhaled slowly before offering me a reluctant smile. "All right. Shall we?"

"Look," I said. "Getting on my grandmother's good side is really easy."

"Oh?" Nina said. "How is that?"

"Simple, doll," I replied. "Have seconds."

With a wink, I unlocked the door and ushered her into the chaos of my family.

And chaos it was.

"*Ziooooooooooo!*"

Two seconds after the war cry, two not-so-small boys shot down the stairs and tackled me on the landing.

"Hey, hey!" I shouted. "Tommy! Pete! Get off!"

"Uncle Mattie! What are *you* doing here?"

"Ma said you weren't coming this week because you're up to no good."

"Did you bring anything from Gino's? Aunt Kate forgot dessert."

"Who's this lady?"

"Did she bring food too?"

Somehow, I managed to peel my two barnacles of nephews off my legs while they continued hurling questions. "Whoa, whoa, whoa, boys. Calm down, all right? Give us a second to catch our breaths."

Tommy and Pete, otherwise known as two of my sister Lea's three sons stood at relative attention while I helped Nina remove her jacket and hung it on the hooks by the door with my own coat and hat.

"Should I remove my shoes?" she asked doubtfully.

I glanced at the scuffed wood floors and the threadbare runner that followed the hall to the kitchen and living room. "Nah, baby. You're good. Nina, these are my nephews, Thomas and Peter Scarrone. Tom, Pete. This is my friend, Nina. Can you animals show her some decent manners?"

Tommy's and Pete's eyes widened as they got a good look at my guest. Hell, I didn't really blame them. She *was* stunning.

They mumbled unintelligibly, bobbing their heads up and down like an arcade game.

I nudged Tommy on the shoulder. "What are you, wolf cubs? Use English, you hooligans."

Both boys blinked at Nina with big eyes for a half-second. Energy vibrated through their small limbs, though I could tell they were at least trying to make a nice impression.

"It's lovely to meet you," Nina said, her gray eyes shining with amusement.

The sound of her voice proved to be too much.

"Nicetomeetyoutoo!" Tommy shrieked, then shot up the stairs toward the bedrooms, Pete hot on his heels.

I turned to Nina and shrugged. "Boys. I'm sorry. I try to teach them some manners, but they're heathens."

She bit her lip. "Livy would probably like them."

The face of her daughter, the little blonde girl I'd only seen the one time, appeared in my mind's eye, as it had several other times since our walk through Fort Greene park the other day.

"She likes over-excited little boys who could double as baby rottweilers?" I joked.

But Nina's face had shuttered. "I think so," she replied quietly.

Her lack of surety broke my heart a little. Of course. How could she really know? I didn't have kids, but I couldn't imagine living hours from mine while they grew up at a boarding school.

Perhaps I'm not a good mother, she'd said.

I didn't believe that. Not for a second.

But before I could say anything more, Lea's voice broke through the hallway. "Mattie, is that you? I thought you weren't coming up here until tomorrow." She waddled into view under the weight of her pregnant belly, then stopped when she caught sight of Nina standing next to me. "I didn't realize we had company."

"Nina, this is my sister, Lea Scarrone," I said. "She's the mother of the herd of cattle upstairs."

"Hey, they're your nephews," Lea said as she accepted my kiss to her cheek. "It's nice to meet you, Nina. I'm sorry if my boys were less than perfect gentlemen, like this one."

She and Nina shared smiles, but not before my sister's sharp gaze caught the diamond on Nina's finger. Yeah, I had a mile of questions ahead of me. No doubt about it.

I set a hand on Lea's stomach. "Any news yet?"

My sister's eyes glowed. "Well, you just missed the reveal, but I think Marie got a video. *Nonna* cried."

"So it's a girl?"

Lea nodded. "Four's the charm, apparently. Mike's disappointed, but I finally get my princess."

"He around? I'll pour him a congratulatory drink."

Lea shook her head. "He had to go back to the garage and finish a job for Mr. Alvarez. But we also announced her name. Guadalupe."

My mouth fell open in shock. That was our maternal grandmother's name. The Puerto Rican one we had met maybe twice in our lives. "Are you serious?"

Lea shrugged. "It's tradition. Frankie already took *Nonna's* name for Sofia, and I didn't want to have two."

"Yeah, but Mom's family—"

"It's already decided," Lea cut me off shortly. She glanced back at Nina's hand. "Do you have kids, Nina?"

Nina's mouth opened. She clearly wasn't used to my sister's frank, curt energy. "Oh, um, yes. I have one. A daughter." She glanced at Lea's belly. "Congratulations."

Was that envy I saw?

"Well, it's another mouth to feed, and it will be all I can do to make sure the boys don't treat her like a football. But I am excited to get some cute baby clothes for once." Lea turned back in the direction of the kitchen. "Come on, there's still some cannelloni on the stove if you're hungry."

I started to follow her, but realized quickly that Nina was frozen in the foyer.

"Hey," I said. "You all right?"

She looked up. Fear crisscrossed her face. It was funny—in those pants, with that shirt, she actually looked a lot like a picture of *Nonna* when she was maybe seventeen or eighteen. All she was missing was a kerchief on her head and a big pair of hoops.

She shook her head, and a lock of hair fell in front of her face. I couldn't help it. I tucked it behind her ear.

"Matthew, maybe I shouldn't—"

"Stop," I interrupted, then took a deep breath. "Listen, I didn't bring you here to make trouble. You said you wanted some Italian food, and this is the best there is. And on top of that…I don't know, doll. I can't shake the feeling like you could use a little family in your life right now. Am I crazy?"

The tension in her face smoothed out a little as I spoke, eventually softening into full recognition.

"Am I that transparent?" she wondered. "That desperate?"

I stroked her cheek, enjoying the feel of her skin under my fingertips. I wanted to kiss her again—shit, I *always* wanted to kiss her.

"Not at all," I said. "People just aren't supposed to be alone. Not all the time. Everyone needs a tribe, baby. You can borrow mine for a while."

"What if—what if they don't like me?"

It was adorable, really. That she could possibly be nervous about something like that. Her eyes, so wide and gray, the color of storm clouds shifting in the wind, blinked up at me. The mask I had seen her wear so many times had dropped, and the vulnerability underneath was painfully endearing.

Her mouth opened, dewy and pink, still stained with the remnants of her red gloss. I swallowed hard.

"Not"—I cleared my throat—"not possible."

I shouldn't have been looking at her this way. I was sidelined. For good. For weeks, I'd been doing my best to separate the night she let me have everything from the rest of my life where I could only take scraps. But right now, compartmentalization was impossible. Right here, in my grandmother's foyer, all I could think about was what Nina would taste like if I stole just one kiss.

I might have been a prosecutor, but when it came to Nina de Vries, I was no better than a common thief.

Except...somehow...she made me want to be better. It was so damn confusing. How could one person make you want to sin and reform all at the same time?

With some regret, I dropped my hand and stepped back. Nina seemed to wilt, but then stood up straight.

"Besides," I said. "We're just friends, right?"

The look on her face said she thought that was about as believable as I did.

But I had to believe it. Because if I didn't, I wouldn't be able to see her again. And that, I wouldn't accept.

Nina seemed to have the same inclination.

"Friends," she repeated. "Okay."

"Well, then." I held out my hand. It was innocent enough. Wasn't it? "Let's go, friend. Come into the henhouse and meet my family."

CHAPTER FIFTEEN

"AHHHHHHHH." I STRETCHED MY ARMS ABOVE MY HEAD AND BEAT MY FISTS lightly on the wall behind me. "*Nonna*, that was amazing. I am so damn full."

"*Zio*, that's a swear."

Beside me, Nina chuckled. It wasn't the first time that night I'd been cornered by my niece or one of my nephews. It was ten thirty at night, and Sofia was still pinging my ass, even half asleep in her mother's lap.

After getting used to Nina's presence, my family had relaxed into their normal chattiness. Frankie and Sofia arrived soon after we did—they sometimes stayed the night on Saturdays to make going to Mass easier the next morning. Apparently Derek had stayed for dinner, but hadn't lingered. Meanwhile, the boys were upstairs watching a movie while the rest of us sat around the big dinner table, listening to Sinatra and the chime of the grandfather clock in the hall.

"Seriously, Sof? Why you gotta do me like that?" I pulled a dollar bill from my wallet and handed it to Frankie, who tucked it in her purse for the jar at home.

"I think she likes watching you more than anything else," Nina murmured with a smile.

I winked. Her cheeks reddened even more—which had already been accomplished with food and wine. And maybe, I thought, a bit of amusement with my crazy family.

"It really was so delicious, *Signora* Zola," she said to my grandmother, who was sitting at the head of the table, looking as satisfied as ever while she nursed her stovetop espresso and watched the kids. She looked the same as ever—a sturdy five foot three in a blue tracksuit topped with a helmet of jet-black hair. Gold and diamond earrings that I recognized as her forty-fifth anniversary gift from *Nonno* dangled from her ears.

Nonna smiled like a satisfied cat. "Good, good. You want more? I can get you more."

"*No, grazie, Signora* Zola," Nina replied quickly. "I'm so full. The third serving really did me in."

I smiled to myself. Nina never had a thing to worry about. When she said she spent a semester in Florence, I knew she would charm the pants off my grandmother. The second *Nonna* heard Italian float out of my dinner guest's mouth, she was already planning our wedding, ring or no ring.

Nonna nodded as she drew her shrewd gaze over Nina for the umpteenth time. Taking her measurements, no doubt. "Okay, no problem. I will send some home with you too."

"I'm never going to fit into that dress now, you know," Nina whispered. She patted her stomach, which looked as trim as ever to me. "It'll have to be let out by two inches. The designer will kill me."

I chuckled. "Wear a bed sheet, then, Roman style. You'd look just as pretty."

Nina's face flushed again. "You're a completely shameless flirt, do you know that?"

I winked, and her blush deepened. She could chide me all she wanted, but the truth was, I'd flirt until my dying breath if it kept her cheeks that color pink. I opened my mouth to tell her just that when the front door creaked open and more footsteps sounded in the foyer.

"Oh my *God*!" screeched a high-pitched female voice. "The train took *forever*, and the game ran late!"

Lea rolled her eyes. "Baby's here."

"Baby?" Nina asked. "I thought all the children were here."

"My youngest sister," I clarified. "Joni is the baby. Although, if Lea knows what's good for her, she won't say that within earshot."

Lea just shook her head as she sat back so Kate could clear her dishes. "It's nothing she doesn't already know."

"Let me help with that," Nina said, standing up to join her along with Marie, though Lea and I stayed at the table while Frankie rocked a nearly asleep Sofia next to *Nonna*, who was strictly banned from the kitchen after dinner.

"OhmyGodohmyGodohmy*God*. I need food!"

Joni entered the living room with the force of a hurricane, decked out in old man sneakers, jeans about three times too big for her, a jacket that barely made it to her navel, and the biggest earrings I had ever seen. I frowned. Seriously, I didn't understand the trends these days. Maybe it made me ancient, but I legitimately did not get how people her age wanted to look homeless most of the time.

"Mattie, put that frown away," murmured Frankie as she swished the wine in her glass.

"Are those acid wash jeans?" I muttered. "She looks like an extra on WWF."

"She looks cute and on point for a twenty-four-year-old," Kate returned as she came to get more dishes.

"Whatever." I stood to wrap my youngest sister in a bear hug. "How's school, Jo?"

"Good, good. *So* good."

Joni brushed off my question in a way that told me she was probably just passing her classes at Bronx Community College. We had barely convinced her to enroll a couple of years ago, and even that was a stretch. She still wasn't finished with her associate's. I tried not to nag, but it was hard not to get paternal with Joni, considering how many nights I literally rocked her to sleep. She wasn't even a year old when our dad died. Two when she lost her mother.

"Did Lea and Mike do the reveal?" she asked as she made the rounds to give everyone kisses. "Do I have a new niece on the way?"

"It's a girl," Lea said.

"Guadalupe." *Nonna* offered the name, though not without a little irritation. I was pretty sure she wanted both her granddaughters to be named after her.

"Ahhhhhh!" Joni flew at Lea with another hug, and Lea's curmudgeonly expression softened.

"You missed it. Of course." Marie bustled around Joni without even so much as a look her way. She and Joni never got along. I was hoping we could save that part of the family dynamic for a night Nina wasn't here.

No such luck.

"It's not my fault the Yankees game ran over, Mar-mar," Joni said, breaking away from Lea. "Just because I can actually get a date on Saturday night doesn't mean you have to be such a brat about it."

"Here it goes," muttered Kate on the other side of the bar as she started scrubbing dishes.

"I am *not* a brat!" retorted Marie. "I just happen to prioritize our family time, unlike some people who still live at home with their elderly grandmother."

"Who is elderly?" *Nonna* demanded. "No one here!" She tossed back the rest of her espresso as if to make the point.

"Hey, hey, hey." I stepped between Joni and Marie, hands out. "Come on, kittens. Chill out. I was late too, Marie, and so were Frankie and Sof."

"Yeah, but *you* guys had good reasons. And you're not late every single week."

"Hey!" Lea's voice cut through the noise, and both Marie and Joni shut up. "Stop. MJ's upstairs sleeping, and we have company."

"What?" Joni asked. "Company who?"

"Her." *Nonna* pointed to where Nina was reentering the dining room. "Matthew brought a girl."

Once again, everyone turned to Nina, though Joni was the only one who hadn't met her.

"*Nonna*," I chided. "Nina is just a friend."

"Oh!" Joni's face was flush with recognition. "Oh my *God*! I mean, I know you! Well, I know *of* you. You're Nina Gardner, aren't you? Eric de Vries's cousin!"

Nina reddened. "Oh, yes. That—that's correct."

"I've seen you on Page Six—oh my God, Kate, her clothes are to *die* for—you would love them."

"Sorry about this," I murmured to Nina.

She gave me a friendly shrug. "It happens."

My brows rose. "It does?" Immediately, I felt like an idiot. I had seen the fifteen years' worth of articles about her in Page Six. Given how lack-adaisical most New Yorkers were about shit like this, it was easy to forget that Nina was actually pretty well-known around town.

Joni, however, just kept fawning. "I *loved* your dress at the Guggen-heim re-opening," she said as she flopped down into Kate's seat and dragged Nina into the one next to her. "Did you get to meet the One Direction guys there too? Oh, *look* at this ring. Kate, did you see her jewelry? These earrings are amaze-balls!"

"They are really nice," Kate chimed in from the kitchen until she caught my dirty look. "What? They are."

"Mattie, you didn't tell us you were dating a *celebrity*!"

Beside me, Nina pinked all over again, and not in a good way.

"We're not dating," I cut in before Nina got too freaked out. "Joni, Nina's married. That's what the rings mean, you goon. She and I are just friends."

"Whatever," Joni swatted me away. "Listen, are you really friends with Taylor Swift?"

With one helpless look my way, Nina was dragged into a long "Who do you know?" about a whole bunch of celebrities. I couldn't lie. It gave me a warm feeling in my stomach, watching her be fawned over the way she deserved, even if it was just because she knew a couple of pop stars. The pleasure from the attention was written all over her face.

"I'll fix you a plate, Jo," Lea said as she lumbered up. "Mattie. You'll help."

I turned. "What?"

But I had seen that look on my sister's face before. Frankie's too. Looked like I wasn't going to avoid the third degree tonight after all.

"Don't start, Le," I said as I joined her in the kitchen.

At the sink, Kate snorted. "Is that possible?"

I ignored her. "She's just a friend."

"Please," Lea said as she pulled the cannelloni across the counter.

"Like I want to get involved in your messy personal life. That's Frankie's job, not mine." She nodded to where Frankie was watching Joni and Kate, Sofia dead weight in her arms. Frankie, however, didn't look particularly happy about what she was seeing.

I gulped. Yeah, that third degree was coming, but probably not until she came home tomorrow night. After hours of praying for me in church. I'd have to promise to come back up every weekend for a month just to make it stop.

"You talked to Ma lately?" Lea asked casually as she spooned a few cannelloni onto Joni's plate.

I stiffened and turned back. So that's what she wanted. "Sure. Yeah. I said hi at Christmas."

"Mattie, that was over three months ago."

I frowned. "What do you want me to say? You know we aren't exactly close."

Okay, that was an understatement. Lea was the only one of the six of us who still kept in regular touch with our mother. And that was more out of obligation to her kids.

"You could check in with her a little more," Lea said. "Not just leave it up to me."

"She still shacked up with that banker in Stamford?" I asked.

Lea eyed me. She knew where this was going. "Yeah…"

"She ever planning on seeing her grandchildren more than once every two years?"

Lea put a hand on her hip. "I doubt you care, but she actually came into the city two weeks ago for Tommy's birthday."

"Too bad his birthday was in October."

"She asked about you."

I scowled. "Did she?"

"Yeah. A lot. I think she misses you, Mattie. Maybe it's time to forgive and forget, huh?"

I fingered my wineglass, measuring the bottom of the goblet. Even looking at it, with this conversation going on, carved a pit in my stomach. Sometimes I wondered if we should be drinking at all, Italian or not. The Zola kids were the products of two fall-down drunks in a neighborhood full of light-weight alcoholics. Joni in particular had never shown much in the way of restraint with anything.

Fuck it. I wasn't my father, who was probably burning in hell for neglect of his family. I wasn't going to lose sleep over his wife, who abandoned hers while she was alive, including a baby girl, not six months after the car crash that killed their dad.

I tossed the rest of the wine back. "Nah, I'm good. Leaving us here was the best thing she did. I'm happy to let her keep it that way."

I took the plate from Lea and started loading salad onto the side, one leaf at a time. My sister, however, just kept staring at me.

"Twenty-two years is a long time to hold a grudge, Mattie."

"Well, thirty-six is even longer to have a drunk for a mother."

"She's been sober for two."

"Yeah, I've heard that before."

"She's trying."

"I've heard that too."

"Mattie, please consider seeing her. The others won't until you do."

I stared at the counter, weighing her words. Lea and I had had this conversation countless times before, and it wasn't fair. My sisters were grown women. They could make their own decisions. It wasn't my fault that the other four followed my lead when it came to our mother. And honestly? If they did? Maybe that was for the best.

"Listen." I turned. "You were ten when Mom left. Maybe you don't remember how many times she and Dad jumped on the wagon just to fall right off again."

"I remember," Lea started, but I had more to say.

"Or maybe you don't remember the way she and Dad used to go at each other like cats and dogs, then come at me when one of them finally ran out. Maybe you don't remember how fuckin' hungry you girls were all the time when she and Dad forgot to make us dinner."

"Mattie—"

"*I* remember, Lee. Because until we moved in here, I was the one who had to clean up after them. I was the one who took the beatings when she and Dad were too pissed to think straight. I was the one who went hungry and begged the grocers for Joni's formula. And to be totally honest, I think forgetting that does a disservice to the only real parents we've ever had, one of whom is sitting at the table right over there!"

"Come on, Daddy was *Nonna's* son! She never wanted us to forget him! And she never told us not to forgive Mom."

"Well, maybe I just don't have the grace that you do." I tossed the salad tongs back into the bowl with a clatter. *"Fuck!"*

"Zio…"

Sofia's sleepy yowl broke through the argument. On the other side of the counter, the chatter around the table had quieted, and Kate had slipped away to give us privacy while we talked. I caught Nina peering at me, worry etched across her smooth forehead, and forced myself to smile until she turned back.

"Mattie, she's better," Lea said quietly once people started talking again. "You think none of us remember when Daddy died, but honestly, we all do. Even Joni and Marie."

I turned. "They were babies. Not even one and two."

"They remember in their hearts."

I stared at the leftover food long enough that Lea relaxed next to me. Out of all of us, she was the most stubborn. Having three boys will do that to you, I guess. Frankie wouldn't have stopped arguing until she chased me out of the house. But Lea just waited me out.

I sighed. "I'm glad you and Mom are connecting if it makes you happy."

"It does. It really does, Mattie. And I think you—"

"But if it were me," I cut in gently, "I wouldn't let my kids within a square mile of her." I shook my head and turned. *"Nonna!* Do we have any *limoncello?"*

At the end of the table, *Nonna* nodded with a raised hand. *"Sì, sì."*

I grabbed the bottle of the sweet homemade liqueur out of the freezer. "I'm sorry. I'm going to go help Nina escape the paparazzi over there, now." I picked up Joni's plate. "Think about what I said. For the little one, eh?"

Lea sighed. "Fine. But you think too."

"Sure, sure."

I returned to the table and shoved Joni to the next chair over so I could be next to Nina while I poured the *limoncello* into the small digestivo glasses *Nonna* had brought out. My baby sister gave me a dirty look, but promptly started shoving pasta and ricotta into her mouth.

"Mmmmm, *Nonna*, it's *so* good!" she cheered.

Nonna just smiled and nudged Joni's cheek, muttering something in Italian that sounded roughly like "beautiful baby devil." Well, if the shoe fits.

"It *was* delicious, *Signora* Zola," Nina complimented my grandmother again. "And I haven't had *limoncello* this good since I was in Italy."

I smirked. Clearly she had been taking notes. Every time she said something about *Nonna's* food, she got extra points.

"*Grazie*," replied *Nonna* with a broad smile. "*Ti darò la ricetta.*"

Nina looked at me. "What did she say she'll give me? My vocabulary's a little rusty."

Frankie's eyes had grown very large. "She said she'll give you the recipe."

Joni looked up. "What? *Nonna*, you won't even give me your *limoncello* recipe, and I live here!"

"Nina helped clean up," *Nonna* returned. "When you do that too, you can have it."

"Ha!" Marie cackled, only to receive another dirty look from Joni.

Nonna turned back to Nina and touched her cheek, lapsing again into Italian, as she often did after a few glasses of wine. "*Guarda questo bel viso. Sembra proprio Grace Kelly, no?*"

Everyone at the table immediately examined Nina more thoroughly.

I chuckled, but nodded. "Yeah, I see it, *Nonna*."

Nina blinked curiously. "I couldn't catch everything. What was that?"

I smiled. "She said you look like Grace Kelly, doll."

When the word dropped from my mouth, a lightning-quick silence swept over the room. I stared at the table, hoping everyone had missed it. Maybe no one noticed. It was that fast.

But when I looked up, it was clear that everyone had. So instead, I focused on Nina.

"She's right, you know," I said, shooting for casual but failing miserably. "You do."

Nina just looked around, unsure why all the attention in the room was suddenly on us. "That name sounds familiar. You mentioned her before, I think. But who *is* Grace Kelly?"

"*What?*" I almost dropped my glass.

"Now you've done it," Frankie remarked.

"Done what?" Nina asked.

"Mattie has a thing for old ladies," Lea chirped.

"Shut up, Le," I snapped. "Grace Kelly is not old." I turned back to Nina. "She's timeless."

"Well, technically, she's dead."

"I said shut up!"

"*Zio...*"

"Here, this should cover me for a while." I threw a crumpled five down the table in the direction of Frankie, who happily stuffed the bill into her dress pocket, then rocked Sofia back to sleep.

"Look," she said. "Here are some pictures."

We all turned back to Frankie, who was holding up her phone so we could see the collage of pictures provided by the internet.

"*Oh!*" Nina said as she accepted the phone. "Yes, of course. I recognize her now." She pointed at one of Grace Kelly at her wedding to the Prince of Monaco. "Did you know that Kate Middleton based her wedding dress on this one? Everyone wanted her to do it like Diana's, but this is much more classic, I think. Mine was a little bit like it too."

I took a long drink of water, ignoring the way my chest ached a little at the idea of Nina in a wedding dress. A wedding that wasn't mine.

"*Nonna's* right. You do look like her," Kate said. "Oh my *God*, Mattie, look at this, they're practically identical here! What movie is this?"

"*High Society,*" Nina read off the screen. "What's that one about?"

"Isn't that the remake of *The Philadelphia Story?* But as a musical?" Marie wondered as she examined her drink.

I nodded. "Yeah. Love quadrangle. She's about to get married, but her ex-husband comes back to get her. Plus there's the guy she's supposed to marry, and another suitor too."

"So she ends up with her husband again?" Nina didn't sound very impressed.

I shrugged. "That's the era for you. Marriage conquered all, don't you know?"

Nina just gave a tiny snort.

"What about that one?" She pointed at another movie picture. "*The Swan*. I like the poster."

"That's her last film," Frankie offered. "I only know because it's *Nonna's* favorite. Isn't it, *Nonna*?"

Nonna smiled. "Yes, yes. I love this movie." She sighed dreamily and sipped her liqueur.

Nina clicked on the film's streaming page. "She's a princess?"

"Well, she becomes one. She took the safe road there too," I said. "Had a brief affair, but went back to the boring prince she was supposed to marry. Sort of like her real life, I guess."

"Oh," Nina closed the window and passed the phone back to Frankie. "Are there any where she doesn't end up with the safe choice?"

"Well, there's *To Catch a Thief*." I smirked. "She hooks up with a cat burglar there. But everyone has seen that movie."

Nina shook her head. "Not me."

"Oh, here we go," Frankie murmured.

"Come on, doll."

With a screech of a chair, I stood and grabbed Nina's hand. Again, that slight shock flew through our fingers. I wasn't exactly used to it by now. More like addicted. But I had other things on my mind than trying to fight it.

"Where are we going?" she asked as I towed her away from the table, ignoring the way three of my sisters' mouths had dropped at the familiar nickname.

"To give you an education," I said. "And get out of this damn henhouse."

"And into the Bermuda Triangle!" Frankie called, breaking the second awkward silence as everyone started to laugh. "Otherwise known as Mattie's DVD collection."

"Hush, Fran," I retorted. "We're just going to my place to watch a little Hitchcock. You'll love *To Catch a Thief*. I promise."

"Your place?"

Nina stopped short and pulled her hand back. Behind her, Frankie's eyebrows practically touched the ceiling. Lea's too. Everyone else just watched curiously.

I knew exactly what she was worried about. And maybe if I'd stopped for half a second, I'd have been worried about it too.

"Hey," I said, reaching out to touch Nina's arm. Innocent. Always so innocent. "It's just a movie. No funny business, I promise."

Nina touched my hand. "All...all right."

———

TEN MINUTES LATER, we had said our goodbyes, even to the boys who were passed out in front of an old *Star Wars* VHS in *Nonna's* room. We were outside waiting for an Uber when the door opened once more.

"Mattie."

I turned around at the sound of Frankie's voice. "Hold on," I told Nina. "I'll be right back."

Frankie was waiting for me at the door, watching Nina warily.

"What is it, Fran?"

"What are you doing?" Frankie asked, as direct as always.

I frowned. "What do you mean?"

"Mattie. You called her 'doll.' Just like...you know."

Yeah, I wasn't getting anything past her. "No one noticed."

"*Everyone* noticed."

I shrugged. What did she want me to say?

"Are you sure it's a good idea?" Frankie tried again. "I know you love Grace Kelly and everything, but bringing her back to our place... this late at night... Do you want me and Sofia to come with you? We don't have to go to Mass tomorrow."

I swallowed. My throat was thick. Was it that obvious what I wanted? Was the tension really that thick my own sister had to point it out?

It took a Herculean effort not to pull at my collar. "Ah, no. I know you want Sof to go to Sunday school and everything. It's just a movie, Frankie. You guys are reading too much into the situation. We'll be fine."

My sister looked like she didn't believe me. Well, whatever. Frankie always looked like that. Over her shoulder, I could see the shadows of at least three other females behind *Nonna's* lace curtains.

"All right," Frankie said finally. "Just be careful, Mattie. Okay?"

"Fran—"

"I mean it," she said firmly. "That one...she's trouble. I can tell by the way you look at her."

"Frankie, I can take care of myself."

"I can also tell by the way she looks at you."

To that, I had nothing. "I..."

"Just be careful," Frankie said again. And then she walked back up the steps and closed the door.

CHAPTER SIXTEEN

It took us a little over an hour to get all the way back to Red Hook. I had considered asking Frankie for the car instead of shelling out for an Uber, but decided I couldn't do that to her and Sofia. It was a long-ass train ride to take with a squirrelly three-year-old on your lap, and they deserved wheels after giving me the house to myself.

To my surprise, though, Nina didn't seem to mind or even argue about the long ride through three different boroughs to get to my house.

"Is there—do you—" I twisted my lips trying to figure out how to say what I wanted to say. "Is there anyone at home waiting for you tonight?"

Nina frowned. "Well, you already know that Calvin is out of town."

I did know. Holy shit, did I know. Just like I also knew that while Nina had checked her cell phone several times over the course of the night, she hadn't received a single call or message.

Again, I couldn't help but think about how I would do things differently. That if she were *my* wife while I was traveling, I wouldn't even be asleep without a very long, probably dirty, likely X-rated FaceTime session. Nightly.

Just the thought made my pants tighten.

"Ah, no," I said. "I mean…like, is there anyone else who would be there? Anyone expecting you?"

Her frown deepened. "You mean Olivia? I told you, she's at school."

"No, I mean—like your doormen. Or, maybe a housekeeper?"

Recognition crossed Nina's face. "Oh! You mean staff. No, we don't currently employ any live-in. Not since Olivia left. I'm considering asking my housekeeper to stay, though, if only to cut down her commute. And it's nice to have someone around."

Currently. I marveled at how the concept could be so normal for her to discuss. The fact that she would potentially hire someone out of loneliness too…the idea cut to the quick.

The car pulled to a stop outside my homely brick townhouse, which was about half the size of *Nonna's* and still took nearly a third of my paycheck for the mortgage.

"This is home," I said as we got out. "No live-in staff either. Just a couple of tenants in the basement and Frankie and Sofia in the upstairs."

"But not tonight."

Our eyes met as the car drove away, leaving us on the street alone.

"No," I said. "Not tonight."

Nina looked around. Red Hook was admittedly a tomb compared to most parts of New York. It was one of the reasons I chose to live here, aside from the fact that I was able to buy before the market shifted. Fifteen years ago, Red Hook was one of the worst neighborhoods in Brooklyn. When I bought, a couple of breweries and a big artist group had just leased some of the more decrepit properties on Van Brunt while the projects to the east were being cleaned up. A few years later, celebrities had moved into the newly refurbished lofts on the water. Just a few blocks away from my house was the Hudson, with a direct view of the Statue of Liberty, and beyond her, the lower end of Manhattan and a distant view of New Jersey. It was gentrified, sure, but for now I liked the relative diversity of the neighborhood. And I liked the quiet. A lot.

"Well," said Nina, her voice low enough that if I hadn't been right next to her and in this part of the city, I might not have heard her at all. "Are you going to invite me in?"

I grinned. She grinned back.

"Sure," I said. "Follow me."

I led her up the steps of the house and unlocked the door, then flipped on the lights to guide her inside. Nina peered into the small, but bright space as she followed me past the stairs down a short hallway.

"Kitchen," I said.

"Do I get the full tour?"

My mouth quirked. "Ah, sure. If you want it. Come on."

I led her back to the foyer and then up the stairs, wincing as the older wood creaked. Normally I was proud of my house. I worked on it nonstop for almost five years, renting out the bottom to offset my mortgage while I put my blood, sweat, and every spare cent into remodeling the decrepit old place. But right now, every stupid imperfection was screaming at me. The uneven trim. The old cracks by the skylight. The squeaky seventh step.

At the top, I flipped on the lights to reveal the bathroom and the two small bedrooms to the right that belonged to Sofia and Frankie. Then we walked down the hall to the master.

"This is my room," I announced as I turned the light on and stepped aside.

Feeling a little bit naked, I leaned against the doorframe while Nina walked in. She moved slowly, with the same expression people have when they look at art. Observing the small, neat space like it was a masterpiece, not the no-nonsense bedroom of a middle-class bachelor.

I didn't have much, and what I did have was just like everything in my closet. Simple. Good quality. Clean and cared for. I didn't understand people who treated their homes like crap. If my grandmother hadn't beaten cleanliness into me, the Marines did it tenfold. I still made my bed with hospital corners.

"The bed set." Nina ran a hand over the gray duvet and white linens atop the simple platform.

I pulled at my collar. Right now I was doing everything I could not to imagine throwing her onto it. Like I had done once before, somewhere else.

"It was my great-uncle's," I said. "He went back to Rome a few years ago, so I refinished it."

Her mouth quirked to one side—not with amusement, I didn't think. More with self-satisfaction. As if she'd known I would say that.

"It's very nice," she said. "I've always liked Danish furniture, actually. I have quite a lot of it myself."

"Is that right?"

Another ache thumped in my chest. I'd probably never see Nina's apartment. Until now, I'd imagined it as some big lonely space in the sky, full of shitty gilt antiques or uncomfortable glass furniture.

But of course, if her husband was gone all the time, it would be a place that Nina had made, wouldn't it? That was what women like her did. They decorated. They hosted. They made and remade their homes (or hired designers to do it). I wondered if Nina was the kind of woman who really put the time in. If perhaps her home was the truest representation of her there could be.

And I'd never see it.

Nina examined the collection of framed photographs on my bureau. "You're very fastidious, aren't you?"

I shrugged. "I suppose I am."

"Not a sock on the floor. Not a speck of dust anywhere." Her lashes cast a long shadow against her impossibly sharp cheeks.

"There's a basket right over there," I said, nodding toward the hamper in the corner. "No reason not to use it."

"You do better than my housekeeper."

"Maybe you should hire me instead."

Nina snorted. As always, it was fuckin' adorable.

She turned back to the pictures and picked up the box at the end of the bureau.

"What's this?" she asked as she looked into the glass.

"A medal." I frowned, a bit embarrassed. Shit, I'd almost forgotten about the stupid thing; a curio box Frankie had made for my birthday a few years ago.

"Navy Cross," Nina read off the certificate in the back. "Is it an important one?"

I shrugged. "Not really." I wasn't surprised by her unfamiliarity. People outside the military generally knew the Purple Heart, the Medal of Honor, and that was it.

But Nina was already on her phone, looking it up. "Matthew, tell the truth. This is quite the honor."

I shrugged again, then moved to stand next to her. "It was nothing."

Her eyes shone again with that same expression as when she called me "Captain Zola." For some reason, I hated it. She didn't know what it really meant. What I was really capable of.

"May I take it out?"

I sighed. "Sure, I guess. There's a latch on the back."

I sank to the bed while she brought the box over to me. I undid the latch in the front and opened the glass so Nina could reach in and gingerly remove the medal.

"For acts of extraordinary valor," she recited, holding it by the pin on the back of the blue and white ribbon while she turned the cross back and forth. She held it up to my chest. "Is that where you would normally wear it? Very handsome."

Suddenly, I felt ridiculous. Like I was a doll, she was toying with me, dressing me up to meet the make-believe princess.

"You want me to role play with you?" I sneered. "Play a little dress up?"

Nina lowered the pin, all amusement gone. "What? Of course not."

"Good, because I'm not doing that. Not for you. Not for fuckin' anyone."

I couldn't help the anger that infected my words. She wouldn't be the only woman who's ever wanted me to put on my uniform in the bedroom. Hell, she wouldn't even be the only one from her neighborhood. There was a reason I didn't actually tell people about this sort of thing.

It was the only role I wouldn't play.

"Matthew, I really didn't mean to offend you."

"Good," I snapped. "Because I'm not interested in playing into people's convoluted sense of hero worship when it comes to this shitty war."

Nina pulled the medal back. "I don't understand. Why are you so upset?"

I yanked off my hat and shoved a hand through my hair. Wine and limoncello had loosened my tongue. And, it appeared, my memories. "Because it's bullshit. It's all bullshit."

"I sincerely doubt that."

"That medal? That was for getting three men out of a burning building in Fallujah."

"I—I don't understand." Nina turned the metal piece back and forth between her hands. "That sounds like heroism to me, Matthew."

"Yeah, but what you don't know is that they were in there on my orders," I said. "I made a bad call. Sent my platoon into the wrong building, straight into an ambush. And two of them died for it. Just like fifteen other Iraqis died after I gave the order to torch the place once I got the others out." It was coming back. Years and years later, these were the memories I could never totally banish. "Some of them were just kids, Nina. They weren't even old enough to grow beards. We killed them anyway."

I bent over and rubbed my hands over my face. Hard. I hadn't talked about this shit for years. Not since that terrible VA shrink pronounced me "cured" and sent me on my way so she could deal with the "real" PTSD cases. The ones whose tours sent them on a long road of substance abuse and self-harm, or suicidal thoughts.

I wasn't lying when I told her my family wouldn't let me go there. If it hadn't been for the sheer will of my sisters, I don't know that I ever would have truly come back from Iraq. And as hard as it had been, I was one of the lucky ones.

When I sat back up, I found Nina still as stone, the cross still cradled in one palm.

"Matthew…" She reached out.

I scowled. "Don't look at me like that, Nina."

But her hand didn't stop moving toward my face.

I leaned away. "I said don't."

"Matthew, please."

"Goddammit, Nina, I said *don't!*"

I pushed her hand away roughly, and she jerked.

"Ouch!"

The cross fell to the rug. Nina clutched her fingers, wincing.

"I seem to have stuck myself," she said grimly, opening her hand. One fingertip was stained with blood where the needle had poked her.

Remorse flooded me. My fault. Again.

"Fuck." I grabbed her hand, and without another thought, put her finger in my mouth and sucked.

Electricity filled the room.

Nina froze. Her eyes met mine. Neither of us blinked.

And yet, I kept her finger in my mouth, sucking gently on its tip. Both loving and hating the way the salty flavor flowered on my tongue. It was its own kind of worship. Idolatry of the worst kind. *Blood of my blood*, said the priest, every damn Sunday. Just like he would tomorrow, whether I was there or not.

> *Take this, all of you, and drink from it:*
> *For this is the chalice of my blood,*
> *The blood of the new and eternal covenant,*
> *Which will be poured out for you and for many*
> *For the forgiveness of sins.*
> *Do this in memory of me.*

I never understood the craze for vampires, the idea of a man drinking a woman's blood. My sisters went gaga for them. Frankie alone consumed a library's worth of those books a year.

Similarly, I'd never understood the whole concept of transubstantiation, though technically as a Catholic, I supposed I believed that I was literally ingesting the body and blood of my savior every time I went to Mass. But here, with one small part of Nina's body in my mouth, one small bit of her salting my tongue, some of that ancient ritual made sense. And for the first time in my life, I understood why marriage was a covenant.

The union of two bodies? That's as holy as it gets.

I released her finger with a pop. Slowly, she pulled her hand back and touched her lips with the finger. The moisture from my mouth wet hers, creating a sheen that was fucking hypnotic.

"This is fucked up," I whispered as I stared. "So fucked up. You know that?"

Her breathing chuffed, like she had just emerged from water. "I—yes. It is. It is fu—fucked up."

I groaned. Something about the word being spoken in Nina's prim voice. It had the same effect as a bit of sauce lingering on her lip. The snort when she laughed. Her perfection marred, and somehow made even more beautiful...because of me.

So fuckin' strange, I thought, somewhat outside the moment. In the rest of my life, I craved order. Cleanliness. But when I was with this woman, I just wanted to make a fuckin' mess.

Was it sabotage?

Or was it that here, with her, was the only place I felt comfortable to be messy at all?

Maybe, another thought occurred to me, *with Nina was the only place I could really be myself.*

The idea paralyzed me. Because if it were true, it was the worst kind of penance. Fall in lust, in need, in love...with the one woman I could never truly have.

I sank to my knees and picked up the medal. Nina crossed her legs, squeezing her thighs together. One foot dangled in front of me, and on a whim, I wrapped my hand around it.

"Matthew..." This time she sounded less concerned. More breathy. Fighting for control, just like I was.

I pressed my nose to her ankle.

"Matthew..."

Still keeping my nose to her skin, I peered up her leg. Nina was looking back at me, bleary-eyed, beautiful, and a bit entertained.

"Matthew," she said gently. "What are you doing?"

I closed my eyes and nuzzled back into her leg as my hand slipped under the hem of her pants. Her skin was so smooth, so soft. Even her ankle smelled good. "Nothing. Just give me a second."

"Matthew..."

"Nina."

"You're..." She sucked in a breath when I wrapped my hand around her limb, testing its circumference with my palm and fingers. "Touching me."

"You act like I'm copping a feel down here. It's your ankle, doll, not your pussy."

Her shoe slipped, dangling for a moment from her toes before falling to the carpet. I watched, hypnotized, as my hand slowly made its way down to cup her heel, then wrapped around her foot completely while I examined her neatly pedicured toes. Christ. Even her feet were beautiful. I understood now why people worshipped at the feet of their idols. I could adore this woman—every part of her—just like this for the rest of my life.

And so, because I could, because I might never have gotten another chance, I kissed her foot. First on the ball, then again on the pad of her biggest toe.

Above me, there was a sharp intake of breath. But I didn't stop. Instead, eager for more, I slipped my tongue lightly over her toes, biting the tips of each, sucking on the smaller one, then the next, one by one until I got to the end of the row. One, two, three, four, five. Then I turned her foot slightly and pressed a long kiss into her elegant arch. It was funny. I'd never had a foot fetish before. But right now I was fucking entranced.

When my teeth closed lightly over her smallest toe, Nina jerked with a moan.

"Matthew!"

I chuckled, then dropped my hand and with an effort that was the real heroism of the night, managed to separate myself from her and stand up.

"It's just a couple of kisses," I said lamely as I pushed my hands through my hair. "A harmless little kiss. Everyone knows that kissing isn't *really* cheating, baby."

It was a bullshit excuse, right down to the generic nickname. But I had to say something, didn't I? If only to wipe that guilt off her face.

"Oh, really? And if the shoe were on the other…foot?"

I couldn't help it. I laughed.

"Matthew!" Nina was trying to be imperious, but by this point, she was laughing too. "I'm serious! If I were your wife, would you be all right if I kissed another man? Even on the—the foot?"

At just the thought, all humor evaporated.

"If you were my wife," I growled before I could help myself, "you wouldn't be able to walk most days. Much less find another man to kiss. On *any* body part."

Nina shied, but then made the mistake of licking her lips as her eyes dropped—only for a half-second—to my waist, where just *how* turned on I was at the moment was no doubt on display. It was taking everything I had not to throw her across the bed like I initially imagined. Show her exactly what I meant. *Remind* her exactly what I was capable of.

———

I KISSED HER AGAIN. I could have kissed her forever. Except I was ready to do so much more.

Nina shrieked when I suddenly flipped her onto her back, a shriek I quickly covered with my mouth.

"Hush," I told her as I picked the rose back off the bed. "Just tell me when I'm doing things right, okay? Or if you want something else."

She nodded, then remained still, only shaking slightly as I started to tickle her body with the rose again. That color. That white. I was addicted to the sight of them together.

This time, however, I followed the rose with my lips, my tongue, my teeth. When it touched her neck, I kissed her there, enjoying the quiver of her body when I left a mark. I paid more attention to her breasts, taking the time to tease her nipples until she was hissing like a teakettle. I followed the petals over her stomach and tickled her inner thighs. And then, with a glance at her eager, open-mouthed face, pressed my nose into that sweet, sensitive spot covered only by a thin bit of silk.

"Oh!" Nina's voice floated through the air.

I chuckled. "Baby, I haven't done anything yet."

"But you will, won't you?" She sighed at the ceiling, falling back onto the bed.

I rubbed my nose back and forth, teasing her clit through the silk.

Nina jerked in response. Her desire was clear through the damp material. Good fucking God. Just the heady scent of her called me home.

"I will, baby," I said as I peeled her panties down her long legs. "Right fucking now."

She was as much a lady beneath her clothes as she was with them on. Trimmed, but not totally bare. I used my tongue, my lips, gently at first. Testing how various places, various pressures affected her. Every woman is different.

Every body responds uniquely. And Nina's in particular deserved the best I could give.

I discovered more about this woman in twenty minutes between her thighs than I had in an hour of conversation. Here she was splayed out for me, naked, unguarded. With each moan, each subtle shake, I learned how she enjoyed pleasure.

———

WE STARED at each other for a good long time. Were we both thinking of the same thing? Those unguarded moments? The way we had both come completely undone for each other?

Seconds passed. Maybe minutes. Both of our chests rose and fell in time with the clock on the nightstand. And then, when my heartbeat dropped to a halfway normal pace again, I finally managed to pick the medal off the bed and put it back on the bureau. When I turned back around, Nina sat with her hands clasped in her lap, eyes closed, almost like she was praying.

"Come on, doll," I said, offering her my hand. "Cary and Grace await. And there's a couch, not a bed. But for both our sakes, we should probably sit on separate sides."

Her eyes opened, once again full of a humor. "Of the room?"

I smirked. "It's a small house, baby. But I'll see what we can do."

CHAPTER SEVENTEEN

STALKING. SURE. YOU COULD CALL IT THAT. I WOULDN'T, BUT YOU COULD. Was I going to sneak into Nina's apartment and stab her? Absolutely not. Was I making my way up to Ninety-Second and Lexington nearly every day to check on her?

Maybe. Okay, yeah.

The worst part about it? I was already trained for it—first as a reconnaissance officer, then as an investigative prosecutor. So it wasn't my fault, really. This was practically second nature. And I couldn't walk away now. Not when my instincts were screaming at me to watch. Something was going to happen.

It started on the couch after Cary and Grace lulled us to sleep. I woke up the next morning with Nina burrowed into my chest, my arms wrapped around her thin frame like I thought she might float away. She snored quietly, her body rising and falling with her breath and mine.

I lay exactly like that for an hour, listening to her slight purr. Savoring the way her scent mingled with mine.

Every morning.

It was all I could think, and the word ached in my chest for the rest of the day.

I wanted to do this every morning.

Her left hand, the one with the rings, lay flat over my heart. But that wasn't what I found myself staring at. Sometime in the night, she had removed the big flashy watch that previously covered up the ring of still-yellowed bruising around her wrist.

I stared at that for another hour. The horse. Petrosinella. It was a good story, but something was still bothering me.

Before I could figure it out, Nina yawned adorably, then started as she realized where she was.

"Oh," she said as she scrambled off me, grabbing her watch before I could examine her wrist more. "I must have—I'm so sorry, I—"

"Relax, doll." I stood and stretched, pretending not to notice how she eyed the way my undershirt rode up. Something told me she wouldn't appreciate being teased with the six-pack she had seen once up close. Not now. Not after last night. Maybe not ever.

I sighed.

We pulled ourselves together, then grabbed coffee at the art studio around the corner. After that, I rode with Nina back to the city. I said I needed to see Jane and Eric and then go back up to help *Nonna* with some things after I took a run around Central Park. Completely false, but she didn't know that.

"Dinner later this week?" I asked as we both stepped out of the Uber on the far side of Lexington, under the shadow of the scaffolding. I jogged in place, like I was intent on warming up. "Without my family this time, I promise."

Nina looked toward her building, as if she expected her traveling husband to appear from its gleaming brass doors. I took the moment to admire her openly. She was a mess. Her pants and blouse were wrinkled from a night on the couch, her hair was tied back, but bedraggled wisps fluttered around her face.

Still the most beautiful woman I'd ever seen.

Maybe even more now.

Something had changed. Something subtle. But here, on this corner, with the city up and about for the day around us…walking away from her felt even more like the most wrong thing in the world.

"I…" Nina turned back to me, looking adorably sheepish. "We'll see.

Calvin comes home this week, but I'm not sure when. We have an event this weekend too, so things will be busy."

"Ah."

Nothing like that name to serve as a bucket of cold water.

I might have wanted forever, but I was only going to get scraps. The sooner I came to terms with that, the better.

I brushed her cheek with a kiss, fighting the urge to linger. "All right, then, doll. You have a good day. I'll see you soon."

Nina blinked, her eyes bright despite the shadows we stood under. "Y-yes. I'll see you soon."

Neither of us moved. I didn't even bother to hide my smile. Nina liked looking at me. Well, I was pretty fond of looking at her too.

"I like you like this," I said, tugging on one crooked strand of hair.

Nina picked it up distastefully. "I look like a beggar."

"You look like an angel."

Her eyes glowed. "Matthew…"

I let the strand go with one last tug. "You, ah, going to go?" I asked with a smirk.

Nina grinned. "I—yes. Okay. Goodbye, Matthew."

And like she was physically tearing herself off the sidewalk, she finally managed to cross the street, looking back over her shoulder every few steps, like she was making sure I was still there. It wasn't until she finally disappeared into her building that I started to walk.

But when I got to the end of the block, I turned right. Then right again. Then right again until I was right back under the scaffolding, staring at the revolving brass doors of Nina's building for another solid hour despite the fact that I had plenty else to do.

I just had the feeling that this was where I needed to be.

———

SUNDAY TURNED TO MONDAY. Monday turned to Tuesday. Then Wednesday, Thursday. And at least once a day, I made my way to the Upper East Side, to that spot under the scaffolding, and watched the front of Nina's building like it was going to tell me something.

Tuesdays and Thursdays she met with her trainer, who came to the apartment. Most afternoons she had some sort of charity board meeting —I caught her once on her way to that. We texted back and forth a few more times, but she continued to put me off about dinner, lunch, whatever else I proposed. She was feeling cagey after the weekend. I started to think that maybe I had gone a little too far.

I was pathetic. I knew it.

But like any junkie, I couldn't stop.

———

ON FRIDAY, I walked out of the NYPD headquarters feeling pretty good about myself. My boss and I had had an excellent meeting with the Chief of Department, and she was on board for the operation at the Met in less than a month. The trap was set. There was no going back now. With a lot of luck (and a leak-proof team), John Carson would take the bait.

I was starting to think we might actually pull this thing off.

My job now was to work with Derek and his team to fulfill the burden of proof so we could indict upon arrest. I needed to get back to Brooklyn, continue going through the mountain of records I'd pulled from Jude Letour's company, and send Derek back to The Hole to watch that safe house until the raid on Roscoe's apartment Monday.

Instead, I caught the 6 train in the opposite direction, then hailed a cab right after getting off on East Eighty-Sixth Street.

"Ninety-Second and Lex," I instructed the cabbie.

The cab driver, a big Slavic guy named Alexei, frowned at me through the rearview mirror. "It's six blocks," he said in a thick Russian accent. "You want to walk?"

Outside, the late afternoon sun was still shining. It would be a killer day for a walk…except I didn't want to be seen.

I leveled my gaze at him through the plexiglass. "Go up Park, hook a right on Ninety-Third, then go down Lex and pull over on the east side of the street."

The driver snuffed, but drove as ordered.

In my pocket, my phone buzzed with a message from Nina. It was a meme of a man sleeping in bed with a giant foot.

Doll: How's your fetish now?

I chuckled. She really couldn't let that one go. I wouldn't get another dinner out of her, but foot memes? Every single day.

Me: Insatiable. You really started a problem for me here.

Doll: I'm so sorry to hear that. Anything I can do to help?

Me: Maybe I should have invited you for pedicures instead of lunch today.

I waited a while, but there was no answer. I frowned at my phone. Not even an ellipsis. Those fucking dots were the worst things ever invented, but at least they told me Nina was responding.
Nothing. *Niente.*

Me: On your way to class?

Fridays, she had told me, were SinCycle days. Some crazy form of rich-lady exercise where Nina paid something like forty dollars a class to sit on stationary bikes in the dark in a room with fifty other women while they listened to techno and the instructor wore glow-in-the-dark Spandex. At least, that was the impression I got based on her description.
"Want me to get you some molly for class?" I joked when she told me about it earlier that week. "Derek could nick some from the evidence locker."
"Darling, if I wanted that, do you really think I would need you?" she had replied sweetly. "Don't you know anything about the rich? We love our contraband."
Both of us ignored the little pet name. Or, you know, tried to.
I peered at my phone, then back at the doors. This was odd. Usually she went to her class in the mornings, not the afternoons. And I happened to know she didn't have any meetings scheduled today.
"Are we going?" asked the driver, itching to move.

I scowled. I didn't know what his problem was—I was paying for him to just sit here. He didn't even have to maneuver through traffic.

"Just a bit longer," I said, still watching the door.

And then, finally, like I had willed her into being, she appeared.

She was as immaculate as ever in a pair of white pants that made her legs look impossibly long, a thin white sweater that hugged every slender curve, and a tawny leather jacket the color of honey. She pushed on a pair of oversized sunglasses, looking exactly like the socialite she was. With a slash of red across her lips—her rebellion. Like she was doing it for me, even when I wasn't there.

Except I was.

I couldn't help it. I had to say something.

Me: Mirror, mirror, on the wall...

I watched as she looked at her phone. A whisper of a smile played over her face, and her reply was instantaneous.

Doll: Doing some fairy-tale reading?

Me: Courtesy of Sofia. She's been asking the mirror in the bathroom all day, but it only tells her one thing. I'll give you three guesses who.

The smile widened. My chest ached. Would she think I was crazy if I got out of the car now and shouted her name? I wanted to keep teasing her until that smile turned into a laugh. I wanted to hear it when it happened.

I really was going crazy.

Me: Seriously, though. Dinner tonight? *An Affair to Remember* is playing at the Film Forum. I have a deposition in midtown, so I'll be in the neighborhood...

Lies. Total fuckin' lies. My work here was done for the day.

Hey. I told you I wasn't a good guy.

I watched as Nina checked her phone again. She smiled briefly, then typed a message. A moment later, my phone buzzed.

Doll: I wish I could, but I have plans.

Fuck. *Plans.* I was really starting to hate that word. But just when I was about to ask her what could be more important than Cary Grant and Deborah Kerr in a movie that could not be more picture fucking perfect for Nina and me to see together, another person emerged from the brick building to stand beside Nina.

A man.

Approximately three inches shorter than the blonde goddess I was following.

Shaped roughly like a wheel of gouda.

Her husband. Calvin fucking Gardner.

I pressed the button of my window, but it didn't move. I slammed my hand on it.

"Yo!" I snapped at the cabbie. "Lower the window, will you?"

"You won't hear nothing," he argued back, but eventually did what I said.

He was right, of course. I couldn't completely hear the conversation taking place across the street. But as the traffic ebbed and flowed down Lexington, which wasn't the busiest of streets in the area, bits and pieces floated into earshot. I pulled down the brim of my hat while I watched and listened.

"I'm sorry, Nina. I just—"

"You can't be serious. Calvin, we are Tier 1 sponsors—"

"—business, not pleasure. I don't have time for—"

"If we don't show…terrible."

Another drove of cars crossed in front of us, to the point where I could only see the tops of their heads as they argued there on the street. Well, as much as people like Nina ever argued. When the cars passed, I flared as Calvin grabbed her wrist and pulled her close, and I watched curiously as she turned her head to the side. Was that a struggle I imagined? Or was she accepting it? I was honestly too far away to tell.

He smashed his mouth onto hers. Nina barely moved. It was wrong. So fuckin' unnatural. Kissing her husband should have been routine, but she was about as responsive as one of the columns behind her. So different than the responsive, pliant woman I had intimate knowledge of myself.

I turned away as my stomach turned too.

She had kissed me before. Slept in my arms only last week. And now she was kissing him. Her husband. *As she should*, I reminded myself.

Fuck.

My stomach felt like it had been punched through.

Fuck this friendship.

Fuck this nonsense.

"Go," I snapped at the driver. "Get going."

"Where?" he asked. "Where do you want to go?"

"Anywhere but here."

Nina and Calvin broke apart at the sudden shriek of the wheels on the pavement. I leaned forward and put my head in my hands, begging the nausea to die down.

"Where we going, chief?" asked the cabbie.

I looked up. Fuck. Yeah, I wasn't paying for an entire cab ride to Brooklyn. I'd already run enough on this guy's meter sitting there like a fool. I needed to get back to my office. To my life.

"Closest subway stop," I said.

He pulled over a few blocks later, and I got out, gulping the air that still seemed stale. I needed to get out of the Upper East Side. I needed to delete Nina's number and pretend this broad never existed.

But as I pulled out my phone to do just that, I found another message waiting for me.

Doll: Plans fell through. I don't suppose you would like to accompany me to the opera instead of dinner?

I stared at the message for a long time, while two trains roared through the grate beneath my feet.

I should say no.

I should do what I had intended to do in the first place.

Say goodbye to Nina Astor de Vries…Gardner.
Go back to being a half-sane man again.
Get on with my fucking life.
Instead, I punched in a very different message.

Matthew: Send me the time and place. I'll see you there.

CHAPTER EIGHTEEN

I HATED BOW TIES. ABSOLUTELY FUCKIN' OVER-THE-TOP *LOATHED* THE THINGS. Regular ties, I could handle. I even knew a few different knots. But these things were made for people with fingers the size of pencils. They were impossible.

"Fucking *fuck*!" I yanked at the black silk strip after screwing it up for the fourth time and scowled at myself in the mirror. I was never going to get this piece of shit right.

"Zio!"

I glared in the direction of Frankie's and Sofia's rooms. I should have closed my door as I finished getting ready for my date with Nina—I couldn't think of it as anything else—but I was already running late.

"On account!" I shouted. "I'll stop at an ATM on my way back."

Frankie appeared in the door with a raised brow. "Dang, big brother. You clean up nice. And where are we going so fancified?"

I took a deep breath and started folding the strips of silk around each other. "Opening night at the opera. Penguin suit required."

Her gaze landed on the top of my head as she crept in. "No hat?"

Gingerly, I reached up to touch my uncovered hair, which I'd combed through with an extra bit of pomade to make it shine. "It's not formal.

No hat required. Can you fix this, though? My fingers are too fuckin' big for these things."

Frankie came around to my front and started retying the bow tie with quick, efficient motions.

"How'd you get so good at this?" I wondered.

I never doubted that she could do it—these were the sorts of life skills that our grandparents would have passed on to us, despite the fact that I had only ever seen *Nonno* wear a tuxedo at a couple of weddings. But her proficiency went a little beyond what a thirteen-year-old girl might learn from her grandpa.

"Xavier had me do it." Frankie's eyes didn't stray from her work. "For his events."

I quieted. Frankie didn't mention Sofia's dad much. I had only met Xavier Parker once or twice when they were dating. He wasn't local, just some rich British guy who did business in New York every so often, then disappeared entirely when Sofia showed up. Never met the family. Never even met his daughter. Scumbag, through and through.

It was too bad, really. Frankie deserved better.

She nodded with satisfaction as she tugged the sides of the bow out through the loop. "Perfect, even if you still look like a wise guy with that flower."

I glanced down at the rose I'd pinned to the lapel on a whim. "A classic's a classic."

"Only if you're about to order a hit."

"Maybe I am," I joked, though I won't lie. Calvin Gardner's face *did* flash through my mind when I said it.

Frankie snorted. "Turn around, *capo*. Your collar is crooked."

I turned toward the mirror so she could flip the stiff fabric over the bow tie.

"There," Frankie said once she was finished. "All better."

But her hands rested on my shoulders, and I found her examining my reflection in the mirror.

"Spit it out, Frankie."

She rubbed her chin. "This is all for Nina?"

"Her husband bailed on this big opening at Lincoln Center. They're major donors, apparently, so she needed an escort last minute." I shrugged. "It's just a favor."

Frankie didn't seem convinced. "Mattie, I..." She tapped her lip. "Don't hate me. But I don't think you should go."

I turned back around to face her. "It's opera, Fran, not the prom."

"I don't mean that. I just don't think you should keep being 'friends' with this one. I see the look on your face. All week you've been gazing off into space. I know you're thinking of her."

I frowned. "Frankie, how many times do I have to say it? Nina and I are *just friends*."

"Because friends go to the opera together."

"They could."

"And friends wear tuxedos and opera gowns when they hang out."

I shrugged. "If the occasion calls for it."

"Hey." She tugged on my lapel. "I'm just saying it because I care. And because I've..." She glanced back toward Sofia's closed door. "I've been there."

That I didn't know. "Xavier was married?"

"Engaged, actually. But still."

"That's why he left?"

She nodded sadly. "Being the other woman—well, in your case, the other man—it never ends well, Mattie. She's going to break your heart. Just like he broke mine."

Anger flowered in my chest at the idea of any man treating my sister that way. But there wasn't anything I could do about it now. Instead, I opened my mouth to say that I knew what I was doing. That things were totally innocent between me and Nina. That we really were purely platonic.

But on the other side of the room, the edge of my Navy Cross gleamed. And I saw Nina sitting on my bed, me at her feet. Worshipping her. What little of herself she had offered.

I couldn't lie to my sister. Not when I couldn't even manage to lie to myself.

"It's just one night out," I said, turning back to the mirror. "A show and then home."

Frankie sighed. "Big brother, you are incorrigible, you know that?"

I bared my teeth. "So I've been told."

BY THE TIME I found my way to the topside of Lincoln Center, it was less than ten minutes to curtain, and the place was crawling with New York's elite. Every elite but Nina, who was nowhere to be seen.

Meet me by the fountain, she had texted. One of the city's universal meeting spots, home to a thousand movie kisses. Suddenly, I was a character right out of *Moonstruck.* Nicholas Cage begging Cher for just one night. I would have liked that movie more if both actors had actually been Italian. Cher might have won an Oscar, but I still thought she sounded like she was doing a bad De Niro impression. Still, I'd lost count how many times my sisters and I had watched the scene where she slaps her lover across the face. "Snap out of it!" they'd all cry in unison. Maybe someone needed to do that to me right now.

"Matthew?"

I turned to find Nina, the spray of the fountain arching behind her like halos. She was wrapped in the biggest fur coat I had ever seen, folds of white mink protecting her slim body against the chilly night. Her blonde hair was pulled back in an elegant twist that revealed her graceful neck and the row of tasteful diamonds at its base. Two others gleamed from her ears, but beyond the slash of red she wore on her mouth, there was no other glitz about her.

She was cool and classic. An old-school beauty.

"Wow," I said. "Nina, you look incredible. As always."

She smiled shyly. "You look lovely too. I'm so sorry, I hadn't thought to ask if you had a tux. I see you found one to rent?"

"Ah, no. It's mine."

I wasn't sure whether to be offended at the assumption that I didn't have my own tux. Honestly, I didn't know many people who did. I had bought this one years ago for the mayor's inauguration ball. Hadn't worn it since, but still.

Nina examined me with a practiced eye. "Of course it is. Kate again?"

I nodded.

"I should have known. Shall we?"

She held out her hand for me to tuck into my elbow. Act the part of the escort. The gentleman.

For once, I was happy to oblige.

"Shall we?" I asked.

We followed the crowds into the opera house, with its familiar arched windows, red carpets twisting around the grand cylindrical staircases, and the famous galaxy-shaped light installations that hung all over the lobby and the concert hall auditorium.

I expected Nina to be stopped several times by patrons, but by the time we got inside, most people had already found their seats. Briskly, Nina led me up the first set of stairs, then took a sharp right toward a door where an elderly usher greeted her.

"Mrs. Gardner. We thought you weren't going to make it tonight."

There, she dropped my arm.

"Hello, Terence. No, I made sure to be here, even if we are a bit tardy."

I waited for her to introduce me. She did not.

"I'm actually glad you were late," she murmured as we followed the usher down the hall. "I can't stand talking to all those people. It's the same horrid conversation again and again."

I nodded, though I couldn't shake the feeling that I was being hidden away. And why not? I was a dirty little secret, wasn't I? Nothing I wasn't used to.

The usher opened the final door at the end of the hall to a balcony separated from the next one by a tall red wall that matched the rest of the theater with its scarlet seating and gold edges. I smiled as I looked around. I had been here a few times, but only when the cheap tickets sold for about forty-five dollars on a good night. This right here was the best seat in the house.

"It's just us tonight," Nina said as she caught me looking around the empty box.

I inspected the six seats. "Really? Seems like a bit of a waste."

She nodded. "Grandmother loved to go, but since she passed, no one else enjoys it. Eric might come occasionally with clients, but he's really more of a theater person."

"Your coat, madam?" the usher interrupted before I could respond.

"Thank you, Terence." Nina slipped the mink from her shoulders and handed it to the usher, who hung it in the back.

"Would you like your customary drinks tonight, madam?"

Nina turned to me. "Would you like some champagne, Matthew? We have donor privileges."

But I couldn't reply. I couldn't fuckin' speak at all. With the drop of mink, a spell had been cast, and I was too entranced to do anything but stare.

Nina's mouth twisted with pleasure. "Champagne would be lovely, Terence. Thank you."

"Very well, ma'am."

The usher closed the door behind him, leaving Nina and me alone in the box. Around us, the theater hummed with the sounds of people chatting. Bells outside announced the show's beginning. But I couldn't register a goddamn thing.

"Matthew," Nina said. "You're not moving."

She was a vision. A sheath of satin poured over her body like water, simple and stark against that pure pale skin I dreamed about each night. It wrapped around her chest to the floor, broken only by a subtle slit up one thigh and two thread-like straps over her dancer's shoulders.

And it was all red. Not just any red. A bright, lustrous crimson, the color of blood. Hearts. Roses.

Scarlet.

"You're...Jesus."

The only part of me that I could move was my hand, and even that I was only able to press over my heart, which gave a thump. Calm. I needed to calm the fuck down.

Nina looked down at her dress and then back up. Tiny dimples appeared outside her mouth, like she was trying and failing to hold back a grin. "It's a bit different than what I generally go for, to be sure. Perhaps I should have—"

"No," I interrupted, then cleared my throat. Awkwardly. "No," I tried again. "You did perfect. Jesus *fucking* Christ, Nina. You are a work of art."

Joy pinked her apple-shaped cheeks. "Matthew."

I crossed the box, thankful that we were sheltered by the balcony above ours. Here in the shadow, none of the audience members could see the desire I couldn't hide.

"I'm not kidding," I said. "I feel like God himself delivered that dress just for me."

Her smile lit up the dark. "Not God. Just Valentino, remember. So you can thank him, I suppose."

"Take the compliment, baby." I tucked a stray blonde lock behind her ear, then floated my fingers over the delicate gems dangling from her earlobe. "If it's the man that makes the clothes, it's the woman who makes the dress. You deserve it and so much more."

Her eyes sparkled brighter than any diamond. "Thank you for coming tonight. I—I appreciate it. More than you know."

My hand lingered around her jaw, and for a second, I considered sneaking a kiss. Given the way her gaze fell to my mouth, I was sure she would let me. But once I opened that door between us again, I was pretty certain I wouldn't be able to close it.

The real question was: did I care?

But before I could tempt fate, the door to the box opened. Terence, with a bottle of champagne on ice and two crystal glasses.

Nina stepped out of reach, hands folded in front of her skirt. Only the flush coloring her otherwise snow-white face betrayed that anything less than respectable had been about to happen.

"Best take your seat, sir," Terence said as he carried our drinks to us. "It's about to begin."

The audience below us quieted as the sparkler-shaped lights dropped, and then rose again before dimming completely. Everyone watched—it was one of the calling cards of the famous venue. But I still only had eyes for one thing. And she was sitting right next to me.

———

I LIKED OPERA. Always had. Like a lot of kids in my neighborhood, I grew up on a steady diet of the Rat Pack and Louis Prima, but I wasn't unfamiliar with the sounds of Puccini or Verdi. There was always a baker or a restaurant owner on the block with a taste for the greats. *Nonna* (along with half the neighborhood) cried when Pavarotti died.

My sisters and I had heard his version of "Nessun Dorma" about a thousand times.

Turandot, of course, was a classic. The Zeffirelli version had been revived here again and again for more than thirty years. I'd seen it myself from the nosebleeds, and even from there, the massive Orientalist set drew oohs and aahs from just about every audience member.

This version, however, was different. Instead of the majestic pieces designed as much or more than the vocal talent, this set was open and shallow. Dark. Simple. Almost unremarkable. And when the company appeared, they were dressed in equally nondescript costumes.

"This was you?" I gestured to the stripped-down version of Peking that was nearly black.

The purpose of the aesthetic was immediately clear: to allow the audience to focus on the music, not just the bells and whistles.

"I was one of the sponsors, yes. It's a limited run." Nina glanced at me. "I only wanted the music, but also the benefit of a full production. Opera is the language of love, you know."

I raised a brow in surprise. Apparently I wasn't the only one having flashbacks.

"SORRY, it must be rather dull for someone like you."

"Someone like me?"

She shrugged.

"Nina?"

She looked up, and the uncertainty there just about killed me. Tentatively, I slipped a hand around her waist and guided her closer. Her breath grew just a bit coarser.

"You could read the damn phone book," I told her. "And it would sound like Puccini."

"Is that a good thing? A lot of people don't care for opera."

"A lot of people are idiots." I smiled. "Opera is the language of love, baby. It doesn't get better than that."

"CAN YOU UNDERSTAND THE LIBRETTO?" Nina whispered as the overture began.

I shrugged. "It's a little harder when it's sung, but I could probably read it." I tapped the small screen embedded in the banister in front of us. "They provide the translation, right?"

Nina nodded. "True." She settled into her seat and crossed her legs, allowing her dress to split over one knee.

I swallowed and turned back to the stage. The only way I was making it through this night was if I kept my eyes trained forward.

And I managed it for the first two acts. Terence interrupted us at both intermissions, refreshing our drinks and making sure everything was in order so we wouldn't have to leave. By that point, I didn't even care that it was probably a ruse to keep me hidden from her friends. Me. Nina. Music, booze, and good conversation? Life was pretty nice from the best seats in the house.

But just as Calaf emerged onto the stage with the memorable intro to "Nessun Dorma," I noticed one thing amiss. Not everything was perfect.

I nudged Nina's shoulder and beckoned her close. She leaned toward me.

"What is it?" she whispered.

"Is your translator broken?" I asked, nodding at the black screen in front of her.

Nina glanced at it with confusion. "What? Oh." She looked back at me. "Oh, yes, I suppose it is." Her smile was almost sheepish. "I was enjoying the music too much to notice."

"Do you want me to translate this one for you?"

It was a stupid request. Obviously, no one really paid much attention to the translations—not if they were here for the music, and—

"Please."

Her bare knee touched mine, and instinctually, my palm fell on top of it so I could whisper into her ear as the tenor began to sing.

"'None shall sleep,'" I said as her hair tickled my cheek. "'None shall sleep.'"

My nose brushed the edge of her ear. She shivered.

"'Not even you, princess, in your cold bedroom.'"

Under my hand, her muscles tightened. Her scent of roses floated around me, making me dizzy. Instinctually, I pulled our legs flush while I continued, spreading my fingers over her knee.

"'Watching the stars that tremble with love, and with hope.'"

Nina clenched her plump lower lip between her teeth.

"'But my secret is hidden within me; no one will know my name.'"

I couldn't help the way my fingers, enjoying the silky texture of her skin, gently caressed her skin, then began, as if of their own accord, slipping down.

"'No, no, on your mouth...'"

My hand was between her legs. Nina sucked in a tight breath. But she didn't move away. Not an inch. Not a centimeter.

"'...I will say it when the light shines...'"

Somehow, while I spoke, my fingers had moved over the curve of her leg, slipped between the folds of fabric. Her thighs rested lightly on either side of my fingers, lithe muscles flexing ever so slightly at my touch.

"'...And my kiss will dissolve the silence that makes you mine...'"

I didn't bother to translate the chorus singing beyond the stage as the tenor took a break. I was too entranced by what, through some miracle, I had been allowed to do.

Her skin was so warm. The theater was so dark. And as the music vibrated through the hall, my hand slipped higher and higher, toward that forbidden space between her legs. Finding that slightly damp warmth that had been calling me home for months.

"'Vanish, oh night...'"

My fingertips brushed a tissue-thin layer of lace. Some delicate fabric, through which I could barely distinguish the soft textures of skin and hair and...Nina.

"'Fade, you stars.'"

Nina's chin tipped into the air as she sighed, no longer watching the performance, though the sound rippled around us. The movement bared her neck and chest all the way down to where her breasts now tested the passion-colored satin. I knew what they felt like. Had memorized the way their soft, supple weight felt in my palm.

It wouldn't be hard to slip one of those nonexistent straps over one shoulder. Bare one perfect pillow. Capture a taut nipple between my teeth.

Instead, I grazed my nose up her neck. Two fingers curved into the lace.

It tore.

Nina hissed.

The rest of the audience was rapt as they watched the singer, but I was only interested in the song under my hands as I slipped one finger, then two into the slick heat that had been waiting for me all night. Maybe all my life. My thumb found her clit and circled continuously while the others moved in aching time to Puccini's masterpiece.

"'At dawn,'" I promised along with the Italian poetry, "'I... will...win.'"

Three fingers now found her depths while my thumb pressed even harder.

"Ahh!"

Nina's voice was an aria that blended with the cry onstage. The tenor's vibrato shook along with the audience's applause and the quake of this woman's body. Nina came there for me in the dark, gray eyes wide as they met mine in the shadows. She opened, legs fully splayed, back arched off the seat as I took her pleasure. For a moment, I considered getting down on my knees for her again. Pressing my nose between her thighs. Tasting that sweet warmth now coating my fingers.

But then, just like the aria, her climax faded. Nina sank back into her chair, gasping for breath. And I removed my fingers, dragging them back down her thigh, over her knee, and then, to my regret, pulling her dress into place.

"Nina."

My voice was barely audible. Much like hers.

"Matthew." She looked at me with eyes full of desire, yes, but also fear.

I wondered if there would ever be a day where she wasn't afraid of me. Afraid of us.

So instead of kissing her, of dragging her out of the booth to continue undoing us both in private, I just leaned closer brushed her hair from her face again. She leaned into my touch.

Something caught my eye. I leaned farther over her. "Wait...your translator."

I sat back up to find Nina's flush rising again, even in the dim light.

"It wasn't actually broken?"

Apparently the light on those things was dim enough that from my seat, her screen was black. As, I realized, mine must have been to her.

"I—no. It, um, it works."

We stared at each other for a long time. Below us, the music grew more frenetic. Nina bit her lip, clearly embarrassed. I didn't know how to tell her that I was equal parts confused and relieved.

After a moment, I just shook my head, then took her hand and squeezed.

"Opera makes people do crazy things," I said. "Let's enjoy the rest and let it be."

CHAPTER NINETEEN

FOR THE REST OF THE PERFORMANCE, NINA'S HAND WAS A VISE AROUND MY wrist. She kept my palm on her knee, but prevented it from moving anywhere else. She didn't look at me, didn't even acknowledge I was there until the curtains had closed and we stood along with everyone else to give the cast an ovation.

I barely noticed. The applause through the house thundered in my ears, but not as loudly as my heartbeat. All I could think about was the muddled cry when she came, the swell of her breasts as she caught her breath, the subtle scent of her that still clung to my fingertips.

I wanted more. I *needed* more. To the point where I couldn't honestly name a limit to what I'd do to get it.

We stayed in the box, hovered in its shadows until the auditorium was nearly empty. Then Nina finally slid her arms into her coat, checked her face in a compact mirror from her purse, and turned for the door.

I couldn't take her silence anymore. Next to the fountain where we'd met tonight, I pulled her to a stop.

"Nina, look. I don't—what happened in there. I don't—I don't want you to think I'm expecting anything else. It just happened. I—"

She cut me off with a finger to my lips. When my eyes met hers, she took her hand away, though her gray eyes were dancing.

"Let's not talk about it right now," she said as she looked nervously around the milling crowds. "Not until we can find someplace...private."

Wait...*what*?

My mind suddenly felt like it was exploding. Was she suggesting what I thought she was? I mean, I wanted it. Good fuckin' *God*, I wanted to rip every shred of clothing off that beautiful body. Continue worshipping her the way I was certain I'd been put on this earth to do.

But I'd made a promise, if only to myself. My faults, the way I coveted this woman—I'd be doing penance for that until the day I died. But for her sake, I could bear the weight of those sins on my own. For her sake, I'd at least try to be better than the terrible man I was in my heart.

That said, if she was joining me on my level...God forgive me, I'd welcome her with open arms.

Nina's eyelids drooped with desire. Every cell in my body stood at attention. I took a step forward, reaching for her hand again, but she dodged my grab.

"Private, Matthew," she repeated as a mischievous smile played over her lips. Her head tilted playfully to one side. "Perhaps the Grace has room for us again."

At that moment, I knew I would carry her all the way down to the Lower East Side again if it meant we could continue what we started in the box.

"Let's go—" I started in the direction of the cab line, but we were stopped immediately at the sound of a familiar voice.

"Nina?"

Nina froze. And I did too.

We both turned.

In front of us, holding the arm of a very bored, very rich-looking older man who perked up considerably when he caught sight of Nina, was someone whose calls I'd been dodging for more than a month now.

"Hello," Nina said as she stepped forward to exchange not-quite-kisses with the woman. "I didn't think you were coming tonight." She did the same with the man. "Kyle, so lovely to see you again. Congratulations on the recent nuptials, of course. Have you two settled in to married life, or does three weeks in still count as the honeymoon?"

"Oh, we're settling quite well," replied the man. "I'm sure this one would agree."

But the woman was more interested in staring at me than answering Nina's questions.

"Zola?"

I swallowed. *Fuck.*

"Caitlyn," I said with a half-raised hand. "Hi, um, how are you?"

Nina looked between us with a wide-eyed expression that almost immediately transformed into that mask I knew so well. Fucking *fuck.*

"You two know each other?" Caitlyn asked.

For once, I was happy Nina had avoided my touch. Well, not happy. Maybe just relieved. Maybe.

"Mr. Zola is a friend of Jane's," Nina said smoothly. "He's also advising the two of them informally about Eric's legal...conundrums."

Caitlyn blinked, clearly recognizing Eric's name as well. "Does he always advise at the opera?"

"Calvin had another unexpected business trip."

"The Swiss bank deal, isn't it?" Kyle shook his head ruefully, but almost admiringly. "Your husband snaked that deal right out from under us."

"He's very good at that," Nina replied. "At any rate, we have the box, and it was just me attending." She shrugged, as if my presence was no better than one of the ushers, then leaned almost conspiratorially toward Caitlyn. "We are rather in debt to Mr. Zola, as it were. I needed an escort tonight, and Eric insisted on—" She tipped her head toward me like she was speaking in code. "I couldn't really say no."

It was fake, of course. It had to be. But I couldn't help the stab in my gut at her insinuation. That I was some kind of fuckin' charity case. No better than a poor relation begging for scraps.

It was all I could do not to walk away right then and there.

Caitlyn's blue eyes flashed back and forth between me and Nina as if trying to determine whether or not the story was true. In the end, she seemed to buy it. Small mercies, even if the lie did make me feel like shit.

"Did Eric make you wear that dress too, poor thing?" She sneered, looking over Nina's red gown where her coat had fallen open. "Let me guess, it's one of his wife's 'designs.' I heard that she's actually designing her own dress for the gala, can you believe it?" She tsked, like she was admonishing a child. "Lord, what a color. You poor thing. Some people really have no taste."

"That's probably because only some people can really pull it off." I nodded at Nina. "Like this one."

Caitlyn's eyes flashed between us. Nina, however, didn't jump in. She didn't say it had nothing to do with her cousin or Jane, nor did she tell Caitlyn to shove her stuffy fuckin' comments up her ass along with the stick permanently wedged there.

Trust me, I knew it was there, too. The woman was stiff as a board in bed.

Instead, Nina just laughed and shrugged as if my comment proved Caitlyn's point about taste. Caitlyn's husband, who looked old enough to be her grandfather, eyed me like I was something on the bottom of his shoe. I fought the urge to tell all of them to fuck the hell off.

"And how do you know Mr. Zola?" Nina pivoted everyone's attention back to Caitlyn.

God, she was good. Turning the question right back onto the interrogator. Intentionally using my last name to formalize our relationship. The only sign of her nerves was the slight flush on her cheeks, which could easily be chalked up to the cold. She was immovable. Implacable. Utterly impenetrable.

Caitlyn wasn't nearly as skilled. Her own cheeks were the color of rosé, and her eyes continued to flicker under the glare of the Lincoln Center lights.

I had never noticed just how much she and Nina resembled each other. They were of similar height, though Caitlyn's eyes were blue next to Nina's gray, and her hair was more of a honeyed brown instead of flaxen gold. And right now, in a light blue dress and a coat that nearly matched her skin, she looked even more Nina-like than the woman next to me.

I preferred my version.

"Oh, we just, um—" Caitlyn stared at me searchingly, begging for help.

But I was more interested in Nina, whose sharp features suddenly betrayed a steeliness I hadn't seen before. To anyone else, she might have seemed perfectly calm. But I knew this woman. I had memorized every plane, every curve, every tick of that immaculate body. And I knew a time bomb when I saw it.

She was mad. Really, really mad.

"We—we met at a fundraiser for the district attorney," Caitlyn stammered. "Yes, just a few months ago, wasn't it, Z?" She turned to her husband. "Well before you and I embarked on our affair, my love."

The old tycoon looked about as sentimental as a doorknob, and as interested in the conversation.

"Did you?" Nina's voice, coated with sweetness, sent a ripple up my spine. "That's incredible. Amazing how many people you meet at those things."

Her subtext couldn't have been clearer. After all, wasn't that the same line she had fed Jane and Eric just a few months ago? Was "we ran into each other at a fundraiser" the Upper East Side's version of "we met at a bar"?

"It really is," Caitlyn said before turning to her husband. "Kyle, we really should be going."

The older man looked bored. "Indeed. You and Calvin will be at the benefit next weekend?"

Nina nodded. "Of course. We wouldn't miss Genevieve's canapes. Caitlyn's cook is the best, Mr. Zola."

And with the exchange of a few more air kisses with Nina, Caitlyn and Kyle left for the long line of limousines and town cars at the end of the plaza—but not before Caitlyn turned back and flashed me a meaningful look. In direct line of sight of the woman standing next to me.

I cleared my throat. I wanted nothing more than to rewind the night by about fifteen minutes, when we could've escaped before we were seen. The next best thing was to pretend the awkward-as-fuck conversation hadn't happened at all.

"Come on, doll," I said as I turned in the opposite direction of the limo line.

But Nina didn't move. She just stood there, staring at the ground for several more minutes, until more of the people who had been milling around the fountain and the surrounding buildings disappeared.

"Nina?" I gestured back toward the opera house. "Let's get out of here. We can catch a cab and loop around. Be at the Grace in less than fifteen minutes."

She finally looked up, and this time the mask fell away. The anger I suspected was there before practically shot out of her like the water from the fountain.

"You must be joking." Then she turned on her heel and strode in the opposite direction.

"Shit," I muttered, then followed her out of the plaza.

I didn't know where she was going, but something told me not to press her. I had done that once before and been slapped for it. Nina and I both had a tendency to lose our tempers. I wasn't exactly sure *what* had happened back there, but I sure as shit wasn't letting it go without a response. Ten minutes ago, we were ready to tear each other's clothes off. Now she looked like she wanted to stick mine through with a knife.

She took the long way around Lincoln Center, shuffling up Amsterdam on her four-inch heels, then back east on Sixty-Seventh. It wasn't until she was across Central Park West with the clear intention of running into Central Park at night—*again*, for Christ's sake—that I tried to stop her.

"Nina!" I jogged to catch up as she started down the dimly lit path into the park. "Come on, let's not do this again."

I looked at her heels. Pretty red things that matched her dress. Fuckin' Christ, I had been *this close* to having those things digging into my back.

Nina stopped about twenty paces in, looked down at them with me, and groaned. "Look at that. *Look* at that! You know, that's two pairs of shoes I've ruined running away from you."

"Then maybe you should stop running," I retorted.

"Maybe you should stop chasing me when I'm angry!"

I sighed. "If it's that important to you, I'll buy you new ones."

"At eight thousand a pair? I shouldn't think it likely."

I stepped back as if I really had been slapped. In all the exchanges we had ever had, the subject of our class disparity had never come up. I felt it, of course. But I'd honestly never thought it mattered. Not with her.

"I—I'm sorry," Nina said almost immediately. "That was uncalled for."

"Yeah, it fuckin' was," I said. "It's not my fault I don't have a trust fund bigger than the New Hampshire state GDP."

This time she was the one to recoil. I took a deep breath. Fuck, we could have this particular argument all night, and it wouldn't go anywhere. Our vast income differences weren't at the heart of what was going on anyway. The only problem was, I didn't know what was.

"Nina," I tried again, this time more gently. "Come on. Let's go somewhere and talk. Somewhere we aren't likely to get mugged. The Grace, remember?"

But when I reached for her hand, thinking that in the dark it would be safe, she scampered back like a wild animal.

"No one is going to get mugged. And you must be crazy if you think I'm going to a hotel room with you after *that*."

"Nina, I know you're not that stupid. But we've been over this. There is a reason why people don't go into Central Park at night."

"Which is exactly why I did," she said. "Because no one *else* in their right mind would follow us in here!"

I held my hands up, talking and moving very slowly. "Whoa, whoa. Come, baby, let's just take a minute to think."

"Do *not* call me that!" she snapped. "You cannot possibly understand what just happened back there. You don't know who that was. What she is capable of. What she will undoubtedly do now that she has seen us."

"Yes, I do."

Nina looked like she was going to be sick. "That's right. I forgot. You 'met at a benefit,' was that it?"

I ignored the question. "Look, you don't need to worry about Caitlyn. I'll make sure she keeps her mouth shut, if that's what's wrong here."

Nina strode toward me. Up close, her body seemed to vibrate. "I'm only going to ask you this once," she said through clenched, perfectly straight white teeth. "How *exactly* do you know Caitlyn Calvert *Shaw*, Matthew?"

I swallowed. I could feed her a line. Make up a story. One that was a lot more convincing than a fundraiser for my boss, who wasn't running for office for at least two more years. Like most lawyers, I was very, very good with bullshit.

But not with Nina. Never with her.

"We slept together," I said. "A few times. The first time, maybe six weeks ago, maybe two months. When I—when I was looking for you."

Nina's lips curled with disgust. "You *slept* with her? What, were you trading one pathetic trophy wife for another? Was she my replacement?"

"A really fuckin' shitty one, yeah," I said bluntly. "I had had too much to drink, I was lonely, and I was tired of pining away for a woman who seemed like she didn't actually exist." I rubbed my face. "Trust me, I regretted it pretty quick. I should have accepted the fact that you are just irreplaceable. I knew it the second I met you, and I've been paying for it ever since."

"Is that's supposed to make me feel *better* about the fact that you screwed the woman who tried to ruin my family?"

My brows screwed up in confusion as another part of the conversation from our first meeting floated back to me. The parts I'd been trying to remember in connection to her inheritance.

———

"I HAD MY HOME, my trust. I could have lived with it. Others, though, especially my—several other people were quite angry. Even my best friend, who tried to ruin the entire wedding."

"Jesus," I murmured. "Not much of a friend, was she?"

Nina shook her head sadly. *"Caitlyn and I grew up together. She even lived with my mother and me for a time when we were girls, and she had a terrible crush on my cousin. But she wasn't a good friend. Good friends don't go behind your back to steal another woman's fiancé. They don't embarrass the entire family to get what they want. It was a complete betrayal of all of us."*

———

"Jesus," I murmured. "You mean she's *that* Caitlyn? The one who—"

"Tried to ruin Eric and Jane's wedding? Yes, that would be her. You should probably know that she's carried quite a torch for my cousin since she was a little girl, and she's made up for his rejection by opening her 'house' to just about any key that tries her lock, so to speak. So you're as much a notch on her bedpost as she is on yours."

"Nina, come on—"

"Is this what you do?" she demanded. "Wander the Upper East Side hunting for vapid rich women to toy with?"

"Of course not—"

"I see what I am to you. Just another one, right? Another desperate, stupid housewife for you to pillage? Another feather for your ridiculous hat!"

"Nina, you know that's not true!"

"Do I?" She tossed a hand vaguely toward the opera. "What makes me all that different from her, Matthew? Honestly. Can you even distinguish between us?"

"Of course I can!" I protested, feeling like I was paddling upstream. "For fuck's sake, Nina, she means absolutely nothing to me, can't you see that?"

"I bet you make us all feel special, don't you?" Her voice was starting to warble, like a spinning top losing its steam. "Tell us we're irreplaceable. Tell us we're extraordinary. Make us feel that for once in our pathetic, lonely lives we're actually lo-loved?"

Her voice cracked on the last word and a tear spilled. My chest felt like it was cracking right with her.

"Doll—"

"Don't call me that!" she shrieked. "I'm not your doll! I'm not your baby, your sweetheart, or whatever stupid names you want to use! I'm not *anything* to you, and now I see that *perfectly!*"

"Goddammit." I grabbed her hand and pulled her back to me, and this time I refused to let go. "If that's what you see, then you're fuckin' blind. I'm right in front of you. I'm *right fucking here*, and I have been since we met. Scraps, though, that's all I get. You're married, with a family, a kid, and I'm the stray dog outside begging for your scraps. And you know what? I'll still take them. I'll take anything you have to give, you gorgeous, pig-headed, frustrating woman. Because I'm all fuckin' yours if you want me!"

"Stop saying that!" she yelled, banging her fists on my chest. "It's not true!"

"It *is* true!" I roared right back. "And I will chase you through every goddamn park in this city until you get that through your beautiful, stubborn head."

Before she could shout back, I wrapped my hands around her jaw and forced her still.

"Listen to me," I said. "Just fucking *listen*."

"What?" she demanded. "What is it you want to say?"

I opened my mouth as a million thoughts raced through my head.

I'm sorry.

I'm angry.

I hate you.

I love you.

But nothing seemed adequate. For the first time in my life, words didn't come. So I did the only thing that seemed to make sense in that moment. I kissed her.

"Mmmph!"

Nina squealed as she shoved me away. And at first, I thought I'd fucked it all up. That she'd run off all over again, and we'd be right back to square one.

But instead, she yanked me back to her and kissed me too. Just as hard, just as unforgiving. Our hands grabbed at each other, yanking on clothes, hair, trying to be closer than humanly possible. Our lips moved, tongues writhed in a terrible war, biting, hating, taking, breaking. God, she drove me crazy. I was so fuckin' frustrated with her.

And the fucked-up thing was, I had never wanted her more.

"Matthew!"

She pushed me away again almost violently, forcing me back a few steps into the night. But instead of running off, she did the exact opposite. She tossed her pristine white coat to the ground and wrenched one delicate strap of her dress over her shoulder, then the other.

"What—what are you doing?" I was still trying to catch my breath.

"Isn't this what you want?" Nina pulled the top of her dress down. Her breasts, as pale and full and perfect as I remembered, toppled gently into the moonlight.

"Nina—"

I wanted to tell her to stop, but at the same time, I wanted more. I was dying to tear the rest of her dress off, had been dying for her since the moment I saw her swathed in red, like a perfect package designed for me to open.

And yet, here, in the park, where anyone could walk through the trees at any moment and see a duchess like this baring herself...I should get her coat. Cover her up, bring her to her senses.

Instead, I didn't move. I couldn't even breathe. I was starstruck. Thunderstruck, even.

"Do it," she ordered, arching her chest toward me. "I know you want to."

"Do...do what?" I croaked.

Nina sank to her knees, and then, to my shock began to undo the front of my pants with quick, efficient movements.

"Nina—shit—you don't have to—oh!"

She pulled me out, and before I knew it, took me deep into her mouth. The sight hypnotized me—this woman, decked out in her jewels and couture, the finest thing New York had to offer. On her knees in Central Park. For me.

My fingers slipped into her hair. I rocked forward. Her jaw loosened naturally, and a low moan escaped from her throat as she took me even deeper.

"Oh, *shit*," I muttered as I watched myself disappear between her full lips.

She stared up at me, two silvery eyes full of frustrated lust. I pushed into her again.

"Is this what you want?" I demanded as instinct began to take over. "To be on your knees? Sucking my cock? Letting me fuck your pretty little mouth?"

She offered a small, infinitesimal nod and sucked harder.

"*Fuck*," I muttered as she started using her tongue, her lips, her hand wrapped around my base to conjure my pleasure, my *need*. What fucking magic was this? I couldn't tell. The woman was a siren in more ways than one.

"Holy...Mary...Mother of...*fuck!*" My head fell back as I stared at the sky. There were stars up there somewhere, obscured by this city, exploding in the universe just like I was in this park. "Oh, *Christ*, doll, I'm gonna come!"

But instead of taking my release in her mouth, Nina pulled me out and started working my cock furiously with her hands. Sliding up and down, then pressing me between her breasts. I looked down, and the sight of myself nested in her perfection was my undoing. *She* was my undoing. Maybe she always had been.

"*Fuck!*" I shouted as I emptied myself onto her skin. Her breasts, her neck, the sleek lines of her collarbones. My eyes squeezed shut, and for a moment, I imagined it everywhere, coating her naked body with my pleasure. Pressing myself deep within her, into the places where some part of me would stay for good. Making her mine. Not just now, but always.

Eventually, her grip softened and released me, and just as gradually, I came down from my high. My heartbeat adopted a more reasonable rate.

I inhaled deeply, then exhaled toward the hidden stars. Then again. And again before I could remember where I was.

"Jesus," I whispered. "That was...you are..."

I looked down, wanting to tell her everything she meant to me. But instead of seeing the satisfaction I felt deep in my soul, I only found misery at my feet.

There, on her knees, on the cold ground of Central Park, Nina Astor de Vries started to cry.

"It hurts," she whimpered, her hands clutching her chest, flattened over the remnants of what I had left there. She curled into herself, rocking toward the earth. "Oh, God, it hurts."

"Fuck!"

Quickly, I put myself back together and lifted her up, then whipped a handkerchief out of my pocket. She shook while I mopped her off, arranged her dress back into place, then pulled her coat, now covered with dirt and dust, back over her shoulders.

"Fuck, fuck, *fuck*, no..." I gathered her closer, pulling her into my arms. Trying to do something, *anything* to stop her tears.

Her fists beat at my chest again, but lighter now. Weaker. Defeated. Eventually they stopped as she was overtaken by tears.

It broke my fucking heart.

"Please," she said as I sank to a bench and arranged her in my lap. "Please stop chasing me, Matthew. My heart can't take it anymore."

"Why, Nina?" I asked. "Why shouldn't I chase you?"

Look at me, I commanded her silently. *Look. At. Me.*

And as if by power of my thoughts alone, she did. Her eyes glowed with sorrow and want.

"Because I know you'll catch me."

Jesus, Mary, it was torture even thinking about being separated from her again. I wanted to get the hell out of this park. I wanted to take her *home.*

"Is that such a bad thing?"

Her eyes were silver pools of pain and sadness. "It is when I want to be caught."

CHAPTER TWENTY

I HELD HER LIKE THAT FOR SEVERAL MINUTES, UNTIL HER THIN SHOULDERS stopped shaking and my shirt was wet through from her tears. We were both wrinkled, dirty messes, but I didn't care. I didn't even care that I was sitting in the middle of Central Park at night or that anyone could come across us like this at any time.

All I cared about was her. Erasing the despair that was breaking us both. Letting her know she wasn't alone. How many times would Nina Gardner allow me to rock her through her tears before she realized what I already knew? There was no fighting this thing between us. There was no fighting fate.

"Come on, baby," I crooned as I stroked her hair. "When are you going to figure out that you and I aren't just some tawdry fling? Since the second I met you, I knew."

"How could you possibly know that?" Her voice was muffled in my collar. "How can you know a future you can't see?"

I gestured toward the sky, toward the dusky corona of light that blanketed New York, even at night.

"We're like the stars, doll. I may not be able to see them clearly, but I still know they're there."

Together, we gazed up at the cloudless sky, wondering at the tiny glimmers that peeked through the city's aurora every so often.

After a few minutes, I loosened my grip on Nina's waist and tipped her chin down so she was looking at me. Both of us had calmed. She didn't seem in a hurry to get off my lap anymore.

"I'm sorry I slept with Caitlyn. Trust me, I regretted it immediately, well before I found out who she was to you." I brushed my thumb over her lips. "Truth be told, beautiful, I regret every woman I've ever been with who wasn't you."

She stared for a long second, then slowly leaned in and kissed me. It wasn't the same angry fight as before. This was desperate. Depleted. So fucking sad.

In that moment, there was only one more thing I could think of to say.

"Leave him," I said as soon as it ended. "I'll take care of you. You have to know that."

I wasn't exactly sure how I'd take care of the daughter of one of New York's first families, but I'd give her the clothes off my back if she needed them.

"Oh, Matthew. It's not as simple as that. This is my marriage, not some teenage crush. Doesn't that mean anything to you?"

"I'm Catholic, doll. I consider marriage a sacrament. But that doesn't mean I think you should martyr yourself to a bad one."

I kissed her again, willing her to understand the truth. Her fingers clutched my lapels like she was afraid I'd disappear, mouth working against mine as if pulling away might kill her. Like we were both thousands of feet underwater, providing each other the air we needed to live.

This is it, I thought. *She gets it. Finally, she understands.*

But when she broke away, my surety splintered all over again.

"I can't." Nina shook her head sadly. "I'm so sorry, darling. I just can't."

"Why?" I asked. "Give me one good reason why you should stay with that neglectful piece of shit?" The words came out more bitterly than I intended, but I couldn't help it. I needed someone to blame, and Calvin Gardner was as good a target as any. I looked at her wrist, the one that had been ringed with bruises. It was pristine now, and there were no signs of others.

"Because I'm not just thinking of myself!" Nina sputtered all over again. She pushed out of my arms and started pacing in front of me. "I have a daughter, Matthew. A little girl who needs her father."

"This is about your daughter?" I couldn't get my head around it. "Nina, I don't want to minimize the needs of your kid, but she doesn't even live here most of the time. I know you love her, but honestly? It sounds like she hardly sees you—"

"We see each other!" Nina insisted emphatically, to the point where I could see I'd touched a nerve. "I visit her in Boston more often than you know. And then she comes home, and I—"

"Okay, okay," I said, doing my best to soothe her fury. "But does she see him—Calvin?" I hated saying his name, but for some reason saying "her dad" felt so much worse. "Does she see him as much as she sees you? Because from what you say, he's gone. A lot."

The look on Nina's face told me I was right.

"So then," I said. "Would it be that different if you and Calvin lived separately?"

"It would be different," Nina said bitterly as she wrapped her arms around her waist.

I frowned. "Why?"

"It just would."

"That doesn't answer the question. *Why* would it be so different?"

"Because Olivia isn't Calvin's daughter!"

She whirled around, a tornado of red and white, then flopped onto the bench beside me. Her face was creased with sadness, and her hair, pulled out when she was on her knees, was half tousled around her blotchy face.

"She doesn't know, Matthew. She doesn't know at all, and I will *not* risk her ever finding out. I don't care what it costs me. I won't do it!"

I blinked while her voice rose to near hysteria. I breathed in. Breathed out. Let the revelations sink in.

Nina had a daughter.

I already knew that.

But her husband wasn't the girl's father.

This I didn't know. And for some reason, neither did the little girl.
Olivia.

The child's face, which I'd only seen for a minute or two, flashed in my mind's eye. She was a looker, all right. As full of sunshine as her mother, though a bit more dark-eyed, more shadowed than the de Vries family's Scandinavian heritage might indicate. And also so unlike Calvin, of course, whose jaundiced paunchiness was about as different from that olive perfection as it got. Probably from her biological father, then. She'd break as many hearts as her mother when the time came.

Nina was searching my face intensely for something. Absolution? Forgiveness? I couldn't tell, but I had nothing to offer yet.

"Tell me," I said. "Tell me everything."

She opened her mouth as if to argue, but eventually, wilted into her seat. "You really won't let this go, will you?"

I tipped her chin up. "Not a chance."

She sighed, but defiantly pulled her chin out of my grasp. "I was barely twenty. On a semester abroad. I studied art history, did you know that?"

I didn't reply. It wasn't much of a surprise, given how involved she was on a bunch of museum boards.

"My professor, he was..." She stared at her hands. "He was very charismatic. Much older than me. Old enough to be my father, even. Worldly. And we—well, I thought it was *we*, but it was really *I* who fell in love. Or what I thought was love." She shook her head. "I was so, so young..."

"And you got pregnant."

She nodded. "But it couldn't go anywhere. He was married too. With two other children, one nearly my age." She wiped a stray tear that hadn't yet dried on her cheek. "Are you ashamed of me?"

"Seriously? You're asking *me* if I'd judge you for being the other woman?"

She chuckled through her sadness. "No. I suppose you wouldn't, would you?"

I didn't laugh. I couldn't really see any levity in this situation. Not yet. It was far too easy to imagine this scenario already. Older European professor spots angelic coed. Seduces her with art, food, wine, and an accent. Then, what, tosses her aside? A woman like Nina de Vries?

"So, then what?" I barely managed to keep my voice level.

Nina shrugged. "Then…I came home. It was May. I was close to two months along, sick in the mornings, and very scared."

"Did you tell your family?"

She shook her head. "How much has Eric told you about why he left the family in the first place?"

I frowned. "Ah…well, not a lot. The basics, I guess."

I knew Eric had left New York when his previous fiancée died. From suicide, which at the time he believed was driven by ongoing harassment from his family because she didn't fit their idea of who was appropriate for their heir. Though Eric now suspected Carson and Letour had been responsible, at the time Nina would have believed the former version too.

I told Nina as much. "Am I missing anything?"

She shook her head. "No, that's about it. But what you don't know is what happened after." She shuddered. "My grandmother, my mother, my aunt—they were all *very* upset about it. Eric took off for over a year before he moved to Boston. No one knew where he was, what he was doing. And all that aggravation and worry…"

"Got put on you," I finished for her.

Nina nodded. "I was the only one left. Eric's father died when we were children. My mother, well, you haven't met her, but if you had, you would know she's utterly useless. Grandmother was always desperate about passing on the family's birthright to someone worthy. She was incredibly angry about Eric's defection. I was already the wrong sex to carry it on."

"Was that when you changed your name to de Vries?"

Nina nodded again. "Grandmother said that one more damage, one more embarrassment…she swore it would kill her." Her hand slipped over her stomach. "So, I didn't tell her what had happened to me. I decided to take care of it."

She sighed, staring at her hand. The big diamond on the left was muted in the dark. I wanted to hurl it into the trees and let the park swallow it up.

She went to a clinic in Queens. A neighborhood where she knew no one, and no one would recognize her. It was harder than it sounded—the de Vrieses had been local tabloid regulars for generations. But outside of Manhattan, after years away at school, Nina thought she might be safe enough to do what needed to be done.

"Again," she said. "So, so naive."

"You were spotted?" I couldn't imagine having to worry so much about being recognized. It did explain why she had the bad habit of running into deserted parks for privacy.

"By Calvin," she said. "He was in the neighborhood looking at an investment. Long Island City wasn't built up yet at that point, you remember?"

"How did you know each other?"

"Calvin was a friend of my father's, and Eric's father too, when he was still alive," she said. "He worked for them before he moved to real estate development. That's why he's always gone, you know. The company he works for now owns property all over the world."

I grunted in acknowledgment. I didn't really give a shit why Calvin Gardner felt he could leave his wife all the fucking time. I just wanted to know why she couldn't leave him.

Nina sighed. "Back then, I knew his face, but I didn't really know *him*. After all, I hadn't seen him in years, and I was just a child then."

When they met again, it was by chance. He saw her approaching the clinic, called out her name just as she opened the door. With her hand at her stomach, there was no hiding why she was there. And so, when he asked her…she told him the truth.

"Why didn't you just tell him you were going in for contraceptives or a checkup?" I wondered. I couldn't help it. The investigator in me had to look at things from all angles.

Nina shrugged. "I panicked. I was young. I hadn't prepared a story. And believe it or not, I wasn't *quite* so good at masking my emotions back then."

I brushed some hair out of her face. "I like it when I can see your emotions, doll."

For a moment, she leaned into my palm. "I suppose that's good, since I can't seem to hide them from you."

I was about to tell her that was fine by me, but then she continued.

"It's hard to explain, but he was just *so* very nice. Kind. Understanding. He knew, of course. Well before I admitted to anything. And I thought, well, there is really only one reason why I would have been there." Nina shook her head. "Calvin would have known I had my own doctor in the city. Someone who could prescribe birth control or whatever other care I needed. After all, what other reason would someone like me be entering a strange clinic in Queens except to have the one procedure most women hide from the world?"

I nodded. It did make sense when she said it like that. Rich girl. Beautiful. Page Six fodder. There wasn't much else she would be getting at a community women's clinic that wouldn't ask for a name or insurance.

"And to my surprise, he offered to come with me. And I—I said yes. It was kind, I thought. I didn't have any other support. We sat in the waiting room together. But when they called my name...I couldn't do it." She swiped a new tear from under her eye. "I just couldn't."

I took her hand and squeezed. "Of course you couldn't, doll."

"I could have," she insisted. "*I'm* not Catholic, you know. I believe in a woman's right to choose. And I don't think it makes anyone a bad person either way. Not matter the reasons."

"I didn't mean it like that. Not all Catholics think of women as vessels, doll. Besides, look at me. Look at what kind of person I am. I would be the last person to ever judge anyone's decisions, good or bad. Especially yours."

Nina buried her nose in my neck, inhaling my skin like I was oxygen.

"Who are you?" she whispered. "Where did you come from?"

"It doesn't matter, baby. All that matters is where I am. Right here. For you."

We sat like that a few minutes more until she could bear to finish.

"Calvin took me home in a car he ordered. Walked me up to Grandmother's flat and reintroduced himself to the family. Said we had reconnected when he was on business in Europe and had kept in touch over the last year."

"I'll bet he did," I muttered. I had an idea about where this was going. Old Calvin saw an opportunity and ran with it.

"I was so stunned, I didn't even bother to correct him. I was so scared..." Nina drifted off as the memories kept coming.

He had come back to call on her, again and again. Daily, weekly. As with her professor, it wasn't hard to imagine. Another older guy, a barely legal girl. The domestic violence bureau, the trafficking bureau—they saw it all the time with different kinds of sexual predators. People who groomed their victims when they were at their most vulnerable. Targeted them when they were scared, isolated, alone.

For Nina, this was the second time that year. She had all the money and privilege in the world, but she was pregnant, terrified of a family who, at the time, she believed was capable of real harm, and desperate to please her grandmother.

Calvin had presented himself as her only ally and gotten a bargain for himself.

"I was almost three months gone when he asked me to marry him. He said they would notice soon, and we could pretend he had actually proposed in the spring. That I wanted him to meet the family and get used to him before we announced." She shrugged. "I was still sick most mornings. Grandmother had already called the doctor. I was a coward for taking the out...but in that moment, I saw a future. I saw a father for my child. I saw a source of pride for my family."

"And for you?" I broke in. "What did you see for yourself?"

She smiled, an expression so impossibly sweet amid the darkness that surrounded us that I couldn't help but smile back myself.

"I saw motherhood, Matthew," she said as her hand lay flat over her abdomen. "I saw love. Real love. For the first time in my life."

We were quiet for a long time, as if both of us were digesting her story, and not just me.

"And the professor?" I wondered. "Does he know he has a daughter here in New York?"

She looked grim. "I thought to tell him, later. The first few years of Calvin's and my marriage were...well, I thought it was a mistake—"

"It *was*." I couldn't help it. The idea of Nina married to anyone other than, well, *me* was a mistake.

The thought surprised me. But also seemed...natural. Soothing, even.

But the idea of her marrying a guy who, from what I could tell, was little better than a sexual predator made me feel fuckin' violent.

"Well, after one particular argument, I told Calvin that I planned to return to Florence and tell Giuseppe about Olivia. I thought perhaps he would help us in the event we were cut off. In the event Grandmother couldn't forgive the scandal."

I wanted to crush the fucking bench under my hands. So close. She had been *so* close to freedom. "Then what happened?"

She swallowed. "He—he died."

My head jerked up. "He *what*?"

She pressed her fingertips into her brow, like she was trying to force the memories out. "Giuseppe died. Honestly, Matthew, I don't know much. The university announced it to the students. He had a sudden heart attack. Died in his bed."

"And he was how old?"

She shrugged. "Perhaps forty-five? It was very unexpected."

"I'll bet it was."

I couldn't stand it. Every instinct I had was on alert. Right when she's about to tell Olivia's dad the truth and leave her bloodsucking husband, the Italian drops dead? It seemed…too convenient.

But before I could press her about it, something else occurred to me. Something that arrested my imagination completely.

"Wait a second," I said. "You said Florence? You were studying in Italy?"

"Matthew, I told you that."

She had, but I'd forgotten the fact in the middle of all of this as my brain made another connection. "So your daughter…she's half Italian?"

Nina's expression softened as she followed my train of thought. "Yes. I suppose she is."

I didn't know why, but that detail gutted me. Italy is a big place, to be sure. And regionally, it's pretty diverse. Different dialects. Different customs. Sicilians are pretty different from Venetians. Neapolitans from Romans.

But for a kid growing up in the Bronx, in a neighborhood like Belmont, the larger connection to the country meant something more, maybe. Being Italian American meant having a community in a city full of people from elsewhere. It was bad enough that Nina had a daughter with another man. But that her daughter shared blood from the same place as the majority of my kin...

I took her hand and played with her fingers. My thumb brushed over her rings. "I was in Italy around that time, you know. Stationed for a bit in Sicily. One liberty across the water...maybe it would have been me."

I shouldn't have said it out loud. There was that sense again, more clearly than ever, that a woman, a life had been stolen from me.

A daughter.

Nina's mouth pressed into a crooked smile. "In another life..."

I exhaled through pursed lips. It was painful, this kind of hypothetical thinking. "Yeah. Another life. But, Nina...what about this one? What about your own?"

Nina bent forward and pressed her face into her hands. When she sat up again, the moonlight cast her face in high relief, revealing streaked makeup and kiss-swollen lips.

"Oh, Matthew, don't you see? I don't care anything about myself. But Olivia?" She pressed a hand to her heart. "She is *all* that matters. And if she ever learned the truth about what she is, it would break her."

"So you'll lie to her instead?"

Nina closed her eyes, as if she were in pain. "I'm already beyond repair, my love. But I won't smash my daughter's heart too."

We stared at each other for a long time. Slowly, I raised my hands and framed her face, examining its flaws, its curves and hues, its complete and utter perfection. The dusting of freckles over her nose. The slight arch of her dark blonde brows. She had a wrinkle just between them— likely it appeared only when she was upset, to match the divot in her bottom lip.

"You're a good mother, Nina," I told her solemnly. "Your daughter's lucky to have one who cares that much about her."

She didn't say anything. But she didn't look away, just let her big gray eyes shine with sadness and pride.

Slowly, because I couldn't help it, I leaned in to kiss her again.

"Don't." Nina's voice was a whisper. "Oh, please, don't."

I considered ignoring her. She stared at my lips like they were the promised land. Every part of her was tensed. She wanted this just as badly as I did. Maybe more. Her mouth was wet and open, her breath coarse, almost feverish.

But there was so much fear in her too. She was still, not even blinking as she waited for my response. A tiny flutter ticked away at her jaw. And if I watched very, very carefully, I could see her entire body vibrating like a guitar string that had just been plucked.

"Nina," I whispered as I pushed a lock of hair behind her ear.

She shivered. "Matthew."

"You don't know what you're asking of me."

She closed her eyes, her long lashes casting a shadow across her cheeks. "Yes, I do. Because I'm asking it of myself."

She wasn't just scared. She was terrified. And that was never, ever something I wanted Nina to feel with me. So I fought against every instinct I had and dropped my hands. I stood up. And stepped away from her.

"I know what it's like to lose a father, even one who wasn't particularly present. I will *not* do that to Olivia. Her happiness—Matthew, it's more important than mine." She touched my lips. "I'm so sorry, my love. But that's all there is to it. I shouldn't have asked you out tonight. You and I...we have to stay away from each other."

"All right," I said, struggling to keep my tone even. My walls were cracking like a teenager's voice. "I'll stay away, Nina."

Her slim shoulders fell in relief, though she rose from her seat. She closed her eyes for exactly three seconds until I pulled the rose from my lapel and tucked it behind her ear.

"Until you ask me not to," I finished softly.

Her eyes opened. "What?"

"I'll respect your wishes. Because I respect *you*, Nina. More than you could possibly know. So I won't kiss you again. I won't call. I won't text. I'll pretend I don't exist in your life." I inhaled deeply. "Until you ask me to."

Nina pulled the rose from her hair and studied it sadly. "Well, then it's settled. Because I won't. I can't."

I touched her cheek, then dropped my hand. "We'll see."

INTERMISSION II

APRIL

She would have walked the rest of the way home on her own, dark or not. But Matthew, despite his earnest promise not to touch her, refused to let her go alone.

Always a gentleman. With a dark side, of course. One that caused him so much guilt, but *oh*, it was one that she adored.

He couldn't have known how close she was to pushing him back into the park. That as soon as she saw the lights of Fifth Avenue, she nearly grabbed his hand and begged him to run away with her. Hide for days. A cardboard box, under a concrete bridge. Out of sight, out of mind. Central Park was the only place where, even for a few scant feet, it was almost as if New York didn't exist.

But she couldn't.

That was her own cross to bear.

He left her when the Met came into view, pressing one final kiss to her palm, then disappearing back into the trees like a ghost. He was a mess—bow tie half-undone, dirty tracks on his dinner jacket, pieces of his glossy hair sticking up on both sides where she'd grabbed it. *She* was a mess, to the point where the doorman would almost certainly wonder if she'd been accosted on her way home. The custom Valentino she'd ordered back in January was utterly unrecognizable, and covering it with her dirty mink coat made no difference. Mud stained the hem and two dark spots from when she had sunk to her knees. One of the spaghetti-thin straps had broken, and the bust was stretched beyond repair.

But as Nina made her way up the streets of the Upper East Side, she barely even noticed her disarray or the occasional horns that honked their awareness. Because walking away from him, even now, was taking every iota of strength she had. Every step became more labored. Her chest felt like someone was standing on it. Her heart like it might explode.

That was the problem with meeting someone who made her feel more alive than she ever had in her life. When he left, it practically killed her. His absence was murder.

Nina stumbled the last few blocks to her building on Ninety-Second and Lexington. She could have called her car, but she couldn't have borne being shut up in the big black Escalade. Another cage. Another jail. Just like this life.

Who was she kidding? Ever since Matthew had admitted to a habit of strolling through her neighborhood looking for her, she had found herself walking nearly everywhere. Poor George, the driver, barely had any work these days. She simply marched wherever she liked. Under an umbrella during a particularly nasty gale. Through the final, late March snow that covered the city just last week.

Now early spring blooms were poking through the dripping remains of winter. Tomorrow, the blue sky would shine, and the sidewalks would be teeming with people. But not with him.

No more.

The thought ached, bone deep.

"Evening, Mrs. Gardner. Are…oh, my, are you all right, ma'am?"

Nina swallowed a snarl. Ten years she had used Gardner, but she'd never liked it. How long had she fought her family to take the name de Vries only to give it up for *that*? Mrs. Gardner. Like the wife of someone who should be tending her grandmother's Long Island estate. The way Celeste addressed her staff without knowing the *actual* person's name.

No, she thought. Gardner was fine. No better or worse than Astor or de Vries or any others she could have ended up with. It was the man who put the sour taste in her mouth. And never more than in the last six months.

"I'm fine, Carl," Nina said to the weekend doorman as he escorted her to the back of the elevator bank. "I just had a bit of a tumble on my way home from the opera, that's all. I'm in a poor mood."

She bit her lip. She wanted nothing more than to curl into herself and speak to no one. But the lack of pleasantries would cause suspicion. She couldn't have that.

So, she tried again. "How was your week?"

"Not bad, not bad. Picked up some extra shifts down at the De Vries Shipping offices like you suggested. Sure will come in handy now that my mother's in the nursing home."

Carl continued jabbering until they reached the service stairs at the far end of the lobby. He pulled open the door, but looked at the concrete stairwell doubtfully, then back at her ruined clothes.

"Sure you don't want to try the elevator today, Mrs. Gardner? Maybe just this once? Manuel can be here in a second."

Nina shook her head wearily, holding back a shudder. He really could not imagine what a horror that would be, particularly tonight.

"No, thank you, Carl," she said. "I'll be fine."

When the door shut behind her, she slipped off her shoes and began the long climb up, up, up to the twentieth floor. She barely noticed the slight burn in her legs by the time she reached the top. She was used to it. She wished she wasn't. Tonight, of all nights, she needed the burn to distract from the facts of her life. From her complete and utter disgrace.

Instead, with every step, it felt like she was carrying an extra weight. Putting her tower on her shoulders instead of ascending it. If only her hair were long enough, like Rapunzel, to ask her dark prince to help her escape the ogre within.

Tears welled as she stopped at her apartment door and slipped on her shoes again. Matthew's face came to mind. The crestfallen expression when he had listened to her story. When she had told him of Olivia's origin, and she could see, plain as day, the idea cross his face.

She could have been his.

How many times had she imagined it herself? A fool's dream, of course. But one she could never shake.

Her damaged heels echoed on the white marble flooring when she entered the apartment. The heavy door to the service stairs shut behind her, and every part of her wilted. She stared at the large bouquet of red roses in the foyer—flowers she had delivered weekly now instead of the usual bouquet of lilies. She approached the table and set the clipped bud from Matthew's jacket in front of them. His flower was wilted and beaten—another reminder of the train wreck of their walk. But she couldn't throw it away. Not yet.

"You're home early."

The sound of Calvin's voice startled Nina out of her mourning. She shut her eyes, summoned the mask she had perfected her entire life, and turned.

"Ah, yes. I wasn't up for donors' cocktails after. Why aren't you in London?"

Calvin shuffled down the hall from the bedrooms. He looked a bit worse for wear in nothing but a t-shirt strained over his overstuffed belly, silk boxers, and the paisley socks he loved from Bergdorf's. Not for the first time, Nina noted how hard her husband tried to look wealthy. And that even after ten years of being married to her, the execution was always off, like a Halloween costume that wasn't quite right.

Is he good to you? Matthew had asked her once.

And like a child, she'd cried.

"They pushed the meeting to next week. I came home to have a damn rest. Good lord, Nina. What the hell happened? You look like a hobo— the doormen must be laughing their asses off right now."

There was no concern in Calvin's voice. No questions about whether or not she was okay. Instead, he was more embarrassed for her appearance. Despite the fact that *she* was the one born and bred in the highest social circles of New York, Calvin was far more concerned with appearances. It was ironic, then, that he never quite got them right.

Nina kicked off her shoes with a clatter and pulled off her coat to set on the foyer table.

"I fell in the park," she said flatly. "Twisted my ankle and rolled down a hill."

"And took your dress and coat with you," Calvin remarked. "How much did that set us back?"

He didn't even wonder why she had been in the park at all. Matthew, of course, would have gone straight to that. Admonished her for being careless, for not protecting her own safety.

It took more energy than normal for Nina not to roll her eyes. Though yes, the dress and shoes were all quite expensive, Calvin had never, not in ten years, adjusted to the fact that even that cost was negligible compared to her actual holdings.

Calvin was a collector. Every month, he glowered at the balances on their bank statements like a dragon guarding its hoard. When Nina was passed over for Eric to inherit the de Vries family's larger holdings, Calvin was furious. Not because he (or Nina) actually had any legitimate interest in running the company. No, it was because those numbers—the numbers that had always belonged to Nina as a result of her grandmother's careful trust planning—would never truly belong to him. As she did not inherit, neither did he.

The truth was, her husband had never been particularly talented at making his own money. Despite working at several different hedge funds, he had failed to rise to the levels of Soros, Shaw, or any of his other contemporaries. His real estate ventures collapsed time and time again. He simply didn't have the touch. His fortune came from Nina's family—a fact of which he was keenly aware and for which he never stopped resenting her. Particularly when he continually lost the small allowance he was granted from Celeste de Vries's estate.

"It's fine. I don't really care for this dress anyway. I only wore it as a favor to the designer."

Lies, all lies.

———

"Do you ever wear red?" Matthew asked as he traced a rosebud up and down her body. "Like this?"

———

From that moment on, she'd never wanted to wear anything else. Although when she bought this dress, she never thought the man who requested she wear red would ever see it, she knew it was the only thing she could wear to the premiere. She had been in love the moment she saw the designs. Adored the woman she became when she put it on.

Someone passionate. Someone alive.

Nina picked up Matthew's flower and started in the direction of her suite. There, if she were lucky, she could draw a bath and scatter these rose petals over the suds. Sink into her memories of his touch. Soak in it as her own private goodbye.

"Well, it's for the best," Calvin said. "You look like a whore in that thing. If I had been here when you left, I would have made you change."

Nina paused on her walk, took a deep breath, then exhaled and kept going. These little possessive streaks in her husband came out from time to time. His most recent project must have done poorly this week. Perhaps that's why his next trip was delayed.

"Why in God's name were you walking home in the first place?" Calvin snapped as he followed her, tension trailing with every step. "Wasn't George there to drive you?"

Now he asks. Matthew's voice, snarling in her head. *Selfish motherfucker. Why wasn't he there, huh?*

"I felt like a walk," Nina replied. "It was very stuffy in the hall."

She felt almost lost as she wandered into her private suite. It was as deluxe as the rest of the apartment, dressed with the same shades of cream, white, and beige. With yet another explosion of red—more roses atop the Majorelle sideboard.

She drifted Matthew's over her lips.

"Roses *again*?" Calvin edged next to her, then plucked the flower from her grasp and wrinkled his nose. "When are you going to get over this obsession?"

It was true. Although she hadn't brought home that first bouquet from the Grace Hotel, she hadn't been able to pass up others. At the store. On the street. New York was full of flower stands she's never noticed before. Every corner deli stacked flowers on its sidewalks, bursting with bright yellows, reds, pinks, and every other dyed color under the rainbow. For the last two months, everywhere she walked, there they were, peeking through the gloom. Friendly scarlet reminders of the fact that she, Nina Evelyn Astor de Vries...yes, Gardner...could still experience passion. Pleasure. Joy.

Even if just for one night.

"I like them," Nina said as she stared at the bud clutched between her husband's fat fingers. Her hands curled with the resistance to snatch it back.

Calvin wrinkled his stubby nose. "Cheap garbage. It doesn't even smell anymore." He tossed it on the sideboard below the array of more fragrant long stems.

Nina picked it back up and held it to her nose. It *was* cheap. Paired with a sprig of baby's breath, it probably cost Matthew a dollar on his way to the opera house. The deli flowers lost their scent before they reached the city and would maybe last two, three days at most after Nina set them in the hideous Baccarat vase Calvin's mother had given them as a wedding present. Her own private joke. The horrible woman had been a social climber of the worst kind, absolutely transparent in her desire for splashy wealth. Gone now, but she would have hated seeing such cheap, ordinary flowers in the gaudy thing.

A pair of thick hands encircled her waist. Calvin's stomach reached the small of her back before the rest of him found her.

Nina shuddered.

"Well, if you're going to wear a whore's dress," he said with breath hot on her neck. "Might as well play the whore."

She tried to shake her head. "Please. I'm very tired."

"Come on, princess. Time to come out of your castle. The common folk need to see you."

It was a game he had always played. She was a princess in more ways than one. The daughter of not one, but two New York dynasties. An "ice princess" too, according to the gossip mags and nearly every man she'd known. Only two had ever succeeded in making her thaw. One had given her a daughter and a broken heart. The other she wasn't sure she would ever get over.

I'll be your friend, Matthew had said.

The fact that she needed one enough to say yes broke her heart even more.

The zipper was drawn down her back. "Let's get this trash off you."

When Nina glanced over her shoulder, Calvin's eyes had that strange glaze about them. She tried not to shrink. She knew what that look meant.

"Oh, please," she whispered. "Please, not tonight. Calvin, I'm so tired."

"Do you really think you can prance around the city in that thing and get away with it at home?"

He whirled her around and shoved her against the sideboard hard enough that the polished teak bit into the small of her back. It would leave a bruise, along with several others come morning.

Calvin took each side of her dress and yanked. The fabric was delicate, but didn't tear.

His expression flared as he shoved the material awkwardly to her waist. Nina resisted the urge to cover herself. It would only goad him more.

Tell him to stop, doll. You don't have to take that.

Except in her heart of hearts, she knew that she did.

Mommy?

There was the other voice that always existed in the depths of her soul. She would never forget that day, only four years ago.

"Mommy? Is Daddy—is he hurting you?"

Calvin froze over Nina, where she was curled on the floor. Her skirt was ripped up one leg, and she would have a nasty bruise over her ribs in the morning. But nothing was visible. Nothing—quite—incriminating could be seen.

Calvin scrambled up, back turned to his daughter as he did up his pants. "Olivia!" he barked. "Go to your room. This is private!"

But Olivia just ignored him and rushed across the room, casting a suspicious look toward the man she knew as "Daddy" before allowing her mother to draw her close.

Behind her, Calvin shoved a thick hand through his thinning hair and shook his head with menace before he looked at Olivia. His meaning was clear. One word, and he would tell her everything. He would break the little girl's heart. And Nina would lose her daughter's trust forever.

Nina pulled Olivia close and peppered her face with kisses.

"No, darling," she told her. "Mommy's fine. I just fell, and Daddy was helping me get up."

"But it looked like he pushed you down. He was on top of you. His hand was—"

"Shhhhh."

Nina kept Olivia's face pressed to her shoulder and stroked her hair so her daughter couldn't see her break. Calvin was now absorbed with his phone, but he kept checking every so often to make sure Nina wasn't saying anything wrong. He, of course, didn't offer the girl the slightest bit of comfort.

"Don't worry, my love," Nina whispered as she clutched the child close. "It will be all right. I promise."

———

She sent her away the next week. They had both cried when she dropped her off at Andover, four hours from the city. But better Olivia shed a few tears than stay here. Particularly if she grew into the girl Nina had every certainty she would.

"What the hell is wrong with this thing?" Calvin pulled and prodded Nina's dress, struggling with the fabric until the bodice was awkwardly yanked over one of her breasts, the rest of her skirt bunched around her waist.

Would he notice the scent of the man all over her? Or would her subtle perfume, the scent of roses, and his own myopia keep Calvin from seeing what was right in front of him—his wife, painted in the colors of another man's pleasure?

He grabbed her breasts with the caress of a toddler. He didn't twist them roughly. Not yet.

He reached down and started playing with himself furiously, but, as she could have predicted, nothing happened.

He would need more.

He always needed more.

And if she didn't give it to him, she would pay the price.

Tonight there was no doubt she would cry by the end. Her emotions were barely in check as it was.

Calvin's tastes, however, meant he would take her tears as a sign of victory, not distress. And with any luck, it would make him more merciful than usual. He never lasted long on the nights when she broke.

"All right," she murmured as she closed her eyes. "But remember, not the face."

ACT III

ARIA

CHAPTER TWENTY-ONE

"UNCLE MATTIE, UNCLE MATTIE, WAKE UP!"

Fifty pounds of solid-brick boy landed on my stomach with a thwack, knocking all the wind out of me before my eyes were even open.

"Christ!" I croaked as I rolled my nephew Pete onto the floor with a thud. "What the hell is your mother feeding you, kid?"

"Right now? Prob'ly cereal." Pete popped up from the Oriental rug looking like a jack-o-lantern with his two bottom teeth missing. "She says it's time to get up. We're leaving in forty-five minutes, and Daddy says God don't like it when we're late to his party."

With a groan, I pushed myself up from my grandmother's sofa and set my feet on the floor, then bent over while the blood rushed from my head. Good fuckin' God. I was really too old to be spending two nights in a row on *Nonna's* couch and *definitely* too old to be this hungover. But the alternative—pacing around my room until I lost my nerve and went back to the Upper East Side to beg—wasn't an option. *Nonna* had taken one look at me when I arrived Friday night, made up the couch, and put me to work for the rest of the weekend. She knew the look of the Zola men when they needed some healthy distraction. I just never thought I'd be one of the ones who couldn't find it myself.

"Mattie!"

I pressed a hand to my temples as my sister bustled into the room.

"Jesus, Lea, I'm up, I'm up. You don't need to yell."

"Mattie, we've been calling your name for the last fifteen minutes. How much bourbon did you put down with the boys last night?"

"Not that much." I eyed the pot she was carrying distrustfully. It smelled like it was full of mushy oatmeal and was *not* doing good things to my roiling stomach. "*Nonna* know you're burning her favorite saucepan?"

"*Nonna* is upstairs ironing your damn shirt like you're a child while I make everyone breakfast," Lea retorted as she stirred the oatmeal. "We're here to walk her to church, like we do every Sunday, and the boys haven't eaten yet."

I noticed she didn't answer the question.

"That looks like puke!" Pete shouted as he screamed out of the room.

"Come eat," Lea ordered me. "The boys say they won't until you do."

I pushed myself off the couch. "Fine, fine. I'm up. Did you at least make some coffee too?"

I followed Lea back into the kitchen, which was crowded with gremlins shoving oatmeal into their faces (and at each other) while Michael, their father, looked at his phone. Tommy made like he was going to fling a glob of that crap at my face until I drew a finger playfully across my neck. He giggled and went back to eating his breakfast.

"*Nonna* said you stayed all weekend," Lea said as she poured my coffee.

I took the cup gladly. Fuck, I needed some caffeine.

"Ah, yeah," I said. "She needed the bathroom re-caulked, so I helped her out."

"Funny, since Michael just did the bathroom for her three months ago. You saying his work was messed up or something?"

Michael looked up at the mention of his name. "What's wrong with my caulk?"

"Cock!" shouted Pete. "Something's wrong with Daddy's cock!"

"Caulk!" Michael snapped at his son. "Caulk, not cock, Pete."

"Cock, cock, cock," muttered MJ, the youngest, while he spooned his cereal happily.

"See what you did, Lea?" Michael said. "Now you got the boys talking about cock on a Sunday. What's Father Deflorio going to say when one of 'em start asking about Jesus's privates in the middle of Mass?"

I cleared my throat. "He's heard worse, Mike. And your, ah, work was fine. Honestly, I think *Nonna* was just a little paranoid about the color."

"She said you showed up late Friday in a tux." Lea examined the undershirt and pair of boxers I'd slept in like they were secretly masking the formalwear I'd fought not to throw in the fireplace.

I took another long sip of coffee before answering. "I went to the opera with a friend. Decided to come up here instead of going home since *Nonna* said she needed some help."

Lea's eyes narrowed like she didn't believe me. I didn't blame her. Considering she and Michael lived only a few blocks away, he was the fix-it guy around here these days, and the fact was a point of pride for both of them.

But I wasn't about to tell her the real reason I'd fled to my grandmother's house on Friday night and made use of my old CUNY t-shirts and hole-ridden sweatpants for two days. I wasn't going to detail how I'd wandered around the botanical gardens for hours yesterday, barely avoided hurling my phone into the fountain, then spent a full hour in confession before drinking far too much bourbon with Michael and his friends. Staying in the Bronx meant I didn't have to go home to Frankie's third degree. It meant I didn't have to watch her with Sofia and be reminded of the cute blonde girl who should have been mine. It meant I could surround myself with errands and church and bullshit conversation instead of the empty white room that seemed so much emptier now that I'd seen Nina in it.

I had to let her go. That was all there was to it. I had to let Nina go.

It just felt like I was tearing out both of my lungs to do it.

"How'd you end up last night?" I asked Michael, avoiding Lea's death glare.

Michael looked up from his phone again. "Ah, shi—I mean, not so hot. Finished the night twenty down."

Lea set the coffee back on its stand with a clatter. "Excuse me? I thought you were watching the game, Michael."

Michael held up his hands in surrender. "Babe, I was with the guys, and you know how it is. Mattie was there too. Just a friendly game of poker, like we always do. Last time I brought home a hundred and you didn't argue with that."

"Mattie, can you talk some sense into him? Remind him that gambling is illegal in New York? Maybe you should call your friends with the NYPD and have them do a raid on Jason Russo's house first Saturday of the month, eh?"

"Can we come?" Tommy asked, and immediately started miming like he was holding a Glock, CSI-style.

"What the hell are you letting him watch, Michael?" Lea started. "First the gambling, and now my baby boy is playing with guns?"

"Lea, it's just boys being boys. He could have picked that up anywhere."

"But he didn't, did he?"

"Christ, Lea!"

"Daddy!"

"I'm going upstairs to change." I turned to leave the kitchen, coffee in hand. I'd been in the middle of arguments like these too many times and had learned when to leave.

Overall, Michael was a good husband to my sister. A good brother-in-law. He was a mechanic and part-time driver who worked in *Nonno's* garage, then took it over after he and Lea got married (much to my relief). He worked hard, supported Lea and the three, almost four kids she'd popped out in eight years, and was as steady as a rock. So he liked to toss in a twenty here and there on a game. I could think of worse vices and had reminded my sister of the fact multiple times.

"Don't take too long!" Lea snapped behind me. "And bring *Nonna* and Joni down with you. We have to leave in thirty-five, or else we'll get stuck in the back! I'm not taking communion after two hundred people have put their mouths on that chalice!"

———

AFTER A QUICK SHOWER, I found my grandmother in her bedroom, the

1950s time capsule that still had the same mahogany bedroom set, the same stack of handmade afghans and lace-curtained windows, the same assortment of prayer candles and saints cluttering the vanity, and the same twelve-inch crucifix nailed over the bed. *Nonna* stood in the center dressed for Mass, as she had every Sunday since we were kids, in a conservative navy skirt and loose sweater, running an iron over my pants.

"*Nonna*, you didn't have to do that," I said as I pecked her cheek.

She smiled. "If I don't, you look like a beggar at Mass."

"A beggar in a tuxedo?"

I peered at the white shirt and black pants she had laid out for me like I was still a kid. Other people might let their kids attend church like they had run off the school yard, but that was never an option for us. Every Sunday, we were up by seven to make sure our hair was brushed, our clothes were pressed, our shoes were shined. The Zolas were nothing if not proud people.

Nonna chuckled. "Don't wear the jacket or the tie. Then you will just look like a waiter, eh?"

I chuckled with her. "Shall I take your order?"

She gestured toward the bed. "Get dressed. We need to talk."

With a rumbling in my stomach, I obediently put on my pants and started buttoning my shirt while *Nonna* put away the ironing board. I could hear the music humming from Joni's room down the hall, layered by the clatter of the boys downstairs. My whole life, this house had been full of noise. Now, though, even after all this time, it still missed my grandfather's voice.

"What are these?" I wondered when I caught sight of a few open cardboard boxes next to the closet, each filled with familiar, slightly moth-eaten clothes. I pulled a cardigan off the top. "Is this *Nonno's*?"

Nonna shoved the ironing board into a now-empty side of the closet. "They are just taking up room. We need the space."

I couldn't believe it. Not because it wasn't time. Shit, *Nonno* had been gone for fifteen years at this point. But in some ways, it felt like it hadn't been long at all. For most of my adult life, we'd mourned him in one way or another. *Nonna* wore black every day for five years. We talked about him constantly, his pictures were everywhere, and his things had remained in this house like he was going to walk in any day and reclaim them.

I stared at the closet, at the yawning space where his clothes used to be. Then I turned away when the rent in my chest seemed too painful to bear, even as his last moments flooded back, just like they always did when I was here.

———

NONNO INHALED DEEPLY *through his face mask. The residue of stunted breath left condensation beneath the plastic. A good sign. He was still breathing.*

He had left the hospital against the doctor's wishes, but no one really blamed him. Mattia Stefano Cristiano Zola had lived well. He had moved across an ocean. Built a business and married the love of his life. Raised three children, mourned one of them, then raised another family of his grandkids. Who could fault the man for wanting to spend his last days in the comfort of his home rather than the cold confines of the hospital?

His last few days had been short. He picked at his breakfast in the morning, the plate of ham, crackers, and espresso Nonna had fixed him since they were teenagers. Then he fell asleep for hours, waking only for a few minutes at a time until sleeping again, off and on, through the day and the night.

Joni and Marie, Lea and Kate—they all still shared the two bedrooms on the top floor, but this was the first time the six of us had been in the house since I'd left for college a few years before Frankie did last spring. Now Frankie was sharing Lea's bed again. I was back on the couch.

We hovered in the hallway, even the little ones. Everyone waiting for their chance to see Nonno's *crooked smile. To share a chat. To say goodbye.*

Nonno *knew too, that these would be our last moments. He had something for everyone.*

"You know what the most important thing in life is, Matthew?" he asked me after finally catching his breath again.

"God? Family? Campari?" I joked. My grandfather loved his aperitivos. *Or had. Once.*

He smiled weakly, but waved his hand through the air like the words I'd offered—the words I'd been taught to say, even half-heartedly, if I knew what was good for me—were an affront.

"No," he said. "Pride, Matthew. All those things, they are important. But nothing matters if you don't have pride for them."

"Father Deflorio said pride is a sin, though," I said, hoping to make him smile again. It wouldn't be me if I didn't argue back a little, right?

"No, no, no," Nonno protested hard enough that he coughed a bit.

"Hey, hey, I was just joking, Nonno. Just breathe. I get what you're saying."

But he wasn't done. "Pride like stubborn, yeah, sure, it's no good. But I'm talking about pride for your life, Matthew. Pride in your work. Pride in your family. Pride in doing things the right way." He shook his hand, the skin over the veins thin as paper. "Matthew, it's the only thing that matters. You understand? Nothing else matters."

He pressed the oxygen mask to his face again and took a long inhale, though his eyes—as green as mine—wouldn't let me go.

"Mattia." Nonna entered the room carrying another tray of coffee and more food. Always food. She asked him in Italian if he needed anything.

"Sit down, cara," her husband replied.

She cocked her head, but obediently moved to his other side.

"Ain't she beautiful?"

Nonno raised a gnarled hand and touched his wife's chin. And Nonna, who never, ever cried, had to look away before the sheen in her eyes turned to something more telling.

"You find a good woman, Matthew, and you take pride in her too."

I couldn't look away. I couldn't stop watching the look on my grandmother's face as she accepted her husband's caress.

"Okay," I managed at the end. "I will."

Nonno nodded while his hand dropped to his wife's lap. She captured it between her own and didn't let it go.

His eyes, though, found mine.

"Good," he said. "Then after I'm gone, I'll still be here. I will still know. So, you make me proud, Matthew. You promise."

I stared at their entwined fingers like they had the secrets of the universe trapped between their palms. And who knows? Maybe they did.

"Okay, Nonno," I said. "I promise."

———

"WE WILL SEND the clothes to a shelter," *Nonna* was saying as she puttered around her vanity. "If you want something, take it, okay? Before you go home. But I saved something else for you."

She turned, holding a small charm. A silver medallion, bearing the likeness of San Gennaro, the patron saint of Naples. I recognized it for another reason, though. *Nonno* used to wear it on a chain under his shirt. He said it made him feel closer to his family and reminded him of why he came here to do better for them too.

"He would have wanted you to have it," *Nonna* said. "I found it in the back and I realized he meant for you to take it with you when you went to the war."

"To Iraq?" A lump formed in my throat as she closed her age-spotted hands over mine.

"You wear it," she said. "The chain broke, but you can find another."

I accepted the charm and was about to put it in my pocket, but on a whim, tugged out the necklace already bearing the white gold crucifix I'd had since my confirmation. Quickly, I unclasped the chain and slid on the tiny medallion to join the cross, then refastened it around my neck and tucked it back under the collar of my shirt.

When I was finished, she tapped the side of my face gently. "Are you okay, *cuore mio*?"

"What?" I looked up from fixing my cuffs. "Yeah. Yeah, I'm fine, *Nonna*. Why?"

She raised a thin dyed brow. Yeah, I wasn't fooling anyone.

"It's that girl," she pronounced. "The skinny one who don't eat enough."

I sighed. "Nina eats plenty. She cleaned her plate three times when she was here."

"Is she Italian?"

"No, her family's Dutch, mostly, I think. Maybe Swiss or German too. They've been here a long time."

Nonna shrugged, making it clear with a single gesture how little *that* mattered.

"Her daughter is Italian, though."

Goddammit. Just the thought of the little girl—Olivia—leaning into

Nina's thigh made that lump come back in my throat. Right along with the urge to sprint back to Manhattan to find them both.

At the word "daughter," *Nonna's* eyes sharpened. "She's married too, yes?"

I wilted. Shit. "Yeah, but—"

"Then you leave her alone, Matthew," *Nonna* cut in as she fixed my collar. "Nothing but trouble there. She's gonna break your heart, if she don't already. Look at you. On my couch two nights in a row. Wrinkled and tired and sad and hungry. *Nothing* but trouble, you see? You need a girl that is better for you than that..."

I stared at the floor, feeling very much like I was fourteen again, absorbing my grandmother's tirades when she realized I was cutting school or getting into fights or any number of things a teenage boy with anger issues could do growing up in New York. She would do this for several minutes if I let her.

"*Nonna?*"

Joni appeared in the doorway, dressed in her Sunday finest as well—well, Joni's version of "finest" was up for debate in my opinion, but she seemed to think her shapeless purple dress was pretty damn nice.

She winked at me, clearly sympathetic about the tongue-lashing.

"Mass starts in less than fifteen minutes," she said. "Lea says it's time to go."

I slipped on the shoes that had somehow been shined overnight, and then *Nonna* and I shuttled downstairs to find everyone dressed and ready. A knock at the door sounded, and Frankie and Sofia announced their arrival.

"Come on!" Frankie called from the foyer. "They've already started ringing the bells."

We all filed to the front of the house, checking shoes, coats, hats, and all the other accoutrements needed to walk the five blocks or so to St. Andrew's.

"The living room is back there," Frankie was saying to a strange girl standing next to her near the door as I grabbed my coat off the rack. "Ah, there you are. Annie, *this* is my brother, Mattie. The one I told you about. Mattie, this is Tino's niece, Annie. She's visiting from Naples for the next few months. Just arrived on Wednesday. *Nonna* asked me to bring her since Tino has to open early."

"Annalisa," said the girl with a thick Italian accent.

"But everyone calls her Annie," Sofia chirped from below, as if it wasn't totally clear.

I glanced at my grandmother, who was watching carefully from the stairs, then Lea and Joni, who also didn't look at all surprised to see this girl. I turned back to our impromptu guest. Tino was eighty if he was a day—I sincerely doubted he cared at all whether his niece was shepherded to church on her fifth day in the country.

Oh, the women in my family were good. Really good.

I traded perfunctory kisses on the girl's apple-shaped cheeks. "*Piacere*, sweetheart."

She stepped back with shining eyes. *Okay*, then.

It was blatantly obvious what was going on here. My sisters, aunties, uncles—hell, pretty much everyone in this neighborhood had been angling me together with neighborhood girls since I got back from Iraq. Even Joni was bringing around her college friends, no matter that I was literally *twice* some of their ages.

This one, though, was genuinely pretty. I'd give them that much. A little young, maybe. I'd guess closer to Marie's or Joni's ages. Petite, with deep olive skin, sooty eyes, and shining black hair that curled around her shoulders. Surrounded by the rest of the Zola women, she fit in. Like one of us.

Annie smiled shyly, but in a way that made it very clear she liked what she saw in me too. "Nice to meet you," she said in stumbling English.

I smiled back. "You've been here four days? Your English is pretty good."

Lea glanced between us before her eyes widened. "Peter Francis Scarrone! You take your grubby mitts off your brother before I have your father take you outside!"

Annie and I watched my sister launch across the room with impressive speed considering her condition, then turned back to each other shyly.

"Kids," I said. "Little devils, sometimes. Especially those three."

Annie giggled in that way girls do when a joke isn't particularly funny, but they want you to think it is. Yeah, she definitely liked me, because that joke was lame as shit.

"I wonder," she said, "if they were the same in America like in Italy. But no. I need to see more, I think."

Not as shy as I thought, then. She was fishing for an invitation. A sightseeing tour around the city. An opportunity to talk that might lead to something...more...down the road.

I swallowed while every other eye in the room landed on me, waiting for my response. There shouldn't have been a problem. After all, I was available, wasn't I? *Move on, move on.* My conscience chimed at me like *Nonna's* grandfather clock. God knew I'd tried. And now I needed to try even harder.

Find a nice girl, Father Deflorio had told me just yesterday when I left the confessional. *Find a good woman, Nonno* had said before he died.

But the question was always the same. How would I treat a good woman when I knew, deep down, I wasn't a good man?

A good man wouldn't have these kinds of thoughts about a married woman.

Lust is a deadly sin. Deep down, maybe mine would be the death of me.

"Matthew?"

I turned to *Nonna,* who was tapping her watch. Frankie and Joni were still watching too.

God bless the Zola women. Harsh saviors, all of them. Maybe my sins would kill me, but they were much stronger. They'd force me to find redemption in the end.

Or so I hoped.

I held out my elbow to Annie. "Shall we, honey?"

Annie blushed. But she took my arm and allowed me to walk her to church, like I really was the gentleman everyone in that house wanted me to be. Not the dirty, no-good sinner I knew I was in my heart. It wasn't the best step in the world, but it wasn't the worst. After all, maybe the thing to do wasn't to wait for change. Maybe the best thing to do was fake it until I actually did.

CHAPTER TWENTY-TWO

"Look, man, I get it. I really do. I grew up in Marcy, used to smoke myself. I *know* what that shit does to your brain. Add pussy to that equation, it's enough to make a man crazy, ain't it?"

Derek sat in the plastic chair, telling lie after comfortable lie to Roscoe Jackson, who was currently quaking in his own very *un*comfortable seat. It was three o'clock on a Tuesday afternoon, and we had been here for nearly four hours. The raid on Roscoe's apartment had taken place over the weekend while I pretended to be a nice guy with my family. Monday's news came as a welcome surprise. Roscoe was held for a full twenty-four hours before we got an extension to ninety-six—just to freak him out. Then Derek and Cliff could get to work.

On the other side of the table sat Clifford Snow, Derek's second detective, who was playing the "bad cop" in a textbook Reid interrogation. They were halfway through the nine steps, and as predicted, Roscoe Jackson was cracking like a nut.

Derek set his hand sympathetically on Roscoe's skinny shoulder. The man was jonesing bad. The raid had gone better than we thought, and Derek was already suffering from intense withdrawals. The idiot had close to 500 grams of crack under his bed, all neatly bagged and ready for sale, but he was obviously pinching off the top for himself. A lot. A simple charge of narcotic use neatly turned into possession with intent to distribute—a felony that could land old Roscoe behind bars for one to nine.

"I got two words for you, motherfucker," said Cliff. "Mandatory. Minimums. We got the bags. And we know about the girls. How many of them know *your* name, huh? How many people you been talkin' to? All it takes is one asshole with the gavel, fuckface, and you'll end up at Rikers with so much dick up your ass, you'll be screaming for your mama by the end of your first *day!*"

He slammed his palm on the table, and then popped his hand into Roscoe's sternum hard enough to shove the guy against the wall. Roscoe's chair hit the brick with a bang, and he whimpered.

"Cliff needs to dial it back," I murmured into a headset connected to the piece in Derek's ear. "The courts are getting even more particular about confessions under duress. Be his friend, King. He already likes your pretty face."

Behind Roscoe's shaky form, I received a hooded look from Derek through the mirrors that hid my presence from the rest of the interrogation room. His meaning was clear: *let me do my fuckin' job, Zola.* And normally I would let him. Derek and Cliff were the best the NYPD had. But we had one shot. The gala was in two weeks. We needed that solid grounds for an indictment, or everything was off the table.

At this point, Roscoe had copped to just about everything we had. The girls. The safe house. But we were missing one thing.

"I don't know," he moaned into his hands, swaying back and forth like he was dancing to a song in his head. "I swear, I don't know. They never told me their names, right? They would just, like, show up. Check over the girls. Tell me to keep 'em locked up until it was time. Keep 'em drugged. Easy, since I got a piece too, right?"

I checked the audio recording for the eleventh time, making sure that it was still on. Roscoe's eyes flew to the left while he spoke—a clear indication, based on the rest of the evening, that he was hiding something.

"He's lying," I said. "He knows. Press him, Derek. He likes you."

"Your sister lives on Crescent, don't she?" Derek set his hand on Roscoe's shoulder again and rubbed compassionately. The guy seemed to find it soothing, but also unnerving.

Roscoe peeked through his fingers. "Wh-what?"

"Over by the park, right? Didn't she move—"

"Yo, man! Don't you touch my s-sister!"

"You better show Detective Kingston some fuckin' respect if you know what's good for you!" Cliff put in with another perfunctory "bad cop" entry.

Roscoe was effectively shook—both by the sudden mention of his sister as well as the continued seesaw of treatment he continued to receive.

"Hey, hey, hey, no need for that, Detective Snow," Derek said. He patted Roscoe's arm. "Honestly, Roscoe, we just need your help. As much with your sister as anyone else."

"What? What d'you mean?"

Derek clicked his tongue with sympathy. "Aw, man, you didn't hear? She's late on her payments to K-Money. Again. Fourth time, apparently."

It was one of many lies we'd told, knowing Roscoe wouldn't know the difference. Derek's reconnaissance had revealed that Roscoe did in fact have a sister who used to live at Cypress Hills, one of the worst housing projects in the city, barely a stone's throw from The Hole. She shacked up for a time with a leader of the Crew, a subset of Crips that functioned as a drug pipeline through the projects of East New York— and likely trafficked other things too. Cast aside, the girl was now prostituting herself about four blocks away to pay for her own addiction.

"I hear too, that K has other ways of getting his money back, right?" Derek cast a meaningful look at Cliff. "How many of the girls are from Cypress, Detective Snow?"

"Seven." Cliff was stone-faced compared to Derek's softer demeanor.

Roscoe began to shake. "What—I?"

"Did you know they were from Cypress, Roscoe?" Derek asked. "Damn, I see you probably did, huh? Shit, man. Intent to distribute *and* trafficking. That's rough. That's at least fifteen or twenty. Maybe life if the judge is a woman."

Roscoe's shaking turned into rocking.

I stepped closer to the window. "Break, goddammit, break."

Derek's eyes flashed at me through the mirror, a clear signal to shut the fuck up.

"All right!" Roscoe shouted finally. "What do you...what do you need?"

"Just a couple of names," Derek crooned. "We need to know who's taking the girls. We need to know who showed up in that big black Escalade, Roscoe. Who's the man in charge?"

"I...I..." Roscoe rocked forward, his face plastered in his hands. When he looked up, his bloodshot eyes bugged out. "And you'll help her? You'll help my sister?"

"We'll help her get what she needs," Derek said smoothly, easily stepping around any commitments. It was one of the worst things about this job. Everyone wanted a favor just for telling the damn truth. But the fact was, Derek's sister was probably no closer to salvation than her brother. I knew the types. They'd both be dead or locked up within a year.

"All *right*," Roscoe said. "All right, I—you promise you won't tell him it was me?"

"No one is going to say who you are," Derek replied, while I stood poised with pen to legal pad. "Who owns the safe house, Roscoe?"

"I—it's a man. Tall, older. Curly, kind of gray hair. Greenish eyes, and a nose like a beak. He only came by the one time to check on things, months ago. Locks, things like that. His name was—shit, man, I don't remember, it was something like Cannon. Chaplin. Uh..."

Derek leaned closer. "Car—"

"Don't," I cut him off. "He needs to say it himself. Come on, Derek, you know better than to feed him a name."

Derek looked mildly disgusted with himself as he straightened. Cliff's face didn't move, but I could tell he was thinking the same thing.

"Carson!" Roscoe pronounced with something weirdly akin to victory. "Yeah, that's it. John Carson! That Jude motherfucker said it, and he snapped at him. But he called him another name too. Titan." He started muttering. "K-Money, he was driving that same truck, a Titan."

"And *that's* how it's done!" I whirled around in victory to face the precinct's chief, who was nodding in approval from the back of the room. "That's it! Mother*fucker*, you got it! Did you hear that? Hook, line, and fuckin' sinker!"

Elation flooded through me. It wasn't a conviction. It wasn't even close to everything we needed to lock up these assholes and throw away the key.

But it was a very, *very* big step.

"Can you describe Jude and Carson for us, Roscoe?" Derek was asking, though I could see him doing his best to hold back his own thrill of victory along with mine.

"Get him to sign," I said as Roscoe continued to talk, pouring forth more details like a faucet that had just been turned on while Cliff scribbled furiously on another notepad. "I'll be back tomorrow morning for the full confession before I head to City Hall. Grand jury, here we come."

Derek's face didn't move while he listened, but his head nodded imperceptibly. Things were on their way. Fuckin' finally.

"Great job, buddy," I told him as I picked my jacket off the chair. I pulled out my earpiece and set it on the desk. I had some news to deliver to two people who really needed to hear it.

CHAPTER TWENTY-THREE

"Damn," I remarked after draining the rest of my wine. "That was really good, Jane. Best way to cap off the day."

Jane smiled smugly as she walked the empty bottle of Margaux to the kitchen. "It's my secret revenge when Eric's late. Drink the rest of his favorite wine."

"Doesn't he usually prefer vodka?"

For no reason that I could see, Jane's cheeks pinked at the word "vodka." "He does," she said carefully. "But usually we have wine with dinner."

I had schlepped to the Upper West Side to give Jane and Eric the latest news about the case (well, so far as I was able). But since Eric was late on his way back from work, Jane and I were left to shoot the shit.

"So," I said, trying for nonchalant but failing miserably. "How's Nina?"

Jane's sharp eyes darted toward me as she popped open another bottle in the kitchen. "Good, I think. To be honest, we don't see her that much. She tends to keep to herself, and she stepped off the committee after I joined. But you already knew that, my fine Italian friend."

I studied the sheepskin rug. "I was just curious."

Jane returned and refilled my glass. "Have a bit of a crush, do we?"

I frowned. I should have kept my mouth shut, but I couldn't help it. "We're just friends. Or friendly. Or, I don't know, were."

Was that true? Not anymore. I had promised her I'd stay away, and so far, I'd kept my word. I hadn't texted. Hadn't shown up on her street. Well, at least not anywhere she could see me.

"I'm surprised the two of you haven't seen each other at more 'fundraisers.'"

I frowned. "Come again?"

Jane rolled her eyes. "Didn't you meet at one?"

"Oh. Right." I sighed. There wasn't really much that got past Jane. I shouldn't have been surprised. Like me, she was trained to zero in on bullshit. Before moving to New York for Eric and getting into fashion design, Jane was an assistant prosecutor in Chicago. From what I knew, she was pretty good at her old job. To the point that, not long ago, I'd offered her a job with me.

"Zola."

I looked up. "What?"

I hated the pity shining through Jane's thick cat-eye lenses. I'd seen that look before. First, when I got back from Iraq and my girlfriend was shacked up with another guy. Then all Sunday afternoon, while my sisters watched me interact awkwardly with Tino's niece.

I fuckin' hated it.

"Look, I get it," Jane said as she sank onto the couch. "Eric said you took her to the opera a few weeks ago. Which was a nice…favor. But let's be honest, the two of you practically fried our apartment with electricity when you ran into each other."

I swallowed about half my glass of wine. I wasn't saying anything.

"But, Zola…you do remember she's married, right?"

I snorted. Did I *remember* Nina was married? Did I remember the flash of the baseball-sized diamond on her finger? Or the scent of her neck when she was panting with desire?

The taste of her mouth, desperate on the street.

Yeah. I remembered Nina de Vries was married. Every. Mother. Fucking. Day.

"You don't need to worry," I replied. "The opera was just a favor, like you said, and I haven't seen her since. I was just wondering because of the case, tying up loose ends before the arrest. We really can't chance any liabilities. You know how it goes."

Jane examined me a bit more before taking a sip of her wine. "Did you know that Nina stayed with me? Before I went to Korea?"

I frowned. "No, I didn't."

Jane shrugged. "She had some kind of fight with Calvin. This was in January, right after New Year's. She wouldn't talk about it, but I think it had something to do with Eric's arrest. Anyway, yeah, she and Olivia stayed here until Liv went back to school. And you know, Livy didn't say a word about her father. He never came to see her once."

The idea made my blood boil. God, I *hated* that guy. Anyone who would neglect that little girl that way...not to mention her one-in-a-billion mother...*fuck.*

"Look, she married him." I should have won an Oscar for my even tone by itself. "I'm sure it was just because they were fighting or whatever. He's probably a good guy."

"Right. Just like I'm *probably* going to turn into Mother Theresa," Jane said.

I raised a brow. "You don't like him either?"

She wrinkled her nose. "I don't know. Calvin's always rubbed me the wrong way. I still don't understand why he and Nina got married in the first place. They don't seem very happy."

"What do you mean?"

She arched a brow while she swirled her wine. "The day before I went to Korea, she sent Olivia back to school. And then she came back here, locked herself in the guest room, and didn't come out for several hours. I swear I heard something like crying in there, but she's very quiet. Discreet."

I swallowed. Yeah, if I knew Nina, she wouldn't have let anyone see her break down. I could easily imagine it too. I had a feeling she cried every time she had to send her daughter away.

Nina toyed with the stem of her empty wineglass, then looked back at me with eyes that, I finally noticed, were slightly pink around the lash line. At some point today, Nina had been crying. Hard.

A pang shot through my chest, and without even thinking twice about it, I wanted to punch whoever had done it in the face. I wanted to find the bastard and wring his fuckin' neck. Shove him to his knees and make him beg for her forgiveness before I taught him some proper respect.

Whoa. That was zero to sixty in about two seconds. I swallowed hard, and this time, I did tug at my collar. I needed to calm the fuck down. Maybe I needed to walk away altogether.

"Matthew," Nina said. "I would—I would like to sit with you, I think. But I just don't have patience for any more small talk tonight. My reserve is simply gone, and I feel I would be very bad company. For anyone."

I set my hand on hers, and we both started like we had been shocked. To be honest, I'm not a hundred percent sure we weren't. A current of something flew through my fingers when they touched Nina's cool skin. Something addictive. Something dangerous.

"Nina," I said slowly. "We can just sit here if you want. I don't mind, really. I was having that kind of night myself."

Her face softened. "Were you?" she wondered softly, almost to herself.

I nodded. "Something just wasn't right."

"No," Nina agreed, her voice quavering. "It wasn't."

———

"Matthew?"

I blinked, shaken out of my memory. Yet another from that first night together. Even then, I'd known that something was terribly wrong, hadn't I?

"Sorry," I said. "You were saying?"

"Well, just when I was about to ask if she was okay, she went out. And she didn't come back the entire night." Jane twisted her bright red mouth around. "I happen to know she did not go home to Calvin that night either. I don't know where she ended up. But I have wondered if you do."

I stared at my glass, studying the way the wine dribbled down the sides of the bowl as I tipped it back and forth. Ironic, really. The day I finished one interrogation, I faced another from the people I was trying to help.

"Why are you telling me this?" I wasn't going to say a fuckin' word, of course, as much to protect Nina as myself. Better to turn it back on Jane.

"Sometimes I wonder if I'm a glutton for chaos." Jane tapped her nail on the rim of her glass. The sound called like a bell. "Honestly? I'm not sure. Nina wouldn't like it."

I didn't have to ask why. Nina was, if anything, an intensely private person. For reasons I was only starting to understand.

"Now, I've only been in this family for a few months," Jane continued. "But one thing I've learned is that things are never as they seem. There's a strong sense of martyrdom in the de Vries DNA. Considering how entitled this family is to the best things in life, Nina seems awfully willing to...settle. And I just think it's strange, that's all."

Calvin's melted-cheese face appeared in my head. It was everything I could do not to scowl like he was there in front of me.

Discretion. I needed to remain discreet. Just like the woman we were talking about. For her sake alone.

"What does Eric say?" I wondered. "About her and Calvin?"

Fuck. I really couldn't help myself, could I?

Jane shrugged. "That we should stay out of it. But he thinks they're a little weird, yeah. Who wouldn't?" She sipped her wine, then set the glass on the coffee table. "Look, there are plenty of women in this weird little world who marry assholes for their bank accounts. But the rich women? It's either gold-digging fuckboys who look good by the pool, or else even older, richer men." She shrugged. "But who's richer than the de Vrieses, huh? Unless Nina walked down the aisle with Bill Gates circa *now*, I really can't imagine what the hell was in it for her with the moldy meatball she ended up with."

I almost spit out my wine at the *way* too apt description. "Jesus, Jane. That's quite an image."

She smiled. "Thanks. It's a special talent."

Before I could offer one of my own, the front door opened, and Eric strode in, looking like he was shaking the weight of the world off his designer-clad shoulders.

"Oh, hey," he said, frowning slightly at the way I'd made myself at home next to their fire with his favorite *vino*. "You're here."

"Just checking in," I said. "We made some progress today. You can blame the wine pilfering on your wife."

"Guilty!" Jane cheered.

Eric nodded. "Just as well. Look who I found loitering on the stairs."

"I wasn't *loitering*, Eric," chided a familiar voice that sucked every bit of hard-won ease out of my bones.

Nina followed her cousin into the apartment, shucking a sleek white coat in the process, which she hung on the rack by the door.

"Jane, I was in the neighborhood, so I thought maybe we could do a fitting now for the gala. I know we're two weeks off, but does that wor—"

Nina froze. So did I. And so did Jane, with a curiously satisfied smile.

Every ache I'd managed to tamp down since I'd last seen Nina sprang up like I'd been bounced off a trampoline. She looked like spring in a form-fitting dress the color of a robin's egg, vibrant enough that it made her gray eyes seem almost blue across the room. Her hair, shiny and gold, was pinned on the side like a 1940s film siren, revealing the slash of red on her lips I'd dreamed about multiple times since that night at the opera.

"Hello, Matthew," she said softly.

I could barely raise my hand. "Nina."

"God, I am *loving* that color on you," Jane said, pointing to Nina's mouth as she got up to get her and Eric some wine. "Where did you get it?"

Nina's hand floated over her lips. Her gaze darted back to me, then back to Jane. "Oh, I—it's just something I picked up at Bergdorf's some time ago."

Because of me? I wanted to ask. But I had a feeling I already knew the answer. The real question was why.

Nina took a seat on the chair opposite me, crossing one long leg over the other, then readjusting again, as if sitting were slightly uncomfortable.

I frowned. "Still taking tumbles in the park?"

Nina's brow crinkled in confusion. "What?"

I gestured at a bruise on her knee.

She immediately yanked the material of her skirt. "No, I dropped a weight on it."

"Your trainer wasn't spotting you?" Eric called from the kitchen.

Nina shook her head. "I was playing Wonder Woman while he was in the bathroom. Stupid, really."

Eric shook his head. "You have to be careful."

Jane didn't say anything as she returned, just narrowed her eyes at the now-covered spot. I was pretty sure I was looking at it the same way.

"Thank you. I will try."

Nina accepted a glass of wine from Eric who then took a seat on the couch next to Jane.

"Well, I guess it's good you're here. Zola has news," Jane said. "Why don't you and Eric talk while Nina and I do the fitting? Nina, they sent the dress here last week. It's in my studio."

"You sure?" Eric wondered, clearly not wanting his wife to leave.

But she nodded her head. I had a feeling Jane didn't actually want to be involved with all things John Carson. While Eric nursed enough of a grudge for both of them, she tended to check out of these updates more and more.

"We'll be back in a few. You can catch me up later." After delivering Eric a brief kiss, she disappeared into another room with Nina in tow.

I watched them go until the door closed. I legitimately wondered if there would ever be a time when Nina's legs didn't hypnotize me into a stupor.

"So," Eric said, jerking me out of my gaze. "News?"

I cleared my throat. "So. Yeah. Ah, I can't go into the details, but I thought you'd like to know we got corroboration. Substantial corroboration. Enough to move forward with our plans."

Without giving away too much of what Roscoe had revealed, I proceeded to outline the basics of what had happened. Eric was a former lawyer himself—he understood the grand jury process enough to appreciate the effort it took to get everything to this stage, even if I didn't explicitly say that was happening.

"My detective—you'll meet him at the museum—is organizing the whole thing with a special NYPD unit," I finished. "It's still pretty hush-hush, so I don't think Carson will find out."

Again, I had my doubts about that, but Eric looked like he needed to hear it.

"Well, there's some good news, at least," Jane said, though her voice didn't sound like it.

Eric and I both turned to where she and Nina stood. Jane's face, normally so expressive, was a blank slate at the prospect of seeing her biological father again. I couldn't blame her. Last time, the man had drugged and abducted her, killed her unborn child, then left her to die. I wouldn't be too excited about his return either.

"It will be all right," Nina murmured, rubbing her cousin-in-law's shoulder. "Matthew is taking care of everything."

I straightened a bit. I was proud, honestly, that Nina had that kind of faith in me. "Jane, she's right. Nothing's going to happen to you or Eric. You do know that, right?"

"I wish I did," she said bitterly. "But sadly, you don't get kidnapped by Daddy Dearest without developing some pretty fucked-up trust issues."

Well. She had me there.

"The entire museum is going to be surrounded by NYPD," I said. "Plus, if I know Eric, he's already hired a platoon of extra security. You'll be fine."

Jane sniffed. "Eric keeps saying that pride comes before the fall. He sounds like his grandmother, may she rest in peace, but he's probably right."

"He *is* right," I said. "But Jane, you used to do this too. The waiting is the hardest part, but every criminal has their weak spot. Hubris gets them in the end. Carson is no different."

I wished I could have told her more. But there was only so much I could say at this stage of the game. And as much as I had my doubts about its plausibility, this big party was looking more and more like the place we'd have to finish things. For better or for worse. I had a feeling that if John Carson slipped out of our grasp there, we'd lose him for good.

"Anything else?" Eric asked.

I finished my wine and reached for my hat on the coffee table. "No, that's about it. I'll need to stop by the museum later next week for a walk-through with Derek."

"Just let me know when," Jane said. "I'll be there every day. I can show you around."

I nodded. "Sounds good. I have my tux ready." I picked up my hat and put it on. "Thanks for the drinks, guys. I'm off."

"Hot date?" Jane joked.

I glanced at Nina, who was watching me sharply. "Ah, no, actually. I just told my sister I'd babysit so she could have a night out."

Nina's shoulders relaxed visibly.

"You're not taking Annie out?" Jane persisted as she gave me a hug.

And there they went, right back up again.

Jane wasn't kidding about the chaos thing. I had told her a little about Annie earlier when we were chatting, a fact I now regretted. A lot.

"No, not tonight. She's a nice girl, though," I said, hoping Nina would think I was only talking about a casual acquaintance.

No such luck.

"His family set him up with this sweet Italian girl," Jane informed Nina in a sisterly fashion. "Don't hate me, Zola, but I looked her up on Facebook. She's super cute! Where are you taking her next?"

"Ah, I really haven't decided. Maybe something after Mass this weekend. She wants American food, so we could hit up a diner or something."

"A diner?" Eric scoffed. "*That*'s the best you can do for a date?"

"I don't know. We could go to Bistro Le Park, I guess—it's getting good reviews. But she's not really the type for fancy things." I shrugged, annoyed at the insinuation that I didn't know how to treat a woman. I did. *If it's the right woman*, I thought, looking at Nina.

Jane nudged my shoulder. "You'd be surprised. If she likes you, she'll be up for just about anything. This one drags me to every fancy restaurant under the sun even though I'd be happy with pizza. I may not know the difference between forks, but the company is all that matters."

Eric offered his wife an uncharacteristic smile. "Thanks, pretty girl."

Like a flower, she bloomed.

"The Cloisters," Nina put in abruptly.

The three of us looked over at her, Eric and Jane ruffled out of their impromptu love-fest.

"You should take her to the Cloisters," Nina said, more quietly this time. "If she's homesick, it's the closest thing to Europe she'll find here."

"What are the Cloisters?" asked Jane, who was still somewhat new to the city.

"It's a castle," Eric said.

"Actually, it's more like a monastery," Nina corrected him gently before turning back to Jane. "It's a museum built in the thirties by J.D. Rockefeller."

"Which one?" Eric interrupted.

"Junior. He had parts of four different French abbeys shipped stone by stone and incorporated into the design." When she caught me looking at her curiously, she offered an adorable shrug. "Art history major, remember?"

"Sounds like a rich guy was really bored and needed to spend some of his dough," Jane remarked dryly.

"Perhaps," Nina said. "The art is nice enough—mostly medieval, if you like that sort of thing. The unicorn tapestries are the most famous pieces there, along with J.P. Morgan's donations. But really, you go for the view, the park, and the architecture. It's quite lovely on a spring day." She sighed. "When I was a little girl, I dreamed I'd be married there."

"Why weren't you?" Jane cut in. "It's a church. I'm surprised Celeste wouldn't have been all right with it, if it's such a New York landmark."

Nina stiffened at the mention of her grandmother. Or maybe it was her actual wedding. I stared at my hands, trying and failing to forget the story she had told me about *why* she had married Calvin "dough-faced near-pedophile" Gardner.

"They eloped, right, cous?" Eric offered.

"Really?" Jane's tone was less admiring, more sharp. Clearly she was having as hard a time imagining the two of them in love enough to run away together.

"I was very young," Nina replied. "It needed to happen quickly."

She stared at her hands. It was her tell, I realized. When she wasn't actually revealing the whole truth. Maybe I was the only one who noticed that she didn't use "I" or "we" with that last statement. There was no personalization of that particular desire. Not on her part.

When she looked up, her mask was laced with pain. Maybe even longing.

"Haven't you been?" she wondered.

I clenched my jaw, then carefully unclenched it once I was sure my expression was under control. "Probably," I said. "Most likely on a class field trip or something like that."

"Take her to the Cloisters, Matthew," Nina said. "You won't regret it."

We shared a long look across the living room until Jane's whispered "whoa" to Eric broke the silence.

"Thanks," I said with difficulty. "I'll, um, see you."

"Wait," Nina called.

I stopped. "What's up, doll?" I couldn't help it. It just fuckin' slipped out.

Nina turned to Jane and Eric. "I'll be back on Monday to meet with the designer, Jane. Matthew, I'll walk out with you."

————

AFTER SHE SAID HER GOODBYES, Nina and I shuffled silently down the big stairs of the apartment until finally emerging outside. The sky had darkened into night, but the scent of flowers was spilling over from Central Park. Or maybe that was just her.

"Everything...all right?" I asked.

I couldn't for the life of me figure out why she had suddenly wanted to walk me downstairs. Unless. Unless she was like me. And six days after she swore we couldn't talk, she was equally desperate even to be next to each other. If only for a minute or two.

"Yes," she said slowly as she glanced at the big black Escalade I assumed was waiting for her. "And is everything well with you?"

I nodded. "Sure, sure. Not much new. Work, family, you know, the usu—"

"And your date."

I pulled off my hat and worked it between my hands. "Well. You couldn't expect me to wait around forever, doll."

Nina cringed, like the pet name caused her physical pain. I wanted to wash my mouth out with soap.

"No. I don't suppose I could." Tentatively, she reached out and adjusted my lapel, her fingers lingering along its edge just a few seconds longer than they should. "You look very sharp." Her voice broke slightly toward the end before she offered a crooked smile. "I'm sure she'll fall right in love with you."

I examined her for a moment more. She was holding back, just like I was. Swallowing back her emotions, like she had done her entire life.

You don't have to do that with me, I wanted to tell her. *Say something. Anything.*

And for a moment, I thought she would. I really did think she might ask me not to go. Those magic words would emerge from those rose petal lips, and I'd break the date and trade it in for the one I really wanted.

The one I could never have.

Her hand dropped. "Good night, Matthew. Have a good time with your girl."

I touched the brim of my hat. "Good night, Nina."

She didn't reply, just disappeared into the car. As I watched it drive away, it was everything I could do not to run after her, slap my palm on the window, and beg her to get back out.

The car turned the corner. Even then I couldn't stop staring. I gulped and turned in the direction of the subway. Good fuckin' God. I needed to get a hold of myself.

But I couldn't. Not quite.

Before I dropped into the train entrance on Seventy-Second, I fished my phone out of my pocket and typed a message.

Me: Still friends?

Her reply was nearly instantaneous.

Doll: Even when we don't talk?

I didn't even need to think about it.

Me: Even then, doll. You need me, I'm here.

As the train was whistling down the tunnel, my phone vibrated with her final message.

Doll: Don't forget to call Annie.

I pulled at my collar. I really was an asshole. Here was Nina doing her best, just like I was, to leave me alone. Move on with our lives. Here she was, giving me legitimately good ideas for my next date with another woman. If she asked me for dating advice, I'd probably tell her to push Calvin off the Brooklyn Bridge.

She was too good for me. I should have known that from the start. Well, at least it still made me want to be a better man, even if it was with someone else.

CHAPTER TWENTY-FOUR

I TURNED OFF THE ENGINE OF MY TEN-YEAR-OLD COROLLA AND ROLLED UP
the window. The silence just continued—I hadn't bothered with music
on the drive from the Bronx. But there hadn't been any conversation
either. I just wasn't feeling all that chatty.

The sun was shining. The birds were singing. I was at a beautiful
park with a beautiful girl. And I'd barely said one word to her since
picking her up from Tino's restaurant.

I stared at the steering wheel and sighed. I'd never hear the end of it
if I didn't at least *try* to make an effort with Annie. Once Frankie heard
me invite the girl out to take advantage of the nice spring weather, she
insisted that she and Sofia could make do with the train so I could have
the car.

"Lea and I will pack you a picnic basket at the house!" she promised
gleefully as we shuffled out of Mass.

I had left the basket with *Nonna* and never mentioned its existence to
the pretty young woman next to me. For whatever reason, I wasn't
thinking much beyond a quick walk through the park. *Funny,* I thought,
as the Cloisters tower rose above us. We were going from one church to
another, essentially, on a Sunday. Like I was trying to remind myself of
the need for chastity.

"You ready?" I said as we unbuckled our seat belts.

Annie smiled shyly. Still in her church clothes—a floaty pink thing the color of tulips and practical shoes that did nothing for her legs—she was smitten and not even bothering to hide it. From the second I spotted her with Tino and his wife in the church, I'd caught her looking at me at least five other times through the service. Sneaking peeks when we were mouthing the homily. Brushing shoulders as we filed up to take communion.

She was clearly interested.

The problem?

I distinctly wasn't.

But things could change. They had to.

"Come on, honey."

I got out of the car, then walked around to offer my hand. She took it, and I tried to ignore the awkward feel of her almost *too* small fingers in my palm as she got out of the car.

We took our time through Fort Tryon Park, which, now that I was here, I definitely did recognize. I could see why Frankie had suggested a picnic. There were plenty of benches looking west toward the New Jersey side of the river. With the sun blinking off the path and flowers abloom through the park, it was pretty fuckin' perfect for a bit of romance.

Like a wedding, starring a classic bride with blonde hair and a groom in a tux. Maybe someone with black hair like mine. Maybe he was me.

What the *fuck* was wrong with me? I'd never been too interested in marriage before, and here I was having daydreams about it like some chick? I was pretty sure if I turned around in that daydream, the woman in it wouldn't be the one walking next to me.

I cleared my throat. "So, this probably isn't much compared to what you have back home," I said as Annie and I walked through the museum's outer gates.

She gazed up at the brick walls and medieval tower. "It is very nice."

Diplomatic, this one. That would serve her well around my sisters.

Annie looked back at me with brighter eyes. "But I come for the company."

Not particularly subtle either.

I mustered another smile. "Me too, honey. Come on, let's see what kind of stuff they got in here."

We wandered through the museum half-heartedly. I couldn't have really told you what all we saw. Some nice glass windows that looked exactly like the ones at St. Patrick's and pretty much every other church I'd seen in Europe. A bunch of statues, chalices, some famous unicorn tapestries that I could not have been less interested in. But I looked because it was better than trying to force a conversation.

While Annie was feigning interest in the big gardens in the center of the building, I suddenly had the uncanny sense that I was being watched. You know, when the hairs on the back of your neck stand up? I tried to shake it off, but I couldn't ignore it. You don't do what I do, grow up where I did, and not develop a finely cultivated instinct for when something is up.

But the arches behind us looking out onto the courtyard were totally empty. No one hiding in the shadows. No one was there at all.

I turned quickly to the other side. I could have *sworn* I saw a blonde ponytail disappear into one of the side buildings. But when I peered closer at the people inside, there were only brunettes. A couple of redheads.

I exhaled while we continued on, Annie blissfully unaware of the paranoia that seemed to be taking me over. Is this what happened when I tried to be a decent human being? I turned into a psycho scared of his own fuckin' shadow?

We rounded a corner, and the feeling came back. This time, however, I turned to see a very *real* familiar face. Only it wasn't the one I had initially imagined.

"Nico," I called out, raising my hand. "Yo! It's Mattie!" I shouldn't have been this glad to see a distant cousin in the middle of a date, but I was. I really was.

Nico turned just before he reentered the museum, but kept his arm securely around the woman next to him, whom I recognized as his wife, Layla. They were an odd pair that somehow fit—he looked like every other guy from the block with a Yankees hat and an arm full of tattoos, while his wife was a more refined type from a much wealthier family on the West Coast. I didn't know her too well, but their story—particularly the parts about how she had helped keep his mother, a Cuban refugee, in the country—was something of legend on my mother's side of the family.

As I watched them holding tight to each other's hands after so many years together, I was riddled with jealousy. These two were the perfect example of love at its finest. How it was never easy. How it was some-times the hardest fuckin' thing in the world. But if you love someone, you never give up on them. Real love means giving everything you are. And if you're lucky, you get it back.

Nico's normally stern face broke into a grin when he caught sight of me and Annie, and he immediately towed Layla across the entire court-yard to greet us.

"Yo, what's good, man? How you been?" Nico reached his free hand around my neck for a quick slap on the back, then backed off so I could trade kisses with Layla.

"Good to see you," she said sweetly. "It's been a while. What, three? Four years?"

"I know," I said somewhat guiltily. "Sorry, I've been stuck in Brook-lyn, working on the house. I bought a place in Red Hook a while back, and Frankie and her daughter are living with me right now."

It wasn't a lie, despite the fact that I went up to the Bronx nearly every weekend, and Kate's shop was maybe ten blocks from Nico and Layla's place in Riverdale. My issues with my mother's side of the family had nothing to do with them.

You see what your grudge is costing you? I could practically see Lea shaking her finger at me.

"Did I hear you guys had another?" I asked. "What does that make, three now?"

Nico nodded. "Yeah. Rafael's our lucky number three." He gazed at Layla, not even bothering to hide his admiration. "This one's a warrior, lemme tell you."

Layla blushed, a bright pink that reminded me of another woman whose skin reflected her emotions.

She always was a pretty little thing, short and solid like a lot of girls from the neighborhood, but with a pair of blazing blue eyes that glowed whenever she looked at her husband.

"Well, you don't look like you just had a kid, sweetheart," I told her honestly. "Nico's a lucky man."

"Hey, hey, easy," Nico joked.

I rolled my eyes. I forgot how possessive this guy was. Well, I couldn't blame him. If I ever looked at a woman the way Nico Soltero looked at his wife, I'd probably never let her out of my sight.

I see the way you're looking at her.

This time it was Jamie's voice reminding me of the truth. I shook his away too.

Layla shoved Nico playfully, then reached a hand toward Annie. "Hi, I'm Layla."

"Sorry," I said while the girls exchanged kisses. "Shit. Guys, this is Annalisa, a family friend from Naples. Annie, this is Nico, my...what, second? Third cousin? Once or twice removed?"

Nico shrugged his big shoulders and pulled on the brim of his Yankees cap. "Who the fuck knows, man? Something. Cousins is enough, right?"

I chuckled. That was how it went sometimes. Big, convoluted families full of aunties and uncles, *zios* and *tías* and *nonnas* and *abuelas*. It was completely possible that Nico and I weren't actually related, but since we saw each other growing up at these family events, we were introduced as cousins, and that was that.

I hadn't been to one of those things in years. And for the first time, it occurred to me that maybe Lea was right. Maybe I was missing out on a bit more than a relationship with my delinquent mother.

"Who the fuck knows?" I agreed. "And who cares? What's going on, man? What else is new?"

"Not much, not much. Layla's an immigration lawyer now at the Children's Advocacy Clinic. I'm at the firehouse in Long Island City. Same old, really."

"Stop being so modest," Layla chided. "He just got promoted to chief!"

"Battalion chief, sweetie," Nico corrected her gently, but his pleasure at her obvious pride was pretty obvious. He shrugged. "It's no big deal."

"Stop it," Layla said again with a glowing face. "I'm so freaking proud of you, I can't stand it."

"Well, it's not exactly having our kids *and* helping other kids find their families again, like you," Nico argued back.

Annie and I watched a bit awkwardly as the two of them bickered over who was prouder of the other.

"Sounds like you're doing good," I said. "Glad to hear it. Time flies. It's crazy."

"Man, don't get me started. Forty-two. I can't fuckin' believe it." He chuckled. "We actually just celebrated our thirteenth anniversary. This is the first we could get some time away from the baby, so we came here." He gestured around the courtyard before his gaze landed on Layla again. "It's one of our spots, right, baby?"

"Right," she murmured.

Nico rubbed his nose to hers before he gave her a kiss just a *little* too familiar for polite company. Maybe for some guys, being that affectionate with their woman would be embarrassing, but in my family, it wasn't that unusual. I grew up with grandparents who were unflinching in their devotion. I wasn't scared of a kiss or two.

Annie inched closer, and her hand sought out mine. Looking for a mirrored kiss. A sweet growl in the ear. A promise of something better, later.

And if it had been six months ago, I probably would have given her what she wanted. I had a whole bag of tricks, little gestures just like the one in front of me that I used to rotate with woman after woman. Usually the types looking for a quick escape or someone to remind them they were more than just mothers or wives.

But Annie wasn't one of those women. And more importantly, I was starting to realize that I wasn't that guy either. Or at least, I didn't want to be.

I didn't want to lie to her. I didn't want to lie to anyone anymore.

So instead of wrapping an arm around her waist and calling her "baby" like she wanted, I offered a brief smile and turned back to Layla and Nico, who started chattering about other family news. He continued to name drop people I hadn't seen in years. Aunties and uncles and random cousins from my mother's side of the family—people I'd all but cut off after she left us.

"Saw your mom a couple of weeks ago," Nico was saying. "*Tía* Alba had another get together. Your sister was there with her kids too."

"Yeah, Lea told me." I didn't mean to be short, but I didn't know what else to say.

Nico clearly noticed. "Sorry, man. I don't mean to overstep."

"No, it's fine. But you know, we don't really get along, her and me."

Nico nodded. "Yeah. Yeah, I know how that goes."

We looked at each other with the silent acknowledgement shared between two people who maybe came from something a little darker than the norm. For a second, Layla looked like she wanted to cry. Annie just blinked, clearly sensing some kind of subtext, but not really comprehending any of it.

"So, anyway," I broke the awkward silence. "It was good to see you, man. We should get a beer or something. Or have you guys over to the house. You and your kids are welcome any time."

Nico returned my handshake. "Yeah, man. That sounds good." He offered Annie another brief kiss on the cheek while I did the same with Layla. "Nice to meet you, Annalisa. Tell this asshole not to steal my favorite place next time, all right?"

Annie's smile was shy as it darted between us. "Um, okay. Yes."

Nico and Layla disappeared into another part of the museum. I watched them for a bit more before I realized that Annie was watching me.

"You, um, ready to go?" I asked, for want of anything better to say. The way she was looking at me was unnerving. Like a puppy begging to be pet. "I actually have a lot of work to do this evening. I need to get you home."

With a bit of regret, she nodded. "Okay."

We walked back the way we came, letting the crunch of our feet on the gravel fill the silence.

Say something, I told myself. *Anything. Don't be an asshole, you fuckin' asshole.*

"What do you think, honey?" I asked suddenly. "Should we go out again?"

What in the fuck? Did I really just ask her that?

Annie shrugged, a lot less enthusiastic than she had been an hour ago. She wasn't stupid, this girl. Naive, maybe. But not dumb. And she deserved better than what I was giving her.

So I stopped, tugging on her hand. She turned, looking a bit more hopeful.

I slipped a hand around her chin and tipped it up, examining her for a moment. I didn't know what I was waiting for. A sign? A lightning bolt? Here I was, with a girl as beautiful as one of the flowers in the gardens outside, ready and willing for me to pluck if I wanted.

"All right," I said, almost more to myself than to her. "How about next week? We'll get dinner. And I won't work after, I promise."

I reached out and brushed a bit of hair from her face. She had nice hair. A shiny, dark brown that curled slightly around her temples. Her face tipped up like she wanted to kiss me. Her lips were thin, but they still looked soft. It might have been nice.

But instead, I dropped her hand and stepped back. "Tuesday?"

Her eyes brightened. "Tuesday. Okay." Then she sighed contentedly. "You are very nice."

Nice? *Nice?*

"You think so?" I felt like a complete fraud. This girl had no idea how completely *not* nice I really was.

"Not like the other boys I know at home," she said. "All whistles and shouts and hands up your skirt."

An opera box. A red skirt. My fingers. Her thigh.

I shook my head again, trying to ignore the want that lanced through me at the memory. No, I needed to stay here. Now. *This* girl. *This* moment.

Tentatively, Annie reached out to touch my shirt. I was still in my Sunday clothes, just like her. Another three-piece suit, light gray, appropriate for spring.

"You are...how do you say...a gentleman, yes?"

She pulled lightly at my tie until it was completely out of my vest. Then she gave it a little tug. And I couldn't lie—it was like a direct line to my dick.

For a moment, I considered correcting her. I thought about shoving her against the brick wall and showing her just how far from a gentleman I really was. I thought about closing my eyes and putting a hand over her mouth, pretending that her scent of gardenias was actually roses and the hair running between my fingers wasn't brown, but blonde.

I could teach this sweet, innocent little girl what a bastard I really was. Hell, maybe she'd even like it. I'd *definitely* like it. And maybe, if we were lucky, we'd like it a few more times, tucked into my bed in Brooklyn or maybe whatever spare room she had above Tino's restaurant.

But then it would be the same as ever. And Annie wasn't one of these unscrupulous bitches dripping in diamonds. She'd wake up worried about the sins she'd committed, whether she'd given up too much of herself too early for a man all too eager to take it. I'd wake up wanting to take a fucking whip to my back.

That's the problem with living a lie. Whether it's a lie to be bad or a lie to be good, it's a lie either way. And it can cost you your soul.

So instead of pulling Annie into one of the shadowed corners of the rebuilt abbey, I gently untangled my tie from her fingers and tucked it back into place.

"Come on, honey," I said as I tucked her hand into my elbow and turned us back toward the car. "Time to get you home."

Annie smiled and walked as if nothing was wrong.

Be good, I thought to myself with every crunch of my feet on the gravel. *You can be good.*

Lies, lies, lies.

If the truth costs your soul, but the lie ruins it anyway, which is the greater price?

I didn't have an answer. But I knew which hurt more.

Women like Annie wanted a certain kind of man. Maybe it was time to make him real.

Well, at least I could try.

CHAPTER TWENTY-FIVE

I DID TRY. I TRIED TUESDAY NIGHT, OVER DINNER AT TINO'S RESTAURANT while half the neighborhood watched. I ordered a *primo* and a single glass of wine and was on my way back to Brooklyn by nine. Lea called me about an hour later wondering why the hell I was so rude.

So, I called Annie again, who asked to see more of the "sights" in New York. On Thursday, after work, we at the Empire State Building to watch the sunset. But instead of kissing her like every other decent man was doing with his date, I said it was too windy and stayed in the shelter until she tired of wandering the deck alone.

She was nice. Too nice. And definitely too patient as she told me bits and pieces about herself that, six months ago, I might have found interesting. She grew up in a house outside of Naples, the only daughter of a mid-level banker and a church-going housewife. She had the idea of being a chef, but her family felt there were more opportunities here if she worked with Tino and went to culinary school. She liked reading Nicholas Sparks (translated into Italian), doing macramé projects, and watching reality talent shows in her spare time.

In other words, Annie was the definition of a good girl. And considering how relaxed she seemed by the fact that I had barely given her a closed-mouth peck over four dates, I was pretty sure she was a virgin too.

And I didn't care. Not one fucking bit.

"How about Chinese?" she suggested.

This time I was holding her hand. My palm was sweaty, but she hadn't wanted to let go since getting into the elevator for the long ride down from the roof. And I felt so bad about my neglect, I let her.

The back of my neck prickled as we walked out to Fifth Avenue. It had been happening all day—while I ran out for a falafel for lunch, and then later when I met up with Annie in this very spot.

"What's that, honey?" I asked as I looked around.

Nothing. Just the normal assortment of tourists and New Yorkers milling in front of one of the city's most famous buildings. A smattering of food and coffee carts packing up for the night, plus the standard hubbub of traffic racing down Fifth Avenue and across Thirty-Fourth Street.

"I said, would you like to eat Chinese food for dinner?"

I raised a brow. This girl loved her Asian foods, according to my sisters. Apparently you couldn't get good dumplings in Naples.

"You know, I'm kind of Chinese'd out, honey," I lied for no good fucking reason. "I had it last night." I didn't. I just didn't want to eat dinner. "Once a week is sort of my limit for that much MSG."

"What is MSG?" Annie wondered.

I shook my head. It was like this a lot with her—constantly explaining what this word and that meant. Her English was generally pretty good—better than my Italian, for sure—but her vocabulary was limited.

"Too much salt," I clarified.

Annie wilted. I smacked myself mentally.

"How about French? There's a decent spot in Park Slope, but it's in Brooklyn. You game?"

"I like French," she agreed. "And I like you. Brooklyn, I will see."

See? Sweet. And pure. And maybe a little bit nauseating.

Asshole. I was such a fuckin' asshole.

I forced a smile. "Thanks, honey. Let's, uh, eat."

———

FORTY MINUTES LATER, we were seated near the back of Bistro Le Park, a new French-American joint in Park Slope that my boss raved about. It was just past five o'clock, and I didn't think I'd eaten dinner this early since I was maybe...okay, since ever. Annie probably hadn't either. The one time I visited Naples, I didn't see a single restaurant that opened before eight for dinner.

Each of us took our sweet time looking at the menu, possibly to avoid talking to each other. I was running out of things to say. I think she was too.

I rubbed the back of my neck. That prickly feeling again. Maybe it was just the universe telling me this was the wrong thing to be doing. Whatever it was, I was getting sick of it.

"Who is that?"

I looked up from my menu. "Huh?"

Annie pointed over my shoulder toward the entrance. "A woman, on the street. She passed maybe five times. To look at the menu. But the last time, I think she is looking at me. There she is again!"

I turned, and that's when I saw a pair of familiar gray eyes peering through the gap between the menus taped to the window, the top of a head of sleek gold hair peeking over the top. It was twilight, and I could barely make out the rest of her through the reflection on the window. It didn't matter, though. I would have known that shape anywhere.

"What the..."

The eyes widened when they found me looking, and immediately disappeared.

"You know her?"

"Unfortunately, I do," I said as I pushed back my chair. "She's—she's involved with a case I'm working on. Excuse me, honey. Order the *coq au vin* for me, will you?"

I tossed my napkin on the table and made my way out to the street. It wasn't until the oak door swung shut behind me that I located a familiar leggy figure skittering down the sidewalk as quickly as her three-inch heels would carry her.

"Nina!" I called.

She stopped, then started walking again. This time faster.

"Oh, for fuck's sake. Nina!" I began jogging. "Wait up!"

She did actually stop at the curb, though I had a feeling it was more to protect her shoes than because I asked her. Or maybe she just realized there was no point. When she turned, her face looked broken. Beaten. Totally defeated. And as beautiful as ever.

And I, like a complete fuckin' asshole, felt alive again.

"I—hello, Matthew."

I came to a stop and caught my breath. "Hello? That's all I get? What are you doing here?"

We were about as far from the Upper East Side as you could get. And that had been by design. I was pretty sure that prickly feeling would only get worse knowing I was potentially only a few blocks away from the woman I couldn't get out of my head. I needed my territory. My borough.

Another thought occurred to me. "Were you at the Cloister on Sunday?"

Nina's extremely guilty expression told me I was right. So, that prickle I felt had come from her, not Nico. My sixth sense about that shit was spot-on—maybe even more accurate because it was her.

"Jesus. I *knew* I wasn't crazy. I kept thinking someone was watching us…"

Again, no argument from her. But I didn't have time to be smug. I was too fuckin' angry.

"What are you doing?" I asked. "Stalking me, now?"

"What? No! Excuse me, I had *plans* to visit the Cloisters last weekend," Nina retorted. "In case you've forgotten, I happen to serve on the board of directors for several organizations."

That tone of voice, the snippy, holier-than-thou dialect that only people of her station ever seemed to know how to use, suddenly got under my skin like never before.

"And does this board meet on a Sunday after Mass?" I asked.

"They could. Not everyone is Catholic, Matthew."

"How about Park Slope, huh?" I pressed. "Are you on the board of some secret museum here too? Is the Met planning to break ground at Prospect Park? Or maybe the top of the Empire State Building?"

"Oh, for goodness' sake, stop cross-examining me, Matthew," she snapped. "I had a meeting in Midtown earlier today. And I heard this restaurant was supposed to be good, that's all."

Christ. She wasn't even denying it. "Where did you hear that?" I asked through my teeth.

"I don't remember."

"Did you hear it from me?"

"When would I have—"

"How about last Monday?"

"Matthew, be serious, do you really think that—"

"Stop fucking around with me, Nina!" I exploded. "I don't know what this idiotic game is you're playing, but you and I both know you didn't just *happen* to be in Brooklyn today. So what the hell are you doing? Why do you keep showing up everywhere I go? Why the fuck are you here?"

"I don't know!" she burst out. "I—I honestly don't! I came home, and there was no one there, per *usual*, not that I found that particularly saddening, if you want to know the truth, and I just—well, I didn't mean to see you today, but you were just there. And you *did* practically shout your intended plans at Jane and Eric's. Was I supposed to think that wasn't for my benefit, or are you just that thoughtless?"

I scowled. Irritatingly, I had actually been thinking of Nina when I mentioned this restaurant to Jane and Eric. "You can't be serious. That was over a week ago. You *told* me to take her there."

"Well, I didn't actually think you would do it!"

I rubbed my hands vigorously over my face. "Nina, Jesus Christ. And so you decided you had to stalk me for the rest of the week?"

"As if you aren't?" she shot back. "Please. I've seen you across the street from my building. Do you think I don't know it's you in those cabs? You're the *only* car not moving on all of Lexington Avenue, and sometimes you sit there for nearly an hour!"

I opened and closed my mouth several times. Fuck. She knew?

Her eyes narrowed to silver slits. "Yes, darling, that's right. I know you're there, just like you know I'm here. Anonymity and distance would mean everything, but we just can't seem to manage it. It's our sad little curse, isn't it?"

"Right along with everything else." I groaned into my hands "Where's your car? We'll have them pick you up so I can get back to the woman who actually *wants* to be seen with me."

Nina's eyes flared before she looked away. "Don't bother. It's ir Manhattan, where I left it. I'll send for an Uber."

"What do you mean, where you left it?"

She looked up from her phone. "I—well, I walked here."

"You *walked*? From where, Manhattan?" The idea was unfathomable.

"No, just from—from another neighborhood in Brooklyn. A tax dropped me." She looked down, almost ashamed. "I didn't want anyone to know I'd come."

I followed her gaze, all the way to her pair of thousand-dollar shoes (I'd wager), completely ruined. Stained and spotted, with chinks in the leather heels and toes scuffed beyond repair. And those were just the shoes.

"Jesus," I breathed. "Your feet. Look at that."

Her feet were puffy, swollen from the walk, and I could see the angry red marks around the edges where blisters had formed beneath the leather.

"Stop." The word carried all measure of shame. Embarrassment Desperation, even.

"Which one?" I asked.

Nina looked up. "What?"

"Which one? Which neighborhood were you in?"

She sighed. "Are you aware that you wield questions like weapons, Matthew?"

I nodded. "Damn well, too. Now answer that one, doll. Which neigh borhood?"

She looked back down at the ground and mumbled something.

"I'm sorry, I didn't fucking hear that. *Which neighborhood*, Nina?"

"Red Hook!" The words exploded like firecrackers. "I went to Red Hook, all right?"

Well, that explained the feet. The two and a half miles or so from my house to Park Slope would have been fine in running shoes. But not stilettos.

"You were in Red Hook."

Her silver eyes narrowed testily. "Yes, that's what I just said."

"For what, the view? The fine company? The bustling social life?"

Nina sighed. "Matthew…you know why I was there."

"No, I don't."

"Yes, you *do*."

"Fuck!" I shouted, startling her back a step, as well as a group of pigeons that had been pecking their way around us.

"Matthew, you don't need to shout."

God, the woman was infuriating. How could she stand there, so impossibly placid, after she had literally stalked me all the way to Red Hook and then walked over two miles in those shoes just to find me? What the hell was going on?

"Look," I said, trying and failing to maintain an even tone. "Nina, I'm on a date. I'm trying to move on because *you* told me to leave you the fuck alone, doll. For once in my life, I'm trying to be a decent guy. I'm trying to be more than just the other man."

"Oh, Matthew…"

There was that look again. She hated when I talked badly about myself, just like I did with her. But this time, her concern wasn't wanted.

I batted it away like a fly. "Did something change? Did I miss something here? Because I meant it, Nina. I'll only stay away from you as long as you ask. But *you* have to keep your end of the bargain."

She opened her mouth to make another cutting reply. And for a second, I thought she might say yes. I *prayed* she'd tell me to leave Annie at the restaurant and go with her. Back to my house, back to some privacy, where we could hash out whatever the hell was happening between us without interruptions. Figure out a future where we didn't have to stay away from each other.

But instead, maybe as my final remark sank in, her upright posture deflated right along with my bravado.

"No," she said quietly. "No, nothing's changed."

"You sure about that?"

Her body shrank even more.

"And where's Calvin tonight? What the hell is he doing letting his wife get blisters chasing another man across the Brooklyn Bridge?"

"I didn't walk across the bridge."

"I'm serious," I said. "What is he doing while you're out here?"

"Don't make this about him."

"Why not? Seems to be he's pretty central in all of it."

"Because it's not about him!" she cried. "It's about *you*, and I don't know what to do!"

"You should leave him!" I shouted. "It's actually pretty damn simple, if you ask me. You don't love him. He obviously makes you fuckin' miserable. So the real question is, why the fuck do you stay?"

Her temper flared. "You have *no right* to ask me something like that. Especially when you know the answer."

"Oh, no? I think I have the right when you're stalking me all over the fucking city, Nina. Good husbands don't leave their wives alone this much, Nina. They don't jilt them at the opera and let other men make them come. They don't make them cry to strangers in the middle of the street either."

"Stop."

"Jesus!" I paced on the sidewalk like a trapped animal. Despite being outside, despite having a million streets to escape into, I really did feel like a lion in its cage. "I've never met anyone so visibly unhappy and willing to do fuck all about it! You have the world at your fingertips, Mrs. Gardner. Why in the hell won't you do anything to take it?"

"Because I don't deserve it!"

"What do you really owe him?" I asked, more quietly this time. "I don't understand it. So he sat next to you at a clinic nine years ago and gave your baby a name. Do you really think that's worth a lifetime of misery?"

"Spoken like someone who has never had to question giving up that life otherwise."

"He is not good to you!"

"And how do you know that?"

"Because if he was, you wouldn't follow me halfway across Brooklyn just because I'm on a date with another woman! Because I'm pretty sure the most graceful woman I've ever met is not as accident-prone as she would like everyone to believe! Jesus *fuckin'* Christ, Nina, how many more times do we have to have this conversation?"

"I DON'T KNOW!" she screeched, making a pedestrian up the street jump. "You make me—you make me do things I *never* would have done before. You make me absolutely crazy, Matthew. Look at me! I don't even recognize myself anymore!"

She pulled a tube of lipstick out of her pocket and hurled it at me. It bounced off my chest and into the street. I didn't even have to look to know the color was bright red. Just like I'd known from the start, she'd worn it for me. Even when I wasn't around.

If I'd ever needed one indication that I'd seeped into her soul as much as she'd become a part of mine, that was it.

I grabbed her wrist. Nina swallowed and wiped at her face with her other hand. One tear, then another spilled over her cheeks.

"I don't want to feel this way," she said in a voice that quavered on the wind. "I thought, maybe if I saw you with her, I could accept that we'll never work. That's why I wandered around that museum like a fool. And watched you at the Empire State Building. And followed you here after I stood at your house like a lunatic wondering if you were...*with*...her." She closed her eyes, like the unspoken image caused her physical pain. "I believed that if I saw you with someone else, then I could finally let you go."

I inhaled. The scent of roses filled my nose, and for the first time in over a week, I felt like I was breathing again. "And is that working out for you?"

"It has to." Nina shook her head sadly. "I have no other choice." She pressed her hand over her face and rubbed her skin until it all turned pink. "*Why*? Why did I have to meet you now?"

I gazed at my hand, wrapped around her delicate wrist. I loosened my grip, but I didn't let go, instead pulling her closer so we stood only inches apart.

"I ask myself that every day," I said quietly.

She swiped at another tear. "Do you?"

"Sometimes I think it would have been better if we'd never met," I replied honestly. "I wish to God I hadn't fallen in love with the one woman on this planet I can never truly have."

Her gray eyes widened, the color of storm clouds. "Oh, Matthew..."

"But then..." I shook my head. The alternative made me feel like there was a knife shoved into my chest. "Nina, then, I'd never have known you at all. And I can't fuckin' fathom a world anymore without you in it. That world…baby, that world's just not worth being in."

I leaned closer. I knew I shouldn't. I was so fuckin' angry with her. My life was fine before this woman entered with the grace of a flower and the blast of a storm. I'd been empty, maybe. But I knew what I was. Who I was.

Now the only thing I could think of was the way Nina tasted after a bottle of wine.

The way her lips puckered just so when she was upset.

The way her lip felt clenched between my teeth.

I didn't really give a shit if there was another girl waiting for me at the end of the block, or another, or another.

None of them would ever be her.

And suddenly, I needed to feel her kiss like I needed air to breathe. I leaned in. But just when my mouth was about to brush hers, she slipped her hand out of my grasp and pressed both of them to my chest.

"No," she whispered. "I—we—we can't. You know we can't."

Rage bubbled up inside me. Was this how she was always going to be? Fuck around with me until we couldn't take it anymore?

Well, good news for her. I was there. This was it. I was fuckin' done.

"You know what, I was wrong. This is worse than not knowing each other. It's so much worse." I scrubbed the almost-kiss off my lips like I was going at one of *Nonna's* pots with steel wool. "Go home, Nina. Get the fuck out of here, out of my neighborhood, out of my fuckin' life. We're not friends—you just nailed the coffin on that one. And come Monday, God willing, all this shit with your family will be behind me, and I can pretend you never existed at all."

I turned and walked back to the restaurant, listening to my heels echo on the pavement while the rest of the world blurred. But before the restaurant door closed behind me, my name floated through the air, a mewl as soft as an abandoned kitten's and twice as broken.

"Matthew."

It took everything I had not to go back to her. But I didn't turn back. Because I knew if I did, I'd be lost for good.

CHAPTER TWENTY-SIX

"IT'S LETOUR. NO DOUBT ABOUT IT. LOOK AT THAT."

Derek handed me a set of pictures as we walked up Fifth Avenue toward the Metropolitan Museum of Art. It was the Sunday before the gala and our planned arrest of John Carson. The grand jury had come through on Friday with the indictment we sought, and now we were meeting at the museum to go through the final plans with Jane and her boss. Derek needed to tour the exhibit and other finalized gala spaces before tomorrow. And as the prosecutor assigned to the case, I was there to make sure everything was done good and legally. There could be *no* chance of any part of this case being thrown out. We were David going up against Goliath. We had one chance to put out the giant's eye.

When he wasn't prepping his squad of NYPD officers, Derek had spent the rest of the week gathering any last bits of information from The Hole that he could add to our case. This morning, there had been a breakthrough.

In the photos, a tall, dark-haired man in a very expensive-looking suit stood outside a big black Escalade, looking from side to side while a few kids from the neighborhood shuttled a row of young women out of the house and into the back of the truck. Probably there to make plans to change the operation, now that Roscoe "disappeared" with our help. Into

a state-run rehab facility, but I wouldn't be shocked if he didn't make i
through trial.

"Yeah, that's definitely the slimy motherfucker," I said, eyeing a
picture of Jude Letour. "Eric showed me a picture of him before. How
you doin', Jack Sparrow?"

Derek chuckled. "He does look like a wannabe pirate."

"It's the chinstrap. Straight out of 2005. Money doesn't buy class
that's for sure. Do you know where he took the girls?"

"Big truck out in Flushing where they unloaded a bunch of other
boxes. One that had plates registered to Chariot. Once it crossed the
Connecticut state line, though, we couldn't follow. The state troopers los
it pretty quickly after."

I perked up. "Chariot? Really?"

"Yep. It looks like a simple trade—Letour and his associates orches-
trate the dissemination of guns to local gangs on behalf of Carson in
exchange for the girls, which Letour and Carson sell outside the U.S. at a
premium." Derek snorted with disgust. "Animals. I'd wager the truck
was on its way up to Maine. Looser regulations up there, and outside of
the De Vries Shipping ports."

"Who is that?"

I pointed to another suit on the other side of the car. I could make out
his shoulder and the edge of his shirt, but his face was obscured through
the tinted windows. He was obviously not one of the local gang
members, but more likely a new compatriot of Carson and Letour.

"I'm having someone in the photography unit see if they can't suss that
out," Derek said. "I don't know if they can, but I'd like to know who it is too."

I held the photo up closely. I could just make out the outline of a
man's face, but there was no way to see who he was. Maybe someone in
imaging could figure it out. Maybe not.

"It's probably another one of those pricks from that Janus society," I
said, handing the photos back to Derek. "Let me know if anything comes
up. Even if tonight goes perfectly, something tells me it's not all going to
end for us with John Carson's arrest."

"Tip of the iceberg," Derek agreed.

He tucked the stack into his bag as we approached the museum entrance. The entire front had been transformed with temporary tents, barricaded press sections, and a huge pink carpet covering the famous steps. I didn't really know much about shit like this, but anyone could see this was a big fucking deal.

"You got any other photos? Or IDs of the kids helping them?" I asked.

It wouldn't do us good now, but discovery was a bitch. And if we got to the kids tonight or tomorrow before the party, there was a chance they wouldn't disappear before trial.

"We got a gallery, Zo, and Cliff is already out there with a team hauling them in. Four members of the Crew, in and out of that safe house like it was a fuckin' merry-go-round. I think they were getting things ready. Waiting for Daddy to come home and say good night."

I nodded. "Good. It's all good. And when he does tomorrow night, you guys can cart his ass straight to Rikers."

"Mr. Zola?"

Derek and I were greeted at the top of the carnation-colored steps by a cute skirt I recognized as Jane and Eric's personal assistant.

"Heya, Bridget. Just here for the final walk-through with the de Vrieses and Ms. Spring."

Bridget nodded with a peppy smile. "Yes, they are expecting you and Detective Kingston. Follow me."

Derek and I trailed Bridget around the gaping halls of the museum. Even if you weren't a museum-goer, you could appreciate the grandeur of the high arched ceilings and stone work, not to mention the priceless art everywhere. Bridget turned down one hall, sidestepping the crews still hard at work on the new exhibits, and led us through an employees-only door and to an elevator bank.

"Don't use that one," she pointed to one of the two elevators. "Apparently, it hasn't been working well, but they haven't put a sign up yet." She wrote something down on her notepad—I guessed a reminder to tell "them" to get on that sign.

We rode down to the basement, then followed Bridget through a maze of corridors to the Costume Institute in the far corner.

"Wait right here, please," she said as she opened the door to a small conference room inside. "Mrs. de Vries is upstairs overseeing the seating with Cora, but she'll be down in a moment."

"Sure, honey. We'll just entertain ourselves."

I winked at the girl, who blushed as if on command before scurrying off into the bowels of the museum to find Jane.

"Now I know why you stay single," Derek said. "If I had women eating out of my hand like you do, I'd never settle down either."

I shrugged. "It's just a matter of meeting the right ones."

"And you haven't?"

I have, I wanted to say. *She just belongs to someone else.* It had been three days since Nina's and my little screaming match on the street. Three days of silence. Three days of trying and failing not to run every part of that tantrum through my head on repeat.

But before I could respond, the door opened, and Jane de Vries entered with another woman I took to be Cora Spring, the editor-in-chief of *Vogue* magazine and director of the event they were organizing.

"Let's get this over with," she said. "I have a million things to do other than walk a couple of policemen around the museum. Jane, thank God you came on. You absolutely saved the Westwood exhibit."

"Just the one," I clarified as Derek and I got up to shake her hand. "Ms. Spring, I'm Matthew Zola, investigator prosecutor with the Brooklyn DA. This is Derek Kingston, chief detective on this case. He's the one who needs the layout for his team tomorrow night. After you're done showing him around, we can all go through tomorrow's plan together. We'll do our best to keep it short and sweet."

"Why don't you come with me?" Cora nodded curtly at Derek. "I'll walk you through the entire setup myself, Detective. That way it will be finished even more quickly." The edge in her voice demonstrated just how much she was looking forward to negotiating a squadron of NYPD in a hall full of celebrities.

"She's pissed," Jane muttered as the door shut behind them. "This isn't exactly what she was expecting when Nina elbowed me onto the committee."

"She seems to like you, though. My sister says that's a miracle in and of itself. She's pea-green with jealousy, by the way. Apparently Cora Spring is a pretty big deal."

Jane gave me a look like I'd grown a couple of extra heads. "Um, she's probably the biggest deal in fashion. The woman has been making careers in this industry for literally forty years. Ever seen *The Devil Wears Prada*?"

I nodded. "Kate made me watch it with her."

"Well, Cora partly inspired the Meryl Streep character. The rest of it was toned down. A lot."

I raised a brow in awe. "I'm surprised she is letting us do this, then."

"Yeah, well, that's what happens when Nina promises to match the net fundraising of the event," Jane replied. "They allow an amateur to help organize the thing and let us do pretty much whatever we want with the rest of it. Like bring my mother and best friend to hang out with the *Vogue* girls during the event."

"Skylar's coming?"

More new developments, and not particularly welcome. Skylar Crosby and Brandon Sterling were good friends from Boston—the reason I had gotten to know the de Vrieses in the first place. Under normal circumstances, I might welcome their presence. But not right now. Not when anyone else might complicate things. Or end up in the line of fire.

Jane nodded. "She and Brandon arrived with my mom last night. They're staying with us, more for moral support. You should come say hi tomorrow. After...everything is taken care of."

I gulped as I returned to one main detail. That Nina was the one who had made all of this happen. I was right, then. She not only turned over her grandmother's coveted spot on the committee out of guilt and love for her family, but also personally greased the wheels for the biggest sting I'd ever been a part of.

Goddamn it. Just when I was almost about to hate her, the woman made it impossible.

"Out of curiosity, how much does an event like this pull in?" I asked. "A few hundred thousand, maybe?" Chump change for the de Vries family, which, according to *Forbes*, was worth billions. The Sterlings too. I wasn't sure how I had come into such close proximity with this kind of wealth over the last several years.

Jane snickered. "Oh, you're funny. This event fully funds the

Costume Institute for an entire year. That doesn't happen on a few hundred grand."

"So, what, then? A million? Two?"

"Well, last year it brought in closer to thirteen."

Thirteen. Million. Dollars.

I never forgot the de Vries cousins had money, of course. Jane was a newcomer, but Eric and Nina both had that quiet elegance that came with a big fuckin' trust fund and the security of knowing neither they nor the generations that would follow them would ever want for anything. But there was a difference, I thought. The de Vrieses weren't just the kind of people who influenced a few people here and there with a couple of extra hundreds folded in their palms. They could move fuckin' mountains if they wanted.

Like this one. Like tomorrow night.

"I know." Jane leaned over and patted my hand like she was touching a small child. "It's nuts, isn't it?"

"It's practically immoral," I said before I could stop myself.

"That's the question. Is it better to attack the status quo from outside, or change things from within if you can get the power to do so?" Jane shrugged. "I haven't made up my mind about it, to be perfectly honest. But I do like the clothes. And the real estate. I don't miss living on an SA's salary, that's for sure." She examined me curiously. "I'm surprised, actually, that you get to be here for the arrest. Is that normal for your office to be this involved?"

"Kings County moved to a vertical system, so as soon as a case moves to prosecution, the same attorney stays with it through trial. And since this case came through me instead of NYPD, due to its special nature, I have more of a right than normal to play bad cop with Derek."

Derek and I had been working together for years designing sting operations, mapping out the criminal rings in Brooklyn. I had gone on more than one raid with him to witness arrests. He kept a bulletproof vest for me in his car. Plus, like a lot of DA employees frequently targeted by New York's criminal underworld, I was already packing most of the time anyway.

"Isn't that dangerous?" Jane hugged herself with a shudder. "Part of me wishes John Carson won't even come. I don't *ever* want to see him again."

I could only imagine what she was remembering. I hoped for her sake she had seen a therapist or someone to help after experiencing what she'd been through. Trauma is trauma, whether it's a war zone or not. Hell, even love could be a war zone sometimes. I was feeling that more than ever.

I shook my head. "I'm usually well outside the line of fire. It's more like coaching from the sidelines, making sure everything gets done according to the rules. Considering the sensitive nature of this particular case, they need me here tomorrow to advise on the legalities of everything. And I need to witness the arrest and maybe even the crime scene if we're going to make an airtight case against John Carson and his cronies."

Jane blew a long stream of air between her lips. "Wow. I'm jealous. Maybe I would have been more excited about my job if I got to do stuff like this."

"Not the same in Chicago?"

She shook her head. "Not even close. The CPD wanted us the hell out of there until it was time to go to court. We were the paper pushers. That was it."

I made a face. "I would have left that too. Sure you don't want to come back? You got your bar exam waived in New York State, didn't you?"

My boss was always looking for talent. I was pretty sure there was a place for Jane on Jay Street if she wanted one.

Jane nodded. "I did, yes." She paused, her bright red fingernails playing over her lips for a moment. "Do you want to know the truth, though? I didn't ever really like it. I went into law and public service to make my dad proud, more than anything else. Not because it was really what I wanted to do."

I considered that. "Yeah, I know what that's like. I sort of did the same thing."

Jane peered at me over her glasses. "Did you?"

I shrugged. "For my grandfather, but yeah. Only it was after he died. He begged me to straighten out my life. Be a good guy, not one of the baddies. There were a lot of the latter running around my neighborhood back then. The last days of the mob, you know, before they were really wiped out up there."

I still remembered sitting on the porch at *Nonna's* while she and the other housewives up and down the block gossiped about all the arrests. One after another, mobster after mobster ratted on each other. The organization hadn't been the same since.

But it was still there. Still powerful. And in some ways, even slipperier, since without as many associates, most of the crime families in the Northeast outsourced the grunt work that had once gone to its own soldiers to lesser criminal groups, like MCs or local gangs. When it came to criminal organization in New York, *Cosa Nostra* was still on top.

"It was all he wanted," I said. "For me to escape that. I know too many guys who went that route. They don't really tell you, but when you grow up with it, you *know* when someone's a wise guy."

I had wondered more than once while Derek was doing his stakeouts in The Hole if he would spot a member of one of the Five Families coming in and out of that safe house. I couldn't believe that ammunitions sales in Brooklyn would happen without the okay of one of the dons.

"Do I seem like I come from a criminal?" Jane wondered in a soft voice.

I looked up. It hadn't occurred to me that she might struggle with a less-than-innocent legacy as much as I did. But of course, that would make sense. The woman had just discovered less than a year ago that half her DNA came from a complete monster. That alone should fuck with anyone without the subsequent trauma he'd inflicted.

I was quiet for a minute before I replied. "My parents abandoned my sisters and me when I was fourteen."

Jane looked up in surprise. "Oh my God. I'm so sorry."

I shook my head. "That's all right. Not really my point. I mean, my dad I guess didn't technically abandon us, but he was a no-good alcoholic, and to be honest, I consider abuse and neglect its own kind of abandonment anyway."

Jane's expression suddenly took on a different kind of recognition. Yeah, after years of working in a DV bureau, she knew exactly what meant.

So I didn't elaborate. "After he died in a car wreck, my mom split. I don't know, maybe it was the grief. Maybe it was knowing she was as good as dead anyway with the amount of poison she poured down her throat every day. But she left me and my sisters to be raised by our grandparents."

Jane opened her mouth to say something, but nothing came out. It happened a lot when people found out this side of my history.

"But you know what? It was the best thing they could have ever done for us." I sat back. "I might come from a couple of derelicts, Jane, but the two people who raised me made all the difference. Genetics is only half the story. And really, I think not even that."

Jane looked like she wanted to argue. It was obvious she'd been wrestling with the question a lot lately.

"I don't know," she said quietly. "I would like to think that...but there are other things about me that...well, I'm nothing like the two people who raised me. Sometimes our reactions to things are just innate. I think that has to be genetic."

"Like what?" I wondered.

Her mouth twisted around. "You know...this is going to sound weird. But sometimes I wonder if my marriage was sort of preordained by my DNA."

I frowned, although the idea of kismet sounded eerily familiar. "How do you figure?"

"Think about it. I didn't even know my biological father, but he was utterly obsessed with my mother-in-law from the time he met her, what, more than thirty-five years ago now? Stalked her through college. Basically created a whole vendetta against the de Vries family because of her." Jane shook her head. "It's madness."

"But what does that have to do with you and Eric?" I wondered.

"I pushed Eric away for years and years. I sabotaged our relationship again and again. And it wasn't because he wasn't good to me. The de Vrieses...well, the thing I know about them is that they are unfailingly loyal. Even to a fault."

A pang lodged itself in the pit of my stomach. "Yeah, I've picked up on that."

"I convinced myself that just because of his past, our future would have been marred," Jane said sadly. "But really, I was scared of myself. The other thing about the de Vrieses is that...they are really intense people."

My entire body felt that down to its core. "Yeah, I've noticed that too."

Jane raised one wry brow. "Have you?"

I didn't reply.

"Well, when I first met Eric...my reaction to him was just as intense. Maybe even obsessive. I couldn't stop thinking about him, hard as I tried. And physically...well, holy shit." She winked. "Sorry if that's a little TMI."

I shrugged. "I've heard a lot worse." Not to mention experienced pretty much the same fuckin' thing with another member of the family.

"But it wasn't just those things, you know? It's like...when Eric is around, every cell in my body turns in his direction. Every single part of me is aware of his presence. It goes so much deeper than just emotions. Than just sex." She shook her head. "And they aren't easy people to be in love with, the de Vrieses. Talk about drama llamas. But they are easy people to love. Do you know what I mean?"

We stared at each other for a long time. I didn't answer. I couldn't answer. Because what the fuck would admitting the truth to this strange woman get me?

"I—I can see that," I said as diplomatically as I could.

Jane waited a moment more, probably realizing I wasn't going to elaborate.

"It's probably just me," she said. "Which is why I wonder, you know? Even now. There's a thin line between love and madness. My fa—this man, Carson. He's pretty fully on the latter side. What if—what if I end up crossing that line too?" She bit her lip ruefully and pulled at her hair, which had been dyed with streaks of red on one side. "It wouldn't be the first time I've been called crazy."

"There's a pretty key difference, though," I told her. "Your father—your real father, I mean. The one who raised you, not just the one who dropped you a set of chromosomes. He must have shown you what love looked like, Jane. That's devotion, not obsession. I see you with Eric. You learned it somewhere. I think you figured out the difference."

When Jane looked up again, her gaze was like Cupid's arrow, straight and true.

"And you?" she wondered. "Have you figured it out too?"

Before I could ask her exactly what she meant, the door to the conference room opened. In walked Cora, Derek, Bridget, and following closely behind was the arrow's target.

Nina.

"I just want to make sure we have all the financials worked out—" she was saying before coming to a halt when she found me at the end of the table. "Oh. Oh, hello."

I tipped my hat at her, but didn't get up. If I did, everyone would see my legs shaking. "Hey, doll."

Before she could answer, I turned back to Jane. "Now that everyone's here, let's get started, shall we?"

CHAPTER TWENTY-SEVEN

"ALL RIGHT," DEREK SAID AFTER GOING THROUGH TOMORROW NIGHT'S PLAN for the fourth fuckin' time. "I think we're good."

I had to give my detective credit. He was nothing if not thorough. Ludicrous as this scheme was, neither of us was willing to pass up an opportunity to bring down one of the biggest baddies New York had ever seen.

But after an hour of pretending Nina de Vries wasn't casting covert glances my way, I could not wait to get the fuck out of that room. For the most part, I had managed to keep my attention on the magazine editor and other committee members instead of the blonde magnet sitting across from me. But I could feel her. Holy *fuck*, could I feel the woman's presence. Calling me. Mocking me.

And after that little stunt she pulled Thursday, the longer I spent in her company, the angrier I got.

Devotion versus obsession. *Have you figured that out too?* Jane had asked.

Had I?

I wasn't sure, any more than I thought the ice princess across from me had. Our attraction *definitely* walked the line of obsession. But devotion? How could I know if she wouldn't let me try? Maybe the obsession I felt for her only came from the fact that I wasn't allowed to practice devotion at all.

But I'd never have the chance to figure it out.

"Good," Cora said as she stood up from the table and checked her watch. "I believe that covers it. Finally. Now Jane and I have about a mountain of things to figure out before we leave tonight."

"Actually, I need to see the last two stairwells, Ms. Spring," Derek said as he and everyone else stood too. "Take some photos, if you're willing."

Cora didn't even bother to hide her sigh.

"I'm going to talk to Eddie in accounting to make sure the transfers have gone through," Nina piped up, and for good reason. The mention of Nina's mountain-sized donation cleared all frustration from Cora's pinched face.

"I'm going to head back to Jay Street, then," I called after Derek as he followed the editor out.

"And don't forget to wear a tuxedo, Mr. Zola," Cora said. "If you absolutely must watch from inside the event, even from downstairs, you'll need to look like a guest, not someone off the street."

I looked down at my suit, which happened to be one of my favorite Armanis, and frowned. Across from me, Nina hid a smile with her hand. She knew exactly how much a cut like that bothered me.

"See you in Brooklyn," Derek said as he followed Cora out the door.

I turned to Jane. "I'll see you tomorrow—hey."

She looked up. Her arms were crossed over her middle, hands grasping her elbows so tightly her fingertips were white. "Yeah?"

"It's going to be okay. One way or another, we'll get the bastard."

Jane exhaled. "Thank you, Zola. I'll see you tomorrow night."

I nodded and left, not even bothering to say anything to Nina beyond a curt nod. What else was there to say? After tomorrow, I'd never see her again. And I really, *really* wanted to believe that was for the best.

"Matthew. Matthew, wait."

I turned around when I reached the elevator bank to find Nina following me briskly.

I sighed. "Nina, what is it?"

She blinked guilelessly, her large gray eyes as wide as the ocean. "It's

—nothing. I just thought I would ride up with you."

I punched the call button. "Fine. Just fine."

We stood there as a few people from the Institute passed us on their way into the office. When the doors shut behind them, leaving us alone in the hallway, Nina sighed herself.

"I—Matthew, I wanted to apologize for what happened on Thursday. For the entire week. I lost control of myself. It was wrong. Please forgive me."

"I'm not a pawn," I said. "But sometimes you treat me like I am. Treat my life like it's there for your fuckin' amusement. But it's not. I'm trying to move on, Nina. Legitimately trying."

The elevator doors opened, and we both entered. It wasn't until they closed that Nina finally spoke, gripping the handrails so tightly her fingertips turned white.

"I know you were trying to move on, Matthew. And believe it or not, I was too. It's just...I felt that I couldn't unless I knew it was real. You. Another woman. I needed to see her just like I know you needed to see me and Calvin."

I scowled at the name. The very sound of it made me want to tear this fucking car apart.

"And how'd that work out for you?" I asked. "What did you think of Annie and me?"

Nina clenched her teeth. "The truth?"

"That's all I've ever wanted from you, sweetheart."

Her eyes narrowed. "Fine. I didn't like it."

"You were jealous."

Her gray eyes didn't move. "Yes. Extremely jealous."

"Crazy jealous?"

She licked her lips, then slowly nodded.

I exhaled a shaky breath. "Well, then you know. You know exactly how I feel every time I even *think* about the fact that you go home to another man every fuckin' night—"

"Matthew—"

"No, I'm going to get this out, goddammit." Now that we'd started, I wasn't stopping now. I took her by the shoulders, letting her know she wasn't going to turn away. Not this time.

But she didn't fight it. Nina, for once, wasn't running away. She was facing the music, listening to every word I had to say.

My gaze floated over her, taking in the glossy gold waves, the crisp red lips, the big gray eyes that in this light almost looked blue. The immaculate white shirt over a spotless gray skirt and the silver-colored heels I knew so well. She was as much a goddess as ever. Impenetrable and cold to some. But to me, there was a fire burning deep under that layer of ice. They say the hottest part of a flame is its blueish center. Nina de Vries wasn't frigid. To me, she was ice hot.

"You really are a siren, you know that?" I said. "Just when I think I *might* have a shot at escaping your thrall, you cast a new spell."

"A spell?" She touched her lips in amusement. "That's quite a compliment."

"Trust me, it's not."

"How's that?"

"Dumb blonde doesn't really suit you, doll. Smart girl like you. I'm guessing you read enough classics at Wellesley to know what happened to men who chased their sirens."

She didn't answer. Of course she knew. Everyone knew.

"They crashed," I said bitterly. "They fell to their watery graves, shredded by rocks while they chased women they *thought* were the loves of their—"

Clunk.

The elevator jolted to a stop, tossing Nina and me both into the air about three inches and then into the walls from the momentum.

"Shit." I strode to the console and pressed the button for the main floor again. The button remained lit, but the elevator didn't move.

I turned to Nina. "Is this—fuck, which elevator did we get on?"

"What? What do you mean?"

"The right or the left?" I shook my head. I was so fuckin' upset with her, I didn't even keep track of which car we'd gotten on. "Is this the good elevator or the fritz elevator?"

"What *fritz* elevator?" Nina's voice rose with panic.

"You know, the one Bridget told us not to use."

"Bridget didn't tell me anything of the sort. I took the stairs down." Her eyes widened. "Is there something wrong with this elevator?"

"What the fuck do you think?" I jabbed at an emergency call button next to an intercom.

All we heard was fuzzy static.

"Goddammit," I muttered as I pulled out my phone. No service, of course, not even Wi-Fi. I turned back to the console and continued pressing different buttons, trying to get a response.

"St-stop that," Nina chided. "You're going to break it."

"If you hadn't noticed, doll, it's already broken." I pushed another. The elevator jolted once more, and then all of the lights flickered off, encasing us in darkness. "*Fuck!*"

Almost immediately, a row of orange-tinted emergency lights flickered on around the floor's perimeter. I turned around to find Nina pressing her head into the metal paneling in the far corner.

"Everything all right over there?" I asked.

I didn't want to be nice. But she looked…off. The last thing from the proud woman I generally knew. Even when she was going nuts stalking me around New York City, Nina never totally lost that queenly self-assurance.

Until now.

She turned slightly. Her eyes were tightly shut, though one tear had escaped down a pink, round cheek.

Every bit of anger I felt evaporated instantly.

"Oh, fuck. Are you—shit, baby, are you claustrophobic?"

Nina was trembling now as she grasped the handrail. "I—yes," she managed. "Y-yes, I suppose I am."

"But I've—you've ridden in an elevator. I've seen you do it." I blinked, thinking of the night we had spent together at the Grace.

The look on her face told me exactly why it hadn't bothered her that night. She had been far too preoccupied to think about anything else besides us.

"What about your building? I'm assuming you don't live on the ground floor."

"The twentieth," she said between her teeth. "And I take the stairs."

"You walk *twenty* flights of stairs every single day?"

She slid to the floor, then pulled her knees to her chest so she could bury her face in her skirt.

"Well," I said more to myself than to her, "that explains why your legs look like that."

"Oh God, oh God," she muttered, rocking back and forth. "You're not here, not here, not here."

"Hey, it's going to be all right, honey—"

"Do *not* call me that," she said. "If you think using the same bloody name you use to address every other woman in New York is going to make me feel better, you are v-*very* mistaken!"

"Whoa, okay. Okay, doll, you got it." I was speaking in a low voice now, crooning like she was a wounded animal. "You just need something else to focus on." I sank to the floor beside her. "Do some, ah, mental visualizing. Like your ideal house. The best place you could ever live."

"I already have the best place I could ever live," Nina snapped. "It's ten blocks away, awaiting my return!"

"How about the best person, then? Your daughter. Think of Olivia, Nina. Imagine she's there, she's waiting for you."

Her face fell into her hands. "My daughter is nine years old and lives in Massachusetts, Matthew. And even if she were there, do you really think being *separated from my child* would calm me down?"

I ground my teeth, but rubbed her shoulder. "Fine, then. Your husband. Think about him."

The eyes peering through her fingers sharpened even more. "You are trying to make this worse, aren't you?"

If she wasn't so visibly upset, I might have laughed. "All right, then. Who? Tell me who to visualize, doll, and I'll help you do it."

The hands at her face dropped a bit. Her eyes shone, gray and wide under the dim emergency lights. As they dragged over my face and eventually down the rest of me, her breathing calmed and the shaking abated. A little. Not enough, but it was something.

"W-who would you think of?" she asked softly.

I exhaled through my nose. "Nina."

"P-please. J-just tell me."

I worried my jaw. "I think you know the answer to that one too, baby."

"That girl?"

I narrowed my eyes. "Annie?"

"Yes," she said, though a little too harshly.

I opened my mouth to say the right thing. The thing I *should* be feeling.

Instead, the truth came out. "No."

Total, abject failure.

Nina sucked in a shaky breath and closed her eyes again. She seemed to be trying to block everything out.

"Do you...would you ever imagine...us?" The words were barely audible.

I stared at my hands for a long time. When I looked up, she was shivering again. Fuck, she really was having a terrible time.

"Yes, I would," I told her honestly. "I do. Sometimes I feel like I never stop."

Her eyes still hadn't opened. But her breathing did ease a bit. "What do you think about?"

"Nina..."

The elevator lights flickered on and off again. Her shoulders began to shake.

"P-please, Matthew," she said. "I...I'm ten seconds from...it's the only thing that..."

"Fuck. *Fuck*, okay, yes, of course I think about us. You want to know the truth? It's all I ever think about, as hard as I try not to."

"L-like what?" Her hands covered her eyes, and she bit her bottom lip hard enough that the skin around her teeth was turning white. "Please!"

"I think about you. Me. Living in my house together." I snorted. "Not that you would ever live there, but still."

"I l-liked your house. It didn't have an elevator."

She couldn't see me, but I had to smile. Even when she was in the middle of a nervous breakdown, Nina wouldn't stand for me making assumptions about her. And she could still crack jokes.

"I'm glad," I said. "I liked how you looked in it too."

Below her hands, her mouth curved into a sweet smile. It was too easy to imagine how it would look in her eyes too—that warmth that she only bestowed on a few.

"I think about us," she admitted.

Fuckin' hell. We really were gluttons for punishment.

I stared up at the ceiling. "What do you think about?"

"S-so much. But I w-want to hear more about you."

"No, I think it's your turn." She needed to get out of her own head. I she talked, she couldn't think about where we were.

"I..." She paused long enough for her teeth to chatter. "I think abou what might have happened if we had met. In Italy, I mean. Be-before."

I swallowed. Hard. Yeah, she didn't want to know how many times had thought about that.

"What do you think that would have been like?" I joked. "Jarhead meets princess? I'm sure your family would have liked that."

"They would have liked it more than what did happen." Her voice was bitter—did she mean her daughter, or Calvin?

The desolation there, though, was harder to take than I imagined. I could deal with her jealousy. And her misery, even—she brought it on herself.

But Nina as a hopeless creature?

It was too much.

Tentatively, I lifted my hand and set it on her shoulder, rubbing slightly, a small gesture of comfort. Instead of pulling away like thought she would, Nina turned into me, burying her nose in the hollow between my shoulder and my neck. I couldn't help but wrap my arm around her completely. I could be angry at her, but I could never fight the peace that seeped through me whenever this woman was in my arms.

It was a small mercy, I supposed, to know I had the same effec on her.

"Do you want to know the truth?" she murmured as she inhaled.

The shaking had stopped. Her hand still gripped the fabric of my sleeves tightly, but her heart was finding an even rhythm again.

"Sure, doll," I murmured as I stroked her hair lightly.

"You're my happy place, Matthew. The only one I've ever known You compare me to mythical creatures, but to me, you're just as dream worthy. Being with you. L-loving you. That's my Eden."

I squeezed her tightly. It was always the same. This same shitty circle Admitting how we felt for each other only to yank it back again.

"Sometimes..." Nina opened her eyes. When she took in the elevato again, she squeezed them shut and pressed her cheek into my arm. "Sometimes I touch myself too. And pretend it's you."

Whoa. Well, that was a little bit different. Just the idea of her doing something like that called up every bit of desire that seemed to be constantly near the surface whenever I was around this woman.

She looked down, clearly having felt that reaction against her leg. "That doesn't disappoint you?"

"That a beautiful woman gets off thinking about me? Ah, no. Not disappointing at all."

"Is that all I am to you, then? Just some beautiful woman?" She sniffed. "I could be anybody, couldn't I? Like C-Caitlyn."

I tipped her face up. "They might as well have all been you. I was thinking of you every time anyway."

"I don't know if I should find that insulting or flattering."

I shrugged. "Maybe both?"

I could feel her cringe against my shoulder. I couldn't help but chuckle. It was nice, in a fucked-up way, to know I frustrated her too.

"If we—if we could—when you think of it—what do we do?"

I stopped stroking her hair and allowed her to roll off me so we could look at each other.

"Nina, do you really want to talk about this?"

"Please. I—I've finally stopped shaking."

It was true. She had. And considering that I had no fuckin' clue when we were getting out of here, I was willing to do just about anything to prevent a panic attack.

"Fine," I said. "I think about kissing you, first of all. When I close my eyes and I kiss their lips, I pretend they're yours."

"But they aren't me," she whispered. In the dim, dark car, her eyes looked like stars.

I shook my head. "Not even fuckin' close, baby. No one holds a candle."

She stared at me for a long time. With tear-stained cheeks and hair tousled over her shoulders, she had honestly never been more alluring. What did it say about me that I found her most attractive when I had messed her up?

I didn't have time to ponder the question anymore, because Nina reached down. And began to unbutton her blouse.

My eyes bugged out. "Nina. Shit. Um, what—what are you doing?"

She looked down, then back up at me. "What does it look like? I'm d-distracting us."

"But—shit, what if—" I could hardly talk. Honestly, I could hardly believe what I was seeing. "There are cameras in here, aren't there?"

She shook her head, but continued to speak calmly. "The cameras are being replaced." She glanced up at the bare corners and shuddered. "The museum director mentioned it at the board meeting last week." She finished with the last button and her blouse fell open, revealing a nude-colored lace bra through which the outlines of her nipples showed clearly.

I knew that bra. It was the same one she had been wearing...that night. Sleek. Subtle. Completely demure, but at the same time, completely seductive.

"Fuuuucccckk." The word came out like a groan. In less than a second, my pants were so tight it was painful.

Nina closed her eyes, shutting out the room, then cupped her breast.

I reached out eagerly. "Let me do that."

But to my disappointment, she shook her head, eyes still closed. "We can't. You know we can't."

"Are you kidding? What is this, some kind of fucked-up striptease?"

"It's better than a panic attack," said Nina, her voice sharpening again in a way that said she wasn't *quite* as in control as she seemed. It was nuts, the way the de Vrieses could turn on a dime like that. Mercurial creatures, all of them.

To be honest, it was almost worse. Being trapped in here with the woman l wanted more than anything but couldn't have, and then, by some insane twist of fate, being forced to watch her pleasure herself while I...just sat by?

Fuck that. I was no spectator.

"You can watch me," she said in that eerie way she had of reading my mind. It was annoying, really. Her eyes were still closed. "And I...could watch you."

Wait...what?

CHAPTER TWENTY-EIGHT

At first, she cupped her breast, then toyed with her nipple through her bra. Swift, sure movements with the efficiency of a woman used to taking care of herself this way.

She leaned against the wall and undid the zipper of her skirt, then pulled the fabric apart over her hips. Nude-colored lace peeked over the top, and I watched, transfixed, as she slipped her hand under its edge and between her legs while the other returned to her breast. Even in the dim light, I could see the way Nina's forehead smoothed as she worked herself into a more relaxed state.

A few minutes later, her eyes opened.

"Go on," she beckoned, her voice light and breathy.

In response, my hands moved to my own belt, though I barely sensed what was happening. She was touching herself. In front of me. In the bottom of the Met, on the floor of an elevator, Nina de Vries was pleasuring herself while she thought of us. Together.

"I..." My hands stilled on the zipper of my pants. I wanted to. Good Christ, I wanted to. But suddenly, something held me back. "You know, doll, I don't know if I should."

Her eyes opened finally, and met mine, straight and true. "Matthew."

"I...I don't want you to do something...else...we might regret."

Hurt crossed her delicate features—because of what I had said last night? I didn't know. I wasn't sure I wanted to.

The hand at her breast reached toward me, and her other stopped what it was doing. She slipped two fingers under my shirt collar so she could pull out the necklace underneath.

"You added something," Nina murmured as she looked at the small medallion that clinked against the crucifix.

"A gift," I said. "From *Nonna*." Who would be very fuckin' disappointed if she knew what I was doing right now.

Nina's thumb brushed over the tiny visage. "A saint?"

"San Gennaro."

Her mouth quirked. "Like the festival. I've been, actually."

"On Mulberry Street?" I knew she hadn't been to the one in Belmont.

She shook her head. "In Naples. When I..." She drifted off, but it was clear she was referring to the year she had spent in Italy. Her eyes lost focus, and when they refocused on me, it was with laser intent. She was still blocking out where we were. How closed-in. How trapped.

"He's the patron saint of blood," I said in a hurry. "Did you know that, baby?"

She looked at the medallion again, and it was clear that we were *both* thinking about the blood I had sucked from her finger in my room. The salty-sweet taste. The drop of her that I had taken inside *me*.

"*Nonna* said he wanted me to have it," I went on, my tongue thick with desire. It was a little weird, sitting here talking about my dead grandfather. But a reminder too. An important one. "He always knew I was a little too hot-blooded."

Like right now. When the feel of her breath this close to mine was making it hard to think, let alone speak.

"It's a good thing. For you. For—" I cleared my throat. "For your soul."

"But it's not just my soul that's worth protecting," Nina said softly as she cradled the two pendants in her palm.

"Ah, doll, you don't have to worry about me."

She inhaled deeply, then leaned closer and gently rubbed her nose against mine. "Don't I, my love?"

I didn't know what to say. This lust-filled moment had become something else. Actually, who was I kidding? It was *always* something else with her, from the second I saw her in the bar that first night. I never wanted to admit that Nina de Vries was possibly my soulmate, if there was such a thing. Because if she was, fate had other plans, giving her to another man.

Now, in the dark, in this tiny cramped box, she wanted to fuck with that fate?

Fine.

I was all out of fight. I wasn't sure if I'd ever had it in me to begin with.

I looked at the cross in her hand. "All right then, worry."

She was pulling slightly, the weight of her hand causing the chain to bite into my neck. It was a pain I needed. A pain I deserved.

"If you want my soul, baby, you better take care of it."

The hand around the cross closed tightly. Nina looked down to where my pants were half unzipped.

"Let me see you."

It wasn't a command. But it wasn't quite a request, either.

Slowly, I finished opening the button and zipper of my pants. Then I pulled the waistband of my boxers down enough to reveal at least an inch of what she said she wanted.

Nina shook her head. "That's not what I meant."

"What, you want more than just the tip?" I joked.

The hand on the chain tightened. The sudden bite made my dick harden even more.

"I want all of it," Nina whispered. "All the time. *All* the time. You have no idea, Matthew."

Now it was my turn to shudder. Our lips were less than an inch apart. "Don't I, baby?"

"But since I can't have it, I want to look. I want to watch. I—" Her eyes flickered around the car as if to remind herself of the circumstances. The reason for breaking her own creed. "Please, Matthew. I n-need it."

Her frank admission—the need that matched my own—was my undoing. I pushed the band of the boxers down completely. I was hard. Really, really fuckin' hard. I had been at half-mast ever since Nina walked into that fuckin' room, but the second she uttered the word "need," I was like a piece of the stone that made up the museum. I didn't matter that I was still so confused. Frustrated. Even angry, deep down. Who the fuck cared? Sometimes angry sex—or whatever this was —could be the best anyway.

She stared at my cock. The tip of her tongue slipped out one side of her mouth and licked the corner. I closed my eyes. Fuck, if I watched that, this would be over before it even started. And then where would we be? Nina lying on the floor, banging on the walls, falling apart because *I* couldn't keep it together?

Not on my watch.

So I looked down instead and found the hand she had slipped back into her underwear moving again.

"You were saying," I broke the silence. "You imagine us. Together What...what exactly do you see?"

Those silver eyes met mine like the tips of a spear.

"You kiss me," she said. "Like you did on the street that time. The first time, not in the hotel room."

"How was that?"

"Like an animal. Like you hadn't eaten for days. Like you were dying for a meal...and I was the sudden feast."

"You were," I growled as my hand wrapped fully around my cock. stroked it lightly, keeping a loose grip. "Then what? Do I take you to hotel next?"

"Oh, no," she said, a small smile playing over her lips. "Then you take me to bed. *Our* bed."

My eyes opened. "The bed is ours, huh?"

She smiled. "It's my fantasy. I can make it ours if I want."

I didn't want to tell her just how badly I wanted that single word to be true. That a part of me had wanted things that were *ours* since the moment I saw her. That I had imagined *our* wedding, *our* home, *our* kids *Our* future.

My hand slowed, so I closed my eyes and leaned back against the wall. "And then what do I do?"

"I don't know, Matthew. What do you do then?"

"Are we switching fantasies?"

Her other hand dropped the cross and slipped back to palm her breast. Through the silk of her bra, she pinched her nipple. Just like I had.

"Yes," she said. "This is *our* bed. What do we do there?"

"Baby, I don't know if you really want to hear what I think about with you. You don't want to know the dirty recesses of this mind."

Her eyes flashed. "Do you want me to have a nervous breakdown?"

I frowned. "No, but—"

"Then for God's sake, Matthew, tell me how you would fuck me."

There it was again. That sharpness. That knife-edge. If I had allowed myself to truly love her, I would have told her straight—I wanted her to cut me again and again.

"Well, for one, I'd pink up your ass quite a bit for swearing like that."

Her breaths immediately grew coarse. The outline of her fingers started to move a bit more quickly. "You don't like it when I curse?"

"I like it too much."

Another flash. "Fuck."

I shuddered from head to toe. My head knocked against the wall, and my hat fell to the ground. "Say that again."

"Fuck."

My hand picked up its pace. So did hers.

"You like it when I'm a bit dirty, Matthew?"

"If I remember correctly, you've gotten a lot dirty with me, doll."

Her mouth spread into an impish smile. "So I have." She glanced down at her chest. "In the park, remember?"

"How could I forget? It was only a few weeks ago."

"You like to mark a woman, don't you? Make her belong to you."

"I like to mark one woman."

Fuckin' Christ, her nipples were practically pointing at me. She was playing with one side viciously, pinching and pulling. Finally, I couldn't help it. I reached over and yanked the silk fabric down so her breasts were bared in the hazy yellow light.

"That's better," I said. "The scene of the crime, so to speak."

Her hand was working furiously lower, but the one at her breast paused, then drifted across her chest, playing over the white silk expanse. "You were here. And here. And here."

Her hand drifted down again, and then grabbed her other nipple and pulled roughly enough to make herself hiss.

"Fuck, that's hot." I couldn't help it. And you know what? She deserved to know.

Her grin would have beat the Cheshire cat's for most satisfied. "Let me see it," she whispered. "I want to see you do it again."

"You want to see me come?"

She nodded.

By some fuckin' miracle, I managed not to. "You first, baby."

She didn't even answer—that's how close she was. Instead, she just gazed at my moving hand, bit her lip, and pinched her clit in the same way that *I* had all those months ago. Was she...was she pretending it was me?

"Am I doing that?" I wondered aloud. "In your mind, baby. Are those my fingers on your clit? On your breast?"

Her eyes met mine like arrows. "Yes," she whispered. "Oh, *God*, yes!"

Her body began to shake all over again, but this time, from desire, not fear. My hand slowed—I could have joined her, but I wanted to enjoy it. I wanted to watch. And I didn't want to miss a second of this woman's pleasure.

Ever again.

When at last she came down from her high, Nina slumped against the elevator's wall, gazing at me through half-lidded pleasure.

"It's your turn, my love," she said softly as her hands came to rest in her lap. "Now, what do you need?"

You. All of you. Not just for now, but forever. For the rest of our fuckin' lives.

"A kiss," I said.

Her eyebrows rose. "A..."

I understood her trepidation. And maybe her surprise too. On the one hand, kisses were some of the most intimate things you could do. Some people said kissing wasn't cheating, but I knew exactly how I felt when I saw Nina's lips on another man's, and it didn't fuckin' matter to me that *I* was the one who had no claim.

A kiss was intimacy. A kiss was passion. A kiss was raw, pure, emotion.

And for the first time with Nina, I wasn't just taking it. I was asking.

Her mouth, those rose petal lips, spread into another satisfied smile. If I hadn't known better, I would have thought she was drunk. Fuck, we hadn't even touched each other, and we were both high as kites.

Slowly, Nina made her way onto her knees. She took my face gently between her palms.

"Just one," she said softly. "One more."

I closed my eyes. I was this close to begging her again. Just one? It would never be enough.

But tonight, it would have to be.

Nina closed her eyes. Her thumbs stroked the sides of my face. Then she kissed me, lips open and full. Her tongue slipped in and twisted delicately around mine.

It didn't take more than a few seconds, but that was all I needed. I was primed and ready, and as she kissed me, I finally took my release. For a few short seconds, it really did feel like all the energy of Manhattan was throbbing through my hand, through my cock. I came into my palm, slamming my head against the wall even as Nina's teeth found my lower lip and bit. Hard.

"Fuck," I whispered as I slowly regained normal consciousness.

She bit my lower lip again—lightly this time—and pressed her forehead to mine. "Thank you."

"For what?" I was still catching my breath, but I had enough wherewithal to speak.

"For keeping me sane."

I opened my mouth to ask "at my own expense?" but before I could, the lights in the elevator blinked on, and the blare of two voices jerked both of us out of our daze.

"Mrs. Gardner? Mr. Zola? Are you in there?"

"Hey, Zola, it's Derek. Are you and Mrs. Gardner all right?"

Nina stiffened and rolled off me while she put herself back together. I quickly cleaned up with my handkerchief, then crawled over to the console and pushed the call button.

"Yes, it's us," I said. "Can you get us the fuck out of here?"

"The FDNY should be here in about ten minutes," Derek said. "Just sit tight. I'll let you know when they're here. If the system goes down again, don't worry. We're taking care of it."

I pressed the button. "Thanks."

The intercom went dead again. I moved back to Nina and slumped on the floor next to her. She stared at me for a moment, but before I could say anything, she surprised me by crawling onto my lap and wrapping her arms tightly around my neck.

"Don't say anything," she said, her face buried behind my ear. "Not yet. Not until they come back."

I did open my mouth to speak, but realized she was right. There was nothing else to say. When New York's bravest finally did arrive, we'd have to pretend nothing happened. She'd disappear into the big black Escalade waiting at the curb. I'd disappear into another subway tunnel that would take me back to my side of the city. Maybe tomorrow we'd meet again, one last time, or maybe we wouldn't.

So instead of trying to tell her sweet things she or I wanted to hear, or argue with her some more about what could or couldn't happen between us, for once in my damned, sorry life, I just let it be, like I had told her to do once before. I wrapped my arms around her warm, thin frame and rocked her slowly at the bottom of the car. I shut my eyes and went back to imagining for just a few more seconds that I wouldn't have to let go.

That this woman was actually mine.

That I wasn't just the other man.

CHAPTER TWENTY-NINE

I GOT READY FOR THE STING AT KATE'S SHOP INSTEAD OF MANAGING IT myself in Brooklyn. It came at the price of having Joni and Marie cooing over every damn lapel and cufflink, but Kate had a new double-breasted tux steamed for me, "on loan only," given the Gucci piece had cost her a small fortune.

"That's earmarked for a premiere next month. I'm going to need it cleaned and then re-steamed for the event," she informed me as she brushed a lint roller over my shoulders. "You break it, you buy it. So don't break it."

"I could have worn my regular, you know," I said with a smirk, for which I received a withering glare.

"You cannot go to the Met Gala looking like an amateur, Mattie."

"I resent that."

"I don't care if you're working. If someone finds out I let my brother go to fashion prom looking like every kid at homecoming, I'll lose my reputation."

She finished brushing off my shoulders, then stood back to look over her work. She had gussied the tuxedo up with some elements that would fit the punk-oriented theme of the night—cufflinks that looked more like

safety pins, a tartan bow tie that matched the pocket square. I didn'
want more than that—after all, I was there to blend in.

"There," she said with a final brush of my shoulders. "You look like
prince. Now you just need a Cinderella to meet at the ball."

Behind her, Joni and Marie melted in a chorus of sighs as I pinned
red rose to the pocket.

"Too bad you couldn't take Annie," Marie said.

"Oh my *God*, they would look *so* good together!" Joni agreed.

I didn't reply as I examined myself in the mirror. After all, this wasn'
play. It was work.

———

I WAS FEELING that now more than ever.

"Holy shit," Derek muttered as we walked up the stairs to the museun
proper from the Costume Institute offices. With every step, we could hea
the din of the party gaining momentum as the guests continued to arrive.

"He's not here yet," I said. "Eric's mom already texted him. She's sti'
waiting for Carson to pick her up."

"Think he will?"

I knew what he meant. Unlike yesterday, when the place was still hal
scaffolding and service vans, now the museum was covered with peopl
Press, paparazzi, fans. Camera flashes I could see from five blocks awa
Music that was blasting louder than any concert at the Garden as som
of the biggest celebrities on the planet paraded down Fifth Avenue t
take the long walk in front of the cameras.

And this had already been going on for hours.

Worry was written all over my friend's face—would he and his tear
be able to manage an arrest with this kind of chaos? And would ou
target even show once he saw the clamor?

I shrugged. "He confirmed with her last night. And the de Vriese
seem to think he likes a spectacle, particularly since he seems to thin
he's untouchable. So we have to plan like Carson will be here."

We pushed through the doors into the museum. At the other end c
the long hall, I could see glimpses of some of the most glamorous peopl

in the world sparkling as they entered the main exhibit. Their voices carried along with the band outside.

Derek smirked. "You look very nice. Like Prince Charming."

"Fuck you." I straightened my bow tie. "You look like Peter Pan's shadow." Like me, Derek had been told in no uncertain terms that he and any other members of his team needed to be dressed like security, in all-black suits.

"Let's hope I can fly if Carson does," Derek replied. "Yo, I never did ask what happened in the elevator with the Ice Queen yesterday. The two of you took off like a shot after they finally got you out."

I kept my eyes trained straight ahead. "Nothing happened. I'm sure you can imagine exactly how much we had to say to each other."

"Is she as shallow as the rest of them seem?"

"They seem shallow?" I got a lot of things from the de Vrieses. Complicated. Moody. Entitled. But shallow? Not so much.

"I guess you wouldn't think so. You like all this fancy shit." Derek gestured toward the art hanging around us. "But don't you think it seems like a bit much? Big fancy party just to raise a bunch of money and look at other people's clothes?" He wrinkled his nose in disgust. "I don't get it."

I shrugged again. It wasn't really something I could explain. I probably wasn't ever going to pay to go into this exhibit myself, but I understood why some would.

"She's not shallow," was all I said as we met the security guard at this corner of the party. "Beyond that, I don't know. But none of them are shallow. And especially not her."

Derek didn't reply—we had approached the split where I'd enter the exhibit proper.

"All right," he said. "I'm heading to security downstairs, and you're supposed to blend in with the other bodyguards in the main banquet hall. You got your piece?"

I pointed at the coiled, flesh-colored wire connected to the earpiece I'd been given, along with every other officer helping with tonight's sting. "I'll let you know if I see him."

Derek nodded. "All anyone has to do is get the fucker alone and out of the crowds. That's the deal we made with Cora. Just let me know if you see us doing anything wrong."

I tapped my fist to his. "See you in a few hours."

"My man. Have fun at the ball, Cinderella."

I flashed my security badge at the guard, then followed the path Cora and the museum director had designated as my route into the event. Through a couple of marked-off exhibits, around the Greco-Roman wing, and then through a back door that would lead me around to the zone designated for security.

And found myself face to face with Nina de Vries.

Every time I saw her, she looked like a vision, but tonight was a whole different story. Her dress was unlike anything I'd ever seen—to meet the requirements of the theme, "London Calling," she wore a vaguely punk-inspired floor-length dress made completely out of chain mail. Each tiny silver link clung to her lithe body, shimmering in the light with every small movement. Her blonde hair was woven back in a thick braid from the crown of her head, but otherwise the only bit of color was the slash of red at her lips and the thick bracelet made of chains and tartan around one wrist. She looked like an otherworldly goddess. Like one of her Viking ancestors on the eve of battle.

The question was, battle with whom?

"Matthew." Her voice was a breath, yet still audible despite the clamor of people behind her.

I stared. "Ah, hey, doll."

I looked over Nina's shoulder before saying anything else that might compromise her. Or me. But there was no one in her wake. No other man but me. And, of course, the occasional chatter in my ear.

"Calvin didn't come."

I raised a brow. "Oh?"

Her shoulders moved up and down in a general shrug. "He said he had some kind of urgent work to do tonight. I really don't know."

"Or care?" I couldn't help myself. *Dick.*

Again, Nina shrugged, but her eyes shone as she looked me over. "You look very nice," she said honestly, reaching out shyly to pull on one of my lapels. "This is different from the one you own. Kate's handiwork again?"

"How does she know about your sister?" Derek wondered in my ear.

I nodded to Nina and ignored Derek. The electricity from her fingers penetrated the layers of formalwear, though the sadness in her voice tempered it some. We couldn't help but touch, even in a room full of people. I fingered the bracelet she wore on her wrist, a gesture to the theme. Upon closer look, the chain and plaid was speckled with diamonds.

"We match," I murmured. The tartan was the same exact pattern as my tie and pocket square.

"So we do."

"Did you and Jane plan it?" Was I so desperate to wish she had?

She shook her head. "It's just...kismet, I suppose."

Kismet. Right now fate seemed downright cruel.

"Well, you look..." I shook my head. I still didn't have words for how she made me feel. "I'm speechless. Really."

Nina hid a smile behind one hand. It took everything I had not to smack it away.

"Don't hide your smile, baby," I told her. "You don't have to be happy all the time, but when you are, you shine."

Simple, but true. Her cheeks turned the color of rubies, and she blinked rapidly, like she was trying to stave off tears.

"Zola." Derek's voice was low, but full of insinuation. *What the hell are you doing?* Packed into just my name.

I cleared my throat. I couldn't offer her my arm—I knew she'd never let me anyway—any more than I could tell her everything i was thinking. Not with all these people, photographers, gossips that might get back to her husband. Not with the squad of NYPD in my ear.

In another life, we were going to these things together. Here, we were oceans apart.

I glanced around as we entered the Egyptian wing-turned-banquet hall, then found the security zone just a few feet away.

"That's my wing," I said, pointing toward them. "Over with the gorillas."

Nina followed my finger, then turned back in confusion. "What? But that's completely outside the event. You'll never enjoy the party that way."

I fought a chuckle. "Sweetheart, this party isn't for me. I'm next step up from the help here. You know that."

"That's absurd," she said. "You won't be able to see anything from over there. You can be my plus-one." She held out a white-gloved hand. "Since mine didn't show. And you...did."

The glove covered everything, and for a moment, I stared at the proffered hand, imagining that her fingers were just as bare underneath as the immaculate white material. Derek might have teased me about a fairy tale, this wasn't the time to pretend. That rock was very real. As real as everything I felt for the woman wearing it.

"Yo. Cinderella," Derek snapped. "What the fuck are you doing? Say yes so you can start looking for Carson."

Love isn't perfect. And you can't choose when it finds you. All you can do is make the best of the choices it gives you.

You can't squander the chances you get. Even if they aren't the ones you dream of.

And in that moment, I knew: married or not, this chance couldn't get away. Not without knowing what I really wanted. How I really felt.

It was time to put cards on the table.

So I tucked Nina's hand into the crook of my elbow, then reached behind my ear to turn off my headset. I'd catch a raft of shit about it later, but it was just for a moment. Not everything needed to be overheard.

We entered banquet area, where more than half of the attendees were milling around the tables while a band, warming up for some pop star, started playing various covers. A few cater waiters had started delivering food, but the actors, celebrities, designers, and other wealthy attendees who weren't quite ready to eat were standing around, drinks in hand, a few even dancing near the stage.

"Would you look at them?" I said, nodding at the masses of shiny people.

We found a table bearing Nina's name along with Eric's, Jane's, and a few others I didn't recognize.

Nina blinked. It said a lot about where she came from that she wasn't the least bit impressed by a bunch of famewhores. Joni would be going *nuts* about now.

"Some of the most beautiful people in the world, all in one place," she remarked.

I sank into the seat tapped for "Calvin Gardner" and flicked the name card off the plate like it was a cockroach. "None of them compares to you, you know. Not even fuckin' close."

Nina sat down as well. "Matthew…"

One by one she peeled off her white gloves and stowed them in the small handbag she had brought with her.

"I'm going to break it off with Annie," I said, glancing around in case anyone else was listening. They weren't. But you never knew.

Nina's brows knit together. "What?"

I took a chance and set my hand on her knee under the table. Where no one could see. She tensed, but didn't move.

"Don't tell me it doesn't make you at least a little bit happy." I ran the back of my thumbnail over her knee. "I think it's the right thing to do, given what happened in the elevator. Don't you?"

Nina watched the progress of my finger with abject fascination. "Matthew, I don't think…"

"Don't do that. Don't start any more sentences with 'Matthew, I don't think.' It doesn't matter how many times you try to think your way out of this, doll. It always comes back to the same equation. You and me. That's it."

Nina sighed. "It's not that easy. The elevator—that wasn't me. That was a nervous breakdown, not—"

"Love? Lust? Fascination? Desire?" I leaned in to catch her scent. Roses. And, if I wasn't mistaken, a whiff of red wine. Someone had been pregaming, huh? Nerves, maybe? "Pretty sure all of those things were present in there."

She jerked away from my hand. "You're pushing me. Stop."

I glanced from side to side, then darted in and delivered a lightning-quick kiss.

"Matthew!"

"What?"

"Why did you do that?"

"Are you really saying you didn't want me to?"

"Well, I certainly didn't ask!"

She was flustered. It was cute. Right here in this room full of glit-

tering chandelier-like people, *I* was the one who could make Nina d
Vries blush whenever I damn well pleased.

I leaned in again, ready to take up the challenge she was throwin
down. But to my surprise, she placed a hand on my chest and pushed m
away.

"I said *stop*," she said firmly. "I understand that you want to have
conversation about the elevator, but this is neither the time nor th
place."

"I disagree. I think this is the perfect time and place."

"And why is that?"

"Because I'm pretty sure there's a good chance that when you leav
here tonight, I may never see you again."

Her full red lips pressed together. But she didn't argue. We both kne
I was right. That if things went the way they were supposed to, the
was no reason for us to see each other again.

I took a deep breath. The frenetic energy of the party was catching, a
was realization that I might be making the biggest arrest of my care
tonight. Under normal circumstances, I might have chalked the adre
aline rush up to that, but since I'd met Nina, I'd been more consume
with a woman than my job. Now, everything felt like do or die. With h
most of all.

"Don't you see?" I asked. "After tonight, I may not have a reason
see you again. It's the *only* time we have. So do yourself a favor, and sto
fighting it, princess."

It was the wrong thing to say. Nina's eyes flashed like the su
blinking off a sword's edge.

"You stop," she said through her teeth. "Stop pushing. Stop inte
rupting me every other sentence. You can't just corner me at a place lik
this and expect me to give you what you want."

"*You* invited me in here! And you corner me every other time," I c
back. "On the street. In the goddamn elevator. You expect me to jum
but now that I'm willing, you bat me away again? I'm just being hone
here, Nina. Are you? With me *or* yourself?"

"That's enough, Matthew. I am *not* doing this right here," sh
snapped through suddenly gritted teeth.

"Nina, please. I'm done playing the martyr, fighting what we bot know is inevitable."

"You don't know that."

"I *do* know that. And I'm tired of pretending like you don't exist when, since January, my entire fucking existence seems to revolve around you. You want to keep it to clandestine hotel rooms? Sneaking a night here and there, lunches whenever we can manage. Fine. We'll do that. If that's all you can give me, I'll fuckin' take it."

She was fighting her damnedest to keep that mask in place as she waved at someone or other across the room. "Well, I won't."

"Why the fuck not?" I demanded.

"Because you deserve more than that!" She looked like she wanted to bury her face in her hands, but couldn't because of her carefully applied makeup. "Because I thought about last night too, Matthew. And in the end, I felt horribly guilty. Not because of Calvin, but because of *you*. You and I—it's not meant to be. I know you think it is, but there is no happy ending for us!"

The statement was a punch to the gut. "I don't believe you."

Nina huffed with exasperation. "You must!"

"Well, I don't!" I protested, suddenly wild as I looked about the crowd.

Her sudden imperiousness sliced through me. She'd had enough? Well, I had too.

I turned back to her, full of stubborn resolve. "Please, doll." I let the nickname slip over my tongue like honey. "I think you and I both know that under the right circumstances, you would do whatever I told you to do."

"Matthew, please!" Nina hissed before lowering her voice to a whisper. "I am not kidding. Aside from the fact that Eric and Jane are about ten feet away, I meant every word I said. I understand that things shifted in the elevator, but you have to leave it alo—"

"Well, hello!"

Jane's overexcited greeting landed in the middle of the sentence like a bomb. It was obvious in one glance that neither she nor Eric were expecting me to be present *inside* the party. But Jane didn't seem particularly surprised to find Nina and me talking.

Eric, however, was another story.

"What the hell are you doing here?" he demanded, uncharacteristically terse, even for him. His meaning was clear. I was supposed to be behind the scenes, not in the middle of them.

It was also the cold splash of water I needed. I was at work. I couldn't do this here. But that didn't mean I wouldn't finish it.

"This isn't over," I said to Nina as I turned my headset back on.

"Yo!" Derek demanded. "What the hell happened to you?"

"I couldn't let the cops have all the fun, could I?" I said to Eric, ignoring my detective's frantic voice. "Granted, I'll have to watch, but Nina was nice enough to help me in."

Eric raised his left brow in the exact same way his cousin did when she didn't believe my bullshit either. "You couldn't just wait over there with the squad cars? Don't you think being smack in the middle of the gala would give the game away?"

I frowned. What the hell was he so uptight about? He knew the plan from the start was to have a man inside the gala to observe, at the very least.

I started to answer, but Jane stepped in. "Eric, why does it matter? Carson isn't coming anyway."

I blinked. *What?*

"He isn't?" Nina looked between them. "Oh, I'm so sorry."

"This is what I've been trying to tell you for the last twenty minutes, man," Derek said in my ear. "Eric's mom got a call just before she left. He canceled. I think someone from the Institute snitched."

"Shit," I muttered, trying to ignore the way Eric was currently staring me down.

I couldn't tell if it was because he thought this was somehow my fault, or if he was pissed I'd wasted twenty minutes talking to Nina, who was currently studying her wedding ring like she wanted to rip it off her finger.

Okay, fine. But I had had my doubts about this plan from the beginning. It wasn't my fault that Carson had decided not to show.

Still, it only meant that Eric and Jane would have to wait even longer for the closure they had both been hoping tonight would bring. My own chest felt a bit heavier as the adrenaline that had previously been racing through my system dissipated as well.

My defenses dropped. "I...no, you're right. I should probably go." I glanced at Nina, who refused to meet my eye. "See you, doll."

Eric and Jane immediately turned toward Nina as I slipped away behind a barrier of elephant palms that blockaded the dining area from the rest of the museum. But even from behind the foliage, I could still hear bits of their conversation floating through the din.

"Nina, what the hell?" Eric snapped. "What were the two of you talking about like that? Where is Calvin?"

"Calvin didn't want to come, and to be honest, I was fine with that. He's a terrible date at this sort of event anyway. Since Matthew is helping to put John Carson behind bars, why shouldn't he have come in? I was just helping."

I smirked. She was a good liar. One of the best. But I did wonder if Eric could see her tells the same way I could, being family and all.

"Matthew? Come on, Nina..."

Yeah, he probably could.

"It's nothing, Eric. Let it go," Jane murmured.

"I'm going to the ladies' room."

I remained behind the palm as Nina rushed past me, her cheeks reddened as she fought to keep her mask in place. On the other side, Jane stepped closer to Eric. If I wasn't mistaken, something like relief colored her features. Out of all of us, she had dreaded this night the most, despite being thrilled about her part of the gala.

"Come on," she told Eric. "It's done for tonight. There will be other chances."

Eric scowled. "Will there?"

"With any luck."

I watched as Eric pulled Jane close, then press his forehead to hers with such open, honest adoration, I knew I couldn't just let things with Nina end the way they had. Maybe she needed to say goodbye.

"Don't even think about following her, Romeo," Derek said in my ear.

I sighed. She was lost already, and there were hundreds of people milling about the place.

"Come down to the security offices," he was saying. "We need to regroup."

CHAPTER THIRTY

THERE WASN'T REALLY ANY REASON FOR ME TO LINGER AT THE PARTY, BUT I did. Derek heading back to headquarters to figure out just where John Carson had gone, whether he was even in the city, and whether or not it was possible for the NYPD to pick him up before he left again. Since I was the only one dressed for it, Derek asked me to stay with a skeleton squad (and be available by cell phone) in case someone of note—namely John Carson or another member of the Janus society—showed up after all. It was a long shot, but I was happy to do what needed to be done for the case.

Who was I kidding? It was for her. It was always for her.

Because it wasn't Eric or Jane or any of their related family that I watched from behind the row of elephant palms.

It was Nina.

I watched as she cut her food into the smallest of small pieces and barely ate any of it.

I watched as she faked smiles to three actors who stared at her tits the whole time (and made me want to punch them in their veneers in the process).

I watched as she got up and danced with Jane with limp, lackluster movements.

It was painful. I knew how that woman could move. I knew he grace, her poise, her bone-deep elegance. Right now she looked like flower deprived of sunlight and water.

These people. This world.

Slowly but surely, they were sucking the life out of her.

Like a voyeur, I watched, until finally, a few hours later, her mas dropped enough that she clearly couldn't take it anymore. She looke over the room, chatted with Jane a moment, and then ducked out in th direction of the costume exhibit again. Likely to grab some peace.

I looked around the room. The event was still going strong, but it wa late. People were going in two directions: toward sleep or delirium. Joh Carson wasn't going to show, and there had been no more from Derel The night was a failure. At this point, I had nothing to lose.

I found her wandering the halls of the exhibit in quiet, standing i front of several large mannequins bearing dresses by someone name Vivienne Westwood, all hanging over steel pipes, behind which flashe black-and-white shots of a bunch of punk concerts.

I peered at them doubtfully. Punk wasn't really an aesthetic I go Ripped clothes. Messy hair. I preferred more classic eras. Tailore clothes. *Nonna* always said I was born in the wrong time period. She wa probably right.

Nina stood in front of the exhibit, staring at one dress in particula that was black and white, but slashed with bright red paint. Like it ha gone through a particularly violent war zone.

"Do you like it?" I asked.

She started, but didn't turn. "Well, no. Truthfully, this designer ha never been my cup of tea."

"But it's interesting," I said as I looked up at the three dresses in fron of her. "It's ugly. But Jane—and the other people—they did kind of mak it pretty."

"Punk was all about pretty-ugly," Nina said, almost more to hersel "It was a whole movement about *not* being perfect. *Not* being wha people expected of you. Breaking the rules for just…one…night."

I stilled. There was something off about her. I couldn't put my finge on it, but it was definitely there.

Then she turned, and I saw why.

Cast in the stark lighting of the hall, for a moment, Nina almost looked like she was part of it. She was dressed in the silver chain mail, but as always, the red across her mouth disrupted the otherwise neutral perfection.

But just like the pictures, the ripped dresses, her perfection was marred—by streaks of makeup, the smear of her lipstick.

Nina hadn't come here for a break. She'd come here *to* break.

And yet, as I looked at her, just like every other time I'd laid eyes on her, the same thought crossed my mind: I'd never seen anyone so goddamn beautiful.

"Whoa, whoa, whoa, baby," I said as I crossed the hall and pulled her in to my chest. "What's going on? What's happening?"

"Oh, Matthew," she whimpered. "Why did you come here? I couldn't—"

"Shhhh," I whispered. "I didn't come to argue. I promise."

"Then what?" she asked. "You say you can't take this anymore. Well, neither can I. But I keep trying to say goodbye to you, and you won't let me!"

"Come on, doll. You can't possibly think this is ever going to go away. We're like magnets, you and me. We keep finding our way back together. And the farther you pull us apart, the more our reunions feel like a crash."

She pressed her forehead into my shoulder. "Crashes break things, Matthew. And ours would ruin people's lives." She shook her head sadly. "I'm sorry. You have no idea how sorry. But I can't give you what you want. My daughter. My family—I told you, I can't split them up."

"I'm not asking you to." I swallowed thickly. Goddammit. Why was this so hard with her? I had been in this position with how many other women and never had a problem with it. I should be able to do it for her too. "You didn't let me finish before. If all I get with you is an eternity as the other man…then yeah, doll. I'll take it."

Nina blinked rapidly, like she was trying not to cry all over again.

"You—you would do that?" she asked.

I tipped her chin so she would have to look at me. "Yeah," I said softly, though the reality of that choice twisted my stomach even more. "For you? I would."

She stared at me for a long time. Then slowly, she framed my face with her hands and pulled me down until we were nose to nose. When her lips touched mine, the kiss was soft and slow, but no less wanting.

"And that," she whispered when she finally let go, "is why I would never let you."

In that moment, I knew without a doubt there was no changing her mind. Just as I knew this would be her response from the beginning. I'd never let Nina cheapen herself in any way for me—why would I think she would allow me to do it?

In reality, I hadn't come here with the intention of sparring again. Or even trying to talk her into being together, one last time.

I had come to say goodbye.

Down the hall behind us, the music shifted. From the hired band this time, a pseudo-punk group doing a slow cover of "Strangers in the Night," of all things.

"You have got to be kidding me," Nina murmured to herself as she looked in that direction.

I cocked my head. "What's that?"

She shook her head ruefully. "My grandmother used to play this song to me when I was little—the Sinatra version, not this of course. And when I met you, I thought of it."

I offered a smile. "Well, it fits, doesn't it? Two lovers meeting randomly. It's sort of our song."

"You do look a little like Sinatra."

"Nah. I'm more of a Dean Martin fan."

She chuckled. "Regardless, it's the hat, you know." But then her expression grew sad all over again. "Except it doesn't turn out 'so right,' does it, my love?" A tear glimmered at the far corner of her eye.

I sighed. "Nina, I'll still have to come by Jane and Eric's. Carson, he's out there. Letour. Those men. I'll see your family. I'll—"

"But you won't see me," she said abruptly, sticking her chin out adorably, like a child with its heart dead-set on a particular toy. "I won't be there. Not anymore. I can't. For *both* our sakes."

That was another thing Jane had forgotten about the de Vrieses. They were proud, sure. But on top of that, stubborn.

And, I was discovering—once they had made up their minds about something, there was no changing it.

"Fine," I said. "I will. On one condition."

Her thin blonde brow rose. "And what's that?"

"Dance with me."

She blinked. "What?"

I held out a hand. "If this is our song, doll, then I think you owe me a dance. Just one before we say goodbye."

She opened her mouth to argue, but then put her hand in mine.

"Yes," she said. "That sounds right."

I pulled her into an easy box step, humming the familiar tune I'd heard a thousand times before. She wasn't the only one with memories of this song. How many times had I seen my grandparents sway around their living room? Hell, *Nonna* had taught me to dance to this song and so many others.

But now I knew I'd never hear it again without thinking of the woman in my arms.

"'Strangers in the night...'" I sang along with the lyrics. I wasn't much of a singer, but I could croon a little here and there.

Nina's eyes closed, and she moved the hand on my shoulder to press over her heart.

"Oh," she breathed. "Oh, it hurts."

I cupped her head and held it close to me. "I know, baby. I know."

In the five months since I met Nina de Vries, I'd been a changed man. But that was a dream. It was time to wake up.

"What's this?" she asked, her fingers rubbing over my chest. "You're so...stiff."

I tipped my head. "Bulletproof vest."

"Oh."

More reality. More reminders of what had to happen.

"If it has to end," I said, not completely sure what "it" was in the first place, "then, can I..." I worried my lips. Was I really going to ask for this?

Yes. Yes, I fuckin' was.

"Can I kiss you goodbye?"

For once, Nina didn't look away. Her eyes simply shone with the longing and sadness that I knew flashed right back in mine.

"Yes," she said. "You may. One last time."

I lowered my head and brushed my lips to hers. Then I covered them completely, relishing in the way her mouth fit to mine with the exactness of a jigsaw puzzle. We stopped dancing and instead just stood there, memorizing each other's tastes with the savor of two people who knew they'd never get another chance.

Because this wasn't a kiss born of fury or lust. It was one of mourning.

And soon, it would be one of memory.

For now, we remained in the moment. Two lost souls, sinning together. Forced to make amends by staying apart.

Much as we might belong together, the world just wouldn't have it.

It was time to accept it and move on.

The song ended, and to my disappointment, Nina pulled away. Several more tears had tracked down her face. She reached up and brushed one from my cheek. I hadn't even noticed it was there.

"God," I croaked. "You are so fucking beautiful it hurts."

And she was, too. Between crying and kissing, most of her makeup was gone, including the red lipstick. And yet, her mouth was still plump and red, almost bruised. *Did I just do that?* I wondered.

"I'll miss you, my love," Nina said softly.

I opened my mouth to say the same. To tell her I really did love her, the kind of love I suspected would last a lifetime. Promise that I'd save her from her tower if she'd let me. Beg her one last time to try. To stay.

But instead, just as I started to say the other word that would end things between us forever, my phone blared into the night.

I closed my eyes and frowned. "Fuck."

"You—I'll leave you to answer that."

"No," I said. "No, just—" I peered at the screen. Derek. Shit. "Just wait a second, doll. This will only take a second—Derek, hey. What's up?"

"Zo, you still at the museum?"

I frowned at the suddenly sharp edge in my friend's voice. "Yeah, I'm here. Was thinking about leaving, why?"

"Is Eric there?"

"Ah, I think so. I haven't seen him in a while, but Jane is still here so…"

Beside me, Nina shook her head frantically. "She left just a few minutes ago, before I walked out. She said she was going home."

"Jane just got picked up by Carson," Derek told me.

I nearly dropped the phone. *"What?"*

"Eric's mom called. They were accosted outside the museum by Carson and his thugs. Jane gave herself up so they would let her go. A couple of units are with Mrs. Keeler and some Russian thug on the south side."

"Holy shit."

Nina watched with confusion, clearly waiting for me to clear things up. She could obviously hear the conversation.

"We're on our way uptown, but it's going to take some time to get back from Brooklyn," Derek continued. "Your squad has been alerted, but most of them are gone. Backup's on its way. Are you still carrying?"

I tapped where my sidearm was strapped under my jacket, though Derek couldn't see me. "Of course."

"Good. Can you find de Vries and check on his mother? He's not answering his phone. No one is."

I glanced at Nina, who was already calling Eric. She shook her head. No answer.

"I'm on it," I said. "Keep me updated."

"My man."

Derek hung up, and with that, I turned to Nina.

"Nina, I—"

"Go," she urged. "Go find my cousins. Keep them safe."

CHAPTER THIRTY-ONE

I EXITED THE MUSEUM AT A JOG, NOT EVEN BOTHERING WITH THE MAZE-LIKE service exit, instead taking the pink-clad steps two at a time through the now-empty press line. Limousines lined up and down Fifth Avenue, their drivers chatting while they had a smoke or leaned against the shiny black doors. They glanced at me as I ran past, but I was too busy with the task at hand to say anything.

I found Eric's mother, Heather, another elegant blonde who had probably been a stone-cold beauty in her day, standing in the company of two officers, one reading Miranda rights as the other locked a pair of cuffs around the wrists of a tall man with a large gash on his forehead.

"Mrs. Keeler," I called as I approached.

She had the look of a woman who, for a few minutes, really wasn't sure everything was going to be all right.

"And you are?" sneered one of the officers.

"ADA Matthew Zola," I snapped, pulling the badge I rarely used out of my pocket. It was heavy, similar to a police badge, and generally I only used it to get into crime scenes. Which, since the perp in custody currently had blood streaming from his forehead, this currently was. "I'm a prosecutor with the Brooklyn DA's office working on a case with this woman's family. And I swear to God, if you ruined a six-month investigation"—I glanced at his badge—"*Officer* Johansson, I'll make sure you're writing traffic tickets for the next three years. I need to talk to Mrs. Keeler here and this gentleman *now*."

Normally I wasn't so confrontational with cops, but I didn't have time for this one's bullshit. Not with so much on the line.

Johansson, thankfully, seemed to understand the urgency. He held his hands up respectfully and stepped aside to give me access to Heather.

"Mrs. Keeler." I reached out to touch her hands. "Matthew Zola. I don't know if you remember me."

She nodded fiercely. "Of course I do. Yes, I do very well."

I gestured at the tall man in handcuffs who didn't look like he was going to talk to me even if I wanted.

I was wrong.

"She attacked me!" he screamed in a loud Russian accent. "That crazy bitch tried to blind me!"

"Easy!" I snapped at him before turning back to Heather. "Mrs. Keeler, what is he talking about?"

"Jane did it!" she said, her voice taking on a hysterical edge. "This man attacked us right here. I was on my way home from the party, and he grabbed me. And then Jane appeared, on her own way home, I believe. A car pulled up, and *that man* and two others jumped out—"

"Which two others?" I demanded, though I was pretty sure I already knew the answer.

"Carson," Heather said. "And that other man. The one with the goatee."

Jude Letour.

"Then what happened?" I urged her on. I had a feeling we didn't have much time to spare.

"Oh, dear Jane. She—she tried to fight them all, valiant girl! She took her shoe—her *shoe*, of all things—and used it to fight this one off!"

I glanced back at the Russian's wound, remembering the sharp spikes lining the heels of Jane's shoes. Yeah, I could eerily imagine someone wielding those things as a weapon. Good on her.

"And after that?" I prodded.

"She left!" By this point, Heather was practically hysterical, which made the cops next to her look around uneasily, as if someone might jump out of the bushes to come after her.

"Ma'am, we really should take the rest of your statement at the station," one started, but she quickly cut him off.

"She gave herself up to Carson and the other one. To—to save me!" Heather choked on the last word. "To save me," she repeated, this time weaker. "She got in their car—a big black thing—and they...they just left me here. With this horrible man, who was supposed to take me to my apartment. Luckily, my son's bodyguards were just down the street, and they found us and held my captor still until these young policemen arrived."

I perked up at the news of Eric's bodyguards. "Was Eric here too?"

Heather shook her head. "No. And poor Jane, if she'd just waited..."

The Russian said something unintelligible, then spit on the ground, dangerously close to Heather's shoe.

"Hey, asshole," I snapped. "Didn't you listen to your rights? Anything you say and do *can and will* be held against you in a court of law. And I should know, because I'm the one who'll be doing it! So show a little fuckin' respect, eh?"

His lip curled with a sneer, but he had the good sense to remain quiet as I turned back to Heather.

"Come on," said the other officer, roughly steering the man toward one of the two squad cars at the curb.

"Which way did they go?" I asked. "We don't have much time here, Heather."

"The traverse," offered the officer after he finished putting the Russian into the back of a car.

I looked to Heather for confirmation. She nodded.

"All right," I said. "I'm leaving. Officers, if you can please escort Mrs. Keeler to the station and take her statement, Detective Derek Kingston will be in touch. Nineteenth Precinct?"

Johansson nodded. "Yes."

"Thank you," I said, already ready to jog again toward the traverse across Central Park. I only prayed I wasn't too late.

"ADA Zola."

I turned impatiently. "What?"

Johansson tapped his belt, and his meaning was clear. I didn't know what I was headed into—did I have the means to keep myself safe?

I opened my jacket to reveal the butt end of the pistol strapped under my arm. "I'm good. Just bring that asshole into custody. We'll take care of the rest."

———

I CAUGHT A CAB ALMOST IMMEDIATELY, and before I even had time to consider where a thug trying to backtrack might go, I had given the cabbie Eric and Jane's address. I took a moment to check the chamber of my Beretta—not standard issue for the NYPD, but the same sidearm I'd carried since entering the Marines fifteen years ago.

"Is that a gun?" demanded the driver once we were moving. "No guns in my car."

I slapped my badge against the plexiglass. "I'm law enforcement, sir. Just keep driving." I replaced the gun in its holster and pulled out my phone.

"Zola?" Derek answered on the second ring. "We're in Tribeca coming up the West Side Highway. What's the status?"

"Jane's with Carson and Letour," I said. "They picked her up off the street, a trade for Eric's mom. She ran into some luck—two of Eric's security were waiting for her along with a couple of patrols who just arrested some Russian goon. Everyone is headed to the Nineteenth."

Derek swore profusely. "Where in the *fuck* is de Vries?"

"I don't know, but he knew something about this. I'm on my way to his house now."

"Zola, don't go in there. Wait for the real cops."

"Derek, I can handle myself. I served for four years, and I've accompanied you on countless arrests in the last seven years, haven't I?"

"That's a lot different than taking on two fucking psychopaths alone, Zola. Don't be a hero, you jackass. *Wait for us!*"

But the car had already stopped in front of Jane and Eric's townhouse, and I was halfway out. If they were up there with Carson and his goons, there was no telling what might happen. I couldn't wait to find out.

"Then get here sooner," I said. "Because I'm here now."

I tossed the cabbie a twenty and jogged up the steps to bang on the front door.

"Come on, come on," I muttered as I banged again. The buzzer was broken—they were in the middle of renovations on the house, and it had been disconnected. "Jane! Eric!"

"Mr. Zola?"

I turned to find Tony, the de Vrieses' head of security, standing on the sidewalk flanked on either side by two other members of their detail.

"Tony!" I looked down the street, but there was no sign of his boss. "Is Eric with you?"

Tony looked up toward the apartment. "He left the party a while ago and asked me to meet him here as soon as Mrs. de Vries left the party."

He looked slightly guilty, like he felt somehow responsible for whatever was happening. At least I knew I wasn't the only one being snowed by Tony's boss.

"So he's here?" I turned back to the door as the other men approached. "Let me in."

"Mr. Zola—"

"Tony, I'm in no damn mood," I snapped. "Your boss gave the slip to investigators from the Brooklyn DA's office and a squad of NYPD. Now his wife is in the custody of a known criminal, and I'd bet my fuckin' job they're up there too. Either Eric has been jerking New York City law enforcement around or he hasn't. And either you want me to help them or you don't. *Which is it?*"

But before Tony could answer, a shot rang through the air from the top of the building. Everyone's heads swiveled upward.

"Fuck," Tony said.

"Unlock the fuckin' door!" I ordered.

In a sudden hurry, he did. That was all I needed to take off up the stairs, all of the security members on my tail.

"Jane!" I shouted. "Eric!"

Our footsteps echoed up the dark, dusty stairwell as we climbed, me and three gorilla-shaped security guards.

"Jane!" I shouted again as I reached the fourth floor and started pounding on their front door. "Eric!"

There was a rumble of voices within—one distinctly male, whos tenor I recognized.

"Eric!" I yelled. "Open the fuck up!"

"Move, sir."

I stepped out of the way just in time for Tony to barrel through th door, not even waiting to unlock the thing, which broke immediately c its hinges.

What lay inside the room brought us all to an immediate stop.

"Oh, fuck," said the second guard.

"Jesus," I breathed. "Holy fuckin' shit."

In the center of the de Vrieses' garish apartment was the body of Joh Carson, lying facedown with a hole through his head, the remains c which was splattered pretty much everywhere.

Eric and Jane stood together beyond him, shaking into each other. I another doorway stood Brandon Sterling, hovering over another uncor scious body that I recognized as Jude Letour while he rubbed his knucl les. It wasn't hard to imagine what had happened. Brandon was a bi guy, no stranger to a good street fight.

Two bodies.

Three people.

A nine millimeter Beretta, an exact copy of my own, lying on th ground.

Fuck.

"Get Letour secured," Eric ordered in a voice that sounded almoi distant while he stroked his wife's hair, seemingly unaware of the fa that she was covered in her dead father's blood.

Shock did that. Cast an eerie calm over the people who should fee the situation the most. I knew it well.

Brandon and the two security guards immediately went to do Eric bidding.

"Where's the Russian?" Eric asked.

"In custody," I said as I pulled out my phone. "We found him wit Heather two blocks from the museum. Jane sacrificed herself to sav your mom."

I continued to look around, memorizing the crime scene while called for backup. Derek was next, but we needed the closest units yesterday.

"Dispatch."

"This is Matthew Zola, Assistant DA for the Brooklyn office. There's been an incident at 17 West Seventy-Sixth Street, Apartment 4. Two men wanted by the CIA and the NYPD have been located. We need help."

Eric and Jane stared at me like dummies while I continued to rattle off codes and directions. As soon as units were dispatched, I called Derek.

"Zo, tell me you stayed put."

"I found them," I said. "I'm at their apartment on Seventy-Sixth Street. You need to get here now. Both suspects are here—Carson, shot at close range, and Letour appears to have been knocked out. I've already called dispatch."

"Holy shit," Derek said. "We're on our way. *Don't* let the local precinct's homicide get wind of this."

"I don't know if that's possible," I said. "Just call and let them know you're coming. This is a mess. A big fuckin' mess."

"On it."

I put my phone away as Tony entered the room, speaking to Eric almost automatically. "Boss. Your mother is safe. We grabbed the Russian outside of the park with the cops."

Eric looked visibly relieved. I had to frown. It wasn't actually Tony who was there, but another few of his squad of security. Which meant that to some extent, all of this was planned. Eric had known something like this was going to happen the whole time.

Quite a fuckin' gamble, putting his mother out there to save his wife. Jesus.

Tony looked around the crime scene with a calculating eye before he walked across the room and picked the gun off the ground. I should have yelled at him to stop, but instead, I just watched in horror as the big man cleaned the weapon with his shirt cuff and then wrapped his hand around the grip, fingers on the trigger like he was getting ready to use it himself.

And then he did. He pointed it at the body once more and pulled the trigger. Everyone flinched. But the chamber was empty.

Eric jerked, even though there were no more gunshots to hear. "Tony. Don't—"

"I had to shoot him," Tony interrupted. "He was trying to hurt you and Mrs. de Vries. It's my job. I had no choice."

"Christ," I muttered. This was beyond fucked up. "Man, you can't just—"

"Tony," Jane said weakly from Eric's grasp. "You're not a cop. You don't have to—"

"It's what I would have done," Tony interrupted. "Please. The DA here called the cops. That's our story, and I'm sticking to it."

I smacked my forehead as sirens started wailing outside the windows. I could *not* be party to this. Surely they had to see that.

And Eric, to my relief, did.

"Well, I'm not."

Eric squeezed Jane to his chest, oblivious to the prints of blood she was leaving there like an inkblot test. Then he got up, went to Tony, and took the gun from the security guard.

The big man had loyalty. I had to give him that.

"I appreciate it, Tony," he said. "But you've helped enough tonight. And it's my weapon. It's my family. It's my right to defend them."

The bodyguard looked like he wanted to argue, like he wanted to argue with all of us as he glanced around the room. I gave him my best "you have to be fuckin' kidding me" expression while Jane just looked like she wanted to throw up. Of course. On top of what she had just been a part of, she was a former DA herself. She knew the exact price of perjury, just as I did.

Tony seemed to relent, then stepped back. "Understood."

Eric walked back to Jane and squatted in front of her, begging her to look at him. There was a dead body on the floor, possibly another in the doorway. But the pull between those two put more of an ache in my chest than the smell of death around us.

"Like the air I breathe," Eric said in a low, intense voice to the wife I knew he loved more than anything.

"Like the water I drink," she whispered back.

Red and blue lights announced the arrival of patrol cars. I exhaled, relieved. Backup. Help.

As knocks sounded at the bottom of the stairwell, Eric turned around with a solemn expression.

"All right," he said with the voice of a man who's been through a battlefield and back again. The voice of someone who has killed to save what was his. "Let them up. Let them see everything this man has brought to my doorstep."

CHAPTER THIRTY-TWO

DEATH IS MESSY. THIS ONE MORE THAN MOST.

I wasn't a stranger to crime scenes, even ones as bad as this. Sometimes I wondered if becoming a criminal prosecutor for the last seven years was my way of dealing with the trauma of war. Like I knew somehow I couldn't switch back to a normal life after being in Iraq, where I was as likely to wake up to a distant car bomb or lose a friend as was to have dinner that night. From the moment I left that world for what I thought would be the more civilized field of law, I wanted to make amends. I wanted to seek reparations.

I wanted justice.

Mostly for myself.

Being a prosecutor in a place like Brooklyn offered a middle ground that maybe felt more reasonable than jumping straight back into civilian life. While my classmates went to larger firms, drafted contracts or tried out advocacy, I interned in the Bronx first, then Manhattan, and eventually with the Brooklyn District Attorney, where I'd worked ever since. The work was addictive, like a halfway house between the horrors of war and the polish of civilian life.

Carson was hardly the first body I'd encountered. Nor was it my first time dealing with the hours and hours of taking statements and going

over them with Derek, the cops, lawyers for just about every rich perso
present, and then both my boss and the Manhattan DA, each looking fc
a full review when they arrived at about seven in the morning.

No one slept. We just slogged through it. Statements were given, the
given again, then given again. Derek had a crack at all witnesses whil
the Manhattan ADA and I jockeyed for interviews. It was only after
was finally able to convince the Manhattan ADA that John Carson
death had clearly happened in self-defense and he shouldn't arrest Jar
and Eric, that I finally left for the day, a briefcase full of statements
review and a month's worth of paperwork to file.

It wasn't until close to two o'clock in the afternoon that I trudged int
my house. Frankie and Sofia were still at school for the day. The plac
was empty. Lifeless. A complete and utter void.

Or maybe it was me that just felt wrong.

Maybe it was the lack of finality that bothered me in the end. Ye
John Carson was dead. The man I'd been chasing for six months wa
gone, likely to the terrified relief of the de Vrieses. But, as Derek kep
muttering over and over again, his death essentially severed any links
the plots we'd uncovered. Letour, who survived with a broken nos
staunchly refused to speak, and without him or Carson, we had no ide
how to reach the middlemen involved in the trafficking scheme unde
our jurisdiction.

Eric and Jane might have found some closure, but our case was sti
wide open.

I lurched upstairs, yanking off my clothes from the night before.
tossed the jacket, vest, shirt, and tie on my bed, then kicked off my shoe
below. Kate was going to kill me, but she wasn't getting that tux bacl
Not with a night's worth of police grime on it.

I ambled into my bathroom and stood at the sink for a long tim
trying to get my head right as I washed my arms, my neck, my fac
again and again. As I pressed the cloth to my face, scalding hot on m
street-weary skin, it all came flooding back to me. Not the night. Every
thing else.

It would happen every so often after a particularly grueling arrest.
few gunshots, a desperate perp. One wrong expression, and I was bac
in Fallujah.

I saw their faces looking back at me.

There were my men, worried about the three we left inside.

There were the kids across the street, peering at us through the windows of the building I'd just ordered blown.

There were the women holding them close, knowledge of their dooms written across their otherwise stolid faces.

For years, I'd tortured myself for their deaths. It was why I had always known, without a doubt, that I'd never be the good man everyone wanted me to be. No matter how hard I tried.

Because being a killer was like being an addict. You could be in recovery for the rest of your life, but it never changed the simple fact of what you were.

When I emerged from the bathroom, I stood in front of my closet for what seemed like hours as the same train of thought cycled through my mind. The way the slumped bodies had brought me back to the scene of my own crimes. I'd never imagined I'd kill again. But I always knew without a doubt I could. Had I arrived a few minutes earlier, would I have been the one to pull the trigger?

Eric had done what he needed to do to protect his wife. He had proven without a doubt that he would do literally anything to take care of what was his. And that included killing a man.

If anything, it made me respect him more.

And I couldn't help thinking of Nina.

The bruises on her wrist.

The too-plump sight of her lips.

The way she cowered from certain kinds of touch, but sought out others like a battered animal.

There was something I was missing. Someone was hurting her. Her husband, maybe. An uncle. Hell, maybe it was Eric himself.

But she had never let me in long enough to find out.

I started to shake as fury at my complete and utter failure really began to sink in.

Make me proud. Nonno's last words.

I tried, Nonno, I really did. I found a good woman, and loved her all I could. But she couldn't love me back, Nonno. What good is that pride, when it only leaves you alone?

I had tried so hard.

I should have tried harder.

I had fought so hard.

I should have fought harder.

For her.

For us.

I turned from the mirror, sickened by my reflection. Maybe *Nonno* was wrong the whole time. Pride was a deadly sin, just like envy. Just like lust. I couldn't pretend not to be a vain man, with my closet full of three-piece-suits, right down to the pants I was wearing right now. Perhaps the way out of this demented existence was to stop caring so goddamn much in the first place.

Pride comes before the fall.

And I had been falling for the last five months in every sense of the word. Smashed by my own cowardice when it came to the woman I loved.

I stared at the simple white walls that framed my bedroom. She had only been here once, but I had never stopped seeing her in it.

Suddenly, though, I hated that color more than I had ever hated anything in my life. Nearly every time I had seen her, Nina had worn some shade of white. Colorless neutrals that forced her to fade away. Only that night at the opera had I ever seen her in color. Seen her look completely and truly alive.

To some, white might be the color of purity. To me, it just looked like a trap. A way to pretend like the rest of the world in its infinite messiness didn't exist.

Blood was red. And it stained too.

Just like the color of her lips after I kissed them.

And without thinking twice, I pulled back my fist and rammed it into the wall as hard as I could. The plaster was thin—I knew because I'd installed it myself. I'd have a hell of a bruise later and my knuckles were already bleeding, but my hand went right through the wall, causing a cascade of dust to fall over my hair and shirt.

"Fuck!" I shouted and punched the wall again. And again. And again, until finally the pain throbbing up my arm overcame the rest of me.

I turned, breathing heavily, and caught a glimpse of myself in the mirror. Gone was easygoing Matthew Zola. Well-mannered attorney. Good uncle, grandson, and brother.

I looked like an animal. A creature ruined. A man at his wit's end.

"What are you doing?" I asked aloud and, quickly, slapped myself hard across the face.

———

"SLAP ME, BABY," *I told her as our pleasure took over.*

"What?" Her voice was heavy with lust, in spite of her obvious confusion.

I took her arms and yanked her up, falling onto my heels so I could drill into her from below.

"Slap me. Hit me. F-fuck, baby. Are you close?"

Her arms were entwined around my neck as our sweat-soaked bodies met. Her head fell back, offering me the white expanse of her neck. I bit one side.

"Oh, God," she moaned. "Oh, God, I'm...I am close. Matthew!"

"Then, slap me." I grabbed her chin and forced her to look at me. "Treat me like the dog I am. Please, Nina. I need it."

———

A MOAN ERUPTED from deep inside my chest. I really was an animal. A deeply, deeply wounded one. And, as always, I had done it to myself.

"You done crying, you worthless fucking POG?" I demanded of my reflection. My eyes wet—from sadness and pain. I slapped myself again and again, taking my vengeance out on my own face instead of the walls I'd worked so hard to build. "Are you done fuckin' crying, you fuckin' pussy? You need a goddamn straw to suck it the fuck up?"

There was no answer, of course. None but the other, unintelligible voice that existed deep in my soul. The one that told me it was time to pick myself out of this shitty spiral and get back to my life. Fix the holes in it, literal and otherwise. Patch the wall. Paint it another color if that's what I needed. And, at long last, move the fuck on.

Spurred into sudden action, I stripped off the rest of my finery and changed into clothes more fitting for a man like me. Twenty-year-old jeans stained with paint, an old undershirt.

Full of intention, I pounded downstairs in search of my toolbox under the sink.

"Fuckin' mess," I muttered as I shoved the garbage pail and various cleaning implements out of the way. It wasn't bad, actually—Frankie and I tried to keep things relatively clean.

A drip of water fell on my face.

"Goddammit."

I pulled out a wrench and immediately flopped onto my back to tighten the leak. It was dirty work, lying under a sink. Grease quickly got on my hands, the white of my undershirt. I didn't care. I didn't care if I ruined this white forever.

Just as I was almost finished, a loud knock sounded on the front door.

"Frankie?" I called out. "Sof? Is that you? Get your key, I'm elbow deep in the damn sink."

The knocking continued, but there were no telltale footsteps outside door.

"Shit," I muttered as I gave one last tug on the wrench, then shoved out from under the sink.

The knocking grew louder. I rolled my eyes. My tenant, who worked a graveyard shift, was probably pissed about the sudden raft of noise.

"Hold on, hold on, Brent," I called as I shuffled to the front door. "Listen," I said as I opened it, "it's only going to be five more—"

But it wasn't Brent at the door. Instead, it was the last person I ever thought I would see standing on my front step today.

Nina stood like an angel, the afternoon sunlight gleaming behind her where it bounced off the harbor in the distance. She was dressed, per usual, mostly in white, with only a slightly smeared dab of red coloring her lips. But little things were off. Her shirt, a white blouse, was untucked and wrinkled, like she had worn it all night. She wore jeans for the first time since I'd met her—skinny gray things that hugged every curve she had, but looked at least ten years old, as if she hadn't worn them since before she had become a mother. Her hair was pulled back into a mussed braid instead of a sleek ponytail.

But her eyes—her eyes were round and wide as they traveled over me, taking in my slovenly appearance.

"Shit."

I looked down. I was dressed for chores, not company. I didn't usually let anyone but my siblings see me like this. Rags, all of them. Fitting for a man who worked with his hands, who spent his days on his back, not at a desk.

Which right now, I supposed, I was.

Maybe that was all I was ever supposed to be.

She held up her hand in hello. Still wordless. But instead of the customary flash there, something else caught my eye. Or, I should say, a lack of something.

Her ring finger on her left hand was bare.

The diamond was gone.

"I, ah, hey, doll," I said as I rubbed my neck. "I—shit, I wasn't expecting you."

In spite of the fact that she had just been hammering at my door like a woodpecker, Nina still didn't speak. Instead, she just stared, looking up and down my body with an expression I couldn't quite read. Horror? Lust? Disgust? I honestly couldn't tell.

I shifted uncomfortably from foot to foot as I stared down at the shirt that was clinging to my torso having been splattered with plaster dust and then dirt and water. "If you give me a minute, I'll run upstairs to clean up."

At the last two words, her gaze found mine again and focused.

"Nina?" I asked. "Hey. Are you all right?"

She blinked. And then, to my complete and utter fuckin' surprise, she lunged.

CHAPTER THIRTY-THREE

THE DOOR SLAMMED HEAVILY BEHIND HER AS WE TOPPLED INTO THE HALLWAY. Nina shoved me against the plaster hard enough that my head knocked against the wall with a thud.

"Nina," I managed between her ruthless attacks of kisses.

It was hard. Oh *fuck*, it was hard. But not as hard as not knowing what the fuck was going on.

"*Nina!*"

With gladiator-level effort, I managed to get my hands on her shoulders and set her away from me. Her rosebud mouth hung open, wet from mine while her chest moved up and down.

"Please."

Her voice was hoarse with want. Her eyes, red-rimmed, flew all over me wildly, desire coloring their deep gray depths. It wasn't a request, but even in the throes of lust, Nina de Vries was ever the lady.

It was everything I could do not to literally drag her down to the floor. Down to my level.

"What are you doing?" I was struggling to catch my own breath.

"I had to see you." She pressed a hand to her chest. "I don't want to talk. I just—I needed—I needed *you*, Matthew."

I licked my lips. She didn't want to know how easy it was for a man like me to lose myself in a woman when I felt like this. With this one, I felt like I was falling most of the time just thinking about her.

And now, for the first time, she was basically writing me a blank check to cash in all my frustrations. To release all the feral rage, lust that we had both been keeping pent up.

For months, I'd tried to be a gentleman for her sake.

But today, when I still had visions of justice and a man's blood on my mind, I couldn't do it.

"You—you don't know what you're asking," I growled.

"Yes, I do." She swallowed, the movement rippling her swan-like neck. "I saw Jane. I saw Eric. Heather told me they came to her house, but only after I saw theirs first. I arrived this morning, when people were...cleaning up."

I winced. I could easily imagine her in her speckless glory, stumbling upon the crime scene when it was still half a war zone. Seeing the bloody remnants of Eric's vengeance splattered over the walls, the fine furniture. Absorbing what happens when a man does what's necessary to protect his own.

"I saw the b-body of that man when they carried him out. He was covered with a sheet, but there was still blood...and something in me... just...snapped."

She mimed the motion with her fingers, though I could see she was shaking from the memory. So was I. Just the thought of her anywhere close to what had happened in that room...I shuddered. I had wondered myself, what would I have done had it been her? I was no stranger to vigilante justice. And with Nina, I had a feeling that the instinct I kept buried deep would fly out of control in the space of a second.

"I saw that man," she whispered. "And then I thought of you there. Maybe even when he died. And I realized...I might never see you again."

"I thought we covered that at the museum."

She shook her head. "For some reason, that's when it sank in. And I couldn't breathe. I just knew I had to come here. I had to f-find you. Matthew, I was wrong. About us. About everything. I always was. It just took me this long to realize it."

I closed my eyes and rubbed my face. How many times had I prayed for her to say exactly this? Come to the same epiphany I'd been having again and again like regular, painful clockwork.

But.

Catharsis only got you so far.

I had a feeling it was too late.

"I can't be a good man for you today, Nina," I said. "Honestly, doll? I'm not sure I ever could."

She closed the space between us again, and with one quivering finger, traced the line of my jaw. Her light touch had every hair on my body standing up straight. With her this close, I stopped being a man. I was an animal caged by the tattered remnants of my own inhibitions. And here she was, trying to break the lock.

"I don't need a good man," she whispered as her lips hovered over mine. "I just need you."

I inhaled deeply. It was like I couldn't get the oxygen into my lungs. "And Calvin?" I could barely say the name without spitting. I had never had so much hatred for someone I had never actually met. That alone would probably be my ticket to hell in the end.

"It's over." Nina's hand floated up and touched her lip. "He doesn't know it yet. But I can't—not anymore." Like me, she inhaled deeply. "Please, Matthew." She was begging now, threatening tears turning her gray eyes silver. "I c-can't breathe, I need you so much."

I sucked in a harsh breath. "I don't think you understand. You're not the only one fucked up by what happened in that apartment. Today... right now? Nina, if I cross this line, I ain't coming back, baby. That's it. Point of no fuckin' return."

I couldn't stop staring. At her mouth. Her neck. The hint of breasts just below her shirt collar.

Slowly, Nina set her hand on my shoulder and leaned in so her lips brushed my ear.

"Then take me," she whispered. "I was yours from the start."

I remained frozen for all of a half-second more. And then, once her words finally sank in, I was all action.

Take me, she said.

No fuckin' problem.

My hand snaked around her neck and yanked her to me for another soul-searing kiss. Not the kind that warms your heart. The kind that fuckin' burns.

I slipped my other hand around her waist to pull our bodies flush. Her mouth opened, and she groaned as our tongues met, twisting, tangling, tasting every bit of the delicious forbidden fruit we were together.

I couldn't talk. I couldn't even think. And I didn't need to, because this was all instinct. Nina was a live wire, mouth open, finger clawing, lips sucking, legs around my waist as she jumped into my willing arms.

"Fuck," I grunted as I flipped her around so her back was to the wall.

She moaned before taking my lower lip between her teeth. She bit. I growled. She knew what a little pain did for someone like me. She knew exactly what it released.

"You better be careful, princess," I rumbled as I ground into her. "You scratch the wolf, you bring out the beast."

Her hand found my face with a sharp slap, and then she grabbed my chin, forcing me to look at her. Her sharp eyes shone with a metallic gleam—that ruthless knife-edge that only I seemed to bring out like this.

My girl.

"Don't call me that," she said, even though her voice was thick with desire. "Not unless you want to get slapped again."

I smirked. "Promise?"

Before she could answer, my hands found her ass and squeezed hard. There was no way she couldn't feel my cock pressing against my pants, just a few measly pieces of fabric between it and the promised land. Nina moaned louder even as she bared her teeth. We were both animals now, wild and lost to our feral natures. Her legs were vises around my hips, so I released her ass long enough to take hold of her shirt and tear. Buttons shot across the room like bullets.

"Yes," she hissed as she took a handful of my hair and yanked. "Rip it off, Matthew. Ruin all of it."

I wasn't sure what she meant. I didn't give a shit either. Because I just needed this woman naked, nothing between us. Pure and bare and laid out for me and *only* me.

For now.

For fuckin' ever.

And I didn't care how many shirts I had to destroy to make it happen.

Her feet dropped to the floor, allowing me to attack her jeans as well, peeling the denim and her silk panties down her long, smooth limbs.

"Take it off," I ordered, staring at her still bra-covered breasts.

Nina bit her lip, then reached behind her back to unlatch the garment. The movement forced her chest out, nipples erect as the silk fluttered to the floor.

"Vixen," I said.

She shuddered, then opened her legs an inch or two. I stared, momentarily entranced by the groomed thatch of dark blonde. Then I took it as the invitation it was and went to work.

She tasted like heaven. A succulent world I'd never stop trying to discover, but also one I knew in the depths of my warped sinner's soul. Nina wrapped one leg around my neck and buried a hand in my hair, urging me deeper with my lips, tongue, fingers that slipped into her slick heat.

"Matthew!"

She didn't even try to stifle her cry. And I didn't want her to. I would do this to her anywhere she liked. And I'd want her to scream as loud as she fuckin' pleased.

She came with a shout that echoed through the halls of my small house, and for a moment, I wondered if the neighbors could hear her. My tenant downstairs. The people next door. Across the street.

I wondered if anyone else knew that I was about to bury myself in Nina de Vries in every fucking way possible.

The idea turned me on that much more.

"Oh, God," she breathed as her voice returned. Her body still vibrated with the last of her orgasm.

I stood and kissed her, letting her taste herself on my lips. Then, before she could stop me, I bent down and toppled her over my shoulder while I kept an arm wrapped around her knees.

"Matthew!" she cried.

I smacked her ass, hard. "Hold still."

She jerked, but didn't argue. I could still smell her desire. So I spanked her again, just for good measure, enjoying the way my palm burned slightly when it made contact with her firm, smooth skin.

Nina sucked in a breath between her teeth. Yeah, she liked it too.

I jogged up the stairs while Nina clawed at my back to keep herself from falling. I kicked open the door to my room, paced quickly across the small space, and dumped her unceremoniously onto the bed.

"You didn't think we were done, did you?" I kissed her again, letting her taste my urgency. My need was pulsing through every vein, every vessel.

"Oh, no," she said as I stood. "I think we have hours still, don't you?"

"Hours?" I grabbed a handful of my undershirt behind my back, ripped it over my head, and flung it across the room. "Try a lifetime, baby. And even that won't be enough."

She sank back into my pillows and watched, unabashed, as I stripped off the rest of my clothes. Her golden hair spread behind her like a halo. It didn't matter where she was. Hotel. Gala. My tiny fuckin' bedroom.

Nina de Vries was a fucking queen.

"You are so goddamn sexy," I told her as I unbuckled my pants. "Do you have any idea what you do to me?"

"Tell me."

I let my pants drop to the ground. "You shred me, baby. All my self-control. All my better instincts. Gone when I see you."

She didn't reply. Instead, as I removed my boxers, her tongue slipped out, a delicate bit of wet pink, like a child upon spying an ice cream cone on a hot summer day.

It's not like she hadn't seen it before. At the hotel, of course. And the park. And just a few days ago, even.

But the elevator was dark, and here we were in the light. Here we had the space to stretch out, body to body. To look. Touch.

Taste.

Nina sat up and moved to the edge of the bed while I ripped off my boxers, kicked them away with the rest. Ignoring the hamper. Ignoring my typical desire to keep everything in its place.

All I needed right now was her.

"I forgot how big you are," she said as she took my cock in her hand.

"You saw it just a couple of days ago."

"It's a little different up close." She drifted her lips over the tip. "Now it's my turn."

I watched, hypnotized by my dick disappearing into her mouth. She was as eager as I'd been, as hungry, practically making a meal of me.

I looked up at the ceiling, trying my hardest not to embarrass myself. Nina had no idea what kinds of depraved thoughts were running through my mind. If she had any clue how I wanted to take her...use her...claim her...she'd run screaming. I knew she would.

Nina released me. "Am I doing this wrong?"

I looked down. "What? No, of course not!"

"Then what are you doing?"

I frowned. "What do you mean?"

"You're not moving. Or saying anything."

"I..." I gulped. "I'm just enjoying it, I guess."

She kissed the very end again. I shivered.

"Fuck, baby," I said, unable to help myself as I rocked forward. "Don't stop there."

"Then use me," she whispered. "I want you to."

She opened her mouth again. But she didn't move. This time, she just waited. For me to take exactly what I wanted.

I slipped my hand around the back of her head and held her in place as I slowly, carefully began to do as she asked.

I closed my eyes and tried to imagine about a thousand other things besides exactly what I was doing: fucking Nina de Vries's pretty little mouth. I had to draw things out. Just a little bit longer.

I failed.

Nina's shoulders sank with relief and pleasure, even as she starting stroking her my base along with my rhythm. A low hum in the back of her throat created a mild vibration as I moved. Using her, just like she said. Just like, God help us both, she wanted.

"Fuck!" I hissed, then pulled out.

"What?" she asked again. "Why did you stop?"

"Because I need more," I snapped. "And I need it right fuckin' now."

I yanked her up and threw her back on the bed, this time crawling over her low, the way I used to crawl the obstacle course, all the way back in basic training. I slid between her legs with clear intent.

"Are you ready for me, baby?" I asked, though I could feel the answer clear enough. She was soaked.

I brushed her hair away from her face, framing its gorgeous shape with my hands. We were so different from this angle. My skin was darker, beaten, weathered even from years of abuse. Hers was smooth and pristine. Did she really want me to mar all this perfection?

"I meant what I said, Nina." I was poised at her entrance, her legs splayed under me. But I wouldn't move. I needed to hear it one more time. "Point of no return. Are you sure that's what you want?"

With sure, even movements, Nina slid her hands over my shoulders and wrapped her long legs around my waist.

"I wanted this before I ever met you," she whispered. "Give me everything you have, Matthew. I already belong to you."

That was all I needed as I shoved into her with a loud groan. She was tight. I was ready. And it took only moments for the two of us to find the natural rhythm that pulsed between us no matter what.

"Is that what you wanted?" I asked her. "Me inside you? Claiming you?"

I didn't wait for her to answer, just took her mouth again. She bit hard enough that I tasted blood, but it only reminded me of hers. So, of course, I bit right back.

Animal.

Barbarian.

Fucking Nina de Vries. Loving Nina de Vries. It was all the same in moments like this. Everything coalesced into one thing: instinct.

"Will you take me again?" she said as our bodies moved furiously. Slick with sweat and hunger. "Every-everywhere?"

It took me a moment to understand what she meant.

"You mean here?" I slipped a hand under her ass and dragged a fingertip over her puckered bud. "Like last time?"

Nina shuddered violently. "Ummmmm yes."

A wicked smile spread across my face before I kissed her again, the kind of kiss that left us both breathless. "Your mouth. Your pussy. Your tits. Your ass. Nina de Vries, I will fuck you anywhere and everywhere. Because this body belongs to me, baby. Don't you forget it."

"Ah!"

She was starting to lose it. My finger continued to tease her, just a little, while I thrust harder. God, I wanted to split her in two.

"I'm close," she cried, back arching toward the ceiling. Her nipples, pebbled with desire, were twin works of art. "Oh, Matthew, I'm so close."

Thank fucking God. I was right behind her.

"Where do you want it now?" I asked.

She liked it when I finished on her. She liked seeing it, just like I did. Physical evidence of the way we fell apart together.

But instead, Nina grabbed my hips and urged me even deeper. "I want you here," she whispered. "As deep as you can go. And, Matthew?"

She pulled me close, and her lips brushed mine again.

"What, baby?"

"I want it now."

The legs around my waist squeezed, showing me just how much she meant it.

"Oh *God*." As my self-control fled, I barely knew my own name.

But I still knew hers.

"Nina!" I cried as my entire body flexed. "Oh JesusFUCK-INGChristNINA!"

"MATTHEW!"

Our names mingled, desperate animal cries echoing off the walls like bells tolling from far away. Nina came with a shriek, me with a howl. I collapsed on top of her, and she welcomed me with bites and scratches. But I thrust home, home, home again, trusting my instincts as they too tolled with the knowledge I'd carry with me always.

This woman.

This union.

This is where you belong.

CHAPTER THIRTY-FOUR

UST LIKE I REMEMBERED, THE WOMAN WAS VORACIOUS. WE WENT AGAIN, nd again, making use of the extra hours we had, making up for the months lost together. I tried to take a shower, but she followed me right n. An hour later, she did the same—I was her shadow. I tried to go downstairs to get us water, but she tracked me to the kitchen like a damn ioness and pounced on me against the fridge.

Is this what it would be like every day? I wondered as we collapsed on he bed after the fourth time.

No. Of course not. No one could spend a lifetime together without getting at least a little sick of each other.

Right about now, though, it seemed fucking impossible.

"I missed you," she murmured. She floated a hand over to my cheek nd traced the line of my jaw with her finger. "Every day I missed you."

I stroked her back, memorizing the way her spine curved gently down, down, down. "Is that why you came? Because you missed me?"

Stupid fuckin' words. They didn't even come close to covering this ind of yearning.

"Believe it or not, I came here to tell you I couldn't see you again. Not s friends. Not as anything. We didn't get to finish our goodbye at the museum before you were called away."

"How'd that go for you?" I was joking, but the truth was, I couldn'
quite register the heaviness in her words. I was still half-dazed from sex.

Nina was serious. Her big gray eyes welled up before she buried he
face into my shoulder. Immediately, I gathered her to my chest. "Hush
doll, hush. Talk to me, eh? I'll make it better."

"I meant it, you know," she mumbled into my skin. Her fingers clung
to my biceps fiercely. She wasn't letting me go. "I couldn't do i
anymore."

"Couldn't do what, baby?" I murmured as I stroked her hair. Lord, i
was so smooth. Like silk. Satin.

"Couldn't s-stop this." With a tiny grunt, she pushed herself up
letting her hair fall over one shoulder while she wiped away one las
tear. "I couldn't stay away from you. I can't fight us, Matthew, thougl
God knows I tried. It's simply…"

"Inevitable?" I suggested as I brushed the hair out of her face.

"It's something."

Her voice was quiet. I knew then she was thinking beyond this room
To the effects our relationship—if that's what I could call it now—woule
have on other people. Her family. Her daughter. Even her cheese fuck o
a husband.

Doubt crept into my heart like a vine. Ready to strangle the new hop
that had bloomed.

"What is it?" she wondered, watching my face as closely as I watchec
hers.

I sighed. Maybe it should have been a comfort to know she coule
read me just like I could read her. But it wasn't. Not when I had to sa
what I had to say.

"Did you really mean what you said before? That you want me? You
want us?"

I had said we were past the point of no return, but even I knew yor
couldn't trust what people promised during sex.

And besides…something was still missing.

Her forehead crinkled adorably. "I—well, yes. Yes, I did."

I cocked my head. "Maybe I need to hear you say it."

"Say what?"

"I think you know."

She took a deep breath. Then another. And another. But she didn't look away. Her silver gaze locked with mine, and I had the strange feeling that if I dared look away, it would be like I was physically tearing off my own limb.

"I love you," she said in voice that was strong. Unshakeable.

My heart exploded, but I didn't move an inch. I sensed somehow that she needed me to be as solid in this moment as I needed her to be.

"And it won't—Matthew, it won't stop," she continued. "Sometimes I feel it so intensely I'm afraid I will drown in it. Like a flood or a tidal wave. Other times it's more like a creek or even just a trickle—usually when I haven't seen you for a long time. But it's always there. Matthew, it's always there."

By the end of her speech, her voice had risen again. Fearing hysterics, I pulled her close.

"I know, baby," I murmured as I covered her face with kisses. "I know."

"Do you?"

She sighed, sounding almost as content as I felt in that moment. Because Nina loved me. Nina Evelyn Astor de Vries loved *me*, no good, lifelong sinner, grade A son of a bitch Matthew Zola.

"I love you," Nina said again, softer. Like a poem. "But, Matthew... do you...Matthew, do you love me too?"

I released her and then moved so that we were lying face to face on my pillow. Then I cupped her face like I was holding a precious piece of art. Which, I supposed, I sort of was.

"Nina," I pronounced clearly, "I wanted you the moment I saw you sitting at the end of that bar. I needed you the second I kissed you. But I loved you...baby, I loved you the moment you opened that beautiful mind of yours and let me in. You say you belong to me? Well, you own me, Nina. That's just all there is to it."

We stared at each other for a few moments, blinking at each other across the bedding like owls.

But in the end, she kissed me, soft and long until we both relaxed.

"It won't be easy," she said after we broke apart. "Calvin will fight it."

"When have I ever backed down from a fight?"

She gave me a look. Of course, the only person she'd ever seen me fight with had been her.

"Is he really that attached to this marriage?"

I fingered her empty ring finger. I wanted to ask why she'd removed it before coming. But there had been enough of hashing out the past. We talking about the future now.

"He's vindictive," Nina said. "And yes...he wants it. For his own reasons."

"Let me guess. Seventeen billion of them."

"Do you really think that's all anyone would want me for? My family's money?"

Guilt lanced through me.

"Shit. Baby, no. I didn't mean it like that. I just—" I shook my head. Fuck, I really stepped in it this time. "I just meant that he never seems to care about you now. He never shows up. He's never around."

Was it my imagination, or did Nina shudder?

"For a long time," she said, "I liked it that way. I didn't mind being alone. Until I met you."

Her smile was so sad, it broke my heart.

"Well, not anymore," I promised her. "You're stuck with me now. He can drag you through every family court in New York if he wants to. But as far as I'm concerned, it's done. All that matters is us, now."

"Us," she repeated. "It's a nice thought."

"You, me. When you're ready, Olivia too."

I thought about telling her that I was pretty sure I'd fallen in love with her daughter too, but in a different way. That despite the fact that I'd only met the kid once, somewhere deep down, she felt like the daughter I was supposed to have.

Another time, I thought. We didn't have to have every life-changing conversation right this moment. We had all the time in the world.

Nina sighed, this time with pure contentment. "I can't wait until she can meet you properly. She's going to be mad about you, I know it." She tipped her face to mine. "Just like her mother."

I cupped her jaw. "Do you know...that sometimes you talk like a fancy English duchess?"

Nina giggled. "I had a nanny from Hampshire when I was a girl. It must have made a difference."

"It certainly does, duchess." I kissed her again. "Talk fancy to me some more."

But before she could, I smothered her face with kisses, delighting in the peals of laughter that came in response like sun-drenched church bells.

God *damn*. I could listen to that sound for the rest of my life.

And maybe, if I played my cards right, I would.

Anything seemed possible now.

On the table, my phone buzzed. I checked the clock. It was almost five thirty—late enough that Derek was wondering when the hell I would wake up. Plus, Frankie and Sofia would be getting home soon.

I sighed. Nothing like real life to burst the damn bubble. But maybe it wouldn't be so bad. After all, the point now was to bring both our lives inside.

I answered the phone. "Hey, man. I just woke up."

Against my arm, Nina gave a light snort.

"Sleep. Yo, that must be nice."

"You didn't get any?"

"Maybe a couple of hours. But I've been in the photo lab with the techs. They had some new stuff to look at from the photos I showed you yesterday. The two in the car weren't recoverable, but they managed to get a decent rendering of the one on the other side."

"Anyone we know?"

"I think you might."

He said a name, and he was right. I did recognize it. And the moment I heard it, my blood turned ice fucking cold.

I sat up in bed, letting the sheets pool around my waist. Nina watched me curiously, though when her eyes alit on the abs I worked so hard to maintain, they brightened with a much different emotion. Greedy girl.

But I was too distracted by the bomb Derek had just dropped to think about round five.

"Are you serious? *Him?*"

"Yeah, man. I gotta follow up more, but you know how these people work. I'll look into it, but he's probably got the attorney general on his side, just like Carson did, which means none of the feds will go after him either. And I don't know about you, but I'm still not convinced the Manhattan DA's not on the take too."

I sighed. Yeah, he wasn't wrong about that.

"It's you and me on this, brother. Otherwise, no one is bringing this organization down. We need to finish this."

I swallowed.

"Get the prints to Tiana and tell her to start drafting an affidavit and the bill," I said. "I'll be at the office within the hour."

I turned off the phone. Dread lodged in my stomach like an anvil. But I had to move. With a hard, hard swallow, I slid out of bed.

"Matthew?"

I grabbed a pair of clean underwear from my bureau and put them on. My chain gleamed with the saint and the cross on the top of the dresser next to the Navy Cross. Symbols of my failed attempts to be a decent person.

I stared at myself, pressing hard on the wood. I was a bad man. A shameless man.

But for her, I had to be better.

This time, there was no other alternative.

I turned to face Nina, but she seemed to be as attracted to me in my boxers as when they were totally off.

I snapped in front of her face. "Yo, eyes up, duchess!"

She grinned, a cheeky thing that made my heart drop. "I'm sorry. It's a bit distracting, you know. You have a *very* nicely shaped posterior, Mr. Zola."

Fuck.

How was I going to do this to her now?

How could I do this to *us* now?

"Matthew?" Now all traces of lust and humor had disappeared. "Who was that? Do you really have to go back to work now?"

"It was Derek."

I rubbed the back of my head, buying myself more time by digging around my closet for a pair of pants and a shirt. For once, I didn't care

bout looking anything more than average. I grabbed the first tie I saw
nd spent much too long making the knot.

Unfortunately, by the time I turned around, Nina was staring like I
vas a package she wanted to unwrap. Good fuckin' God. Was there
nything I could wear that wouldn't write *sex* across that beautiful face?

"Nina!" I barked, unnecessarily harsh.

She blinked, then cowered, almost like she was afraid. *Shit.*

"What is going on?" she asked. "You're acting very strange. And you
—do you have to go back to work?"

"That was Derek," I repeated as I sat on the bed. "He—he found
omething. And yeah, I have to go in."

She frowned. "Want to tell me about it?"

I shook my head. "I probably shouldn't...it's part of an investigation
ve were running. Part of the one with John Carson."

She tensed. We both did. That ghost would take more than a few
ours to exorcise from everyone's lives.

"But he's dead," she said. "What does it matter now?"

"It matters because he didn't work alone." I blew out a long breath,
rying to figure out what I could say. And what might get me fired. Dread
ugged me like a straitjacket, so tight it strangled. "It was..." I swallowed.
I can't believe I'm going to fuckin' say this. But, Nina—baby—doll—"

She shied, like a horse who knew she was going to be hit. Fuck, I
ated to think she could ever fear me.

"It's your husband, Nina," I said. "It's Calvin. He's under investiga-
on for conspiring to traffick minors as sex workers through a Brooklyn
afe house."

I rubbed my face. Fuck, I shouldn't have even told her that, but she
vouldn't let it go unless I did.

Just like I knew she wouldn't say anything to him either.

"Calvin's under investigation for sex trafficking?"

Was it my imagination, or was she not particularly surprised to
ear it?

I peered at her. "I'm afraid so. I'd ask you not to say anything, but
onestly, he'll find out by tomorrow, most likely. We have enough to
ndict now as it is."

"I see…" She blinked. "Well, obviously I won't say anything. Bu
what should I do? Bring my things here? I could stay here for a while, i
you're—if you're open to it—"

"Nina," I interrupted. "Baby, I don't think you understand. You hav
to go. You have to go back home."

Her eyes widened. "What? *Why?*"

"Because," I said. "I can't protect you from this investigation. Bu
being married to Calvin…" I shook my head as a wave of nausea cam
and went. "That will. If you're shacked up with the investigating DA
that puts the whole case at risk, including Jane and Eric, who ar
currently claiming self-defense against the leader of the operation. You'l
get called as a witness. You'll be torn apart on the stand. But if you're
with him…well, you get spousal privilege. They can't touch you."

I took a deep breath, then said the single hardest thing I'd ever said ir
my life.

"You have to go home, Nina. For your sake, you have to remair
another man's wife."

EPILOGUE

NINA EVELYN ASTOR DE VRIES GARDNER SAT AT HER VANITY IN A CREAM silk dressing gown, hair tied back at the base of her neck while she removed the diamond earrings. Heavy, gaudy things. She'd always hated them, the way they pulled at her earlobes and waved around like flashlights. Calvin had been so proud to give them to her for their second anniversary. Back then, she had been barely twenty-two. Too coy and shy to ask him where she might return them for something more tasteful.

So now she wore them, most often when she knew the sight of anything else would enrage him. They didn't, however, mask the new cuts and bruises flowering at the base of her neck, where he had grabbed her.

She had never seen him that angry. Or that willing to take it out on her.

"It's your cousin," Calvin had snapped as soon as he had been released from the local precinct.

As Matthew had promised, the arrest had happened quickly. It also happened in public. Ten NYPD officers had stormed the private offices Calvin rented in midtown. They had handcuffed him roughly and brought him to the local precinct, where he was held while a Brooklyn

Executive Assistant District Attorney named Matthew Zola had presented a case to the grand jury.

The indictment had been swift and immediate.

Charges of racketeering, trafficking, and bribery.

Nina had been the one to post bail.

It had been all over the news. Page Six was going to have a field day for weeks.

But it wasn't until they arrived home that Calvin snapped. He had seen her in her finery for the benefit she had left to bring him home. Another red dress, a Vivienne Westwood she had purchased almost immediately after leaving Matthew's house.

Calvin had taken one look at her in her scarlet couture and completely snapped. Accused her of mocking his current condition. Shouted that she had never had any respect for him in the first place, so he'd have to teach her some.

He had dragged her into her suite, thrown her against the eighteenth-century armoire, and proceeded to slap her silly until her ears rang for another hour.

It might have been over if she had just given him what he wanted. Sex. Tears. Both.

She simply couldn't.

Not for him. Not anymore.

Perhaps that was why, for the first time in ten years, Calvin had broken his only promise. Not the face. Never the face.

Not, apparently, anymore.

Nina touched the bruises forming just under her jaw and under one ear. There was a small cut there from Calvin's ring, but the rest would cover up well with concealer. She removed the jar of stage makeup from one drawer and started to dab on the heavy mask.

"Mommy?"

Nina jerked around to find Olivia standing in the entrance of the room, watching her with big, dark eyes. Her daughter was heading back to school after Memorial Day weekend.

She looked so much like her biological father sometimes, Nina was honestly surprised no one had yet asked if the child was even Calvin's. Of course, most people saw the identical blonde hair, long limbs, and slightly too-long de Vries nose and looked no further. But a closer inspection would have revealed the girl's chocolatey dark eyes circled in shadows, as opposed to her mother's gray and Calvin's blue. They might have noticed the olive tone of the girl's skin, compared to Nina's peachy cream complexion. They might have noticed that neither the shape of her lips nor the arch of her brow looked a thing like Nina's or Calvin's.

She looked like her father. And really, she looked like Matthew.

There had been times, of course, when she had imagined the two of them together. The first time was when they had actually met there on the street. Nina wondered if Patricia, the nanny, had noticed the resemblance at all. After that, when she had seen enough of him with his niece and nephews to know he would be an outstanding father. And then when she had confessed her daughter's parentage, the queer look on his face when he suggested shyly that in another world, she might have been his.

Since then, Nina had allowed herself to imagine the three of them the way she had always dreamed for her daughter.

A family.

Maybe one day.

"What—Mommy, did someone hurt you?"

Olivia crept into the room and pointed at Nina's cheek. Nina turned to the mirror and found that, yes, she had missed a spot.

"I smacked my cheek on one of the brass poles of the awning," Nina fibbed quickly as she dabbed on a bit more makeup. Cakey stuff in the beginning, but if she blended it well, it wouldn't look too horrid.

The bigger problem was that the slightest touch sent needles of pain through her cheekbone. She hoped Calvin hadn't cracked it.

"You're so clumsy, Mom."

Olivia laid her head on Nina's shoulder, and for a moment, Nina placed her hand on the little girl's cheek and held her close. Tomorrow, Olivia would go back to Massachusetts. It was worse every time she left, but there was no other option. Nina certainly couldn't bring up her daughter in this house.

"Can I sleep in here with you tonight?"

Nina's stomach churned. At nine years old, Olivia was getting too old for sleepovers with her mother. She knew it too, which was why Nina knew she only ever asked for them when she was worried about something. When Calvin had been unnecessarily cruel to the girl, who reached out to him as any child would in search of their father.

"Of course, darling," Nina said. "Go put on your pajamas and brush your teeth. I'll meet you back in here."

Once Olivia was gone, Nina examined her face again. She never slept with makeup on, but she couldn't risk Olivia seeing what had happened. It was just a chance she would have to take for some much-needed closeness with her daughter.

Because after tomorrow, it would be back to normal. Back to being totally and utterly alone.

Nina pulled her phone out of her vanity drawer. Her fingers hovered over the buttons as she opened a text chain.

She shouldn't. But she knew she would. Because she had meant what she said. She couldn't fight it any longer.

In this world, Nina felt like she was drowning. Matthew was the only fresh air to be found.

Nina: I need to see you. Tomorrow. Please.

It took a few long minutes of staring at the moving ellipses, but he did reply. He always did.

Maya: I told you. We can't.

Nina: You told me that, and then we saw each other the next day. I need to see you.

More ellipses. More wavering again and again. Nina turned her face to the side to examine her makeup. If she kept it up, no one would notice while the bruises healed. Except maybe Matthew.

If she were smart, she would cancel this plea.

Maya: Our place at eight. I'll be in the back.

Nina: Envy. See you there. x

———

To be continued in…

THE PERFECT WOMAN
June 2020

Preorder here: www.nicolefrenchromance.com/theperfectwoman

Need more Nina and Matthew now?

Read their FREE first night together at the Grace Hotel, three months earlier in **THE SCARLET NIGHT**: www.nicolefrenchromance.com/thescarletnight

Catch up with Jane and Eric's story here, beginning with **THE HATE VOW**, now free in Prime Reading and Kindle Unlimited: www.nicolefrenchromance.com/thehatevow

(Keep reading for a sneak peek!)

ACKNOWLEDGMENTS

I sat down the other day and sketched out all the things that have happened to me over the course of writing this book. It was a lot. More than I really expected. During this time (approximately six months), I experienced the death of my grandfather and the passing of one of my best friend's husband, my son's transition into one new school, and then another, a severe allergic reaction during the holidays, a basement that flooded four times within the span of as many weeks (yes, we lost most of our furniture, but thankfully, not our keepsakes), and then a move to a new home.

It's been a LOT. But you've hung in there with me. And for that, I have some special thanks:

To my readers, especially the diehards (you know who you are): you've been patient. Matthew Zola came into your lives, what, three years ago now? You've been asking for his story ever since. And then to have it delayed multiple times...and then, on top of that, for it to be "this" kind of story?

Saints. All of you.

To my alpha readers (Patricia and Danielle): your constant cheerleading keeps these stories going, this one more than most. I doubt I could have finished it without you. And for the **beta readers** who took this on and took the time to give me feedback while reading (Erika and Shauna in particular), thank you for alllllll you notice. You take a half-decent book and make it sing. Additional thanks go to **Talia** from **Red Hot Ink** Book Blog for checking my Italian—both the language and customs.

To my outstanding editorial team, Emily Hainsworth and Judy Zweifel, thank you for being so flexible and working with my nutty schedule for the last year. I could not do this without both of your expertise and eagle eyes. Additionally, thank you to my publicist, Dani Sanchez, for directing my madness when my plans seemed to be changing, on average, about once a week. You save me constantly.

To author friends who cheer me on, listen to my gripe, sometimes read chapters, or just say hello when things are REALLY happening, your support means everything. This goes times a million to Laura Halloran (I LOVE YOU, my seeeeester), Jane Anthony, Kim Loraine, Harloe Rae, Claudia Burgoa, Parker S. Huntington, and Maya Hughes.

Last but not least, to my family. To Trish—thank you for believing in me enough to join me in this venture! Your cheerleading means the world. To my kids, for humbling me and being a constant source of joy and pride. And to the Dude, for inspiring Matthew more than you know and letting me drag you all the way to Arthur Avenue and for sitting through Turandot at the Met in the name of research. I love you. You are home to me.

Made in the USA
Las Vegas, NV
02 July 2024